PEMBERLEY IN PERIL

A Pride and Prejudice Vagary

Arthel Cake

ISBN: 1973801086
ISBN 13: 9781973801085

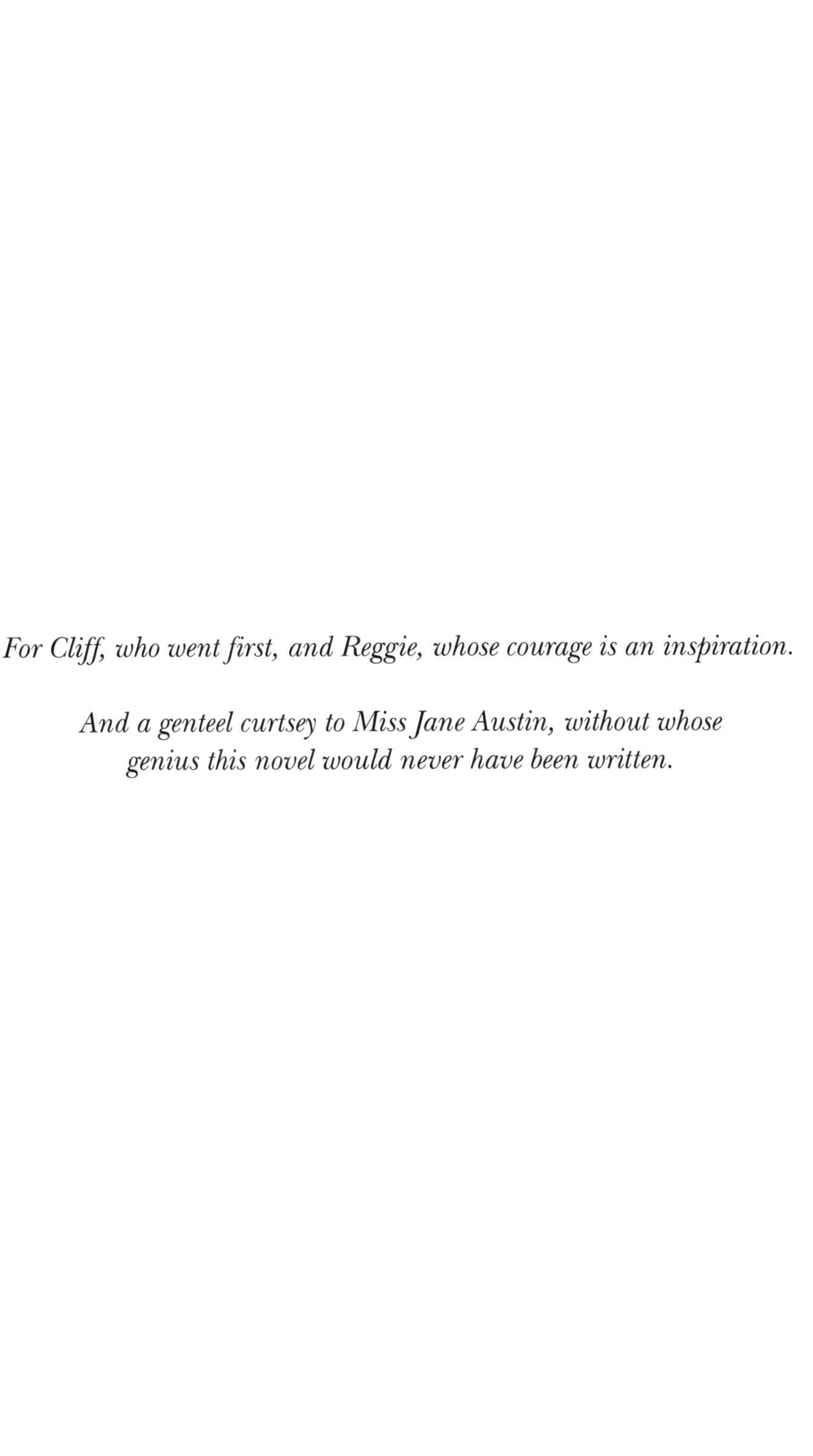

For Cliff, who went first, and Reggie, whose courage is an inspiration.

And a genteel curtsey to Miss Jane Austin, without whose genius this novel would never have been written.

CONTENTS

CHAPTER 1

FATE STEPS IN

What fate imposes, that men must needs abide;
It boots not to resist both wind and tide.

—William Shakespeare
Henry VI, Part 2

George Darcy leaned on the rail fence enclosing a paddock at his Derbyshire estate of Pemberley to watch his son, Fitzwilliam, put a magnificent stallion through its paces. The recently acquired horse stood fourteen hands at the withers; it was luminous gray with a mane that fell to the shoulder and tail that nearly brushed the ground, both floating like banners as it moved. After another ten minutes, Fitzwilliam dismounted and led the horse out of the paddock. He slapped the glossy neck lightly and handed the reins to a waiting groom. The man led the stallion toward the stables. No groom at Pemberley needed instruction on how to care for its horses, and Fitzwilliam stopped beside his father with only a satisfied glance at his newest acquisition.

"Are you sure you will be able to honor your promise to Richard of the first male foal?" Mr. Darcy teased.

Fitzwilliam grimaced and then shrugged. "He was the one who found Sultan; he deserves his reward."

Fitzwilliam was glad to have received a letter from his cousin colonel Richard Fitzwilliam several months ago, as mail from the war-ravaged continent was uncertain and battles had raged up and down the Spanish peninsula and into Portugal. After assuring his cousin that he was well, Richard went on to the gist of the letter.

> *There is a lull in the fighting at present, and General Crawford gave me three day's leave since my regiment had seen heavy fighting. I was directed by a Spanish soldier to a local horse breeder, Don Ignacio Gallardo, who is selling off his bloodstock to recoup losses from the "requisitioning" of many of his horses by the French army.*
>
> *I thought to acquire another mount, but none of his stock is trained as a war-horse. However, he has one of the most magnificent stallions I have ever seen. His sire was an Andalusian of the old breed, with none of the Carthusian blood, and his dam an Arab mare with bloodlines back to the horses the Moors brought into Spain. The price is beyond my means, but if you wish to acquire the stallion, Don Ignacio will hold him until I can confirm the purchase. If you do purchase Sultan, as he is called, I will take the first male foal he sires as broker's commission.*

A cavalryman raised with horses and horse breeding, Richard had an eye for horseflesh that was at least equal to his cousin's. The horse was everything Richard had said, and despite the difficulty in transferring money to the war zone and safely transporting the horse to England, both father and son were pleased with the result.

The two men strode toward the house, but Mr. Darcy slowed his pace before they reached the rear entrance and said, "Walk with me."

Instantly his son's face blanked to an emotionless mask. For a moment, George Darcy wondered if Fitzwilliam would refuse, but he knew that his son would never show him such disrespect or rudeness. They passed the rear of the manor and continued toward the lawns. Fitzwilliam gazed straight ahead, for once not noting the beauty of the extensive gardens for which Pemberley was famous. Fitzwilliam was certain that he knew what his father wanted to discuss. He realized this conversation was unavoidable, a fact that made it no easier or more pleasant.

They made their way across the lawns toward the glittering motion of the lake; two tall, lean, broad-shouldered men, the elder's hair streaked with silver, the younger with the spring of youth and health in his step. Near the lakeside, George Darcy approached a marble bench and sat, indicating that his son join him. When they were side by side, he gazed for a time at the shimmer of water before turning to his son.

"William, it is time we spoke of a subject you have avoided for too long and I have not pressed you about. However, new circumstances have precipitated this conversation."

Something in his father's voice made Fitzwilliam turn to study his face, apprehension tightening his chest. George Darcy had shown unusual reactions of late. Fitzwilliam had attributed them to the strains of the harvest and tried desperately not to read more than that into them. Fatigue, shortness of breath, and lack of stamina had never plagued the Master of Pemberley before, and Fitzwilliam was not a man to lie to himself.

George laid a hand on his son's arm and said quietly, "I am going to London tomorrow. While there, I will consult Sir Ansel McQuary."

"The heart specialist?" Fitzwilliam barely whispered the specialty of the famous surgeon.

"Indeed. You have noticed that lately I have not been myself. I had hoped that it was only the additional work of the harvest, but in the past week I have had an episode of pains in my chest that leads me to believe my heart may be involved."

"Why did you not tell me or at least send for Dr. Morrow?"

Fitzwilliam's voice sounded harsh with concern. He felt like a man thrown suddenly into deep water, numb and struggling to get his bearings. His body had become a great hollow full of disbelief, anger, and pain. For a dozen stuttering heartbeats, he was unable to speak, his father's words finally penetrating the wall of shock that immobilized him.

"I cannot be certain," the older man added quickly seeing the fear in his son's eyes, "until I see Sir Ansel. But whether it is my heart or not, it makes the matter of your marrying imperative."

Fitzwilliam opened his mouth to reply, but his father's raised hand halted the words.

George Darcy continued slowly. "I have always been friendly with your uncle Lord Henry, and I see Richard almost as another son. But Maresford is as greedy as his grandfather. Your cousin is not content to inherit the earldom; he would like nothing better than to take over Pemberley as well. You are my heir, but even though you are young, the future belongs to no man. Pemberley is entailed to 'heirs of the body' and not to 'heirs male of the body,' as you know. Georgiana is too young to marry, although I have no doubt that Maresford would offer for her if he thought it brought him a step closer to taking over the estate. If you marry, especially if an heir is born in the first year, the viscount will have little chance to accomplish his ambition, whether I am with you or not."

Fitzwilliam closed his eyes, his head bowed. The thought of his father dying numbed him with grief too great for words.

He knew his cousin Richard's older brother, Nicholas, Viscount Maresford, was not a man he could admire, nor did they travel in the same circles. The idea of Georgiana married to his dissolute relative was nauseating. Fitzwilliam looked up, pale and tense. It was strange, he thought disjointedly, that his father looked no different than he had at the paddock.

"I want a clear answer from you. Will you marry your cousin Anne?"

Fitzwilliam called on all his hard-won self-command to speak evenly. "No, I will not. Nor does she desire the match. It is only her mother's control over her that keeps her from openly rejecting the idea."

His father nodded. "You know that I support your decision. Anne may or may not be as ill as Catherine thinks, for I have often wondered if much of her illness is not a way to escape her mother's despotism. But she is certainly not in any way qualified to be mistress of Pemberley or run a household as complex as this one, having neither the vitality nor any training or experience. Nor has she had the society that would allow her to act as your hostess or to assist Georgiana when she comes out. And there is always the question of bearing a healthy heir and surviving the birth."

Fitzwilliam did not respond, his gaze toward the lake but turned inward. The light wind in the trees sounded like distant voices mourning. It was too great a burden to consider marriage now with this news of his father's illness, but he was realist enough to know the matter must be faced. He had known that he could not escape marriage forever, nor did he want to. But he had never found a woman who met his standards of both beauty and intelligence. Perhaps the memory of his mother, who died when he was sixteen, made him reject ladies whom most men of his station would wed without a second thought.

With no reply from his son, George Darcy's expression grew stern. "You have been out in society for six Seasons, William. You have met countless young ladies of wealth and position, and despite the greedy mamas and insolvent fathers, many would have made you adequate wives."

"Mother was not 'adequate,' " Fitzwilliam said. "She was not only beautiful and the daughter of an earl, she was kind, bright, witty, interested in the world, not just the newest fashion or who is involved in crim con with whom."

His father nodded. "Yes, she was special, and I adored her. But she was a rare gem in our world. There are others, I am sure, but they are not easy to find."

"Father, I have made an effort to choose a wife, but the ladies are all the same. They fawn and simper and behave as if they were nothing more than pretty dolls with heads full of air. I do not want the kind of marriage most of my acquaintance have, barely acknowledging their wives after an heir is born. I could not live in such an empty sham!"

Resentment had crept into his son's tone. George Darcy moderated his own impatience, understanding that it was not the subject that caused Fitzwilliam's anger. The father remembered his feelings at his own father's last illness—the helplessness, the sense of impotence to change the inevitable.

"I do not say you have not looked for a bride or that your assessment of the ladies of the *ton* is not valid. But even if my problems are not as bad as I fear, there is no more time to seek perfection. Therefore," George Darcy continued straightening up, at once the Master of Pemberley, "while I am in London, I mean to contact several acquaintances and find a young lady suitable as your bride. While I am gone, I want you to consider what I have said. I do not like to force you to accept my choice, but I see no other means of securing Pemberley's future."

George Darcy rose, and his son stood up, conflict evident in his expression. His father rarely imposed his own decisions on his son, but when he did demand obedience, Fitzwilliam complied.

Torn between anxiety, shock, and resentment, Fitzwilliam did not reply but returned to the house at his father's side in silence.

⸻

"Lizzy, please accompany me to my study. I need to speak to you."

Her father's voice had a quality that Elizabeth Bennet knew meant it was not an invitation but a summons. She said, "Yes, Papa," and followed him from the dining room. Her mother's self-satisfied look followed her. It was not an uncommon expression when Mrs. Bennet anticipated her second daughter being set down, but it vexed Elizabeth anyway.

Mr. Bennet, never loquacious, had been unusually quiet at dinner. The conversation of his wife and youngest daughters had followed its usual pattern of fashion and gossip, without his wry comments. Elizabeth was certain that she knew the reason he called her into his sanctuary. Her mother had undoubtedly confronted him as soon as he had returned from his law practice with her latest complaint that Elizabeth had discouraged a suitor. In the past, Mr. Bennet had not taken his wife's diatribes any more seriously than her other dissatisfactions, but of late, he seemed more inclined to react seriously when his favorite daughter refused to allow a young man to call on her.

The study was large by town standards, paneled in walnut with glass-doored bookcases built into three walls. Lamplight glinted on gold lettering and softly glowing leather bindings. The room smelled of books, beeswax candles, port, and, faintly, cigars. Mr. Bennet indicated a leather chair before his desk and took his place behind the polished walnut expanse, tenting his fingers on the leather top.

"Your mother tells me you have discouraged Mr. Whitford from calling on you."

Elizabeth simply nodded, hands clasped in her lap. Her father regarded her more sternly than she remembered since she was a girl, and a swift chill passed through her.

"I cannot say I entirely blame you. He is a pleasant young man with a fine estate and good prospects, but I expect too mild mannered for you to respect him."

"He is pleasant," Elizabeth agreed reluctantly, "and I like him. But he expects me to have no opinions on life or politics or anything but clothes and dancing. I would stifle in a year with him, nor would he be happy with me. Mama does not care what I want in a husband; she only wants me out of the house!"

Slowly Mr. Bennet said, "Jane came out three years ago. She married Mr. Bingley six months after the Season ended. Mary did not want a Season. She now has an informal arrangement with my junior partner, Mr. Cranshaw, a thoroughly suitable young man. Kitty came out last Season, was engaged two months later, and will marry in the spring after the new Season ends. You came out with Jane, and to date you have turned down two offers of marriage and several requests to call on or court you.

"I agree," he said, holding up a hand to stop any protest, "that Mr. Holcomb was not marriage material and wanted an entry into my social and political circle, but the others seemed suitable if you were willing to make an effort to get to know them."

Elizabeth dropped her head and stared at her hands, twisting in the skirt of her gown. At length she said, "I want to marry for love, and I have not found a man I can love. I do not want a marriage of convenience, or a marriage of...of inequality of mind or heart. I do not want a husband who cannot appreciate that I am an individual, not just a body for bearing children, and who cannot respect my abilities and my opinions. I do not want to be poured into a mold and told to be happy with it!"

"I understand that you do not want a marriage like your mother's and mine or like those of too many of the *ton*. But not all marriages are so unequal. Even some arranged marriages grow to include love."

She did not reply. Mr. Bennet sighed.

"You know that I wish you to feel affection for your husband, but affection is not everything in marriage. You are two-and-twenty, and while that is hardly on the shelf, the offers are not coming as often as before. A gentleman of my acquaintance told me in confidence recently that his son was interested in getting to know you until he spoke to several of his friends, who informed him that you seemed to find nothing to admire in any young man. I am sorry, Lizzy, but you are acquiring a reputation for wanting so much in a suitor that no one can meet your expectations."

Elizabeth felt tears prickle her eyes. Her father was rarely disappointed in her, and his censure hurt her deeply. Was she too particular about what a husband ought to be? Many of her friends were married or engaged to men she would not have considered and were seemingly happy with their lot. Should she bow to the inevitable and accept a man just because he evinced an interest in her, knowing that marriage meant changing to meet his expectations and denying who she was in the process? Her spirit rebelled against the idea, but when her father continued, she felt her resistance turn to disquiet.

"An old acquaintance from Cambridge came to see me this morning; Mr. George Darcy of Pemberley, in Derbyshire. I have invited him to dine with us tomorrow. I know you will treat him with respect, as that is your nature as well as training. However, I also want you to engage him in conversation."

Elizabeth was puzzled. She knew the name; everyone in society knew the name of Darcy, but if this man had gone to university with her father, he must be at least as old as him and not someone her father would consider as a suitor for her. A sudden thought struck her with almost physical force. She raised her head, alarm in her stiff posture.

"He...he has a son, does he not?"

"Fitzwilliam Darcy, his only son. There is also a daughter about Lydia's age."

"I have never met the gentleman, but he has a reputation for being excessively proud. Cecilia Benham-Stout told me that he associates only with his relatives and a few close friends. She once was at a ball that he attended, and he danced only two sets, one with his cousin and one with his aunt, and left shortly after."

"He spends much of the time at the estate in Derbyshire or one of the other smaller estates they own. He will inherit great wealth and property when his father passes, and Mr. Darcy is concerned that his son marry and produce an heir. I speak plainly, for I respect your intelligence too much to paint a romantic picture."

Mr. Bennet leaned forward over the desk and held his daughter's gaze. "If Mr. Darcy finds you suitable, I shall initiate a betrothal. I am sorry, Lizzy, but I know as certainly as I know anything that spinsterhood would be the destruction of you. The young man is honorable, educated, responsible, and intelligent. He took a first in history at Cambridge and is exceedingly well-read. He may not be sociable, but with a wife's influence, that can change or at least be modified. I—"

Elizabeth came to her feet, her hands clenched into fists at her sides. Her cheeks burned, but she felt chilled and shaken. "How can you do this to me, Papa? How can you condemn me to a marriage I do not want with a man I do not know?"

"Because I love you, child," he replied gently. "I will not see you waste your youth awaiting a great love that may well never come. You are not impractical, nor a dreamer, but if you lock your mind on an image of an ideal husband and exclude any who do not meet that ideal, you will find yourself unable to accept anyone. You know what I say is true. I have kept some track of my old university acquaintances. I know that both Darcys are greatly admired for their honor and abilities. It is a good, even a great match.

"Now," he said, rising, "I want you to spend the rest of the evening quietly thinking about all I have said. Good night, Lizzy."

It was a dismissal she knew better than to ignore. She left the study without a response and almost ran to her room, wishing with all her soul that her dear Jane was still there for her to pour out her heart to. Her dearest sister was in Hertfordshire at the Bingley estate of Netherfield Park, a short distance from their own modest estate of Longbourn, expecting her first child in three months.

By the time Elizabeth closed the door behind her, tears ran down her cheeks. She groped blindly for her handkerchief and fell onto the window seat, burying her face in her hands. She had never thought her father would do such a thing. He had always been opposed to arranged marriages; to force her into such an engagement went against the nature of their relationship. She felt abandoned and betrayed and totally lost.

When the bitter tears ceased, Elizabeth wiped her eyes and contemplated her options. If she refused the match, she knew her father would not turn her out, but he would have to send her away, most probably back to Longbourn or to her aunt Phillips in Meryton. The widow of her mother's next elder brother would welcome a companion. Elizabeth would find herself back in the society of the small market town with the people she had known most of her life. She liked their neighbors, but there were no likely prospects for marriage among the estate owners of the area. Had there been, she would have found a suitable match before now.

Elizabeth sat for some time, wondering what she was to do. She had no intimate friends, only acquaintances, and not many of them, for she had no patience with the false friendships of the *ton*. Elizabeth preferred her aunt and uncle Gardiners' circle of friends and a few unconventional ladies from her own circle. She meant to speak to her aunt Gardiner, but Jane's calm appraisal and gentle advice were what she desired more than anything. She could not visit now, however a letter would reach her sister in a day or two. With a practical purpose at hand, Elizabeth moved to her writing desk, took out paper, and dipped her pen into the inkwell.

In the downstairs hall, Mrs. Bennet slipped out of the drawing room the moment Elizabeth reached the top of the stairs and hurried to her husband's study. She knocked on the door, barely awaiting his summons before entering the room. He looked up from the papers he was sorting with resignation and a hint of vexation at her precipitous entrance.

"Yes, Mrs. Bennet?"

She seated herself before his desk, her gaze sharp. "You spoke to Lizzy. I hope she did not convince you to allow her another Season. She has had three already, and it is time for Lydia to enter society. She will need a new wardrobe if she is to meet all the right people and attend all the important festivities, and there will be other expenses. Lizzy has already had her share."

Her husband studied his wife with a combination of irritation and impatience. Frances Gardiner Bennet was still handsome in middle age, her fair hair covered by a cap of fine lace, her face barely lined, her figure only a bit plumper than when they had married. It was her personality that had suffered from time, growing more irritable and acerbic with the years and her disappointment with the lack of a son to carry on the Bennet name. The daughter of a wealthy merchant, she had never become accommodated to the life of a society matron and had instead retained a sense of inferiority in spite of her husband's position as both a gentleman and an extremely successful solicitor.

"What we spoke of is between Lizzy and myself, Fanny. As for Lydia, she is sixteen years old, too young in my opinion to come out."

Mrs. Bennet pruned her lips. "Kitty came out at seventeen. Why cannot Lydia?"

"Because her age may be sixteen but her behavior is nearer twelve. When I deem her mature enough, she shall have her Season."

"But she has met a charming gentleman at Lady Arthur's when she called on Miss Arthur with her friend Lettie Gradison. He was quite attentive, although Lydia thought him a little older than she would wish, as he is a friend of Miss Arthur's brother, Sir Colin."

"I do not consider that a particularly favorable recommendation. And I am sure," Mr. Bennet opined, "that charming gentlemen will not be in short supply anytime soon. Lydia will wait another year. Now," he continued, tone forestalling any protest, "I have something to impart. I met a gentleman today whom I knew at university, and I have asked him to dine with us tomorrow."

Mrs. Bennet's interest was piqued. "Do I know the gentleman?"

"No. We have not kept in close contact. But he is in town for a se'nnight, and I wish to renew the acquaintance."

"May I know his name?"

Mr. Bennet said with mild reluctance, "Mr. George Darcy."

"Darcy?" Her face instantly took on an expression of intense interest. "The father or the son?"

"As we were at Cambridge together, I can assure you it is the father."

She nodded rapidly. "Oh yes, of course. But there is a son, is there not?"

"There is. He is in Derbyshire at the estate. He rarely visits town. As it is harvest time, he is fully occupied, with his father away."

"Very well." Mrs. Bennet sounded vaguely disappointed. "I shall speak to Cook."

She rose and bustled to the door. Mr. Bennet sighed. He rubbed the bridge of his nose, a sign that he was troubled. This match, if it came about, was a very good, even a great, one. He had no illusions that in spite of his daughters being gently born and having respectable dowries, the small size of his estate and his lack of noble or even great connections limited the gentlemen who might offer for them. Mr. Bennet wanted his favorite daughter well placed in marriage, and Mr. Darcy offered a solution he might never have achieved on his own.

He returned to his papers with a shake of his head. He would have to warn Mr. Darcy to mention his son as little as possible until matters were more finally settled. Fanny had an infallible nose for an unattached young man, especially one with a fortune.

"Did you get me an invitation to the Gradisons' ball?"

Sir Colin Arthur poured brandy into two glasses and handed one to his friend, a man he knew as George Winter. In his various forays outside the law, George Wickham had used several aliases; however, Winter was his favorite. He fancied the name described his character; nor was he mistaken, for he was cold and pitiless.

"My invitation is for myself and a guest, so there will be no problem," Sir Colin drawled. "With my mother making noises about their daughter, they will be happy to see me, whomever I bring."

Sir Colin finished his drink and set the glass down on the sidebar. His sitting room was furnished with leather chairs and polished mahogany tables, carved and gilded, the walls papered in a hand-painted Chinese design of pheasants and woodcocks amid greenery. Everything spoke of money spent lavishly but with conventional taste. Since boyhood, he had never been denied anything he had wanted; the result was a young man spoiled, self-absorbed, and arrogant, who felt himself above the ordinary rules and strictures of society.

Winter smiled to himself. As long as Sir Colin continued to gamble and lose, he stood to make a profit from both his enterprise with the young nobleman and from his entrée into high society.

"What do you think of Miss Gradison?" asked Sir Colin. "She has twenty thousand pounds and a nice lot of jewelry from her grandmother's estate. At present, Father is not pressing me to marry, but if he finds out how deeply I am in at White's, he will be livid. Twenty thousand would clear that with most of it leftover."

"You would have to wait until after the marriage." Winter contemplated his glass, swirling the amber liquid. "That could take six months or more. By then your creditors are likely to be on your heels."

Sir Colin said sulkily, "What else am I to do? I can hardly ask Father for an advance on my allowance. He is already unhappy that I go through it so quickly."

Winter drank thoughtfully. A slight smile turned up his mouth. He was a handsome man of six-and-twenty, dressed in the latest fashion. He projected assurance and a smooth charm that easily gained him entry to the lower levels of the *haute ton*. If there was something of the libertine in his demeanor, Sir Colin would not have noticed.

"I may know a way for you to accumulate some quick cash, but it takes daring to accomplish. I do not think you would relish the idea."

Sir Colin drew himself up. "I have never been accused of being faint of heart."

"Um. Let me consider the matter, and we can talk later if you still are of the same mind."

Sir Colin huffed but only said, "We had better dress if we are to meet Harvey and Sutton-Wilde at the Valkyrie."

Satisfied for the present, Winter threw back the rest of his brandy. "I wonder if Hilda will be free tonight? She is remarkable in bed." He left the room smiling at the forwarding of his plans. *The hook is in. Now I have only to reel in my fish and wait for the opportunity to put my plans into action.*

The morning after the interview with her father, Elizabeth desperately wanted to talk with her aunt Gardiner. Upon reaching Gracechurch Street, she was unreasonably annoyed to find that her aunt was out and not expected to return before afternoon. Accompanied by the maid she shared with Mary, Elizabeth vented her frustration by means of a brisk walk in the small park near the Gardiners' home. By the time they took a hackney cab home, Elizabeth realized the absurdity of feeling vexed because her aunt was not available for her unannounced call and returned herself to reasonably good humor.

The remainder of the morning was spent in assisting her mother to prepare for the evening. Mary and Kitty helped as well, while Lydia amused herself looking at fashion plates and complaining because she was not yet out and could not attend balls, like the Gradisons'. Kitty attempted to reason with her, only to have Lydia toss her magazine on the floor and reply petulantly.

"It is all very well for you to talk of patience, Kitty, for you are already betrothed and will marry in the spring. But Papa will not even allow me to have my coming out for another whole Season! Lettie is to come out this Season, and she will not be seventeen until April. I will be seventeen in March. It is not fair! You came out at seventeen. Why cannot I?"

"Perhaps," Kitty said as she bent and retrieved *La Belle Assemblée* and placed it on a table as she sat down, "because you do not behave as if you were ready to join society or marry. A Season means more than parties and balls; it means that you are ready to take on the responsibilities of a husband and family. To manage a house and host social events and oversee your husband's comfort and your children's education. Can you do all that?"

Lydia tossed her head. "I shall have servants to do my bidding, for I will not marry a man who is not rich, and I am sure I shall find one easily. Sir Colin's friend finds me a most pleasant companion; he told me so. He is too old, of course, but very amusing."

"I hope you observe the proprieties with him, Lydie." Kitty regarded her sister gravely. "Sir Colin does not have the best reputation, and for his friend to single you out is dangerous for your reputation if it is noticed and spoken of."

"Oh, poo, Kitty, you are beginning to sound like Lizzy. I was calling on Miss Arthur and her mother with Lettie. We were all together. There was nothing improper at all."

Lydia thought it best not to mention the impromptu walk in the garden with Mr. Winter, Lettie, and Sir Colin. After all, there were four of them, although not always close together.

Kitty stood. "Very well, Lydie, as long as you remember that if you want to make a good marriage, your reputation must remain unblemished. I promised to help Mama with the arrangements for dinner. I am sure she could use your help as well."

Lydia also rose, straightening her gown. "With you and Lizzy and Mary, I do not think she needs me at all. I will go to my room and rest for a while."

Kitty watched her sister walk from the room with an exaggerated sway that caused her skirts to swish around her ankles. Kitty knew that "rest" meant Lydia had acquired a new novel she wished to read.

"Thank you, Papa, for not allowing Lydia to come out yet," Kitty murmured with a sigh.

The morning after the Gradisons' ball, George Winter woke past noon. When he had dressed, he came downstairs to find Sir Colin in the empty dining room, a cup of cold coffee before him and a scattering of newspapers on the table. Sir Colin's eyes were puffy, and there was an unhealthy pallor to his skin. Winter poured himself a cup of coffee at the sideboard and sat opposite his host, watching the expression of mingled excitement and apprehension on the young nobleman's face.

Sir Colin Arthur glanced up from the newspaper he was perusing. "There was a burglary at the Gradisons' last night, during the ball. Mrs. Gradison lost over three thousand pounds' worth of jewelry. It had been locked in her dressing table during the festivities so that she could return the gems she was wearing to the bank with the rest the day after the ball. Someone seems to have climbed the tree next to the house and come in through a window. The drawer was forced and the jewel box broken. A magistrate is questioning all the servants who were in that part of the house, as the window had to have been opened from the inside."

He flung the paper aside. Winter said casually, "Careless of the lady. And a social disaster for the Gradisons, although profitable for whoever took the jewels."

Sir Colin rose abruptly. He walked to a sidebar, poured two glasses of brandy, and returned to the table, setting one in front of Winter. He drank his own in two gulps, shivered and leaned across the table, his voice dropped to a rough whisper.

"When?"

"Tonight." Winter sipped the brandy. He was enjoying the younger man's discomfort. As long as it did not become panic, it kept the little fish under his control.

Lowering his voice again to a murmur, Sir Colin said, "How much will we realize?"

"Nothing near their worth. Half the value if the fence is in a good mood. The stones will have to be recut and reset, and the settings melted down. They'll probably go to someone in Amsterdam. The Dutchman is not generous, but he is safe. He will not grass on a client. He wants to hang no more than you do."

"Shut up!" Sir Colin wiped a hand across his face. "Sorry, old man. It's just my nerves. I have a terrible headache, and I have never done anything like this before."

"Neither have I," Winter lied, "but they say that practice makes perfect."

He would never have agreed to Winter's plan if he did not need money so badly, Sir Colin told himself. Sweat prickled his forehead. Viscount Maresford had been pressing him over his losses at whist, and it was almost time to renew his membership at White's. A fellow had to play cards after all, and there were the races at Newmarket and an occasional impromptu bet on a whimsy. Only, he had such rotten luck lately. Even George seemed to win more often than he did.

Sir Colin went to renew his brandy. A chill ran over his body. Half of fifteen hundred pounds was enough to satisfy his loudest creditors, but unless his luck at cards improved soon and dramatically, he might be forced to participate in another episode like the one last night. He had no doubt George was willing, but was he himself prepared to face the unimaginable calamity if he were caught? Still, it had given him a sense of excitement he had not felt in some time, rather like the end of a hard-run race.

Winter finished the brandy and leaned back, a secretive smirk on his face. He was not about to share the butter with the fool in equal parts. Winter knew that the fish was well and truly hooked. Besides, he was enjoying the game. He only needed to keep Sir Colin on the line until the chance arose to make his fortune. At that point Winter would be certain that his cat's paw took the blame and that he was well out of London.

CHAPTER 2
PROGRESSIONS

Although Mrs. Bennet had little knowledge and no understanding of the world at large, within her realm of home and society, she was entirely competent. The dinner she put on for her husband's university friend consisted of three superb courses and a dessert course. Mr. Bennet seated their guest on his right, with Elizabeth next to him. Mary sat to Mr. Bennet's left with Kitty next to her and Lydia next to Elizabeth.

Remembering her father's instructions, Elizabeth sought for some way to begin a conversation. Mr. Bennet made no attempt to engage Mr. Darcy in a discussion of the war or economics, leaving Elizabeth no alternative but to speak or be indefensibly rude. When Darcy smiled at her, she found her voice.

"I have never been to Derbyshire, Mr. Darcy, but I have always wanted to visit the lakes. Mr. Wordsworth's poetry is a great favorite of mine."

"He lives near Wyndemere," the gentleman replied. "We had the pleasure of meeting Mr. Wordsworth last summer. We have visited the lakes many times; it is not too far from Pemberley. It is beautiful country, and the Peak District is quite spectacular. You would enjoy it, I am sure."

Elizabeth ate a little of her *ragout de poulet* without tasting it. Mr. Darcy was really quite charming. She wondered if his son resembled him, with a chiseled profile, strong jaw, and dark eyes. At that moment Mrs. Bennet entered the conversation. Her voice had a shrill note to it that she had never successfully moderated. It made Elizabeth flinch.

"That is your estate, Pemberley, is it not, Mr. Darcy?"

"It is." He turned his attention to the lady of the house with quiet courtesy.

"It is very large, I believe? It must be difficult for a man to manage the domestic arrangements without a wife."

Elizabeth saw their guest's nearly imperceptible wince at the mention of his late wife, but he said as calmly as before. "I have a very competent housekeeper who has been with us for over twenty years. It is not a burden, I assure you, madam."

"Do you farm much of your land?" Elizabeth put in quickly before her mother could ask how many rooms the manor contained and how they were furnished.

"About half is under cultivation. There are extensive woods as well. We also run sheep and a small herd of cattle for meat and dairy products, and we breed horses. Do you ride, Miss Bennet?"

"Yes, sir, I do. My father bought my first pony when I was six."

Mr. Darcy nodded approval. "My daughter, Georgiana, is very fond of riding. There are many wonderful prospects to be found on the estate that can only be reached on horseback."

Fish was served, and for a time, the conversation moved to other matters of a conventional nature. Mr. Bennet took part in forwarding the exchanges. Over the venison, which Mrs. Bennet proudly proclaimed to be from their estate in Hertfordshire, the matter of the French embargo on British goods and shipping arose.

"I think it a terrible shame," Mrs. Bennet proclaimed with a sniff. "One can hardly get anything from France anymore, lace or wine or anything."

"I imagine it is not any easier for those who make their livelihood by producing and selling goods," Mr. Bennet responded mildly. "It is no easier for our own people, with so much of the national product going to the war effort. The prices of wheat are rising to the point where many of the poor will not be able to adequately feed their families."

"We have been attempting for some time to maximize production at Pemberley, for the sake of our tenants as well as the estate in general," Mr. Darcy responded. "With the war taxes, we have no desire to burden our people any more than necessary."

Elizabeth felt a warmth for the man beside her she had not expected. She said, "My father initiated the Scottish system of crop rotation several years ago, and wheat production has already increased by forty percent."

"We also use the Scottish system," Mr. Darcy said. "It has proven its worth over time. Our wheat yields are consistently seventy percent higher than they were when we began, over a decade ago."

"Lizzy," her mother's voice was almost angry, "I am sure Mr. Darcy does not want to hear your opinions on matters best left to gentlemen."

"On the contrary." Mr. Darcy smiled at Elizabeth with approval. "I am gratified that a young lady takes an intelligent interest in a matter vital to the economic success of any estate."

Elizabeth colored. Her father diverted talk back to neutral subjects, but Mrs. Bennet continued to throw an occasional vexed look at her second oldest daughter. How was Lizzy to attract a man—any man—when she would meddle in the male province? Certainly Mr. Darcy was a trifle old for Lizzy. But he had a son, and if she was ever to expect an introduction, she had better convince Mr. Darcy of her suitability as a wife and mother. To that end, when the men had enjoyed their port and cigars and rejoined the ladies in the drawing room, Mrs. Bennet addressed her least-favorite daughter.

"Lizzy, why do you not play for us? I am sure some entertainment would be agreeable to our guest."

"I would enjoy hearing you play, Miss Bennet," Mr. Darcy assured her. "My daughter has a passion for music and plays whenever she can, but she presently only performs for family."

Elizabeth looked at her father, who nodded slightly. She rose and went to the pianoforte at one side of the room. As she passed Mary, her sister said, "Shall I turn the pages for you?"

"Yes, thank you."

The warmth Elizabeth felt for her sister at that moment eased her tension and allowed her to seat herself at the instrument with composure. A piece by Pleyel that she had been practicing was on the music rest. Elizabeth let her fingers rest on the keys as Mary sat beside her, and then she began to play and sing. When she reached the chorus, Mary joined in, her lower soprano complimenting Elizabeth's sweet, clear tones. They finished to applause. Elizabeth next selected a sonata by Mozart and finished with a Scottish reel she played from memory.

Mr. Darcy said as she rejoined the others, "You have a remarkably fine voice, Miss Bennet, and your duet with Miss Mary was delightful. I hope to have the pleasure of hearing you sing again one day."

"Thank you, Mr. Darcy," Elizabeth replied quietly. "Perhaps you will."

Fitzwilliam Darcy waited at the foot of the main stairs in front of Pemberley House as his father's coach proceeded along the driveway. A lookout had sent word that the coach was on its way, and he wanted to be ready when his father arrived. For a week,

Darcy had worked on estate business and mulled over the idea of marrying a woman he did not know, and the prospect was no more appealing to him now than it had been that day by the lake. Perhaps he could convince his father to allow him a month or two to survey the prospects and hopefully find someone tolerable among the sisters and cousins of his acquaintances.

Fitzwilliam was at the door as the coach stopped rolling. A footman jumped down and raised the steps. Fitzwilliam opened the door himself and waited for his father to emerge. For several moments, nothing happened, and Fitzwilliam's heart clutched in his chest. Then George Darcy stepped out of the coach and descended heavily to the ground, where once he would have jumped out, disdaining steps.

Fitzwilliam hesitated to offer his arm as his father straightened. "Welcome home, Father."

"Thank you, Son."

Fitzwilliam waived the coach on and turned back to the house at his father's side. They entered the large foyer with its pale walls and delicately painted, coffered ceiling depicting classical scenes. George Darcy made his way to his study across the marble floor that gleamed in the subdued light. Once inside he took a chair before the fireplace where a small fire burned against the autumn chill. Fitzwilliam brought two brandies and sat in the other chair, unwilling to speak. His father's face had a gray cast that sent a shiver down his spine. He knew before the other man spoke that the news was not good.

George Darcy sipped his drink and stared at the fire snapping over a small pine log. Drawing a long breath, he said, "As you must be aware, my condition is not as I had hoped but as I feared. I have an affliction of the heart. Sir Ansel had a medicine made up for me that will ease the pains when they recur, but there is no practical treatment. He refrained from predicting how long I may have; however he advised me to put my affairs in order."

Fitzwilliam swallowed hard and blinked rapidly as tears threatened for the first time since his mother had died. "Is there nothing else we can do?"

Noting the plural, George smiled wryly. "I am to worry as little as possible and avoid strenuous exercise. Good advice, but hardly unique."

He drank the rest of his brandy, set the glass aside, and turned to face his son. "William, this news affects both of us. You know what we spoke of before I left. It is even more imperative now."

When his son made no reply, he continued with more authority, "Fitzwilliam, I want you to understand. I have been forcibly reminded that no man owns the future. In other circumstances, you might not marry for another ten years and still produce an heir. But with Maresford in the picture, if something happened to you, Georgiana would be left defenseless. As co-guardian your cousin Richard would try to take care of her. However, he is away much of the time and he is not married. Even if she were married to a good and worthy man, it would mean the end of the Darcy name. I suppose it is selfish of me, but I do not want that."

"No more do I," Darcy said without inflection. His father never used his full name unless the matter was of the greatest importance. "It is not that I do not want to marry, but the idea of taking a wife I know nothing about, have never even met, however worthy, is—distasteful."

George Darcy sighed inwardly. "You feel I have taken away your power of choice. Since you reached your majority, even before that, I have never interfered in your private life. But I feel you can no longer afford to wait for the perfect wife."

Fitzwilliam recognized the truth of the statement, however much he disliked it. He might refuse, but it would be a betrayal of his family and, worse, of his father. He raised his head to meet George Darcy's eyes. "I will do whatever is necessary, Father."

There was nothing for George Darcy to say to that. His son was a man of impeccable honor, once his word was given he would not break it. George nodded. "While I was in London I renewed my acquaintance with a gentleman I knew at university, Thomas Bennet. He is the senior partner of Bennet, Delibes, and Cranshaw. He also owns a small estate in Hertfordshire that has been in the family for five or six generations. The gentleman has five daughters." Ignoring Fitzwilliam's grimace he went on. "The eldest is married to a gentleman in Hertfordshire, the middle daughter has an informal agreement with the junior partner, Mr. Cranshaw, and the next youngest is betrothed to a Mr. Cowper. The youngest is not yet out."

"And that leaves the second-eldest lady."

"Yes, Miss Elizabeth Bennet. I met her when I dined with them. She is quite attractive with the most remarkable eyes I have ever seen."

"How old is she?"

"About two- or three-and-twenty."

"And she has all but one other sister married or betrothed? Why is the lady herself not taken?"

George Darcy considered his answer. "She is not the usual society miss. Her manners are perfect, and she is quite charming. But she is also well read and more aware of the world than most ladies. Her father has encouraged her to reason and think critically. It sets her apart and is not attractive to the gentlemen of the *ton*. She plays the pianoforte quite well and sings in a beautiful soprano. I have no doubt her mother has made certain that she is versed in household management. More than that, a single dinner did not divulge. Oh, and she rides."

Fitzwilliam raised an eyebrow. "What are you not telling me?"

Again his father hesitated. "I cannot say with any certainty. But I know that Miss Elizabeth has opinions, and I believe she does not appreciate having them ignored or dismissed out of hand. She may also be a bit stubborn. Her dowry is twenty thousand pounds, and as there is no heir to the estate, she will receive a portion of the profits if it is sold after her father passes."

"Adequate, but not out of the ordinary. I have heard of her father's firm; he handles legal matters for a fairly large number of the *ton*. His reputation is excellent. Are there any other drawbacks to the match?"

George Darcy held out his glass, and his son rose to refill it. Now that Fitzwilliam had committed to the match, the young man's reason assumed control submerging emotion, at least for the time being.

When he returned, his father said, "Mrs. Bennet's father was in trade. Her brother now owns the company, Gardiner Imports. He is reputed to be quite wealthy and known as an honest and reliable merchant. Georgiana and your aunt Madeleine have bought from his warehouses, along with other society ladies and the best modistes. Personally I have no objections to the man, but you may feel differently, although you have always been liberal in your friendships."

Fitzwilliam shrugged. "I admit that I would not care to have a fishmonger in the family, but I see no reason to judge the man without having his acquaintance. In any event, I intend to spend most of my time here rather than in Town. Do you think Miss Bennet would object to that?"

"As she is not particularly involved with the *ton* and is used to the country, I see no reason why she should object. You will have to ask her yourself."

Fitzwilliam watched as his father drank a little more of the brandy and leaned his head back against the leather chair. How much longer would he have this man's advice and counsel, his unconditional love? How much longer before there was no one to turn to except Georgiana, and she dependent on him for support? She would need someone to help her as she matured from girl to woman, especially if her father was taken before she was ready to step into the role of a lady of society. He needed more than a mother for his children and a mistress for Pemberley and their town house; he wanted a partner, a companion, a friend, and a lover. A woman who knew more of life than how to decorate his arm and defer to his every opinion, a woman who did not expect him to regulate her life. Yes, he was able to provide the luxuries a lady of the *ton* expected, but he did not want a wife who was willing to substitute material goods for affection and esteem.

Thus far he had failed to find a woman who came even close to meeting his idea of a wife in spite of six Seasons of debutantes and their aggressive mamas. One or two had come close, but always there was the sense that he was not seeing the real woman, only a portrait, posed for maximum effect but empty of warmth or veracity. The rest were so many china dolls, lovely to look at but with heads empty of substance. This Miss Bennet might well be headstrong and contrary. But at least she was not just one more prettily decorated confection, or his father would never have chosen her.

George Darcy pushed himself out of the chair and stood still for a moment, gathering his strength. "Have Martin pack your trunks; you will leave for Town tomorrow and stay until the arrangements are completed for the wedding."

At the look of resignation on his son's face, he said with a smile, "Miss Bennet is indeed worthy, and I believe you will find her something of a challenge, not a bad thing in a wife. Look on the bright side, Son. Marriage to a strong-willed woman will never be dull!"

CHAPTER 3

CONFERENCE AND CONSOLATION

The morning after the dinner for Mr. Darcy, Elizabeth was still in the breakfast room when Mr. Hill announced her aunt Gardiner. Elizabeth sprang up and ran to embrace the woman she thought of as a second mother. When she was released Mrs. Gardiner stepped back to survey one of her two favorite nieces, still holding Elizabeth's hand.

"Lizzy, you look as if you have not been sleeping well. I am sorry I was not at home when you called yesterday I was at a meeting of the board of the foundling hospital. Mr. Mars said you seemed upset. Is something wrong? It is not Jane, is it?"

Elizabeth shook her head. "No, she is well as far as I know. It is something concerning me." She glanced toward the door. "Mama will be down soon. Would you mind if we walked in the park? We can talk privately there."

"Of course, my dear. Get your things, and we will go immediately."

As soon as Elizabeth retrieved her shawl, gloves, and bonnet, the two women walked several blocks to the main entrance of

Hyde Park together. Elizabeth said nothing until they sat on a bench in a sheltered area. There were several horsemen on the broad expanse of Rotten Row, grooms exercising their masters' mounts and one or two riders out for a morning canter. The sound of hooves on the sanded ground made a counterpoint to Elizabeth's swirling emotions.

Mrs. Gardiner studied her niece's strained expression before asking softly, "Why do you not tell me what is bothering you so deeply?"

Elizabeth said with suppressed anger, "I am to be married—to a man I have never met! Papa arranged the betrothal with the son of a gentleman he knew at Cambridge, a Mr. Darcy."

"Darcy? Mr. George Darcy?" Mrs. Gardiner could hardly suppress her amazement.

"That is he. Do you have his acquaintance?"

It would not be impossible for the Gardiners to know a member of high society, as they moved in circles considerably better than the average tradespeople, if not the equal of the *haute ton.*

"No," Mrs. Gardiner hastened to assure her niece. "However, Mr. Darcy's son is well known to most people who follow society activities. He has participated in a number of Seasons without marrying or becoming betrothed. He is said to be not sociable and rarely attends the exclusive gatherings of the *ton.* His uncle is the Earl of Matlock. I believe he has a younger sister but no other immediate family except his father."

"I met the elder Mr. Darcy at dinner last night. He is dignified but amiable, not self-important as I expected. But his son may be nothing like him."

"Or he may. Lizzy, why did your father arrange this marriage? I thought he was against such practices."

"So did I," Elizabeth said with barely restrained bitterness. "Apparently he is tired of sending me out to find a husband only to have me reject the young men who want to call on me and the two who offered for me. I could hardly believe it. I feel as if someone should be running me around the yard at Tattersall's: brood mare for sale, not too old, good teeth, acceptable conformation, owner tired of maintenance."

Before her aunt was able to reply, Elizabeth burst into tears. Mrs. Gardiner put an arm around her niece's shoulders but let her cry until she quieted. Elizabeth pulled out her handkerchief and wiped her eyes.

"I am sorry, Aunt. There has been no one I can talk to. No one else knows. There will be no announcement until the younger Mr. Darcy arrives and calls on me. It may be because Papa does not wish to listen to Mama's effusions, but it may also be he thinks I will still reject the betrothal."

"Would you do that, Lizzy?" her aunt asked seriously.

Elizabeth hesitated. "No, I cannot. There is bound to be talk, even if no open scandal occurs. I cannot risk the damage to my family. And if I do not marry Mr. Darcy, I know I will be sent back to Meryton, perhaps forever."

"I am sure Mr. Bingley and Jane would welcome you staying with them."

"No," Elizabeth said firmly. "I could not do that. Mr. Bingley would never countenance my paying my own way, and I cannot be a permanent guest in my sister's home. Besides they are just starting their family. I refuse to add a complication to their lives."

One of the grooms in the livery of a Personage rode by them at a little distance, urging his horse to a pace faster than allowed in the park. Mrs. Gardiner waited until the disturbance passed, to ask, "It is settled, then?"

"Oh yes, it is settled. Papa says he does not want me to waste my youth waiting for an ideal man who may never come. He believes that I am not made for spinsterhood, that it would destroy me. I do not want to remain unmarried, but I have always said I would only marry for the deepest love. That choice has been taken away from me. At least," she added softly, "Jane married for love."

"She did indeed," Mrs. Gardiner agreed. "But you must know such marriages are rare. I was extremely fortunate to meet your uncle, but even though I was attracted to him I cannot say that I was deeply in love when we married. He is a good, kind man, and that was sufficient to earn my respect and esteem. True affection came later. I have never been sorry that I accepted him."

"At least you were not forced to wed him," Elizabeth said. The breeze wavered on the brim of her bonnet, tugged a strand of curling dark hair loose, and played with it merrily.

Mrs. Gardiner felt a great sadness at the defeat in her niece's voice. "Have you thought," Mrs. Gardiner lay a hand on Elizabeth's arm, "that Mr. Darcy may feel the same way?"

Elizabeth's head jerked up; she met her aunt's eyes, her own full of uncertainty. She had not considered her proposed fiancé's feelings in the matter. "No, I had not."

"He must be near thirty. When his father passes away, he will inherit vast property and wealth. Most men of his station are married soon after they enter society, unless there is a reason for them to reject marriage. Mr. Darcy has no such reputation for dissolution or wanton behavior. From what I have heard of him, he is quite the opposite. Perhaps he, too, has waited for a particular sort of woman to wed and not yet found her. If his father is determined to have his son married, he may have done what Thomas did and looked for a suitable bride. I doubt Mr. Darcy would defy his father; most young men would not. But I also doubt the marriage was of his choosing."

Elizabeth looked away over the shimmering water of the Serpentine. Swans floated like small white clouds on its surface, while ducks foraged among the grass and reeds along the shore. She felt weary all at once, her anger spent. When she did not respond, Mrs. Gardiner continued, watching her niece's face.

"Lizzy, you are one of the strongest ladies I know. As difficult as this is for you, I know you will find your way through it. Why do you not wait and see what sort of man Mr. Darcy is before you reject him because of your father's actions? You may find that matters are resolved far more happily than you expect."

Elizabeth contemplated her aunt's advice. If she had no escape from this marriage, at least she might look for the good in her betrothed. If she was able to respect him, it would make the situation easier for both of them.

"I shall try, Aunt."

Elizabeth hugged her aunt. They rose, and Mrs. Gardiner accompanied her niece back to the entrance of the park. She knew how stubborn Lizzy could be; if she determined not to like the young man her mind would not be changed easily. It was a brilliant match, of course, but Lizzy was not materialistic. As they reached the Bennet House, Mrs. Gardiner hoped Lizzy would take her words to heart and give Mr. Darcy a chance, for her own sake as much as his.

Mrs. Bennet was in the breakfast room when she heard voices in the hall. She popped the last bite of her muffin into her mouth, swallowed her tea, rose from the table, and hurried to the drawing room. Elizabeth had rung for tea. She returned to the sofa and sat beside Mrs. Gardiner. Her mother gave her a look of rebuke as she seated herself in a chair across from them.

"Why did you not call me when my sister Gardiner arrived, Lizzy? I suppose you have told her all about last night's dinner?"

"No, Mama, I thought you would wish to do that."

Mrs. Bennet's expression moderated. "Oh. Well, then, I shall do so."

She proceeded to recount the entire evening's activities—what every course consisted of, how Mr. Darcy looked, how he dressed, and what she had gleaned about his estate.

"He is a true gentleman," she said at last. "He engaged Lizzy in conversation, and he might have spoken more to her if she had kept to ladylike subjects instead of talking about revolving crops and wheat prices. Mr. Darcy has a son, you know, and he is not married. But I doubt Lizzy will ever meet him now, much less have a chance to secure him or any other man of wealth and status."

Elizabeth colored but said nothing. Mrs. Gardiner deftly turned the subject to Kitty and her upcoming wedding. Even though it was nearly six months in the future, Mrs. Bennet was already making plans for the celebration. Mrs. Gardiner listened with half a mind to the monologue of warehouses, modistes, menus and guest lists. She was fond of her sister-in-law. She knew that Mrs. Bennet loved all her daughters, but her attitude toward Elizabeth had always disturbed Margaret Gardiner. At times it took all her control not to speak out.

Elizabeth simply did not fulfill her mother's notion of feminine behavior or interests. It had been a point of friction between them since Lizzy was a child. Jane, Mary, Kitty, and even in some part Lydia, were ladylike in their interests and pursuits. Mary read extensively, chiefly books of self-improvement, although since her informal arrangement with Mr. Cranshaw, she had taken more interest in her appearance, choosing more modish coiffures and dress styles. The three oldest daughters all played the pianoforte and sang; all did needlepoint and embroidery. Jane painted moderately well, and Kitty drew very well, while Mary had no interest in art. Lydia did not play although she sang quite well and followed fashion avidly, even though she was not out and was not allowed to wear the revealing dinner and evening gowns worn by her older sisters. Other than reading every new novel she could lay her hands on, she had no interest in literature, or expanding her mind.

Elizabeth was the exception; she did not fit Mrs. Bennet's notion of a lady. She read history and science, perused her father's newspapers, and preferred Shakespeare to novels and opera to pantomime. She loved to walk whenever possible and cared little for fashion, and while she played well and sang beautifully, she lacked what her mother considered the necessary skills for obtaining a husband, namely deference and flattery.

After half an hour of Mrs. Bennet's raptures over the dinner with Mr. Darcy and Kitty's wedding, Mrs. Gardiner rose to leave. Elizabeth offered to walk her out while her carriage was brought around. As they stood in the foyer, Mrs. Gardiner took Elizabeth's hand and leaned to speak softly so that she should not be overheard by the waiting footman.

"Lizzy, whatever happens, your uncle and I will support you."

"Thank you, Aunt." Elizabeth felt her throat tighten. "You have always been so good to me."

Mrs. Gardiner squeezed her hand and stepped back. The footman opened the door, and she proceeded out to her waiting carriage, hoping with all her heart that young Mr. Darcy had the perception to appreciate Elizabeth's intellect and not try to shape her into someone she was not and could never be.

The town house on South Audley Street was one of the finest ones built there; a tall, narrow structure of brick, two stories above the ground floor with attics at the top. It had been built in the second quarter of the previous century, and no expense had been spared. The creamy brick was of the finest quality. The pitched slate roof had a heavily leaded valley to protect from leakage, and there were dormer windows in the attics to ventilate the servants' rooms. The recessed sash window frames and paneled front door were painted dark blue. A fence of iron palings set the property off from the sidewalk, with a driveway opening instead of a gate, wide enough for a carriage to pass through. A small front-garden area bloomed with late color.

In a sitting room on the first floor, an elderly woman surveyed the prospect of the square across the road with clear gray eyes. Her ice-white hair was drawn up in a simple knot and braids, her gown of deep-purple silk beautifully made in the style of an older generation. She was Lady Agatha Quintain, widow of the renowned painter Sir Cedric Quintain. Like its owner, the room was furnished and decorated in a more severe style than currently popular: delicately carved rococo shells and curves, walls, dadoes, and doors painted white with gilt decoration, the carved mahogany chairs and sofas upholstered in silk.

Several paintings occupied the space above the picture rail, landscapes in the manner of Turner but with a softer palette. Above the carved white-marble fireplace, a white-painted and gilt chimneypiece held a nearly full-length portrait of a young woman in a simple country dress of sprigged muslin, auburn hair falling around her shoulders. She held a single red rose in one hand. Clear gray eyes arresting in their strength looked out from a face too sharply cut for conventional beauty. The painting breathed vitality, life, and love. The painter had been no stranger to his subject.

A knock caused her to call in the butler, who bowed and advanced to stand beside her chair. She gazed up at him with a quizzical expression, one brow raised.

"Yes, Mr. Hughes?"

"A letter has arrived by express, my lady." As stiff as a new recruit facing a general, he presented the missive on a salver.

Lady Agatha took up the letter, realizing from the weight that it was at least two pages. The return direction was only "The Vicarage, Kympton, Derbyshire" and only her name and direction were on the outside. Lady Agatha hesitated, holding the letter in both hands. Kympton was a name she had not seen in many years. The fact that it had come by express rider made it of some importance. Curious but not alarmed, she broke the simple seal and said without looking up, "Is the messenger waiting for a reply?"

"No, my lady."

"Very well. I shall ring if I want you. Thank you, Mr. Hughes."

The outer page was not long, written in a clerical hand. It said simply,

> *My dear Lady Agatha,*
>
> *The enclosed was found among the papers of the late Mr. Tweed, rector of Kympton, Derbyshire. It contained instructions to forward same to you by express upon his death. Mr. Tweed was the rector here for nearly forty years and a man of integrity and piety. I trust the enclosed is to your benefit.*
>
> *Yr. humble servant,*
> *Joseph Keene, Vicar*

The enclosed document was not the letter she expected but a signed and witnessed statement. The writing was solid, if not polished, and perfectly legible. The signature, however, was shaky, the writing of a very old or very ill woman. As she read, a gray fog slowly surrounded her. It brought with it a paroxysm of fury, grief, hatred, and despair as real as the memories it raised.

When her surroundings became clear again, Lady Agatha sat rigid in her chair, the papers still clutched in both hands. Her muscles ached with tension; she heard the blood rush through her temples like water over a weir. She began to take slow, deep breaths, forcing her body to ease. When she was once more in command of herself, she sat for a long time with her eyes on the window without seeing the scene beyond the panes. So much was explained by this simple missive, so many years of rejection, denial, and pain.

To her benefit? Her mouth twisted; tears misted her eyes.

After several minutes, Lady Agatha's gaze rose to the portrait of her younger self. She stared fixedly at it for long minutes, her mind reverting to another time.

Are *you still looking over me, Cedric? What should I do? It is so long past time for any amends to be made, even if the years might be brought back again. Shall I act, or shall I simply burn this and let the dead past bury its dead? You were always so logical, while I acted on impulse and emotion. I have learned better over the years, but still I cannot forget or forgive. This opportunity for redress has been handed me as a gift. Tell me what to do, my dearest love.*

There was no answer. At length Lady Agatha rose and rang for her maid. The woman, who was only a few years younger than her mistress, came in with a smile. "Are you ready to return to your rooms, my lady?"

Agatha nodded. "Yes, Marie. I will rest for a while before dinner."

She required solitude, Lady Agatha thought. Time to consider and decide what she wanted to do. She must not act in haste, she told herself. No one else knew the truth; that was to her benefit. No one would realize her motives if she took advantage of this gift from a dead man. Lady Agatha put the letter in the pocket of her gown. Leaning a little on her walking stick, with her maid in close attendance, she left the sitting room that seemed to echo with silent voices behind her.

Before he left London, George Darcy had informed the staff at Darcy House that his son would be arriving within the week, so when Fitzwilliam Darcy entered the town house on Grosvenor Street, everything was in readiness for his comfort and convenience. His sister would not be home from the seminary until later in the day; until then there was no one he needed to see immediately. After he had washed off the dust of travel and allowed his man Martin to bring him a pristine coat and exchange his boots for house shoes, Darcy went downstairs to the library. The dark peace of the large room with its shelves and cases of books, its world globe on a separate stand, and its glass case of special manuscripts soothed him, as it always did. Darcy took a chair in one of the two window bays and leaned back, trying to sort and order his roiling thoughts.

He had been raised to duty and responsibility since childhood, and groomed to take over management of the Darcy estates and interests whenever his father relinquished them. Darcy prided himself on his logical mind and rational habit of thought, but the crisis facing him now submitted to neither. For more reasons than privacy his father wanted no one to know that he was very ill. There were opportunists who wanted nothing more than a sign of weakness from the patriarch of the Darcys to attack the family like ravening dogs. Once Fitzwilliam was firmly in charge of their affairs, if word of his father's illness leaked out it would not be a matter of serious concern.

And that led him to thoughts of his arranged marriage. He must call on the lady and judge what he faced with his bride-to-be. Fitzwilliam doubted that his sister knew anything of Miss Bennet, as Georgiana was not yet out and her circle of friends was limited to other young ladies at the seminary and a few family acquaintances. His aunt Madeleine might have some information. Surely the lady attended parties and balls, even if she was not deeply involved in the *ton*. His aunt was an excellent judge of character, especially in women. He determined to call on her in the morning. He would then visit Mr. Bennet at his office to ascertain when it might be best to call on his fiancée.

His father had indicated that the betrothal was to remain secret until the marriage settlement was drawn. Fitzwilliam knew that it was to give him a chance to adjust to the idea of marrying a lady he had never met and to find out something about her before the matter was irrevocably determined. But was it not that now? Even if he found Miss Bennet unsuitable, there would be no time to go through another Season of searching for someone more compatible, with no guarantee of finding her. No, he was committed by fate to wed this lady. All he could do was hope that she proved to be a lady he could respect. That would have to serve the place of affection, at least for the present.

Weary from long nights with little rest, he dozed off, only to be abruptly wakened by a knock on the library door. Darcy got to his feet as Mr. Burgess, the town house butler, entered.

"Colonel Fitzwilliam, sir."

Richard Fitzwilliam walked in past the butler and crossed to his cousin, his hand extended. They shook hands with the warmth of brothers, and Darcy indicated a sideboard holding decanters and glasses.

"Brandy or whiskey?"

"Both," Richard joked.

Darcy brought back two brandies, indicating the other chair in the bay. They sat, and Richard took a swallow of his drink, raising an eyebrow. "I hope this is prewar French, or I might have to arrest you for trading with the enemy."

"Definitely prewar," Darcy assured him. He sipped his own brandy while Richard studied his cousin's face.

"I am the one who has been in battle, but you look like you have been through hell, my friend."

Darcy took another swallow and felt it burn the back of his throat. He could put Richard off, but his cousin would persist until he knew everything. They had grown up together, Richard two years older. They had been inseparable until Richard, a younger son, had graduated from Cambridge and taken up a commission in the army. He had risen through the ranks from lieutenant to colonel on his own merit, refusing to allow his father to buy his advancement. Even though they only saw each other when Richard was on leave, the bond was as strong as it had ever been.

"It is Father." Darcy set the glass aside, his eyes fixed on his hands clamped together between his knees.

"Uncle George is not ill, is he?"

Darcy tried to force the words out. His throat felt as if it had closed. Instinctively Richard reached out and gripped his cousin's shoulder.

Darcy said, "Terminally."

Richard drew a sharp hiss of breath. His hold tightened, but he did not respond, letting Darcy find his way to explain what had happened.

"His heart," Darcy said woodenly at last. "Sir Ansel McQuary confirmed it a fortnight ago. I do not…do not know how long…"

Richard sat back. He had seen enough death in the past few years to drive many men mad. Soldiers who lost lifelong friends, cousins, brothers, and even sons. While he felt compassion for their grief, Richard had hardened himself to the fact that men died in war. This was different. Not only because this was someone of his own blood, someone dear to him who suffered, but also because this was the uncle he admired and respected. Unlike Richard and his father, Fitzwilliam and his father were close. Losing all that George Darcy meant to him would wound his son in ways that might never be healed.

"Georgie does not know."

It was a statement, not a question. Darcy shook his head. "She will have to be told later, but not now. She is nearly finished at the seminary. When she leaves, we will return to Pemberley and remain there until…until the end."

"Is that why you are in town, then?"

Darcy dropped his head into his hands for a time. When he straightened, he said, "No. There is something else."

Frowning, Richard watched Darcy closely. "Do you want to tell me?"

With a mixture of disbelief and resentment, Darcy said, "I am to be married."

"Pardon me? You are to be what?"

"Married."

Richard rose, took both glasses, and refilled them. He came back, put Darcy's glass into his hand, and took half of his in a gulp. Resuming his seat, he said, "When did this come about? And do I have the lady's acquaintance?"

"Before Father left for town he told me that he wanted an heir at Pemberley and that I had spent too much time searching for a bride. He has arranged a match with the daughter of a man he knew at Cambridge and has kept some track of since, Mr. Thomas Bennet of Bennet, Delibes, and Cranshaw. And, no, you do not know her. Neither do I."

Carefully Richard asked, "Is this because of his...illness?"

"In part. I am sorry to say it. But Father knows that Nicholas wants Pemberley, or whatever of it he can get his hands on, and if there is not a new heir soon, he will try to force a marriage with Georgiana. Father will never consent to it, nor would I. But it could well lead to a family split. If I marry, even if there is no heir immediately, it will stave off any plans Nicholas may have."

The colonel replied, "You do not know my brother as I do. Our grandfather had much of the raising of him, thanks to Father's disinclination to stand up to the old man, and Nick is as greedy and unprincipled as grandfather ever was."

"I would never see him marry Georgie," Darcy said in a hard voice. "But life is uncertain, and if anything were to happen to me before I produce an heir, she would become the prey of every potential suitor who wants Pemberley. If Nicholas offers for her, your father will undoubtedly support him."

"I imagine so." Richard kept his voice neutral.

Slowly Darcy said, "There is an alternative."

Silence dropped between them. At last Richard responded, "I have thought of that."

"Georgie is fond of you. It is a good match for you and security for her. There would be no concern about her future or how well she was treated."

"I am fond of Georgie as well, but I am also twice her age. I do not believe she considers me in the way a woman considers a husband. She is not even out yet. She ought to have her Season. She may find someone she wishes to marry. To take that from her on the chance of your premature demise could cause her to bitterly resent both of us. No good start to a marriage."

Darcy studied his cousin closely. "Forgive me, but is there a prior inclination?"

Richard shook his head. "No one in particular. With my army pay and my allowance, I can live comfortably. But I cannot take a wife without some other source of income, and that means a lady with property, a large dowry, or both."

"I understand your reluctance. Perhaps you will keep it in mind?"

"As you wish." Richard finished his drink and continued, "So you have not met the lady yet?"

"No. Father dined with the family while he was here. He said Miss Bennet is well read and aware of the world and has a beautiful singing voice and amazing eyes. She is also likely to have 'opinions,' whatever that means."

"Lord help you if she's an adherent of Mrs. Wollstonecraft." It was not entirely a jest.

Darcy shrugged. "It is done. I will call on her father tomorrow at his place of business and probably meet her the day after. There is to be no word of the engagement until after the settlement is drawn. I do not believe Father chose her at random. There must have been something about her that led him to believe she will be a suitable wife and mistress of Pemberley; however, I do intend to call on your mother tomorrow as well and ask if she knows the lady or anything about her."

"If anyone does, it is Mother. Take care, though. She is not easy to deceive in matters of the heart." Richard rose. "Why do you not dine with us tomorrow? I can give you my valuable support and divert her if necessary."

"Very well." Darcy walked him out into the entry hall. "How long are you in town?"

"I am not sure. Officially I am on leave; unofficially I have business at the War Office that I cannot discuss."

Darcy nodded. "I will see you tomorrow evening, then."

They shook hands again, and Richard left. Georgiana's companion, Mrs. Annesley, came downstairs at that moment and greeted her employer's son cordially. She was on her way to bring Georgiana home from the seminary and did not linger. Darcy sent word to the kitchen that he and his sister would dine in the small breakfast parlor, and then he went into the study to look at any post awaiting his attention. He had not intended to tell Richard about his father, but the words had come out in spite of his resolution. His cousin was the one person Darcy could speak to with absolute honesty. That trust, built by years of companionship and mutual support, was precious in a world where even family was not always to be relied on.

Darcy closed the door behind him and sat behind the massive mahogany desk. He had a feeling that he was going to need Richard's unwavering strength badly in the days to come.

CHAPTER 4

HONOR AND DECEPTION

"Paste!" Sir Colin's voice slid up the scale, his face red with fury. "What do you mean, 'paste'? Lady Swandon has one of the finest collections of jewels in the country; how can they be paste?"

"Because," Winter drawled, "she has one of the finest collections of jewels in the country. The originals are probably in a bank or safe somewhere."

Sir Colin's eyes narrowed. "I don't believe you."

Winter made an elaborate display of reaching into his pocket, drawing out a small velvet bag and opening the drawstring. He dumped the contents onto the pedestal table between them. Set in what appeared to be gold flowers were a number of diamonds surrounding a central ruby. Sir Colin touched the necklace carefully. He raised his head to look at Winter's half smile, his eyes narrowing.

"It looks fine to me."

"That is why you are not a jeweler—or a fence." Winter took a small hammer from the dish of nuts on the table. With sudden vicious force, he smashed the ruby to scattered bits. "Paste."

Sir Colin swore. He was not original, but his vocabulary expressed his opinion of Lady Swandon and her jewels adequately. Winter gathered the remains and returned them to the velvet pouch. Sir Colin collapsed into his chair.

"What about the settings?" he asked suddenly.

"As fake as the gems. Not worth melting down. A beautiful job, though. A real master made these."

"Damn the master! And damn you! I've made promises, and now I can't pay. Maresford will have my—"

"A sad fate." Winter's insouciance infuriated the young nobleman, as he knew it would. He was growing tired of the whining and the tantrums, even though they were proof of how deeply ensnared Sir Colin was. "There may be a way out."

"How?" Sir Colin was instantly attentive.

"I have a small amount put aside. I can loan you enough to buy a little more time. The Little Season will be over in a few weeks; there are bound to be several large balls and soirees before then. Not all society women are careful enough to have copies made of their jewelry; they enjoy showing themselves off in the originals too much."

Winter leaned toward his companion, lowering his voice even further.

"All we need are one or two big hauls, and you can pay off your debts, with some leftover."

"What do you get from this if we succeed?" The question was asked in a manner just short of insulting.

"Enough to do some traveling in style. I have always wanted to see Scotland."

"All right. I shall accept invitations to all the best entertainments. I…I have no choice."

No, you do not, Winter thought, concealing a satisfied smirk. *You are in deep water, little fish, and a pike is about to swallow you whole. The Dutchman gave me enough for the settings to tide you over, and I am out nothing but time.*

"Talking of entertainment." Winter's lips lifted in a feral grin. "There's a place I know of in Whitechapel. I do not think it would suit your refined taste, though."

"Girls?" Sir Colin's face reflected salacious interest as well as hesitation.

"Young girls. Quite young. Fresh off the post chaise from the country. The proprietor has an abbess pick the ones least likely to be missed. She offers them work as maids." Winter chuckled. "They do not remain maids for long. If you see something you fancy, you can bid for the privilege of introducing her to the rites of Venus."

"Are...are the girls willing?" Sir Colin licked dry lips.

"Rarely. That is what provides the entertainment. Of course, participation is limited to his wealthier clients, and you are a little young for the sport."

Sir Colin drew himself up. His breathing had quickened, and Winter saw other signs of his interest. "I am not inexperienced, George. I will go with you."

"Then let us have an early supper at Antoine's. You will need your strength."

Winter laughed to himself as he went to his rooms to dress. He would not disabuse Sir Colin of the notion that the girls were newly garnered from the numbers who flocked to London to find work in the grand houses of the wealthy. The owner of the place kept these events to a small number of select men who paid well for the experience. The owner was not about to waste unspoiled girls on a few drunken "gentlemen." All but one or two of the girls were women from another of his houses, made to look as innocent as possible. *No small feat,* Winter thought.

The men were usually half-sprung when they arrived, and the brandy and whisky sold on the premises guaranteed that, by the time the bidding started, the men participating were likely to spend outrageously for very little. The rest of the audience watched, drank, shouted advice, and sang bawdy songs. Winter did not participate, preferring his carnal encounters to be of a more private, and less expensive, kind. He held the men who came and the women in equal contempt. It was simply a means to secure Sir Colin tighter on the hook.

Winter had once said to George Darcy when the man he hated more than any other had accused him of corrupting innocents, "There are no innocents. Only those who have not discovered the extent of their appetites." Sir Colin was in the process of making that discovery. And tonight would not be the end.

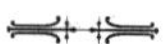

The offices of Bennet, Delibes, and Cranshaw at the Inns of Court were larger and better appointed than Darcy expected. A middle-aged clerk led him from the quiet reception area to a private conference room. He was offered a variety of drinks and an apology that Mr. Bennet was detained with a client. Darcy surveyed the room as he waited. The furniture was highly polished oak and leather. A Wedgewood vase of bronze chrysanthemums centered the oblong table, and there were paintings in the spaces between bookcases and tall, narrow windows. Darcy recognized a racing scene by John Nott, as well as one of horses by Gilpin, and a Turner landscape over the fireplace. Everything spoke of subtle but expensive taste. Darcy began to feel that the situation might turn out well after all.

The clerk brought tea and biscuits. Darcy was just finishing his first cup when the man returned and led him to Mr. Bennet's office. It was furnished in the same manner but with a more Spartan sensibility. The only painting was another Turner above the fireplace, a seascape of ships in a storm. Several miniatures rested on the solicitor's large mahogany desk with a gold writing set of pen, inkwell, wax softener, and seal. There were no other decorations. Like the rest of the offices it gave a sense of quiet seclusion. Clients instinctively knew they were in the presence of confident, solid competence.

Mr. Bennet was standing to meet his guest. He matched the office well, Darcy thought. A man of about his father's age, a little above middle height with a mane of silver hair and clear, dark-blue eyes that assessed the younger man at a glance. They bowed to one another, and Darcy took the chair before the desk.

"May I offer you some refreshments?"

"Thank you, no," Darcy declined, and the two men gazed at one another, Mr. Bennet with professional serenity, Darcy aware that he was being weighed in some private balance and not comfortable with the feeling. It caused the reserved mask he usually wore to fall firmly into place. After what seemed a long pause, Darcy said, "I wanted to meet you, Mr. Bennet, before I called at your residence. I realize the awkwardness of the situation and that you may have questions for me or matters you wish to discuss privately."

"Very civil of you, Mr. Darcy. I appreciate your position. You may have questions for me as well."

The older man leaned back a little in his chair. His voice had the timbre of a professional speaker. "I remember your father well from our time at university. He was not only a scholar, he was the finest rider I ever knew and a prime fencer. Do you follow the noble sport, Mr. Darcy?"

"When I can. I fence at Angelo's when I am in town. Most of my time is spent at Pemberley or at a small estate my father owns in Staffordshire. Is Miss Bennet inclined to country living?"

"Very much. I have heard that the gardens at your estate are nonpareil. She will enjoy them, as she likes nothing better than to be out of doors." Mr. Bennet looked to his hands resting lightly on the desk's mirror-polished top. "I was surprised when your father called on me to see that he looked quite tired. He always had boundless energy. But we all grow older."

Does he suspect that something is wrong? Darcy wondered. *If he does, and he is not a dull man by any measure, it would provide him an advantage in the provisions of the settlement.*

"It is the harvest, I think. He oversees everything himself, although I do as much as I can."

"Allow me to be frank, Mr. Darcy." Mr. Bennet leaned forward, holding the young man's gaze steadily. "You have been out in society for some time. You have your choice of the young ladies of the *ton,* yet your father must arrange a marriage for you with my daughter. If there is a reason for your reluctance to marry, please tell me. I will hold your answer in complete confidence."

Darcy felt his face heat. "I have not found a lady among the debutants of the *ton* who meets my requirements in a wife."

"And those are?"

"Intelligence, kindness, and empathy for others. I do not want a pretty decoration; I want a wife who can be my companion as well as fulfill the other roles necessary to the mistress of Pemberley. I do not want to spend my time ordering her days for her. I especially do not want a wife who is only happy in Town, whose only interests are fashion and entertainments and gossip about who is engaging in an affair with whom."

Finding that his tone had grown more heated than courtesy permitted, Darcy apologized. Mr. Bennet waived it away. After a pause, Darcy went on in a quieter voice, "I mean no disrespect, Mr. Bennet, but I understand that Miss Bennet has also been in society for several Seasons and that all but one of her sisters is either married or betrothed. Is she disinclined to wed?"

"She has her own requirements in a husband, which I shall let you discover for yourself. The last man who offered for her, by the way, was Mr. Leslie Hatfield. I was no more in favor of the match than Elizabeth."

"I have some slight acquaintance with Mr. Hatfield. I will only say that I would not allow my sister to marry him."

"Is there anything else you wish to know, Mr. Darcy?"

Darcy was about to reply in the negative when he suddenly realized that he did not know one important fact. "Is Miss Bennet aware of the arrangement?"

Mr. Bennet nodded. "She is. My daughter is an intelligent woman. I would never attempt to manipulate her."

Warning number one, Darcy thought wryly. "She is not opposed to your choosing her husband?"

"'Opposed' may not be the proper word. Elizabeth is of an independent nature. She accepts my decision; however, she will need to decide for herself if she finds you a suitable husband. Convincing her will be up to you."

Warning number two. From some note in Mr. Bennet's voice, Darcy wondered if the man was much given to irony in his private life. "I was under the impression that our betrothal was already decided."

"It is, insofar as I am concerned. However," Mr. Bennet said, considering the young man before him seriously, "you should know that if Elizabeth is irrevocably against the match, I will not force her to wed. I treasure her too much to consign her to a lifetime of resentment and regret. That would not be fair to either of you."

Warning number three. "My father has said there is to be no announcement until the settlement contract is drawn. Under the circumstances, I believe a fortnight should be sufficient for Miss Bennet to decide if she will have me."

Mr. Bennet's lips twitched up at the corners. "That time should indeed be sufficient. Why do you not dine with us tomorrow if you have no other engagements? My family will think it a courtesy call since they met your father when he was in Town recently."

"I shall do so. Thank you, sir." Darcy rose and extended his hand.

Mr. Bennet walked Darcy out himself. When the young man had departed, he returned to his office with a thoughtful expression.

They are far better suited than I expected. Too well suited, perhaps, for either of them to recognize the fact. Well, well, we shall have to wait and see.

CHAPTER 5
DISCOVERY

Dinner at Matlock House had been a quieter affair than usual, in spite of Richard's presence and Nicholas's absence. Viscount Maresford was dining with friends at White's, no doubt followed by an evening of gambling at the card tables, if not by some less savory pursuit. Darcy was grateful not to have his cousin present. At family gatherings Nicholas always seemed to find a subject to quarrel over with his father or with Richard, if his younger brother was at home. His mother was reduced to keeping the peace as best she might, with the assistance of his sister, Sofia. The meal usually ended in discomfort for everyone present.

The food was as excellent as always. The earl engaged Darcy in political discussion until Richard brought up the subject of the Spanish stallion. Talk moved to horses and the breeding of heavier, healthier draft animals for both military and civilian hauling. When the ladies left them to their port and cigars, the talk turned more personal.

"Well, William, why are you in town at this time of year? You're usually at Pemberley until the harvest is finished. Looking for a bride again?"

The joke came far too close for comfort, and Darcy took a swallow of his wine before replying neutrally, "I have some legal matters to deal with for Father. The harvest is in for all intents and purposes. Standish can handle anything that arises now."

"We saw George when he was here a couple of weeks ago," the earl continued. "He looked fagged to death. Don't know why he doesn't let you take over managing the small estates at least. You do most of it now in any case."

Darcy drank a little more of his port. He felt Richard's eyes on him. "My father is used to taking charge of everything to do with Pemberley. I do manage the Staffordshire estate; they are mining a high-grade clay there that we sell to Wedgewood, among others. The Scottish estate takes less management; our steward does well with only minimal oversight. I expect that Father will begin to transfer more responsibilities to me now that the harvest is in."

"I dam' well hope so. You tell him I said it's time he took it a bit easier."

"I will," Darcy agreed.

When they joined the ladies, the earl left for a meeting with some of his political cronies, which meant "port and plots," as his younger son called it, until late in the night. Richard led the conversation in the general direction he knew Darcy wanted, asking his mother if she intended to hold any large parties before the end of the Little Season.

"I shall have a musical evening," she replied, "and perhaps a garden party if the weather allows or some sort of soiree. We have already hosted two balls. I do not know if I am ready for another, especially in view of what happened at the Gradisons' ball the other night."

Sofia shook her bright head. "What a shame to have the house burgled when one is entertaining. But I hardly think a thief would dare such an outrage here."

"It was the second robbery in three weeks," Lady Matlock said thoughtfully. "And there is a rumor that some jewelry was stolen from Lady Swandon's home during a soiree the other night. But she only keeps paste copies in the house, so I imagine they did not report it."

"I hope we have another ball," Sofia said wistfully. "I do love to dance."

"And you do it beautifully." Richard made a gallant little dip of his head at his sister, who dimpled. "Speaking of dancing and balls, someone mentioned a lady to me the other day, but I do not have her acquaintance. I wonder, Mother, if you know her?'

"What is her name?" Lady Matlock looked at her son with interest.

"Miss Elizabeth Bennet."

His mother pondered the name for a short time, her brow slightly furrowed. "I do not have the lady's acquaintance, but I have seen her at various social functions during the Season. She has been out for three years, I think."

"What is she like?"

"I know the lady you mean," Sofia said suddenly. "Her father was born a gentleman and inherited a small estate in Hertfordshire when his elder brother died."

"Yes," Lady Matlock agreed. "He is a well-known solicitor; some of our friends are clients of his. The young lady is the second daughter of five. Her elder sister married several years ago. If you had ever seen her, Richard, she is the one you would be inquiring about. She is quite beautiful—a tall, statuesque blonde with a sweet, gentle nature. Lady Hamilton was thinking of her for her son Ronald, but she married a newly made landowner who lives near their estate."

"Her sister?" Richard persisted.

"Small, fair, a mass of very dark hair, and the loveliest eyes. She dances very well indeed and is said to be witty and lively."

"But she is not married."

"No," Sofia put in. "She is of an independent character, not something that attracts the men of our social station."

"She has a respectable dowry," Lady Matlock continued, "and she is gently born. If you would like it, I can invite her to one of the entertainments."

"Let me think on it," Richard replied and moved the conversation to another subject.

Exiting his coach at the Bennet residence the next afternoon, Darcy thought that the information from his aunt and cousin added very little to what he had known of his bride-to-be. He still felt a residue of resentment for the situation, although his training and nature would not allow him to show it to Miss Bennet or her family. What was done was done. It was his duty to make the best of it.

A very proper butler answered his knock and ushered him into a pleasant foyer of pale plastered walls and honey-colored wainscoting. Several landscapes and still lifes caught the muted light from the fanlight over the front door and the two tall, narrow windows flanking it. The butler took his card but led Darcy directly to the drawing room, where the family awaited him. They rose at his entrance, and Mr. Bennet came forward to make the introductions.

"Mr. Darcy, may I present Mrs. Bennet and my daughters Elizabeth, Mary, Catherine, and Lydia?"

Darcy bowed. He had a brief impression of a plump, pretty woman of middle age with suppressed excitement in her glance, three young ladies of varying ages, and a fourth standing a little apart. She was indeed small and fair, her hair coiffed more simply than he might have expected, the color of burnished ebony. When she straightened and her eyes rose to his, his breath stopped.

Remarkable eyes, loveliest eyes. The words spun through his mind. They were the color of wood violets, flecked with blue with a thin black ring around the iris. He had met ladies with violet eyes before, if rarely. But these were the pure color and Darcy thought, as he struggled to respond in a rational manner, that a man could fall into those eyes and drown.

"Mrs. Bennet, ladies, it is an honor to meet you."

Elizabeth colored and dropped her gaze. The ladies seated themselves and Darcy took a chair near the sofa where Elizabeth and her next eldest sister sat. Mrs. Bennet rang for refreshments, while Mr. Bennet engaged their guest in general conversation. When tea arrived and was served, Darcy turned to Elizabeth. She kept her eyes modestly downcast, a modesty Darcy was thankful for. Knowing she was aware of the reason for his call, he tried to find something to say to her; alas, his faculties had deserted him.

Say something, man; you are acting like a dolt. Ask after her interests; do not just sit here until you embarrass her!

"My father mentioned that you liked the poetry of Mr. Wordsworth, Miss Bennet. I had the honor of meeting him when we last visited the Lake District. Do you agree with him that poetry 'takes its origin from emotion recollected in tranquility'?"

"I like to think the first part of his definition is more accurate: 'the spontaneous overflow of powerful feelings.' Certainly his famous elegy is full of vivid images and almost overwhelming reflections."

Darcy realized without conscious thought that he had cited one of the so-called graveyard poets, undoubtedly in response to his father's condition. "Indeed. Have you any other favorite poets, Miss Bennet?"

"Other than Shakespeare, I have read generally from many poets: Coleridge, Dryden, Gray, Donne, Milton, Dante, Herrick, and Homer in translation, although my father reads Greek and can appreciate Homer in the original."

Taken a little aback, Darcy saw the corners of her mouth turn up slightly and wondered if she was teasing him. It was not a sensation he was used to; oddly, he found he did not resent it.

"A comprehensive list," he observed. "You must read a great deal."

"Oh yes, when I am not walking or engaging in more feminine pursuits."

"Such as, Miss Bennet?"

"Needlework, netting, knitting, tatting, dancing, and the usual skills expected of a young lady."

Darcy wondered if she was actually attempting to display her irritation at what must seem to her to be an examination of her worth as a wife. Aware that her mother had cleared her throat meaningfully, he said calmly, "You also play and sing very well; my father was impressed by the beauty of your voice."

"I…thank you, Mr. Darcy. That was kind of him."

"I am sure that Lizzy will be happy to perform for you after dinner," Mrs. Bennet put in with a repressive look at her daughter.

"If she would give me the very great pleasure," Darcy replied, watching Elizabeth's face.

She looked down, so he was unable to read her expression. Her voice told him nothing. "Of course, Mr. Darcy."

Mr. Bennet entered the conversation at that point, and Elizabeth was relieved of any further discussion with her presumptive husband. He had certainly not reacted as she had expected he would to her nearly impertinent listing of her accomplishments. He seemed to be making an effort to be civil. Remembering her aunt Gardiner's advice, Elizabeth resolved to restrain her vexation and allow Mr. Darcy to reveal more of his character before making any decision about their chances of a harmonious if not affectionate marriage.

Dinner progressed in the same manner, with Elizabeth seated next to Mr. Darcy. She had a momentary sense of déjà vu as she glanced aside at him. It left her no doubt that the elder Darcy had looked exactly the same thirty years ago. She blushed at the thought that a son of theirs might bear the same resemblance.

Unaware of the cause, Darcy noted her heightened color. He remembered his aunt's description and thought that it had not done Miss Bennet justice. She had a clean profile of delicate bones, creamy skin, and a mouth he felt an urge to kiss totally out of proportion to the fact they had just met. Her hair curled despite a maid's best efforts to control it, an escaping wisp caressed her slim neck. Her figure was not full, but it was light and pleasing. Most remarkable of all, she had a mind Darcy wanted to explore.

Mrs. Bennet had made an extra effort with the meal, presenting a delicate soup jardinière, red mullet with cardinal sauce, oyster pate, croquettes of sweetbreads, lamb cutlets in a cream sauce with truffles, asparagus, peas, roast saddle of mutton, salad, a mayonnaise of fowl, macédoine of fruit, meringues à la crème, ices, cheese, nuts, and fresh fruit. And an appropriate wine with each of the courses. It was far less elaborate than a formal dinner party would have required, but designed to impress nonetheless. Darcy praised the food, as had his father, and made light conversation with Mr. Bennet and Elizabeth.

Lydia, having been warned by both her parents not to speak unless spoken to, kept silent through most of the meal. However, repressing Lydia for any length of time was a chancy proposition at best. Darcy had determined that he wanted Georgiana to meet Miss Bennet and mentioned casually that his sister was finishing her time at a ladies' school in Town.

"Oh, la, I went to a seminary," Lydia suddenly interjected, causing all eyes to focus on her, not all complacently. "It was boring, trying to learn so many things I shall never need to know. I left last spring, and I am much happier at home. I should like a dancing master, though," she added as an afterthought.

"I wager the headmistress is happier too," Mr. Bennet said dryly.

"Oh, she was sorry to see me leave. When I spoke to her, she paid me a compliment. It was in Latin or something; I cannot remember all of it, but I think it was 'Beneficum invite non…' something or other. I am sure it was a compliment, because she smiled as she said it."

"Beneficium invito non datur," her father corrected (a benefit cannot be bestowed on an unwilling person). "I quite agree with her."

Darcy understood that the headmistress was using the words in their literal sense, rather than the customary interpretation: "a generous gift always comes with a quid pro quo." Uncertain how, or even if, he should respond, Darcy took a sip of wine.

As he did so, he heard Elizabeth murmur, "Where ignorance is bliss, 'tis folly to be wise."

She looked aside sharply as he sputtered and swallowed the laugh that threatened to explode along with the wine, which brought on a fit of coughing. Darcy snatched up his napkin, but a look of horror suffused Mrs. Bennet's face at the thought of her prize guest choking to death at her table. She half rose from her chair, her voice shrill as she watched Darcy color with embarrassment.

"Oh, dear, Mr. Darcy, are you well? Mr. Bennet, Mr. Bennet, do something!"

Darcy straightened, trying to keep his countenance. "My apologies for alarming you, Mrs. Bennet," he said as soon as he was able to speak. "I am quite well. A little wine went down the wrong way."

"I rather think it was a little quotation," Mr. Bennet said sotto voce. To his wife, he replied, "Calm yourself, Mrs. Bennet. All is well."

The butler brought Darcy a clean napkin. Darcy shot a glance at Elizabeth. She had the grace to blush, but merriment danced in her eyes. Normally Darcy would have been vexed at the loss of dignity. Instead he found himself smiling at her. He badly wanted to say, "I shall get you back for that," as he would have to his cousin Sofia, but it would be totally improper except to a relative or close friend. He returned to his meal, content. Elizabeth Bennet was like no other woman he had ever met. Her wit was natural, quick, and without the meanness that characterized the snide remarks of the *ton*. The prospect of taking her to wife seemed more appealing than he could have hoped.

Lady Agatha looked up at a familiar tap on the sitting-room door and called her butler in. He crossed to her chair and stood, waiting for her to indicate she wished him to speak.

"Yes, Mr. Hughes?"

"I initiated the inquiries you requested, my lady, and I have some news regarding the gentleman you inquired about."

"And that is?"

"My sister-in-law's cousin is Sir Ansel McQuary's secretary. He worked late one night last week. As he was leaving Sir Ansel's residence, he saw a hackney cab pull up and a man exit the vehicle. He recognized the man and waited on the opposite curb in case Sir Ansel should call him back. When Sir Ansel himself answered the door, the secretary went on, as he felt the meeting was a private one."

"And the man was Mr. George Darcy?"

"Yes, my lady."

"How late was this visit?"

"About ten at night. The next day the secretary mentioned to Sir Ansel that he had noticed a cab pull up as he was leaving and wondered if it was an emergency. Sir Ansel informed him that it was a social call, and the matter was dropped."

Lady Agatha took in the information silently. A man did not visit a specialist at that hour of the evening in a hackney cab when he kept a carriage unless he did not wish the visit to be noted. *So George Darcy has an affliction of the heart. I do not blame him for not wanting it known. I wonder if his son is aware of it?*

"Further, my lady, Mr. Fitzwilliam Darcy is now at Darcy House for an indeterminate stay."

She nodded. The butler stood at attention, his eyes fixed in the middle distance, waiting his mistress's orders. He had been with her since before her late husband died some twelve years ago. Hughes had no complaints. She was a generous employer and fair in her dealings. He knew that there had been some great rift in her early life, but that was none of his concern. His only responsibility was to run the household in an efficient manner and carry out her ladyship's orders to the best of his considerable ability.

"Mr. George Darcy dined with his brother-in-law, Lord Matlock; visited his family's solicitors; and called on Mr. Thomas Bennet at his offices. He also dined with the Bennet family."

Mr. Hughes delivered his report in the same manner he might have informed his mistress of any household matter. Lady Agatha sat quietly for a few seconds.

She said, "Marlborough, Marlborough, and Hamlin have been the Darcy's attorneys for donkey's years. I doubt they mean to change, despite Mr. Bennet's reputation."

"It is said to be the renewal of an acquaintance going back to Cambridge."

"Such acquaintances are either kept up or dropped," Lady Agatha declared firmly, "not renewed after a quarter century." She tapped thin fingers on the arm of her chair. *What is George Darcy up to? First Sir Ansel, then his attorneys, and then Mr. Bennet.* "What do you know about the Bennet family?"

Hughes straightened his already-ramrod posture. "Mr. Bennet has a wife, five daughters, an excellent practice, and a spotless reputation; he is wealthy and respected. The eldest daughter is married, the middle daughter unofficially being courted by Mr. Bennet's junior partner, the next youngest betrothed to an estate owner, the youngest at home. The second eldest is unmarried."

Lady Agatha stared at the portrait on the mantelpiece. She had begun; she was not one to quit before the matter was concluded. "Find out who Mr. Bennet's connections are, who his friends are, whom he can call on if he requires help."

"Yes, my lady."

"I also want you to find out what you can about the comings and goings of young Mr. Darcy. I know the Darcy servants do not gossip about the family, as most servants in wealthy houses do, but you seem to have sources of information that would turn a Bow Street Runner sea green with envy. I want to know whom he sees and what he does." She considered for a moment and then added, "Bring me my lap desk."

"Yes, my lady." Hughes bowed, retrieved the little rosewood desk, saw that everything was arranged for his mistress's convenience, and left the room.

Lady Agatha's writing was like the woman herself, delicate, finely formed, as firm as it had ever been without any of the tremor or spidery lines that come with age. When she had sanded and sealed the missive, she rang for Hughes. Her jaw had a determined set her late husband had known well.

"Send this with a footman," she instructed, handing the butler the letter. "He need not wait for a reply."

"Yes, my lady."

Lady Agatha closed her eyes, leaned her head back, and sighed. *Am I doing the right thing, Cedric? How I wish you were here! Not a day goes by but I long for you, for your love, your intellect, your devotion. I will proceed, but I am not certain at this late day that the game is worth the candle.*

⁂

Elizabeth pinned her hat in place and looked at her image in the cheval glass in the corner of her room. Her riding costume, while not new, had not been worn above twice. It would have to do. She was not a woman who enjoyed primping. Her mother had reprimanded her often enough, especially when they spent summers at Longbourn, that she dressed no better than the maids. It was not true, but Elizabeth did tend to pay less attention to her appearance than her sisters, with the exception of Mary.

The thought of sisters led her mind to Jane and the letter she had received from Hertfordshire shortly after the elder Mr. Darcy's visit. One passage in particular stayed with her:

> *If Papa is determined on this course of action, my dearest Lizzy, you have little choice but to agree. However, I cannot believe that he would force you to wed a man you found truly objectionable. Have patience and assess the young man carefully. Remember, his own father is imposing the marriage on him, as Papa is on you. If you give him a chance to display his character, you may find that he is a worthy match.*

First her aunt and then her beloved sister. Well, Elizabeth thought as she left her room, she would do her best. She heard voices in the entry hall and paused at the top of the staircase. Mr. Darcy and a man in regimentals had been confronted by her mother, who was attempting to herd them into the drawing room. Elizabeth started down the stairs, making enough noise to attract the group's attention.

Mr. Darcy looked up, and she saw him stiffen. His companion turned, also looking up at her, an appreciative grin spreading over his square face. She wore a riding costume of gray-and-black-tartan skirt that came nearly to the ankle of her boots, a white silk blouse and dark-red velvet short jacket trimmed in black soutache braid and frogs in the military style currently popular. A black felt hat with a red cockade sat at a jaunty angle on her dark curls.

"Good morning, Mr. Darcy." Elizabeth curtsied as he bowed.

Darcy found his voice, although it was a trifle weak. "Good morning, Miss Bennet. May I present my cousin, Colonel Fitzwilliam of the Household Guards?"

Colonel Fitzwilliam bowed over her hand. "I am pleased to make your acquaintance, Miss Bennet."

"Thank you, Colonel."

Mary had come downstairs quietly and stopped beside her sister, who said, "May I present my sister, Miss Mary Bennet? Colonel Fitzwilliam."

Introductions completed, Mrs. Bennet immediately attempted to lead the party to the drawing room, but Elizabeth forestalled her. "We have to leave if we are to reach Hyde Park before it becomes crowded, Mama."

"Yes, yes, but surely the gentlemen will dine with us?"

Darcy glanced at Richard before he said, "That is very kind of you, Madam. We will be pleased to accept."

"Wonderful! Go along, then, Lizzy, Mary. Do not keep Mr. Darcy and Colonel Fitzwilliam waiting."

Together the four left the house. A groom held the bridle of a handsome sorrel gelding hitched to a smart little gig. Darcy glanced at it as he handed Elizabeth in. Richard did the same courtesy for Mary. The groom passed Mary the reins, and the two men mounted their horses, the party heading out into the street. It took them ten minutes to reach Hyde Park and the broad drive called Le Route de Roi, somehow corrupted over time to Rotten Row. There were a few riders and one or two carriages, but it was far from busy. Mary drove to the stables, and Elizabeth allowed Darcy to hand her down instead of leaving the vehicle on her own, as was her wont.

She retrieved her mount, a gray mare that showed both Arabian and Andalusian bloodlines, and led it to a mounting block. As she started to step up on the stone square, she suddenly felt two large, strong hands circle her waist and lift her into the saddle. Automatically Elizabeth hooked her leg around the horn and settled into the leather. Then she looked into Darcy's face, his eyes full of mischief.

"When ignorance is bliss, 'tis foolish to be wise."

In spite of her shock at his boldness, at that moment Elizabeth liked him immensely. She raised one eyebrow. "'Mend your speech a little, lest it may mar your fortunes.'"

He chuckled. She turned the horse into the Row, and Darcy mounted, following to where Mary waited in the gig. Richard had watched the interaction without understanding it. He glanced at Mary, sedately guiding the small conveyance along. Her face was not plain, but lost in the physical beauty of her sisters, she was undoubtedly considered the least attractive of the five. Richard admired her fine profile and soft brown eyes.

"You do not care to ride, Miss Mary?"

"As the riding horses are boarded here, I felt it better to drive to and from home." She glanced up at him. "Are you stationed in London, Colonel?"

"Not at present. I am on a short leave from my regiment."

She hesitated and then said shyly, "There is something I have always wanted to ask a military man."

"Ask whatever you like, Miss Mary. If I can answer your question, I will be happy to do so."

She glanced up at him, and something in his chest kicked him hard. "Why is the place where you dine called a 'mess'?"

"If you had ever eaten army food, you would not have to ask."

Mary looked at him in some confusion and then laughed brightly. "I do not believe you."

Richard chuckled. "And rightly so. The word is from the Old French *mes*, meaning a portion of food. Similar to English 'mess,' meaning a portion of soup or porridge."

Mary nodded. "Is the food really so bad?"

"It is not *haute cuisine*, but generally it is not bad. Of course when we are engaged in a campaign, we frequently eat whatever is available."

"You have been involved in the war on the peninsula?" Her tone had become suddenly serious.

"Yes."

"I cannot think of anything more terrible than war," she said softly, "especially on civilians caught up in it against their will."

"It is indeed a terrible thing, Miss Mary, but sometimes unavoidable. Napoleon will take over the entire continent if he is not stopped. His real goal is to invade England. If that happens, even more people will suffer."

She nodded. Her eyes went to her sister and Mr. Darcy, who had drawn ahead of them by a short distance. She tapped the sorrel with the reins, and the gig speeded up enough to bring them closer to the pair. Richard wondered if he had offended her, but in the next moment, she raised her eyes to him again.

"'And they shall beat their swords into plowshares, and their spears into pruning hooks.'"

"I hope it may be so," Richard replied, although he had seen too much of life to believe it.

"You intend to leave your career one day, Colonel?"

"If I can. I am a second son. If I marry well, I will be able to resign my commission and take up another occupation. Politics, perhaps."

"Oh, do not do that." Mary's lips turned up in a smile. "Not if you wish to leave war behind."

Richard laughed aloud. He remembered suddenly that he was supposed to be observing Miss Bennet, and with a bow to his companion, he jogged forward to take up a position on Elizabeth's far side. He was beginning to wish that the Bennets were a wealthier family. Miss Mary appealed to him more than any woman of his recent acquaintance. She would have a dowry equal to that of her sisters, but it was still not enough to allow him to support a wife and family in more than moderate comfort. In any event, she was being courted by her father's junior partner and unlikely to consider a man ten years older than herself, even if his father were an earl.

CHAPTER 6
SCHEMES

The knock on the door of Lord Matlock's study was perfunctory. Nicholas St. George Fitzwilliam, Viscount Maresford, entered the room with his usual studied insouciance before his father summoned him. The earl sat behind his massive desk, a tray of documents at his right hand that he had not touched. His face was set in stern lines familiar to the members of the House of Lords when Lord Matlock debated a serious matter. Nicholas strode to the sidebar and poured himself a brandy. When he turned, his father indicated the chairs in front of the desk.

"Sit down, Nicholas."

Still unconcerned, his eldest son dropped into a chair and took a long swallow of his drink. "I assume you want to see me, Father."

"I would rather not," Lord Henry said shortly, "but again necessity outweighs inclination."

"Oh Lord, what have I done now to disrupt the smooth flow of family life?"

Lord Henry's hand came down so hard on the polished mahogany that Nicholas jumped enough to spill a little of the brandy on his coat. He swore as he brushed at the superfine with his handkerchief. When he looked up, his father regarded him as if he wondered who this insolent puppy was.

"Countess Lavigne."

Nicholas briefly closed his eyes. His mouth lifted in a smirk. "A nice little bit of muslin. What about her?"

"The count," his father said, his words spaced out, "is ready to cause a diplomatic incident. Do you have any concept of what that will do to our relations with the few French émigrés who are actually in a position to assist this country in fighting Napoleon?"

Nicholas shrugged. "I doubt the count is of more use in the war than in his wife's bedchamber. It was she who began the affair."

"And you who pursued it. Are you really that stupid, or is it just that you cannot resist the chance to prove your irresistible charm with any woman who takes your fancy?"

Nicholas was having trouble controlling his anger. He set the glass down on the desk without concern for it marring the surface and leaned a little forward. "I had no idea that bedding a willing woman was to cause so much consternation. If her husband wishes to call me out, I will make her a charming widow."

"You fool." Lord Henry's voice sunk to a cold growl. "I believe you have no idea what sort of political chaos a duel with the count would cause. He is the single most important representative in England of the anti-Bonapartists. What you suggest could well be considered treason. I cannot believe a man of your age and education would allow his carnal appetites to override his judgment to such an extent."

The word "treason" penetrated Nicholas's self-assurance. He stared at his father, his face showing a flicker of succeeding emotions: fear, anger, and resentment. "Who has spread this story? The countess or her husband? I shall deny it!"

"After you have bragged about it to your associates, I doubt a denial will be believed by anyone."

"Is that how you came to hear about it?" His face darkened. "My stalwart brother, I suppose? Or was it that old monk, Darcy?"

"I do not need informants when the count has gone to the minister. It will take every political favor I can call in to keep the matter from exploding into a full-scale scandal. And that brings me to the reason you are here. I have had my fill of your exploits, Nicholas. You have the next Season to find a wife and settle down. Otherwise I will cut off your allowance and seriously consider the remainder of your future."

Nicholas came to his feet, his face suffused with fury. "I am your heir; you cannot do this to me!"

"You had best remember who controls the money in this family. You are not the Earl of Matlock yet." Lord Henry met his son's eyes with steely purpose. "That is all. You can go now."

Nicholas read the adamant purpose in his father's face, picked up his glass, and hurled it at the fireplace. It shattered into sparkling shards. He stalked to the door, turned back, and said in a hiss, "I will *not* be dictated to. My life is my own. I will live it any way I choose."

"Then," his father told him quietly, "you will live it on whatever funds you can obtain without my help."

Retaining a modicum of self-preservation, Nicholas did not quite slam the door. Lord Henry looked at the ring etching the dark surface of his desk and wiped at it ineffectually with his handkerchief. He rang for the butler, shook his head, and picked up the first document on the waiting stack.

It was the second time in a week that Lydia Bennet and her friend Miss Gradison had called on Lady Arthur and Miss Arthur, and she was a little worried that the ladies were beginning to wonder at the number of visits. Sir Colin and his friend Mr. Winter joined the group after a few minutes. Mr. Winter took a chair next to the sofa where Lydia sat with Lettie. They engaged in desultory conversation while tea was served, before Mr. Winter leaned a bit toward Lydia and lowered his voice.

"I understand that Mr. Darcy dined at your residence recently. Is he a friend of your father?"

"I believe they were acquainted before the elder Mr. Darcy visited London several weeks ago. He also dined with us. He is quite handsome for an old man, but he spoke mostly with my father and my sister Elizabeth."

Mr. Winter nodded. "I expect he is not a very amusing guest. What of his son?"

"Oh, he is very handsome and dresses extremely well," Lydia replied with more enthusiasm than consideration, "and he is supposed to be very wealthy. But he is very dull. He and Lizzy talked of poetry and horses, and I do not know what all, for I was not listening. He and his cousin took her riding yesterday in Hyde Park with my sister Mary as chaperone. I was not yet up when they left. Then both gentlemen dined with us."

She did not see the sudden flash of interest in Mr. Winter's languid blue eyes. "Indeed. Which cousin was that? He has several."

"Colonel Fitzwilliam. He wore his regimentals; they are very handsome."

"Yes, he and Mr. Darcy are very close. Is one of them paying court to your sister?"

"Oh, la, I do not know. It is all very recent, and Lizzy seems not to like most young men she meets. I might have allowed Mr. Whitford to court me if he had asked. But I am not out yet, so I cannot go to balls and soirees and meet young men."

"What a pity." Mr. Winter smiled in a way that made Lydia feel shivery all over. "You would be the most beautiful lady ever to grace such gatherings."

It was gross flattery of a kind Mr. Winter rarely used anymore, but it was totally suitable for Lydia Bennet. She simpered, and her friend cast them a look that warned Winter he was going too fast.

"You are not allowed to socialize with anyone but family, then? But surely you must hear of the balls and other affairs that go on. What a pity you cannot enjoy them yourself."

"Oh yes. I follow the news of the *ton* closely." She cast a swift glance at Lettie Gradison, who was engaged in a discussion with Miss Arthur of a new gown, before lowering her voice. "My friend told me of the robbery at her residence during the recent ball there. The magistrate thinks one of the servants was in league with the burglar and opened a window for him. Can you imagine anyone climbing a tree to the second floor without falling? He must be very agile."

"No doubt. I hope the incident does not curtail further social gatherings. The Little Season is almost over."

Lydia's piquant face suddenly took on the look of someone with a secret to impart. She said in a conspiratorial whisper, "Do not tell anyone, for invitations have not yet been sent, but Lady Wendover is giving a ball for her daughter Euphemia's engagement to Lord Coughlin-Hervey. She is to wear the Kalimar Diamond, but with the recent robberies, no one is to know until that night."

Mrs. Arthur, distracted from the latest fashion by the tête-à-tête between her guest and Mr. Winter, cast a cold eye on that gentleman. With a murmured, "I shall not say a word," he rose, bowed, and excused himself on a matter of business. Sir Colin rose and followed him.

"I cannot fathom what you see in that chit," Sir Colin declared as Winter guided him through a side door into the back garden. "She is pretty enough but as dense as a brick wall."

"And that is exactly why she is so very useful." Winter looked casually around the relatively small space and moved closer to the fountain. At his gesture, Sir Colin joined him.

"Did you learn anything of interest?" Sir Colin asked.

"Indeed. I learned that we are going to have the opportunity of making a bigger profit than in any of our previous endeavors. You have heard of the Kalimar Diamond?"

"Certainly. Lady Wendover guards it like her hope of Heaven. It never leaves the bank vault unless it is accompanied by paid guards."

"It will leave the vault and make its way to the Wendover mansion for a ball she is giving in the near future. No one is to know about it. But Miss Lydia cannot keep a secret, and apparently neither can someone at the Wendovers'."

"I have heard of no ball the Wendovers are giving." Sir Colin looked skeptical.

"Nor will you until the invitations go out. I am sure you will receive one. Make absolutely certain that you accept. As it is an engagement ball, most guests will be focused on the happy couple. Lady Wendover will want to make a splash by wearing the diamond."

Sir Colin scowled at Winter. "So how will you take the diamond if she is wearing it?"

Winter's vulpine smile raised the hackles on the back of Sir Colin's neck. "I shall explain everything to you later. For now, let us go in and have a drink to celebrate the occasion of our coming achievement."

Lady Claudia Swithenhurst rose to greet her caller enthusiastically. After bobbing a quick curtsey, she took Lady Agatha's hand and led her to a carved and gilded sofa, seating her with great ceremony. As soon as she rang for tea, Lady Swithenhurst seated herself in a chair facing her guest, a wide smile on her round face. Her day gown was a confection of silk in several colors emblazoned with gold thread. Lady Claudia's figure, barely confined by her stays, gave it the appearance of a hot air balloon about to ascend.

"My dear Lady Agatha, how wonderful to see you. We have not talked since the Academy show last year. How are you keeping?"

"Well enough for my age. And you, Lady Claudia?"

"Oh, quite as usual. I gad about all the time, so many things to see and people to keep up with. Have you been to any entertainments this Season?"

"Not yet. I am rather sorry I missed the Gradisons' ball; it seems to have been rather more exciting than usual."

The dry tone of her voice was not lost on Lady Claudia, who produced a girlish giggle that made her caller wince. "Oh my, yes! The burglary. It has completely ruined the remainder of the Season for the Gradisons. And have you heard what happened at Lady Swandon's last week? She was robbed but only of paste reproductions. I imagine the burglar was unhappy when he found out."

If there was a scrap of gossip to be found, Lady Claudia's infallible nose for scandal would ferret it out. It was Lady Agatha's only reason for the visit. Tea was served with several kinds of small cakes and tarts. While Lady Claudia made inroads on the sweets, they spoke of various mutual acquaintances, the current rumors circulating about engagement and weddings, and the Prince Regent's latest extravagance. Setting aside her teacup, Lady Agatha spoke casually, although her sharp gaze belied her seeming disinterest.

"Someone told me that Mr. George Darcy was in town several weeks ago. I hardly believed it; he so seldom comes to London since his wife died."

"Indeed he was in town. Lady Markham saw him at Hatchard's bookshop. She said he looked very tired. The harvest, I suppose, although Pemberley produces as high an income as any estate in England."

"Legal business, I imagine."

"Perhaps, perhaps not." Lady Claudia suddenly set her teacup on a small table and leaned toward her caller with a self-satisfied little smile turning up her rosebud mouth. Lady Agatha always thought that the woman resembled a humanized rose with her too-bright hair and not-too-subtle cosmetics.

"This is strictly between us, dear Lady Agatha, but it is too intriguing not to share. Do you know who Thomas Bennet is?"

"The solicitor. I do not know the gentleman personally, but I am aware that his legal firm handles the business of a number of the higher-ranking members of the *ton*."

Lady Claudia nodded rapidly. "Well, his only unmarried daughter who is out may be on the verge of making a spectacular match. She has been seen riding in Hyde Park with, oh, you will never guess whom."

"I am sure I will not." Lady Agatha made an effort to control her vexation. "Why do you not tell me, Lady Claudia?"

"Mr. Fitzwilliam Darcy! Henry Farraday saw them several days ago. Miss Bennet was riding a beautiful Arab mare; that was what caught his attention. Her sister drove with them, and Mr. Darcy's cousin colonel Fitzwilliam was also in the party."

"A ride on Rotten Row does not make an engagement, my dear. Perhaps it was the colonel who is finally in the marriage market."

"No, no, that is not all. Mr. George Darcy visited with the Bennets when he was here, and now his son is in town. Well, one can draw the obvious conclusion."

Lady Agatha wanted badly to say, "Obvious to you, perhaps." Instead she said, "Well, I suppose it had to happen one day. His father may wish to retire and allow the son to take over management of Pemberley. Many men do at his age."

The conversation wandered for another quarter hour before Lady Agatha took her leave. On her way home, she hardly noticed the crowds of people, riders, carriages, street vendors, drays, and pedestrians all about their individual business, as unaware of her as she of them. She saw a pattern to the information she had gained. Lady Agatha knew little of the Darcy family after her marriage. Alexander Darcy had one son, George, who had married the younger daughter of the Earl of Matlock. They in turn had one son and a daughter who must not yet be old enough to come out. Other than bits of gossip over the past few years, she knew nothing of the present heir to Pemberley, except that he was considered one of the most eligible bachelors in England. She knew even less of his father. A situation she must remedy. She would find out more about Miss Bennet as well. Knowledge, she thought as the barouche pulled into the drive on South Audley Street, was indeed power. The best way to obtain knowledge about members of the *ton* was to mingle socially with them.

In her sitting room half an hour later, she had perused the social news in the *Morning Post* and made a short list of ladies she intended to call on. As much as it went against her character to seek out persons she held in contempt, it was the quickest way to find out what she wanted to know. Her name still had considerable cachet, enough to easily admit her to the drawing rooms of the upper levels of society. She rose, rang for her maid, and began to plan the next several days' activities.

"Well, Richard, what do you think of Miss Bennet?"

The two cousins sat in Darcy's study over brandies. It was late. The fire in the grate was burning low while chill from the cold evening outside seeped into the room. Richard leaned back in his chair and stretched his legs out to the red glow. Darcy looked tense, he thought, as if his opinion of the lady were more important than Richard thought it ought to be.

"She rides very well."

"Indeed. But I could hardly say, 'Miss Bennet, I greatly admire your seat.'"

Richard chuckled. "No, I suppose not. Well, a ride, some conversation, and a dinner are not enough to reach any ironclad conclusions, but I will say one thing."

"I sincerely wish you would," Darcy rejoined with some annoyance.

"Very well. She is intelligent, clever, witty, and I believe, steadfast. If her elder sister's beauty rivals Helen of Troy, then I would cast Miss Bennet as Penelope."

"The wife of Odysseus. Are you casting me as the man who wandered many years to find his home?"

Richard contemplated his glass. "Is that not what most men do who desire to marry? Seek a home?"

Darcy made no reply. He stared at the pulsing coals, his mind in turmoil. Yes, Miss Bennet was all those things and more. She was kind, sensitive, caring, brave enough to be different, and unashamed of it. With a deep sense of shock, Darcy realized that she was the wife he had described to his father. Her willingness to tease and debate and her thirst for knowledge excited him. There was so much they might explore together. If her nature also held the passion he sensed in her, it would be truly the perfect match.

"Darcy?" his cousin questioned.

He came back to the cooling room with a jolt. "Thank you, Cousin. I believe," Darcy said as he stood, "I will retire now. Stay here tonight if you like."

"Thank you. I will take you up on the offer."

They climbed the stairs, Richard to the guest room always ready for his occupancy, Darcy to his chambers in the family wing. His man Martin assisted him to remove his elaborately tied cravat and closely fitted tailcoat. Darcy dismissed him as soon as the valet had finished his duties. He wanted to think in solitude. Darcy contemplated another brandy, rejected the idea, and got into bed. That morning in Hyde Park came back to him vividly. Richard had ridden at first next to the gig, giving him time to speak to Miss Bennet alone. After he had admired her mount and told her of the stallion he had acquired, silence had fallen for several minutes.

"Is that a family tartan?" he had asked at last for want of anything better to say. "I did not know that there was Scottish blood in your family."

"Only a very small amount," she replied, looking sideways at him in a manner that made his heart speed up. "My father's maternal grandmother was a Douglas. I liked the pattern, and my uncle obtained the cloth for me."

"Mr. Gardiner?"

"Yes." She seemed unsurprised that he knew of her relations in trade. "I am very close to my aunt and uncle. I could never give up their society."

"I see no reason why you should," he said and was rewarded by a quick glance of approval.

"Many, if not most, of the *ton* look down on those in trade. I know that not all merchants are honest, but neither are some of their customers. I do not call it honest to purchase merchandise without paying for it or to pay for it months, if not years, later, as is the habit of not a few wealthy men."

"No more do I. It has never been a practice of my family."

"I had not thought it was." She hesitated before she went on, "It is a way the *ton* shows its contempt for those they consider beneath them. They do not seem to think that tradesmen have families they must feed and clothe and house. It is easier to lose their money at the gaming tables than pay their just debts."

A certain anger had grown under the level tone. Darcy knew this was something she felt strongly about. It was his own opinion as well. However, he also knew that few merchants would proceed against one of the gentry or nobility for payment, as it was likely to stop others from seeking their custom.

"Has your uncle suffered much loss in that manner?"

"Not as much as some. If he is kept waiting too long, he refuses to sell to the same person without payment when the purchase is made. It has not always made him popular, but his goods are so much in demand that he has not suffered from the practice."

Darcy smiled. Her uncle must be a shrewd businessman as well as an honest one. "I should like to meet your uncle and aunt," he said.

Elizabeth turned a little to regard him levelly. Whatever she saw in his face reassured her. "I shall be happy to make the introduction, Mr. Darcy. I believe you will like them. My aunt is involved in charity work of a sort not many high-ranking ladies of society care to engage in. She sits on the committee that oversees the Foundling Hospital. Lady Warrington is the chairwoman. Perhaps you have her acquaintance?"

"I know who she is; we have never met. She has a reputation for good works and for speaking her mind."

"I admire her," Elizabeth said firmly, as if she thought he might disapprove of the lady's character. "She cares about the children, when so few do. It is so much easier to look away than to make an effort to help."

"I think you are much like her."

"I do not know how much like her I may be, Mr. Darcy," she answered wryly, "but I have been known to speak when I ought to keep still, at least according to my mother."

It had been a revelation. That she cared about the foundling children was evident; he found it an indication of a kind and caring nature. Miss Bennet would be a loving mother, as well as able to care for Pemberley's tenants in her role of mistress, not from a sense of noblesse oblige but from honest concern for their welfare. She would also want to help the poor of the parish, whom the Darcys had always felt obligated to assist. He made a mental note to send a bank draft for one hundred pounds to Lady Warrington with a request to maintain his anonymity.

Richard had arrived then, riding on Miss Bennet's far side. With a twinge of unfamiliar discomfort, Darcy had seen the admiration in his cousin's eyes. They trotted along in companionable silence until Miss Bennet, wanting to say something, turned her head to Richard.

"You are a member of the Horse Guards, I see."

"I am."

"You have seen much action lately on the peninsula. I expect you are glad for a little time to rest between campaigns."

If he was surprised that a lady knew how deeply his regiment had been involved in the Peninsular War, he did not show it. "Any chance to come home is always welcome. Do you follow the war news, Miss Bennet?"

"I read my father's newspapers. I am sure they do not tell us everything, but one gets a general picture of the progress of the army. I have read that Napoleon is likely to invade Russia. Do you not think it very late in the year for such a campaign? I have read that the winters in Russia are very harsh, and to move so many men and so much materiel seems an impossible task."

Richard's expression wavered between shock and respect. Respect won. "I can only say that Boney has made mistakes before. This may well be his fatal mistake."

Darcy took up the conversation at that point, asking Elizabeth if he might introduce her to his sister. She agreed with obvious pleasure, and the talk moved to general topics. She seemed more comfortable in his company than at first, Darcy told himself. He pondered how to spend more time with her without a constant chaperone listening to their every word. Tomorrow he would see what play was performing at the Royal Opera House. If it was suitable, he would ask her and her family to attend with himself, Richard, and Georgiana. In their private box under the cloak of the noise always present at plays, they might have as close to a private conversation as anywhere. If they were noticed, so much the better. Darcy was tiring of the charade that he was only acting as his father's envoy to the family of an old acquaintance.

Worry for his father was a constant dark fog in the back of Darcy's mind. The sooner the engagement was announced, the sooner the wedding arrangements could be made and they could return to Pemberley. Darcy prayed there was enough time for them to live as a family before the inevitable happened. The thought raised another question: when should he tell Miss Bennet about his father's illness? Or ought he to tell her at all?

In spite of his troubled thoughts, Darcy fell asleep at last, his dreams drifting to a promontory on Pemberley land he often visited. The view swept out over miles of country to the high moors in the north and the peaks to the south. Only in this dream, he was not alone. A woman leaned against his side, her small body warm within the circle of his arm. She looked up at him, her wonderful eyes alight with love, and smiled. Her name passed his lips even in sleep: Elizabeth.

Viscount Maresford had dined at White's and now sat at a table in the paneled cardroom with Sir Colin Arthur and his friend, Mr. Winter. They had played two hands of loo, one of which Winter won and the other Maresford. Sir Colin had begun to drink heavily, his face growing ever more sullen as the evening progressed. Winter watched both men unobtrusively. He judged that Maresford was angry as well but not over the cards. Intrigued, he decided to find out what had upset the nobleman.

"You seem piqued tonight, my lord," he ventured as the viscount poured another glass of premium brandy. "Perhaps you are in need of feminine company?"

"That is the last thing I am in need of!" Maresford drank off the liquor in two gulps and poured another. "That [he used an epithet no gentleman ever used to describe a lady] Countess Lavigne has advertised her crim con to the entire *ton*, and my dear father is threatening to cut off my allowance if I do not marry by the end of next Season."

"I see no problem with that," Sir Colin said, reaching for the brandy bottle, "since you will be an earl one day. There are plenty of ladies more than willing to wed a man of wealth and status."

"And once you are wed," Winter put in with a smirk, "your wife will hardly be in a position to object to any of your 'activities.' "

Maresford shook his head. He was a large, fair-haired man with features already a little blurred by liquor and indolence. Despite his size, Winter mused, the viscount was already running to fat rather than muscle. He was known as a fine shot, but Winter doubted that his reputation was much more than Maresford's well-known braggadocio.

"I need more than a dowry. I need a wife who brings property to the marriage, preferably one who has not slept with half the men of my acquaintance."

"Have you anyone in mind?" Winter asked. His ever-present instinct for his own advantage was alerted. "Sir Colin's sister comes out next Season."

Sir Colin glared at his friend. Maresford shrugged.

"She is a pretty girl, but I require more than she can offer. No offense, old man," he added to her brother. "Hell, I'd offer for Sofia if she wasn't my sister. Forty thousand pounds goes a long way to make up for a lack of property. If my cousin Georgiana Darcy was out, she would be perfect. She's young, beautiful, well protected, and if her brother dies without an heir, she'll inherit Pemberley. What a prize that is!"

"Would her father approve?" Winter asked.

"No. He disapproves of cousins marrying, although it is perfectly legal."

He disapproves of a good deal more in your case, Winter thought. "Well, that is too bad, as I hear that Fitzwilliam Darcy may soon marry."

Maresford's face took on an ugly look that erased any sign of breeding it might usually show. "Damn him! Who is the woman? Do I know her?"

"I doubt it. She is the daughter of the solicitor Thomas Bennet. Young Darcy has been seen in her company of late, along with your brother, the colonel. Perhaps he is the one interested in Miss Bennet."

"He!" Maresford scoffed. "He does not make enough in his fancy uniform to sustain a wife, let alone a family. He barely lives decently with the allowance my father makes him—which will cease when I am Earl of Matlock."

Mr. Winter shrugged. "She has a nice dowry. Not a fortune, but a careful man might invest it well enough to bring in a moderate income."

Maresford shook his head in disdain. "Richard is in love with war. He will die in battle or in poverty, and I care not which." He finished his brandy and set the glass aside. "You said you might help me with Miss Darcy. How?"

Winter considered the best way to explain his knowledge of the family. He said, "I used to visit a friend from university at his father's estate. It was not far from Pemberley, and of course, we socialized with all the local gentry. I have not seen Miss Darcy since she was, oh, nine or ten. She was always a shy, obliging girl. If I were able to renew the acquaintance, I might be able to influence her in your favor."

"She will never go against her father."

Forgotten, Sir Colin suddenly said, in a voice too loud for the refined presence of the room and its other occupants and slurred a little by too much liquor, "There're other ways to force a woman to marry you."

Both of his companions looked at him as if the table had addressed them. The viscount scowled. Then his brow cleared, and his expression became speculative. Winter's smile was nasty. He purposely lowered his voice.

"If there were no other way, the Darcys would do anything to avoid scandal, especially where Miss Darcy is concerned."

Maresford rose abruptly, looking down his nose at Winter. "Call on me when you have made progress with the lady. Or, better yet, send a note, and we will meet here or elsewhere that we can talk privately."

He sauntered from the room, nodding once or twice to men he knew. Winter watched him go with a knowing smirk.

"Can you do it?"

Winter shrugged. "I can make the attempt. I shall have to take special care; she is watched constantly by her companion, and at present with her brother in town, she will be particularly sheltered. But there are ways."

Sir Colin leaned back in his chair. The brandy came, and he poured his glass full again, passing the bottle to Winter. "I expect you know them all."

"Yes." Winter stared absently at his glass. "And in this case, I will particularly enjoy employing them."

CHAPTER 7
ADVANCES

By the time Lady Agatha finished her rounds of calls, she knew very little more about young Mr. Darcy's situation than when she had left Lady Swithenhurst's, although she had a better idea of the general impression of his character or, rather, the character he presented to the world. He was considered upright, honorable, and a man of principle. He did not drink to excess, rarely gambled, and did not keep a mistress, patronize brothels, or engage in affairs with the widows and grass widows of the upper social strata. He did not exceed his income. This might have seemed a given, considering the general opinion that Pemberley brought in ten thousand pounds a year, unless one knew the habits of some young men of fortune. He was thought of as proud and cold, even forbidding, to anyone but family and a few intimate friends. *A Darcy indeed*, she thought sardonically.

Miss Bennet was a respectable young lady, a nominal member of the *ton* by birth but not active in society. Her mother's brother owned a large, successful import business and probably other investments; her father was an extremely successful solicitor. She had four sisters and no brothers. Her mother was genteel but silly, and Miss Bennet had rejected at least two marriage proposals after three Seasons in the marriage market. *My only real accomplishment for all the tea and cakes I have consumed,* Lady Agatha mused, *is an invitation to the Wendovers' ball, which I plan to attend. Perhaps Mr. Darcy and his presumptive fiancée will be there, and I might get a look at them.*

Lady Agatha sipped her tea and looked unseeingly out of the window. The initial conflagration of emotions from the letter had sunk to a molten core, like the heart of a furnace. She had to know the truth before she made an irrevocable decision.

Cedric, my beloved, I have begun on this journey to the past, but I cannot see my way clearly. I need to know about this heir to Pemberley and if he is to marry the young woman. Is she willing, or has her father chosen the man whose will she will spend her life subjected to? I feel as if I have stepped back in time. If this ball shows me no more than I have learned already, I shall have to make the trip; there is no help for it. I shall have to return to where I had sworn I would never set foot again. Cedric, Cedric, am I wrong to go on? Will revenge finally ease this pain that is ever with me?

She put her head back and closed her eyes, but the images she saw behind the fragile, blue-veined lids were from long ago. Half an hour later, Marie found her sleeping. She stood looking down at her mistress, her face troubled. She had served Lady Agatha for twenty years. Whatever drove her was like nothing in the past, not even the death of her husband. Marie left her mistress alone and quit the room on silent feet. Whatever it was, she could only wait and hope that nothing irreversible came of it.

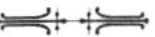

Elizabeth was in the process of writing a letter to her sister Jane.

> *I am making an effort to give Mr. Darcy every opportunity to reveal his true nature. At present I have nothing of importance*

> *to complain of. He has invited our family and our aunt and uncle to share the Darcy box at the Royal Opera House tomorrow night for a performance of Shakespeare's* A Midsummer Night's Dream. *As you are aware, Mama does not care for the Bard's plays, preferring a pantomime or farce, but she has agreed to go because of the source of the invitation. We shall be quite a party, as Miss Darcy and Colonel Fitzwilliam are also included.*
>
> *Lydia chooses to remain at home in spite of Mama's insistence that she go. Since she left school, her life has become a round of shopping, social calls, and novels. She resents Papa's decision not to let her come out next Season with her friends and grows more irresponsible by the day. She has made a great friend in Lettie Gradison, and both seem to be close to Miss Arthur, on whom they call at least twice a week. Lydia speaks of a man she sees at the Arthur's, a Mr. Winter, who is a guest of Sir Colin Arthur. She declares that she only sees him in company and that he is too old to interest her, but his name comes up frequently enough to belie her words. I asked her who the gentleman is, and she only says that he is Sir Colin's friend and a gentleman.*
>
> *Heavens! With Sir Colin's reputation, the man might be a Newmarket tout! I feel I should speak to Papa about it, as he has been exceptionally engaged in work of late and not as aware of matters at home as usual, but I dislike causing the upset it would bring.*

When Elizabeth finished and sealed the letter, she took it downstairs and put it with the outgoing post. Mrs. Bennet heard her in the hall and appeared at the drawing room door, rather like a plump jack-in-the-box. She hurried to her daughter, a missive in her hand that she waived back and forth. Her face was a little flushed and her eyes wide with excitement.

"Lizzy! You are invited to the Wendovers' ball! Oh, my dearest daughter, I am sure it is Mr. Darcy's doing. He is growing attached to you, I know it. The Wendovers' ball will be one of the crowning events of the Little Season. You must have a new ball gown; we shall go tomorrow to Madame Colette and order it. I am sure she will have all the latest fashion plates, and you will need new slippers to match. You can wear Grandma Bennet's pearl eardrops and pendant; they become your coloring so well. Oh! What a social triumph!"

Elizabeth extracted the invitation from her mother's fingers and read it. Mrs. Bennet firmly believed that she was entitled to read any communication to one of her daughters, even those obviously intended for the Miss Bennet alone. If she had not been engaged in writing to Jane, Elizabeth would have followed her habit of intercepting the post to extract any correspondence addressed to herself. The missive was indeed an invitation to the Wendovers' ball, written in a polished hand and addressed to "Miss Elizabeth Bennet" at their direction. With a sigh, Elizabeth put the invitation in the pocket of her gown. From now until the night of the ball, her mother would fuss and flutter, issue directions she frequently rescinded half an hour later, and generally upset the household for no practical reason. It cemented Elizabeth's decision not to speak to her father about Lydia and Mr. Winter.

"My brother and sister Gardiner will be here for dinner, along with Mr. Darcy. You had better go upstairs and rest before it is time to dress. Be sure you have Meg style your hair properly; you know how it slips out of pins if she does not put enough in. Go, go."

Elizabeth went. In her room, she took off her slippers, lay on the bed, pulled the quilt over her, and stared at the canopy. She was certain that the invitation was indeed Mr. Darcy's doing, as she did not know the Wendovers, who were at the uppermost level of society. Elizabeth had no doubt that he intended to escort her to the affair. Was this his subtle way of indicating that they were a couple? She moved restively under the coverlet. She was growing tired of this charade; perhaps he was as well. They were to be married. Whether she found him a suitable husband or not was immaterial.

It was far too early to feel anything approaching affection for him, but Elizabeth found that she liked him quite well. He possessed more humor than she had dared hope, and this boded well for their future. He was intelligent, knowledgeable in many areas, and willing to listen to her thoughts on any subject they discussed without patronizing her or dismissing her ideas. She admitted to herself that he was extremely handsome, and while Elizabeth had never considered it a prerequisite in a suitor, it was an agreeable bonus. He was coming tonight specifically to meet her aunt and uncle Gardiner. Her future as Mrs. Darcy might not be as difficult as she had expected.

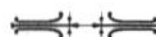

Mr. Darcy arrived at the Bennet residence an hour before dinner, alone. The invitation had included Miss Darcy, but he was reluctant to expose his shy, sheltered sister to the full force of the Bennet family, including the relatives in trade, until he was more certain of the climate. When the butler announced him, Darcy stepped into the drawing room to find Mr. and Mrs. Bennet, Elizabeth and her sisters, and a couple who might have stepped out of any fashionable setting. The man was in his forties, his brown hair graying at the temples, above middle height and solidly built. His wife was a few years younger, a bit older than Darcy; her face was kind and intelligent, attractive without being conventionally pretty. Her hair was not quite auburn, a sorrel brown that glowed in the light.

Mr. Bennet performed the introductions. They sat, and Mrs. Bennet rang for a maid to bring port and Madeira for the gentlemen and sherry for the ladies. They discussed current events in the capital, and Mrs. Gardiner took a part, along with Elizabeth. Darcy began to see the resemblance of minds between aunt and niece. He did not doubt that Mrs. Gardiner had been a longtime, beneficial influence on Elizabeth. Certainly her manners and speech more resembled her aunt's than her mother's, for which Darcy was grateful.

The conversation turned to the play. Mrs. Bennet was happy to know it was a comedy, as she felt that the Bard's tragedies were rather vulgar. Elizabeth blushed a little for her mother's comment, but Darcy only smiled at her.

"My aunt Lady Catherine de Bourgh has the same opinion. She is even more severe on Ben Jonson. She has managed her daughter's estate of Rosings since her husband passed some years ago and feels that Jonson's theme of women requiring men to guide their actions is insulting."

"I have not read above three of his plays," Elizabeth replied, as Darcy was looking at her. "However, I find I agree with her. He is not so much insulting as patronizing. He poses that women are incompetent and require men to make their decisions and manage their affairs, or they will surely get into difficulties."

Her eyes sparkled. She raised an eyebrow, and her lips turned up at the corners. Darcy was enchanted. "How does one measure competence, then?" he asked.

"By the decisions a woman takes in her life, by her level of maturity. Many a widow manages her own finances after her husband's death, and does so to her credit. Given the opportunity to enter professions now denied women, I believe the general opinion of women's competence would be vastly changed."

Darcy was given no chance to reply. Mrs. Gardiner, seeing Mrs. Bennet swell with indignation and alarm, quickly took up the conversation.

"Whatever your thoughts on his plays," she said, giving Elizabeth a warning look, "Jonson wrote very lovely poetry. 'To Celia' is a most beautiful declaration of love."

"'Drink to me only with thine eyes, and I will pledge with mine,'" Darcy quoted. "'But leave a kiss within the cup, and I'll not ask for wine.'"

His vibrant baritone shivered through Elizabeth's body. She colored but could not take her gaze from his. She struggled for a comment, finally saying in a low voice, "I wonder if Celia appreciated the sentiment?"

"I can only hope that she did. It would be devastating to spend such passion on an indifferent lady," he replied.

"It is a very pretty sentiment," Mrs. Bennet agreed, still a little stiff. "I prefer it to the sonnets of Shakespeare. I always think the dark lady cannot be a respectable person."

Elizabeth did not know whether to laugh or roll her eyes. She caught her aunt's glance and shook her head slightly. The gesture broke the tension Darcy's words had engendered, allowing her to continue conversing with tolerable composure. The remainder of the evening passed pleasantly. Mrs. Gardiner played after dinner while Elizabeth sang, and then the two ladies joined in a duet of an old folk song, "The Yellow-Haired Boy." Darcy returned late to Grosvenor Square. Tomorrow he meant to speak to Georgiana. He did not intend to tell her of his coming engagement, only to prepare her to meet Elizabeth Bennet and her family. He believed his sister would like Miss Bennet. Once she was comfortable with the lady, it would be time enough to prepare her for the announcement.

That brought Darcy to the decision that it was also time to consult their attorney about the marriage settlement. He was tired of waiting with his father's health casting a pall over his days. Sometime in the next few days, Darcy intended to find a few private moments to speak to Miss Bennet about declaring their betrothal and setting a wedding date and place. There was, after all, no uncertainty that they were to marry. He only hoped that she was agreeable to his request. Darcy was beginning to hold Miss Bennet in high regard. He was also beginning to believe this marriage might be more agreeable than he had dared hope when he had come to London.

CHAPTER 8
FAMILY CONSIDERATIONS

"Well?" Viscount Maresford leaned forward over his beefsteak and scowled at Winter. "What have you accomplished?"

Winter picked up his glass, filled it with his host's whisky, and took a sip. "I have the matter in hand. Miss Darcy is to attend the theater this evening and meet the Bennets. Miss Lydia Bennet is remaining at home at my request. It will be easy enough to persuade her to assist me in finding out where Miss Darcy goes and whom she sees. Sooner or later an opportunity will arise, and you can step in to take advantage of it."

"It had better be sooner rather than later," Maresford growled. "If Darcy marries, there will be another heir, and that ends any thought of taking over Pemberley. What about Darcy's fiancée?"

Amid the cacophony of male voices and the clatter of cutlery in the busy chophouse, their talk was virtually impossible to overhear.

"Miss Bennet." Winter took another swallow of whisky. "Her reputation is spotless. If anything, she might be described as overly fastidious about male companionship. She has been out for several years, and four or five men have courted her, two who offered for her. But she has turned all of them down."

Maresford grunted, swallowed, and drank off a large gulp of whisky. "I know one fellow she turned down, Hatfield. Nothing wrong with the man."

"Nothing but the fact that he drinks, gambles, and wenches to the point that when he finally achieves his inheritance, he is unlikely to retain anything to inherit."

"Hell, any man who is a man does the same. Hatfield's a bit on the wild side, but I like him."

Because he loses bets that you gull him into when he's fuddled enough to take you up on them. "I am meeting secretly with Miss Lydia tonight while her family is out. I will see what I can accomplish toward your commission and let you know as soon as there is anything to report."

"Do that, Winter. And don't take a bloody year about it!"

Winter finished his drink, rose, and walked away from the table. His progress was not noted except by a nondescript patron sitting in a dark corner. The man had already paid for his ale so that when he rose a few moments later and walked to the door, he might have been invisible. The street outside was dark except for the dull yellow glow of street lamps that barely penetrated a chill fog. He saw Winter near the far end of the block and took on a slightly irregular gait as of a man in his cups but still able to navigate.

His quarry paid no attention to anything around him, but his seeming nonchalance did not fool the follower. He held back until Winter crossed the street and hailed a hackney cab. The man looked around as the cab pulled away, saw an empty sedan chair at the curb, and ran for it. The bearers picked up the poles as he got in. He spoke to the bearer in front, and the chair jerked forward, both men picking up a good pace.

Their fare kept his eyes on the hackney as best he was able, inwardly cursing the brown murk that drifted out of alleys and cross streets, obscuring his vision. The chase, if so it might be termed, seemed to last for an hour, although the actual time was much less. The chair halted abruptly and descended to the ground.

"Up there, gov. Big house second from the corner."

The man from the chophouse handed the bearer some coins and walked briskly down the sidewalk, like a man heading home after a long day. He expected to see the door of the residence open to admit his quarry, but the facade was dark except for a small lamp burning in a tall glass window next to the entrance. Speeding up his pace, he reached the corner, quickly looked both ways without any sign of Winter, and cursed softly. At that moment he realized that the entrance to a mews opened part way along the side street.

Careful of his footing on slick cobbles, the man hurried to the mouth of the mews and turned in. Stables and carriage houses fronted on the driveway, a night lamp burning behind the closed doors of one or two indicating that the owners were gone for the evening. He inched forward as he approached what he figured to be the rear of the house where Winter had left the hackney. A low susurrus of voices halted him. He crept closer, aware that if he were seen, there was no place to hide himself.

It took him a half minute to locate the speakers. Winter stood in the mews, inclined a little forward toward the woman on the other side of a gate. She was tall and full figured, light from the rear of the house limning her and faintly picking out Winter's features. A shawl wrapped around her upper body, but her hair shone brightly. The man was unable to discern her age, except to know she was young.

Winter was obviously trying to convince her of something. *Probably the obvious*, the man thought with disgust. She seemed to waver and then nodded. The man tensed; he dared not interfere, or he would lose a greater prize than a foolish woman's virtue. But Winter bowed, kissed the woman's hand, and made to leave. Afraid that if he hurried away the motion would catch Winter's eye, he retreated silently from the faint radiance outlining the pair and slipped across the drive to the clotted shadows of a large carriage house. Crouching, he waited. Several minutes later, Winter came down the drive, whistling softly. The tune was a barracks song with predictable lyrics.

Pleased with yourself, are you? Enjoy it while you can. Your rope will run out soon enough. And old Jack Ketch is waiting at the end of it.

The man rose to his feet, waited half a minute, and followed.

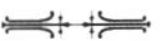

Georgiana Darcy entered the breakfast parlor where they often dined when they were alone and found her brother already waiting, immaculate in evening dress. He smiled the special smile he kept only for her as she came to the table, and held her chair as there was presently no footman in attendance. With her pale hair, milky skin, and soft hazel eyes, Darcy thought, she lacked only a heavily brocaded gown and a jeweled hairnet to have stepped out of a portrait by a Renaissance master.

"I wanted to speak to you privately before we eat," he said as he resumed his seat at the head of the table. "You know we are joining the Bennet family tonight at the Royal Opera House. Mr. and Mrs. Gardiner will also be attending. They are Mrs. Bennet's brother and sister-in-law. Mr. Gardiner owns Gardiner Imports."

"Oh yes, I have met the man," Georgiana replied. "When Aunt Madeleine and I went shopping at his warehouses he attended to us personally. He is very dignified, and he was most helpful."

Darcy nodded. "You are a step ahead of me then, Georgie. I only met the Gardiners at dinner last night. Do you know any of the Bennets? Miss Elizabeth Bennet in particular?"

Georgiana's forehead drew into a slight frown.

Darcy asked, "Is something wrong? You look perplexed."

"No, brother, it is just curious. Papa asked me the same question."

Darcy drew in a deep breath. *Of course. That was the connection. His father had found a potential bride for him but wanted information he was unable to ask anyone else about.* "What exactly did he ask you, Georgie?"

"If I knew of Miss Bennet. I do not have the lady's acquaintance, but I went to school with Annabelle Nash-Trevane. Her elder sister, Annette, is a great friend of Miss Bennet. She married Mr. Trowbridge last year."

"Mr. Trowbridge, the MP who is a colleague of Mr. Wilberforce in the antislavery movement?"

"Yes. That is how Annabelle's sister and Miss Bennet met; they both support the antislavery cause."

Darcy nodded. "That is all you know of Miss Bennet?"

"She is said to be of an independent nature. Her father is a solicitor, and she has sisters but no brother. There is a small estate, in Hertfordshire I believe. That is all I know."

Darcy considered his next words carefully. "I want you to get to know Miss Bennet, Georgie. She is a worthy lady; I think you will like her."

"I am sure I will," Georgiana said automatically. She felt a pang of anxiety at her brother's words. "Will I be going to the theater with you?"

"No. I will be collecting the Bennets. Richard and Sofia will call for you." He rang for the footman to begin serving dinner.

Georgiana kept her eyes on her plate as the soup was served. When the footman retreated, she said in a hesitant voice, "I know one day you will marry, William. I hope your wife likes me. I do not think I could bear being separated from you as some sisters are when a brother marries."

Darcy reached out and covered her hand with his. "You will never be separated from me, sweetling. I could not marry a lady who did not love my sister."

Smiling, Georgiana returned to her meal, but doubts remained. She had never wished William to marry a lady of the *ton*. The cruelty of their gossip alarmed and frightened her, nor did she trust the declarations of friendship from those who sought her out. She had observed how quickly those supposed friendships changed when the advantage of socializing with her brother did not occur. And yet this unknown lady presented another reason for apprehension. Georgiana's instincts told her that William had a more than casual interest in Miss Bennet. She only hoped with all her heart that the evening went well and Miss Bennet was amiable.

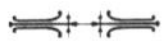

Catherine Bennet had felt ill all day. Not of a strong constitution, she frequently suffered with her courses, and today had been worse than most. The cook had prepared a tea of white-willow bark for the cramping, and at last Kitty, as she was called in the family, fell into a light sleep. The creak of the door to the garden woke her. She roused, wondering without real interest who might be leaving the house at that hour. The only other family member at home was Lydia. None of the servants had business in the garden at night.

Instinct sent her out of bed. She slid her feet into her house slippers, wrapped her robe around herself, and went to the window. Since she had been sleeping in a darkened room, her eyes were better accustomed to the night shadows than they might have been. That was how she discerned a figure melting into the lush tracery of wisteria by the gate into the mews. Alarmed, Kitty left her room and hurried down the hall to Mary's room. It was the only one overlooking the area around the gate. The fire in the grate was banked, the air chill. She crossed the floor silently and drew back the drapes enough to see into the mews. Her breath caught as she recognized Lydia standing at the gate, talking to a man on the other side.

Kitty pressed closer to the cold glass, wishing that she dared open the window enough to try and hear their conversation. She did not think she knew the man, but in the dim glow from the lower windows it was impossible to be sure. He seemed to be asking Lydia for something, or attempting to persuade her, for she shook her head several times. At last the man smiled, his teeth flashing briefly, caught Lydia's hand, and kissed it before straightening and striding down the driveway toward the street at the end of it.

Lydia turned and hurried back to the house. Her mind in turmoil, Kitty was about to turn away from the window when movement in the mews had her once more pressed to the panes. An indistinct, dark figure emerged from the side of the stables and glided after the first man. Kitty released the drapes and stood hugging herself, a sob rising in her throat. She knew her younger sister was impulsive and presently angry that she was not treated as a woman, but to commit such an impropriety could ruin not only her own reputation but also those of all her sisters.

And who was the second man? A confederate of the first or someone watching him or Lydia? She had to tell their father, she thought; there was no help for it. But if she did, Lydia would be in terrible trouble. Kitty was not sure what their father might do; she only knew it would be severe. Growing up, Kitty had been close to her younger sister, sharing much the same outlook on life. School had changed Kitty. She realized that she must take on responsibilities with adulthood, that being a woman was not all privilege; it was also duties. Lydia had not learned that lesson. She had always been her mother's favorite. The special treatment she received led her to think herself exempt from the rules that governed other young ladies.

Cold with shock, Kitty heard a furtive step in the hall. She opened the door of Mary's room in time to see Lydia slip through her bedchamber door and close it noiselessly behind her. Suddenly decided, Kitty crossed to Lydia's room and knocked once on the door. When there was no answer, she turned the knob and went in. Lydia stood by her bed, her face pale in the candlelight.

"Oh, Kitty, you gave me a start! What are you doing here?"

"What were you doing meeting secretly with a man at this hour?"

Lydia's mouth fell open; she raised her hands as if brushing away a gnat. "I do not know what you mean, Kitty. What man?"

"The one in the mews. The man at the gate. I saw you from Mary's window, Lydie, so do not lie to me."

Lydia turned away, her voice defiant. "I did nothing wrong. We were just talking."

Kitty closed her eyes in disbelief. Anger began to erode her control. Her voice sharp, she said, "You met with a man, alone, in secret, at this hour of the night. Do you really believe that was not wrong? You know better, Lydia. It is a gross impropriety, and if anyone else saw you, you could be ruined and the family with you. Did you not think of that?"

"Well," Lydia said, flouncing to sit on the side of the bed, "no one but you saw me. So it does not count."

Kitty went to stand over her sister. She said in a tone that Lydia had never heard from her before, "Listen to me, Lydia, and listen well. I am to be married next spring to a gentleman whom I esteem very much. A scandal would force him to withdraw from the betrothal. Mary will probably marry Mr. Cranshaw. What do you think your actions could do to her future? And Lizzy has attracted the attention of Mr. Darcy, a very wealthy, very respectable gentleman. Are you really so childish that you think only of yourself and not of your sisters? Give me one valid reason that I should not tell Papa of what you did the moment he arrives home."

Tears filled Lydia's eyes and fell onto her dress. Kitty handed her a handkerchief and waited. She was well aware that Lydia was able to cry at will.

"I meant no harm, Kitty," the younger girl sobbed. "Mr. Wi... the gentleman was only acting for a friend. His friend is in love with a...a young lady of my acquaintance, and he wished me to tell him of any soirees or excursions she is invited to so that his friend might obtain an introduction. His intentions are honorable; the gentleman swore it."

Kitty softened her voice a little. "Lydia, any man who entices an unmarried lady to speak to him in secret is no gentleman, and I doubt his friend is either. I want your solemn promise that you will not participate in this scheme, nor will you meet with this man or any other alone unless you are married to him. If you do—and I shall find out, I promise you—I will go straight to father. You know how he will take the information, do you not?"

Wide eyed with fear, Lydia nodded her head rapidly. "You will not tell him now, will you, Kitty?"

With a sigh, Kitty said, "No, not now. But I shall tell him if you break your word. Now promise me."

"I p...promise," Lydia said in a strained voice.

"Very well. Goodnight, Lydie."

Chilled by more than the cold of the hall, Kitty returned to her room and bed. She remained wide awake for a long time, unable to banish the images in her mind. Had she done the right thing? She knew that much of the blame for Lydia's attitude belonged to their mother. But her sister was sixteen years old; she understood the rules by which society operated and the penalty for breaking them. Lydia was selfish and shallow, but she was not stupid except where her own desires were concerned. Kitty resolved to watch her sister closely and to do as she had threatened if she saw any sign that Lydia betrayed her word.

In her room, Lydia Bennet made ready for bed. She would have liked to call the maid she shared with Kitty, but she did not want to deal with anyone else, even a servant. Thank Heaven it was Kitty who discovered her rendezvous with Mr. Winter and not Lizzy! Lizzy would have told on her immediately, and she did not want to think of the consequences. *Another school,* she thought with a shudder, probably far away from the pleasures of London. Kitty had given her a chance to save herself, one she meant to use to the fullest.

As for Kitty's accusations, Lydia thought as she plaited her hair, Mr. Cowper was in love with her; he was not going to ask to be released even if there was a scandal, and she doubted Mary cared all that much for Mr. Cranshaw. He hardly ever called, and Mary did not appear to mind. Finally, if Mr. Darcy wanted Lizzy, he could have her for all Lydia cared. She could lecture him for a change.

She was *not* childish, Lydia told herself. Mr. Winter admired her; he told her she was a beautiful young woman who ought to be out in society, enjoying life. It was such a small thing he asked of her, after all, just a little information about Miss Darcy. And if she encountered the gentleman Mr. Winter represented and they fell in love it would be very romantic. Humming, Lydia blew out the candle, got into bed, and fell asleep.

Instead of calling at the Bennet home the following day, Darcy waited on Mr. Bennet at his offices. As Mr. Bennet was not currently engaged with a client, he saw Darcy at once. His expression was neutral as usual, but with a question in his eyes. Darcy took the indicated chair, refused refreshment, and gathered himself.

"I have called today, Mr. Bennet, to advise you that I have instructed my solicitors to draw up the marriage settlement for Miss Bennet. I think you will find the terms satisfactory; however, I am open to any amendments or changes you wish to make. I intend to speak to Miss Bennet today about announcing our betrothal and setting a wedding date. I see no reason to delay longer, and I believe she will agree that as the matter is already fixed, there is no reason to wait."

Mr. Bennet removed his spectacles, rubbed the bridge of his nose, and replaced them. It was a gesture that was not unfamiliar to the courts. "As you have not yet consulted my daughter, I can only say that if she agrees, I have no objection. As for the marriage contract, I will review it, of course, but I have no doubts that it will be more than generous."

"I have come to admire and esteem Miss Bennet, and I can assure you that she will want for nothing as my wife, nor will any children of the marriage, whether the heir is male or female."

Mr. Bennet looked momentarily surprised. "Pemberley is not entailed to the heirs male of the body?"

"No, sir. There have been male heirs since the beginning, but if I should die before producing a male heir the estate would devolve on my sister."

"I see," Mr. Bennet said slowly. "So it is rather imperative that you produce an heir."

"It is my wish, of course, but if God does not grant us a child, it will not affect my feelings for my wife or her status."

Mr. Bennet smiled. It was a paternal smile that reached out to Darcy in a way he would not have expected from anyone but his father. "I think I have chosen well for my Lizzy."

Darcy rose, and Mr. Bennet again walked him out to the reception room before returning to his office. His fears about trusting his favorite child to a man he did not know were fading. Darcy was a good man. He sincerely hoped that Lizzy would be happy with him. He did not want any of his daughters to marry a man she was unable to respect if not love.

In his carriage, Darcy was able to concentrate on what he meant to say to Elizabeth, as he had begun to call her in his mind. He no longer had concerns about the settlement. Mr. Bennet was an ethical gentleman who would not use any suspicions about George Darcy's health to increase the bride's fortunes. The next challenge that faced Darcy was his approach to his fiancée. As the carriage rolled through the constant surf of sound that was London's life breath, he decided that a direct approach was best. Surely she had known from the beginning that theirs was not to be a long courtship. If she agreed, the announcement would be in the *Morning Post* the day after the Wendovers' ball.

The butler opened the door of the Bennet home and bowed him in. From the level of noise emanating from the drawing room, Darcy's first impression was that some family crisis was in progress. At his raised brow, Mr. Hill smiled slightly.

"Mr. and Mrs. Bingley arrived a short time ago, sir. Please follow me."

The drawing room was in controlled chaos, with Mrs. Bennet fluttering and expostulating, her handkerchief in constant motion, her voice even higher and more incoherent than usual. On a sofa, Elizabeth sat holding the hand of the most beautiful woman Darcy had ever encountered. In spite of her obvious condition, she might have been carven by Phidias, so classic was her beauty. Elizabeth looked up at that moment and caught his eye with a raised brow. Darcy colored and then stepped forward as Mrs. Bennet finally noticed his entrance.

"Oh, Mr. Darcy, welcome, welcome! My eldest daughter and her husband have just arrived unexpectedly from Hertfordshire. I am all every which way, but we are always so happy to see you. You must meet them. Lizzy, introduce your sister and brother to Mr. Darcy."

Elizabeth, who had already risen and curtsied to Darcy's bow, introduced Jane Bingley to Darcy and turned to a sandy-haired young man who waited patiently with a happy smile. "Mr. Darcy, may I present Mr. Charles Bingley of Netherfield Park in Hertfordshire. Mr. Darcy of Pemberley in Derbyshire."

The two men bowed. Darcy's swift assessment saw a gentleman of middle height, well dressed, with an affable expression on his good-natured face. They exchanged the usual pleasantries as tea arrived. When Darcy took a chair at Elizabeth's end of the sofa, she leaned a little toward him, lowering her voice.

"Do not worry, Mr. Darcy. I have spent my entire life seeing men react to my sister's beauty. It does not bother me, for she is every bit as sweet as she is lovely."

Distracted from his original intention of speaking to Elizabeth about their betrothal, he looked for something to say to Mrs. Bingley, who was smiling serenely at him.

"Are you staying in Town long, Mrs. Bingley?" he asked.

"At present our plans are to remain until spring. Mr. Bingley has opened our town house. I shall be glad to have the holiday season with my family and his."

Elizabeth gave Darcy a swift glance that told him her thoughts were also on their coming announcement. Would she wish to postpone the marriage because of her sister's arrival? It was even more imperative that he discuss it with her now than before. Mr. Bingley's voice interrupted his thoughts, and he turned his attention to the gentleman who was shortly to become his brother-in-law.

"We had not been introduced," Bingley said, "but I remember you from university. My first year was your last. We moved in different circles, however I have never forgotten the beautiful black stallion you rode. I never saw a finer animal."

"Erebus. He is still my favorite mount."

Bingley said a bit wistfully, "I always wished I had conjured up the nerve to ask you if you might sell him to me, but I expect my question would have been in vain."

"It would. We have bred horses at Pemberley for several hundred years. He is one of the finest in memory. There are several of his offspring available at present. Perhaps we can discuss the subject later?"

Bingley beamed. "I would be delighted to."

Jane leaned forward enough to address Darcy across her sister. "I have heard of Pemberley. I am told the house is magnificent and the gardens more so."

"The gardens are indeed wonderful," Darcy replied with a glance at Elizabeth. "They are the product of many years' effort by the family and our gardeners. Some species of plants exist almost nowhere else in England."

"I am only leasing Netherfield Park at the moment," Mr. Bingley said, "so we have not made any extensive changes in the landscaping. If I purchase it, I shall look for someone to plan out the gardens and park who uses nature and natural features as much as possible."

At that point, Mrs. Bennet interrupted the exchange with a panegyric on the garden at Longbourn, allowing Darcy to speak softly to Elizabeth. "I saw your father this morning. I need to speak to you in private."

Her eyes darkened with what Darcy read as alarm, quickly gone. Her chin rose, she replied as softly, "Yes, Mr. Darcy, we do need to talk. I shall excuse myself shortly, and do you meet me in the library."

Darcy straightened. Mrs. Bennet had moved on to the Wendovers' ball and Elizabeth's invitation. With a smile and a word to Jane, Elizabeth excused herself and left the room. Darcy waited until Mrs. Bennet was deeply enmeshed in an elaborate description of a piece of Belgian lace to rise and quietly exit the drawing room. He found Elizabeth waiting before the fire in the library grate, her arms crossed around her body as if she were cold. She turned as he came in leaving the door half-open. Darcy was unable to read her expression except that she was tense.

"You wished to speak to me, Mr. Darcy?"

"Yes. It is about our betrothal."

Something flickered through her remarkable eyes. Pain? Fear? She drew herself up.

"You wish to withdraw, Mr. Darcy?"

Startled, Darcy said more emphatically than he intended, "Good Lord, no! I wish to announce it."

Elizabeth shivered. She dropped her gaze for a long moment as Darcy moved closer.

He said quietly, "I am sorry, Miss Bennet, if my request to speak with you gave you the wrong impression. I feel that there is no reason to delay the announcement of our engagement."

Elizabeth allowed her heart rate to calm before she replied.

"I, too, am tired of the deception that we are only acquaintances, although in practicality, it is true. As the marriage is already agreed upon, I see no reason to delay. That was what I wanted to speak to you about as well."

At last she raised her eyes to his and found a dark fire in their depths that set the blood pounding through her body. Her voice stumbled. "It…it will take at least a month to purchase a wedding gown and trousseau, but any time after that will be acceptable for the wedding."

"You wish to be wed here, then?"

"Do not you? I know it is a long trip from Derbyshire for your father, but my entire family is here."

Darcy paced away. He stopped at the window that looked out on the side garden and stared sightlessly at the large redberry bush twittering with birds. "There is something I must tell you, Miss Bennet. I had hoped it would not make a difference; however, I see it is unfair of me to ask you for concessions without a valid reason."

Elizabeth moved closer, studying his chiseled profile. "What concessions?"

"That we marry as soon as may be. My father will not be traveling to London; I will not ask you to marry at Pemberley, as I know your sister is unable to make such a journey."

Elizabeth saw pain grip his tall frame and instinctively reached out and laid a hand on his arm. He said in a voice roughened by distress, "My father is...gravely ill. I do not know how long..."

Darcy fought for control. Elizabeth felt the grief he did not express. Had it been her father, she knew that she could not have contained it. She said nothing, but as he turned to her, she stepped into his embrace. For what seemed an eternity, Darcy held her soft body against him, his face buried in her hair. At that moment Darcy wanted nothing so much as to kiss her sweet lips for the comfort she offered him, but he knew it was not the time.

At last, drawing back, she said, "The trousseau is not important. I can be ready in a fortnight, although my mama will be devastated. Papa can deal with that. What of the banns?"

"I can obtain a special license, so the reading of banns is not an issue. If your trousseau is not complete, you can buy whatever you like later. I should have told your father at once," he added heavily, "and I should have told you. I will tell him the next time I see him. I hope it will not change anything."

"No, it will not," Elizabeth reassured him. She felt his anguish and remorse so strongly it made her question her feelings for him. He was offering her an honorable way out at a cost to himself and his father she could not fully comprehend. And she found she did not want it. "Today is the nineteenth of October. We can marry in the second week of November."

Darcy stroked warm fingers gently down her cheek. He hesitated, looking intently into her eyes. "I know we are obligated to wed, but I still feel it is only right that I ask you. Miss Bennet, will you do me the very great honor of becoming my wife?"

Elizabeth heart began to beat very fast. This was more than she ever expected, more than a simple proposal. This man was offering her his life. She looked up into his face, waiting, unsure.

"Yes, Mr. Darcy, I will."

"Thank you, Elizabeth."

Her given name on his lips sent a frisson down her spine. In three weeks, she would be a married woman; they would be man and wife in every sense of the words. Almost with relief, Elizabeth heard her aunt's voice in the hallway calling her.

CHAPTER 9
A MOST UNUSUAL BALL

The Royal Opera House was crowded with patrons in couples and groups, all, it seemed, talking at once. Amid the cacophony, Darcy guided his party up the grand staircase to their box, walking with Elizabeth on one arm and Georgiana on the other. Immediately on seeing his sister, he had realized that she was very nervous and had tucked her hand under his elbow to steady her. Behind them, the Bennets, the Gardiners, Mary Bennet, Richard, and Sofia followed like a neat procession of female birds in colorful feathers with accompanying black-and-white males.

Darcy had eyes only for Elizabeth. She wore a gown of pale-green, gauzy silk in the current empire style that emphasized her slim body, her dark curls piled up behind a silver tiara set with small emeralds and citrines. In contrast to Georgiana and Sofia, both of whom had the Fitzwilliam height, Elizabeth seemed almost diminutive, her head coming barely above his shoulder.

In the box, Darcy effected introductions, impossible in the main entry below. When Georgiana and Elizabeth straightened from their mutual curtsies, Elizabeth smiled at the young woman with a genuine warmth that could not be mistaken.

"What a lovely gown, Miss Darcy, and the color becomes you so very well."

Georgiana murmured thanks but made no other reply, desperately seeking something to say. She had carefully selected the gown she wore, a creamy sprigged muslin in the newest fashion. She appreciated that William did not insist that she always wear white as befitted a girl not yet formally out in society. With her pale hair and milky complexion, she felt that white made her look like a wraith in a Gothic novel.

Elizabeth stepped closer, still smiling. "I have seen you at Madame Colette's shop. Not having your acquaintance I had no idea who you were. I believe you frequent Hatchard's bookshop as well."

"Yes." Georgiana glanced at her brother, who was speaking with Richard and Mr. Gardiner. Finding no help there, she said in a breathless voice, "The music. I…they have a large selection. And they can order what I want if it is not available in their shop."

Sofia came up to them as Elizabeth said with interest, "You play the pianoforte?"

"Yes. And the harp, but not as well."

"She plays very well," Sofia put in. Elizabeth shifted her position slightly to include Sofia in the conversation. "Do you play, Miss Bennet?"

"Yes, but not as well as I would like. My favorite master moved to Italy last year, and I do not have the discipline to practice as much on my own."

"Signor Donatello?" Georgiana inquired.

"Yes. Do you know him?"

"He was my music master for two years. He was very good. I do not like my new music master nearly as well."

Sofia watched Elizabeth converse with Georgiana on music, her passion, offering a comment here and there. The two ladies' eyes met once and Sofia smiled, understanding Elizabeth's purpose in drawing the shy girl out by using her favorite subject. As the warning bell for the performance sounded, Darcy came up to them and seated the three in the first row of chairs, with Elizabeth between Georgiana and Sofia. The other ladies occupied the rest of the front row; Mrs. Gardiner next to Sofia, then Mrs. Bennet, and then Mary. As they took their seats and settled for the play to begin, Elizabeth looked across the pit to the opposite boxes. She had been to the opera house many times, and the pageantry of humanity it offered never ceased to fascinate her.

She turned in her seat to where Darcy sat behind her. "Mr. Darcy, do you know that elderly lady in Mrs. Montague's box? She has been staring at you or perhaps us?"

After a brief casual glance, he said, "No, I do not believe I have ever seen her before."

"Women are always staring at my cousin," Sofia murmured to Elizabeth. "The lady is elderly, not dead."

Elizabeth's silvery laugh caught Darcy by surprise, shivering over him in a wave of pure desire. Startled and embarrassed, he turned to Mr. Bennet, who was watching them with raised brows.

"There is an elderly lady in Mrs. Montague's box, sir. Do you know who she is? She seems to have an interest in our party."

Mr. Bennet looked to the box in question. The woman's aristocratic face was turned to their box, her expression unreadable. She was dressed in pale-lavender silk in a classic style that emphasized her white hair, drawn up in a simple knot. Mr. Bennet turned back to Darcy.

"If I am not mistaken, that is Lady Agatha Quintain, the widow of Sir Cedric Quintain, the portraitist. She is rarely in society since her husband's death some years ago. Mrs. Montague's grandfather was one of Sir Cedric's first and staunchest patrons and supporters."

"I suppose that explains it," Sofia said, and the conversation faded as the curtains opened on the court of the Duke of Athens.

At the interval, they did not leave the box. Darcy had arranged for champagne to be brought in, and the party stood or sat and talked as they enjoyed the refreshments. Richard and Mary joined Sofia and Elizabeth. Sofia looked across to the Montague box, but Lady Agatha was no longer there. With a mental shrug, she put the incident out of mind and turned her attention to Elizabeth.

"Are you attending the Wendovers' ball, Miss Bennet?"

Elizabeth glanced involuntarily at Darcy. "I am. Mr. Darcy kindly arranged an invitation."

Sofia cut her eyes at her brother. "Lady Wendover will be thrilled. The idea of Darcy voluntarily attending one of her balls will be the high point of her Season. They are deadly boring," she added. "Not that Darcy would notice; he finds all social events of the *ton* boring."

Richard chuckled. He looked at Mary and asked, "Are you also attending the Wendovers' ball, Miss Mary?"

"No," she replied calmly.

Realizing his error, he said swiftly, "Would you like to attend? Lady Wendover is an old family friend. She will be happy for another lady to bore."

"I…I could not impose," Mary said, a light flush coloring her cheeks.

"It will not be an imposition," Sofia told her with a smile. "She delights in crowds, and if Richard goes, she will be doubly delighted."

"I shall see to it," Richard said firmly, closing the discussion.

Nearby Mrs. Gardiner watched the interplay with a soft smile. She had never been comfortable with Mr. Cranshaw's halfhearted pursuit of her niece, believing it to be a method of ingratiating himself with Mr. Bennet and more so with Mrs. Bennet. Mary had certainly never responded to him as she was responding to Colonel Fitzwilliam. Perhaps this was the catalyst needed to give

Mary the confidence she required to reject Mr. Cranshaw's efforts. Mary was not unattractive, but she was so used to being compared to her sisters that she believed herself plain and unlikely to find a husband on her own merits. If she was not mistaken, Mrs. Gardiner thought, Mary might soon find herself the object of a suit by a gentleman with much besides position to offer.

"I am not to speak with you alone."

Lydia Bennet kept her eyes downcast as she sat on the sofa with Mr. Winter in his usual chair next to her. She lowered her voice even more. "My sister Kitty saw us talking the other night. She will tell my father if I have private conversations with you, and I do not know what he might do to punish me."

Winter drew a breath through his nose before replying. He must not seem angry, or this silly chit was unlikely to confide in him again. Instead he said soothingly, "She is right, you know. Our conversation was harmless, but it might have looked improper to anyone who saw us. Are you going to withhold information about Miss Darcy as well?"

Lydia hesitated. "She told me I was not to assist you in any way, but I do not see the harm in telling you what you might well find out from someone else."

"Exactly. My friend is love stricken and only wants an opportunity to meet the lady. It is rather romantic, do you not think?"

"Oh yes! That is exactly what I told Kitty. Only I did not use your name or Miss Darcy's."

"That was very discreet of you, Miss Lydia." *And lucky for me.* "You are a most intelligent young lady, as well as beautiful."

Lydia simpered. Winter took the conversation in another direction, hardly attending to what he said, having carried on such tête-à-têtes many times before. A combination of flattery and mild flirting sufficed to satisfy ladies like Miss Lydia, allowing his mind to work on another level at the same time.

Miss Gradison was giving indications that it was time to leave when Lydia suddenly said, "My sister is attending the Wendovers' ball tomorrow night with Mr. Darcy. He has been calling nearly every day. I think he has a *tendre* for her."

Instantly all of Winter's attention was on the chattering girl. He said, "He is courting her?"

"I do not know. Nothing has been said, but he escorted her to a play the night we met in the garden, along with my parents, my sister Mary, my aunt and uncle, and his cousins. It was Shakespeare, I think. And I heard her say he arranged the invitation to the ball, because we do not know the Wendovers."

Lydia rose as her friend made her goodbyes to their hostesses. This was manna from Heaven. He bade Lydia goodbye with half a mind and left the room. This news was something he needed to reflect on in private. It opened all sorts of possibilities, both for profit and failure. Winter had intended to attend the Wendovers' ball as Sir Colin's guest, but with Darcy in attendance that was impossible. He had to come up with another plan.

Pacing his room, Winter contemplated his next move. If he was unable to attend as a guest, he must find another way to be there. Sir Colin was growing more and more unstable as days passed, and he had no more in the way of money to pay his mounting debts. Added to that, his drinking had reached a point that made him unreliable, a sure way for them to find themselves exposed and arrested, and the thefts were a hanging offense.

Winter threw himself into a chair and stared at the empty grate. The room was cold, and no fire had been laid. There was not even any coal to make one. *Damned footmen*, he thought, *lazy bastar...*footmen! With a huge society affair, the Wendovers were certain to hire or borrow extra help. And no one noticed a footman in livery and a powdered wig. Winter grinned. If he was careful, he would be as safe as if he were invisible.

He needed a suit of the Wendovers' livery and a wig. Winter knew that footmen usually slept in the basement of a house, their livery and other supplies kept in pantries that were seldom locked. He knew just the man for the job too. Rising with new vigor, Winter put on an old coat and hat he kept for such moments and slipped out of the house by the servants' stairs. A quick trip to Whitechapel, a few coins, and he would have his disguise. And the Kalimar Diamond.

Lady Agatha Quintain sat in one of the chairs placed around the ballroom at the Wendovers' palatial town house for mothers and others who did not participate in the dancing. It was not far from the open door to the gardens, and the night breeze wafted the odors of jasmine and late roses into the already-warm room. Lady Wendover had personally seen to her comfort, knowing that the presence of the reclusive widow was a true social triumph. Between Lady Agatha and the attendance of the illusive Mr. Darcy and his cousin Colonel Fitzwilliam, the hostess could barely contain her excitement to see the society columns in tomorrow's *Morning Post.* She was sure to be the talk of the *ton.*

Darcy and Elizabeth arrived with Lady Sofia, Colonel Fitzwilliam, and Mary as the last guests went through the receiving line. Euphemia Wendover was a plump girl of twenty, dressed in a gown of gauzy blue silk and wearing an overage of sapphire jewelry. Her betrothed smiled inanely as he accepted congratulations on his forthcoming marriage.

After introducing the sisters to their bubbling hostess, who made certain that the huge diamond around her neck was fully appreciated, Darcy guided Elizabeth toward the ballroom.

Immaculate in evening clothes, he made an imposing figure. Elizabeth felt a stir of emotion composed of excitement, expectation, and pride. He was easily the most handsome man in the room; Elizabeth would not have been human if she had not felt gratified that he was her escort. The emotion was deepened by the looks directed at them from a dozen ladies of the *ton*, envious, surprised, disbelieving, one or two positively vitriolic.

Her chin rose at the implied hostility, but her stomach tightened. *Get used to it*, she told herself. *When you are married, this will be the reaction you face, at least in the beginning.*

As if reading her thoughts, Darcy smiled down at her. Elizabeth colored, but he only held her arm a little tighter against his body. She had taken special care with her gown and hair, the curls grouped around her face and the remainder of her hair drawn up in a woven knot surrounded by small braids into which white ribbon was wound. Her dress was also white, a very fine, thin velvet enhanced by silver embroidery on the bodice and hem. She wore an antique pearl pendant and earbobs and pearl pins in her hair. Darcy noticed that her day dresses had more modest necklines than current fashion, but tonight her gown exposed the swell of creamy breasts and her smooth arms from the tops of her long gloves to puffed sleeves.

In her seat near the door, Lady Agatha watched their entrance. *He is certainly a Darcy*, she thought. *They are all handsome devils.* The lady on his arm interested her more. Small, slim, with a mass of curling dark hair, and an intelligent face in which remarkable violet eyes took in the room with cool assessment. *She is not overwhelmed by him, nor is she impressed by the glitter of the assembly. A woman of spirit. He will not easily overmaster this one.*

Lady Wendover had rejoined her guests and now signaled for the musicians to begin the first set. Darcy saw the anticipation in Elizabeth's face and spoke softly beneath the quieting clamor of the crowd.

"May I have the honor of the first set, Miss Bennet?"

"You may, Mr. Darcy."

She put her hand in his and was led to the forming set. Three large chandeliers with multitudes of crystal drops showered light on the dancers, catching shards of color from jewels, shimmering over silks, velvets, muslins, richly dark on the gentlemen's evening coats. Elizabeth saw Colonel Fitzwilliam and Mary take their places several couples down the line. Mary looked happier than Elizabeth remembered seeing her. She felt a warm glow of gratitude to Darcy's cousin. Mary was too much ignored at home.

The musicians began to play. Lady Wendover liked to feel that she was just a bit progressive, to which end she did not have the ball begin with a minuet, a tradition most country and some city balls still followed. The dance was a galliard, nearly as stately but more demanding of concentration. Elizabeth moved with a natural grace and a love of the dance that drew the usually reluctant Darcy into the joy she felt. They finished the set with Elizabeth glowing. She took Darcy's proffered arm and accompanied him off the dance floor to the chairs along the wall.

"Would you like a glass of punch or lemonade, Miss Bennet?"

"No, I thank you." Elizabeth saw the elderly woman she had noticed at the play sitting with an empty chair next to her. "I believe I shall sit down for a few minutes."

"Very well. I want a word with my cousin."

Darcy saw her to the chair, bowed to Lady Agatha, and went in search of Richard. Her gray eyes interested, Lady Agatha looked up at Elizabeth and said, "If you will forgive the impropriety of an old lady, I shall introduce myself without standing. I am Lady Agatha Quintain. And you, I believe, are Miss Bennet."

Elizabeth curtsied. "I am honored to meet you, my lady." She took the chair, flat backed in the chinoiserie style with a seat upholstered in patterned silk.

"They are not what one is accustomed to," Lady Agatha indicated the chair, "but quite comfortable when one grows used to them."

"They are called 'scholars' chairs,' are they not?"

"Originally. The current Lady Wendover has a passion for chinoiserie, as you can see by the number of japanned tables and cabinets and painted hangings adorning the regal Palladian walls. Not to my taste I am afraid."

"I like the Palladian," Elizabeth ventured. "Our home is a modified Queen Anne, and I also find that pleasing."

Lady Agatha nodded as if something had been confirmed. "You have a classical taste. It is not so much found in young people these days. My late husband was a classicist. Our taste always agreed."

"I have seen some of his portraits. They are the most wonderful I have ever encountered. The people seem to step out of the frame; they are so lifelike. There is nothing false about them. One feels as if one spoke to them, they might answer."

Lady Agatha tilted her head a little to one side. Against her intentions, she was beginning to be drawn to this lovely young woman. "You have an extremely attractive escort, Miss Bennet."

"Yes." Elizabeth blushed lightly. "Mr. Darcy."

"He is little in society, I understand. You have achieved a social triumph."

Elizabeth shook her head. "His father and mine are old acquaintances. I have…"

Whatever Elizabeth might have said was lost in the approach of a young man in well-tailored evening dress. His brown hair lay in fashionable curls around a face already flushed with drink; an elaborately tied cravat fell to the top of his white-satin waistcoat. He bowed to Elizabeth as she rose and curtsied as minimally as courtesy permitted.

"Miss Bennet."

"Mr. Hatfield." Elizabeth resumed her chair. Beside her, Lady Agatha watched the exchange with growing interest.

"I suppose," the gentleman said without the usual inquiries as to her and her family's health, "it is useless to request a set?"

"Yes, Mr. Hatfield, it is."

He sneered openly. His voice took on an insinuating tone just short of open insult. "You have found a gentleman more to your liking, I see."

Elizabeth's chin rose, although her voice was calm. "No, Mr. Hatfield, you are mistaken. You were never to my liking. And if you have any further comments to make, I suggest you address them to Mr. Darcy, as he is about to join us."

Hatfield looked sharply over his shoulder. Seeing Darcy making his way through the guests toward them, he said shortly, "No, Miss Bennet. I am not fool enough to have a man with Darcy's mastery of pistol and sword call me out for insulting his—friend."

With a mocking bow, he left them. Elizabeth fought to compose herself before Darcy reached them. Again Lady Agatha found herself admiring Miss Bennet's strength of character. Many debutantes would have poured out their distress at such treatment whatever the consequences. Darcy shot a sharp glance after the departing gentleman as he stopped before the two ladies.

"Shall I have a word with Mr. Hatfield, Miss Bennet?"

"No, thank you, Mr. Darcy. I am perfectly capable of dealing with Mr. Hatfield."

Lady Agatha waited for Darcy to swell up like a pouter pigeon, the usual male reaction to being told their lady did not need a dragon slayer at the moment. To her surprise, he only nodded.

Intrigued, she said to Elizabeth, "Will you introduce your escort to me, Miss Bennet?"

"Certainly. Lady Agatha Quintain, may I introduce Mr. Fitzwilliam Darcy of Pemberley in Derbyshire?"

Darcy made an elegant bow. Lady Agatha appraised him frankly but without visible emotion, as a painter appraises a subject. "I am pleased to make your acquaintance, Mr. Darcy."

"It is my honor, Lady Agatha. I have always admired Sir Cedric's work; it is certainly the equal, if not the superior, of any other portraitist of the last century."

"Thank you, Mr. Darcy. He was a great painter and a good man. Miss Bennet also admires his work."

His eyes sought Elizabeth. "Miss Bennet has exquisite taste."

"Cedric would have made a very good job of her," Lady Agatha mused. "He preferred painting women. He found them more complex than men."

"My father attempted to have Sir Cedric paint my mother's wedding portrait," Darcy said quietly, "but he had so many commissions it was impossible. My father has always regretted it."

The musicians began to ready their instruments for the second set. Colonel Fitzwilliam arrived with Mary and bowed to Elizabeth and Lady Agatha, who acknowledged him with a dip of her head. Mary glowed. Her muslin gown draped softly over her womanly figure, a butter yellow trimmed in lace with a wide gold sash. She wore yellow topaz and citrine jewelry that emphasized her warm coloring.

Darcy said, "Miss Mary, if you are not engaged for this set, may I have the honor?"

She stared at him for a second and then offered her hand. "You may, Mr. Darcy."

"Miss Bennet, will you give me the pleasure?"

"Thank you, Colonel Fitzwilliam." Elizabeth had risen when her sister arrived. She gave Richard her hand, curtsied to Lady Agatha, and allowed him to lead her onto the floor.

Lady Agatha did not watch the dancing. Her attention had been captured by a movement at the near side of the room. Lady Wendover was talking to another lady and a youth, the Kalimar

Diamond throwing sparks at every gesture of her shoulders and beringed hands. A footman stood stiffly just behind her, as if awaiting a command.

Lady Agatha studied his face. In powdered wig and livery, he looked very much like any other footman in attendance, but there was something about his posture that made her uneasy. A painter in her youth and married for many years to a man trained to see the nuances of personality in body movements and posture, she found herself thinking that he lacked the demeanor of a trained footman. His hands were clenched at his sides, his shoulders stiff. Lady Agatha caught a glimpse of a heavy gold ring on the middle finger of his right hand as he shifted position slightly. Something was wrong, although she was unable to say exactly what it was.

In the company of Lady Atwood and her son, just back from his grand tour, Lady Wendover was extremely pleased with the progress of her event, not least because Mr. Fitzwilliam Darcy was in attendance with Miss Bennet, the lady whose name had begun to be linked to his by the latest gossip. She had also garnered Lady Agatha Quintain, a social triumph in itself, as Lady Agatha never attended large social gatherings. True, she had hardly left her seat by the French-style door to the garden. But she was there, and that was all Lady Wendover required. The magnificent diamond hanging around her plump neck was a finishing flourish to the evening. Yes, it was all going very well indeed.

The thought had barely crossed her mind when a loud shriek snapped her head around. A lady was bouncing up and down near the middle of the lines of dancers just formed for a quadrille, waving her arms wildly and screaming. Lady Wendover immediately wondered if she was having a fit of some sort. She did not feel a man move close behind her or the slight tug on the diamond pendant's chain as very small, very sharp clippers cut a single link. When she took a swift step toward the confusion ruining her ball, the pendant slid down her décolletage and lodged in the top of her stays. Rendered immobile, Lady Wendover could only clutch her bosom and watch the proceedings in horror.

On the far side of the room, the young lady was still shrieking. It had begun when another female guest pointed a shaking finger at Miss Bentley-Stokes's gown. Miss Bentley-Stokes had followed the path of the finger and found a large black spider clinging to her silk skirt. She had proceeded in the way of startled ladies to scream and shake the silk wildly, dislodging the unfortunate arachnid onto the immaculate black breeches of her recent partner. The gentleman, unable to see the creature clearly and not wishing to exhibit undue agitation, began hopping in place and slapping at his breeches with a gloved hand. This succeeded in knocking the spider—which, while as ugly as all its kind, was quite harmless—onto the floor, where it proceeded to use all eight legs to scuttle through a forest of silk and satin toward the nearest exit. The spider's progress inspired the nearby ladies to begin an impromptu tarantella, shrieking and shaking, while the gentlemen stomped the floor at random, giving the impression of a primitive mating ritual. By this time the spider had somehow avoided all attempts on its life and secreted itself in the darkness of the heavy velvet drapes against the wall, no doubt grateful to be alive and in one piece.

At this point Lady Wendover regained the power of speech. She called loudly for her husband, who was summoned from the cardroom. Miss Bentley-Stokes was assisted, shuddering, to a chair and fanned by a friend while her partner went to get her a glass of wine and himself a quick brandy. Euphemia stood, clutching the arm of her betrothed, and looked wildly for her mother while Lady Wendover sent Mr. Wendover to soothe the guests. As he departed on his errand, she made her way very carefully toward the door to the hall.

"You," she ordered the footman waiting just outside the door, "get my maid and the guard. He is in the senior-staff dining room. Hurry!"

Winter said in a disguised voice, keeping his head lowered respectfully, "Yes, my lady, at once."

Carefully Lady Wendover walked toward the ladies' retiring room, clutching the pendant to her body. She was humiliated by the incident in the ballroom. Something must be done to save the evening, or she would be made a laughingstock by the papers. Her beautiful social triumph was rapidly descending into disaster. Absorbed by her thoughts and fear that she might not be able to wear the diamond for the rest of the night, she did not see the footman come up behind her on stealthy feet. After a swift glance up and down the hall, Winter struck her a sharp blow over the ear with his fist. Lady Wendover was aware only of movement to her right and a blasting pain in her head that lasted for a second before she lost consciousness.

Breathing hard, Winter bent and rolled her over with an effort. With a single movement, he ripped her gown down the front and retrieved the diamond from her underpinnings. Shoving it into his waistcoat pocket, he made for the stairs. He was out of sight in half a minute, walking swiftly along the upper hall to the room he had located as Lady Wendover's dressing room. As he neared the door, a heavyset man stepped out, scowling at him. Winter halted abruptly and turned back to gesture the way he had come.

"Madam wants you downstairs, sir. There is some trouble about the diamond she is wearing."

The guard nodded and strode past him without a second glance. Wearing a tight smile, Winter entered the dressing room, passed through to the bedchamber and threw open the window. He tore off the wig and coat and then tossed them into the garden below to be found later. In shirt and breeches, he passed back down the hall as a loud commotion erupted from the ground floor. Still grinning, he hurried down the servants' stairs to where he had left his regular coat in a pantry. Affecting a slight stagger in the event he was observed, he exited the house and let himself out the rear gate into the mews.

After two blocks at a fast walk, Winter slowed, laughing out loud. By God! He had gulled them all, even Darcy and his blasted cousin, the bloody colonel. No one noticed a footman! Winter slowed his pace, found a hackney cab, and gave a street in Whitechapel. He would see the Dutchman tomorrow night, but tonight he wanted a woman and a number of drinks. Sir Colin could wait for his return and sweat a little. There would not be many more nights to wait before it all crashed down on his dupe's head. Winter chuckled and called to the driver to whip up his horse.

CHAPTER 10
PROGRESSIONS

The chaos in the ballroom had just quieted when the hired guard appeared in the doorway to the central hall, his face pale. He looked around the room, located Mr. Wendover, and bulled his way through the reassembling guests to where the host was quietly instructing the musicians to play something lively. Without preamble, he grabbed Mr. Wendover's arm and whispered loud enough for those nearby to hear him easily that Lady Wendover had met with an accident and required a doctor. A scream from the hallway affirmed his words. There was a startled silence before host and guard rushed to the doorway. A maid appeared beyond the opening, both hands over her mouth, her eyes wide and terrified.

Darcy took Elizabeth's arm and walked her quickly back to the side of the room. "Please stay with Lady Agatha, Elizabeth, until I find out what has occurred."

For a moment, Elizabeth bridled, but reason told her that he was right. Lady Wendover was virtually unknown to her; her presence would offer no help or comfort. She nodded and watched him walk swiftly away, joined a moment later by Colonel Fitzwilliam. Mary came up to them, shaken but in control. Lady Agatha smiled up at her.

"Introduce me to your sister, please, Miss Bennet."

Elizabeth did so. Both ladies remained standing, throwing swift glances at the hall that was now the focus of everyone's attention.

"Well," Lady Agatha commented wryly, "this is certainly the most memorable ball I have ever attended."

"The most unsettling, at least," Mary commented.

Elizabeth said nothing. Her face was withdrawn, as if her thoughts were concentrated on something that troubled her.

"What are you thinking, child?" Lady Agatha asked quietly.

"The Kalimar Diamond. She should not have worn it at such an event with the burglaries that have been happening lately. I find the idea of a spider attaching itself to a lady's skirt in the middle of a ballroom very unlikely. I have spent nearly every summer of my life in the country, and spiders are generally reclusive. It would hide from the noise and people."

"You are perceptive, Miss Bennet. It would indeed, unless she brought it in with her, which is even more unlikely."

"You believe someone purposely put it on her skirt for a jest? How awful!" Mary shuddered.

Lady Agatha said, "No jest, Miss Mary. To a very real purpose."

Rumors were flying with phenomenal speed through the crowd. Lady Wendover had been attacked; the hallway was awash in blood; she was dying; her clothing had been torn off her, with the usual implication. Euphemia, Elizabeth noticed, had not gone to her mother but remained in the center of a group of friends, sobbing into her handkerchief. Poor Miss Bentley-Stokes was quite forgotten. Elizabeth was unable to see either Darcy or Colonel Fitzwilliam, but she heard someone giving what appeared to be orders. After five minutes, the colonel entered the room and halted just inside the doorway.

"Ladies and gentlemen, may I have your attention." His voice carried easily, the habit of command bringing every head in the room toward him. "Lady Wendover is not badly injured. A doctor has been summoned and a magistrate. The Kalimar Diamond has been stolen."

"The footman," Lady Agatha said involuntarily.

Elizabeth looked at her with a certain discomfort. "The police have investigated the servants at the other residences that were burgled; none of them was involved."

"You misunderstand. The man was pretending to be a footman. He wore the costume, but there was something not right about him. It is easier for a trained servant to pass as a gentleman than a gentleman to pass as a servant."

Darcy came in and walked directly to the three women. He said, "I will see that you are taken home, ladies. The ball is over."

"No doubt." Lady Agatha took up her walking stick and started to rise. Darcy offered his arm, and after a brief hesitation, she accepted the assistance. Her eyes fell on his gold signet ring. She drew in a sharp breath, her eyes meeting his.

"The ring. That was what was wrong with him; he wore a ring!"

"Who wore a ring?" Elizabeth asked quickly.

"The footman. I knew there was something wrong about him. He was nervous, keyed up, the way no professional servant would be. And he wore a heavy gold ring on his right hand. No footman on duty wears jewelry."

"If you will excuse me for a moment, I will advise Colonel Fitzwilliam of this."

Darcy left them. Watching him stride confidently away and observing Elizabeth's face, Lady Agatha found herself uncertain for the first time since she had received the priest's letter. Surely this was not her domineering father all over again. She perceived no arrogance, only a reserve that she understood and approved of. Such a man was not raised by a domestic tyrant. Perhaps the Darcys had changed; certainly he treated Miss Bennet as an equal, without any of the patronizing attitude she remembered so bitterly. Did they know the truth? That was the question she must have answered.

Lady Sofia joined them at that point. She looked as cool as usual, but there was a shine to her eyes that told of emotional distress.

"Lady Wendover is not badly hurt," Elizabeth told her at once. "But the diamond has been taken."

"I do not wonder. I am only glad that she has not been badly injured."

Lady Agatha turned to Elizabeth, "To be clear, Miss Bennet, I do not automatically blame a servant when something goes wrong. This is a very clever thief and a ruthless man. He will not be easily apprehended. Let us be thankful that he took a gem and not a life."

After seeing the morning papers the next day, Lady Wendover might not have agreed with her.

⁂

In a modest coffeehouse not far from Covent Garden, a man sat at a battered table, his face stony, a half-eaten roll and a cup of thick coffee before him. Hunter, as the man called himself, had also read the morning papers. He had watched the Arthur town house until nearly dawn, but only Sir Colin had gone out, coming back earlier than expected. There was no sign of his quarry, no evidence that Winter was not in the mansion. From his viewpoint, Hunter was not able to see every door. But if Winter had come out to the street, there was no way he could have gotten past undetected, and no riders had left from the mews. The only person who had emerged during the evening was a footman on an errand.

Hunter stiffened. A curse spat from his lips. He slammed his fist on the table hard enough to slop some of the coffee onto the stained surface and over a page of newsprint detailing the Wendovers' ball and the theft of the Kalimar Diamond. A footman. The clever sod! Who looked twice at a footman? Thinking back, Hunter realized now that the footman did not return. Of course, he might have been from another residence, waiting for a response to a message, but he had not arrived from the time Hunter began watching the house at dusk, and that was a matter of several hours. Too long to wait for a return message.

What now? Winter had most probably already seen the fence he used, and without trailing him, Hunter had no way of knowing which one of several high-end fences had his custom. Better to stick to the man and wait a little longer. Winter was greedy. There was bound to be at least one more major social event before the Little Season ended; that was Hunter's best chance to catch Winter in the act.

Hunter pushed the coffee away, rose and tossed a coin on the table. Sooner or later, he told himself, sooner or later, he would watch Winter swing, even if the crime he died for was not the one that had sent Hunter on his trail like the hounds of Hell.

Colonel Fitzwilliam entered the breakfast parlor where Darcy was breaking his fast and poured himself a fragrant cup of coffee before sitting next to his cousin.

"Ambrosia," he muttered as he drank deeply. He rubbed a hand over reddened eyes. "I have been up all night with Magistrate Siddon, who is an ass. I told him of Lady Agatha's observation, and in spite of the fact that a wig and livery coat were found under an open window, he said, 'No offense to the lady, but women are fanciful creatures, and no gentleman would stoop to impersonate a footman.' As I was unable to convince him I left off." His face registered disgust.

"It is always easier to blame the servants, when in fact most servants have no idea of how to dispose of expensive jewelry. This thief is a professional."

"Indeed. I spoke to several of the footmen and maids, and no one noticed a footman with a gold ring, which they would certainly have done. He hid out until his confederate caused panic in the ballroom and then struck and was gone."

"How is Lady Wendover?"

"Recovering. The blow only stunned her. She was more concerned with her diamond and the gossip that will ensue than a headache. However," Richard added, rose, and went to replenish his cup and fill a plate with food, "there is a small cut on her temple that looks to have been made by a ring."

"So Lady Agatha was right."

"Apparently. That may be why the man has not been spotted in the houses he robs. Footmen are never noticed, especially when there is a large social gathering."

He started on the food hungrily. Darcy sipped his own coffee, considering. "I doubt he has used the disguise every time. He is more likely to have attended as a guest. It would be interesting to know which guests have been at all the houses that were robbed."

"Um." Richard swallowed. "The guests will all be the same people. The magistrate might ask for guest lists, but I assure you he will not. He categorically refuses to believe anyone from the *ton* is involved."

"And yet we all know men who are deeply in debt to the moneylenders and not scrupulous about how they find the funds to pay their debts."

"Indeed. Yet how many will risk a capital crime to recoup?"

Darcy shrugged. "We will have to let the law look into this. Lord Wendover is influential., I am sure he will demand action. Perhaps the chief magistrate will step in."

"I am sorry you had so little chance to dance with the lovely Miss Bennet," Richard said between bites. "When is the announcement to be?"

"I had planned to speak to Mr. Bennet about that today. Miss Bennet has chosen the second week in November. I wish to wed as soon as possible and return to Pemberley, and she is in agreement."

"She knows about Uncle George?"

"Yes. She is a woman of compassion; there is nothing selfish about her. I find myself a most fortunate man."

Richard helped himself to another plate of food and more coffee. At Darcy's raised eyebrow, he said in mock defense, "I am a soldier. I eat whenever I can. Besides I do not want to insult your cook."

Darcy smiled. He said as Richard dug in, "You appear to know Lady Agatha Quintain."

"You do not? She is a Darcy on her father's side."

Darcy stared at his cousin in disbelief. "No, I did not know. She said nothing when we were introduced."

"I do not know the entire story, you will have to ask Mother. But Lady Agatha and your maternal grandmother were good friends as girls. Alexander Darcy and Lady Agatha were twins."

"Then how is it she has no contact with us now?"

Richard shook his head. "Again I do not know. Her father had a reputation as a domestic tyrant. There was some scandal when she was young. Mother probably has the entire story."

Darcy rose as Richard finished his meal, stood, and yawned widely. "I have to get home. I need about ten hours' sleep, and Mother will want to know the details of last night that Sofia has not already told her."

"I will call on Aunt Madeleine either later today or tomorrow with Miss Bennet. I want them to meet before the betrothal is formally announced. If the opportunity presents itself, I shall ask her about Lady Agatha."

"Good." Richard accompanied Darcy to the entry hall. "I am sure she will be enchanted with Miss Bennet."

Darcy saw his cousin out and returned to his study.

As he began to sort through the waiting post, he wondered what had alienated Lady Agatha from her family. Even if she had fought with her father, surely after his death, she could have sought a reconciliation? Darcy put it out of mind for the present. He doubted it was of any consequence after so many years. If Lady Agatha wished to maintain her privacy, he would not intrude.

Darcy sincerely hoped that his aunt Madeleine liked Elizabeth. Not only were Lord and Lady Fitzwilliam socially powerful but his uncle was also the head of the Fitzwilliam family. If they accepted Elizabeth, most of society was likely to follow, making her life as his wife infinitely easier. His aunt was a fair woman, unlike her sister-in-law, Lady Catherine de Bourgh. He trusted her judgment. Still Darcy felt a small wave of uneasiness. He could only wait and see her reaction to his marriage and his bride.

"Where the *bloody* hell have you been?"

Sir Colin stood in Winter's dressing room, red faced with fury, his fists clenched at his sides. Winter adjusted his cravat in the mirror over a side table without turning. He said coolly, "I required a little recreation after the events of the evening."

"Whoring while I sat at home, not knowing if you had been taken or not. Damn you, Winter, you were to come straight here!"

Winter swung around on the younger man, who backed a step at the look on his face. "I go where and when I please, Colly.

You had better get hold of your nerves; you are becoming more liability than asset."

The menace in Winter's voice was unmistakable. Sir Colin swallowed hard and moderated his tone. "I was concerned that someone might have realized you were not one of Lady Wendover's servants."

"Not likely. After the chaos our little friend caused in the ballroom, no one was looking at just another footman. Even Lady Wendover spoke to me without realizing I was a total stranger."

He walked to the door with Sir Colin trailing him anxiously. The young nobleman said in a strained tone, "What about the Dutchman?"

"I shall see him tonight. We can expect a good sum from the diamond, with a word of caution. Even more than the other swag, it will have to be smuggled out of the country to be cut down and reset or sold to someone who will never wear it in public."

"George, I need that money." Sir Colin dropped his voice to a murmur. "I have to give Maresford something on account at least. He's threatening to go to father. If he does, I shall be in the most terrible trouble. I promised him I would not gamble beyond my means the last time he paid my debts of honor, but I cannot resist. It is as if something grips my mind, and I must play just one more hand!"

"A common failing." Winter descended the stairs and entered the breakfast parlor. "Have a brandy to settle your nerves, and let us contemplate our next adventure."

"Next? I thought this was the last one."

"The Little Season is drawing to a close." Winter poured two brandies and put one in Sir Colin's shaking hand. He felt only contempt for the boy, none of which showed in his expression. "You need more than you will realize from last night, not only to pay your bills but also to make your father believe that you have not broken your word. There will be at least one more large ball, and I think I know who will host it and why. You will like the irony, my friend."

Sir Colin sat at the table and drank like a man dying of thirst. "How can you know that?"

"I saw Mr. Darcy last night, although he did not see me. He is smitten with the lovely Miss Bennet. If their engagement is not announced in the next few days, I will be astounded. Lord and Lady Matlock will wish to host a ball in honor of the betrothal. You can pay Maresford back with his family's money."

Sir Colin half rose. "No! They will expect something of the sort and be on guard. There must be another way!"

Winter walked to the table, set his brandy glass down, and gripped Sir Colin's coat, bringing him the rest of the way to his feet. "Listen to me, Colly. I began this venture to help you pay your gambling losses and for enough money to retire to Scotland in style. Neither of us is quite at that point—yet. We are *both* going to finish the course. If you even think of grassing on me, I can assure you that you will never live to go to court. Am I making myself quite clear?"

Terrified, Sir Colin stared into a face that had suddenly become a mask of evil. He tried to speak through a constricted throat, finally nodding acquiescence. Winter released him with enough force to send his chair tipping sideways. Sir Colin grabbed the table to steady himself, snatched up his brandy, and emptied the glass. Winter picked up his own glass, smiled blandly, and made a toast.

"To our future success."

Darcy arrived at the Bennet home in the late afternoon. When he entered the drawing room, he found Mr. and Mrs. Bingley with the ladies. Elizabeth sat with Jane on the sofa as they had done for so many years, each with an arm around the other's waist. Their obvious affection for one another brought Georgiana sharply to Darcy's mind. Elizabeth was the sister she had never had, the sister she longed for. He bowed as both ladies stood to curtsy. Mr. Bingley also stood and bowed, his amiable face wearing a smile.

"It is good to see you again, sir," he said as they all seated themselves. "We hardly had a chance to speak before."

Darcy found himself drawn to the open manner of the younger man. He said, "That is easily amended. Are you staying long in town?"

"Until spring." Bingley glanced at his wife with a brief flicker of concern. "The winter planting is well in hand at Netherfield Park, and I can make the trip easily in four hours if the weather is good."

"You are purchasing the property?"

Bingley's smile turned wry. "I would like to, but the owner is reluctant to part with it, as his son is currently second officer on a man-of-war. Depending upon the outcome of hostilities, he wishes to give his son the option of resigning his commission and taking over the estate. I understand your estate is in Derbyshire, Mr. Darcy?"

"My father's estate, yes. It is in the Peaks District. My father is there now, overseeing the last of the winter planting." Darcy saw Elizabeth cast a swift glance at him. He went on, "Perhaps when you are able to travel, you will allow us to host you at Pemberley?"

Delight filled Bingley's face. "We should be honored, sir."

Jane smiled at Darcy, her beautiful features transformed into a painting by Quintain. "I, too, thank you, Mr. Darcy. It is most generous of you."

They heard the front door open and steps coming down the hall. Mr. Bennet entered the room and bowed to the gentlemen, who rose to return the courtesy.

Darcy waited until greetings were finished, and then requested a brief meeting with the solicitor. Anticipating the subject of the conference, Mr. Bennet led Darcy to his study and closed the door. Darcy took the chair before the desk as Mr. Bennet seated himself behind it. The two men looked at one another, and Darcy cleared his throat.

"I have spoken to Miss Bennet. She agrees that it is pointless to wait longer before announcing our betrothal. There is also another factor."

Darcy paused, straightened a little. "My father has an affliction of the heart. While he was in London, he saw Sir Ansel McQuary, who confirmed the condition. He may have weeks or months, but there is no treatment and no cure. I apologize for not informing you of his condition at once. I have also told Miss Bennet. It does not affect her decision."

Mr. Bennet nodded gravely. "I anticipated something of the sort. He looked ill when he was here. And so you have decided to go ahead?"

Mr. Bennet watched Darcy, understanding the cost to the young man of making this disclosure. Darcy's eyes were dark with pain although his voice remained steady. Mr. Bennet's estimate of his future son-in-law rose.

"I expect you will wish to marry sooner than the usual courtship period."

"Yes, sir. Miss Bennet has chosen the second week of November. She knows it will not give her time to purchase a full trousseau, but anything that is needed she can obtain after we are married. I am sorry to disappoint Mrs. Bennet regarding the celebrations that are normally part of an engagement, but I cannot delay any longer than necessary to return to Pemberley."

Mr. Bennet said with a certain irony, "Mrs. Bennet rather enjoys being disappointed. She will manage quite nicely; do not let it concern you."

He leaned back a little in his chair and studied Darcy openly. "I admit that I am not altogether happy to lose my favorite daughter, but I do not believe I could have entrusted her to anyone more worthy."

"Thank you, sir." Darcy shifted in his chair. "May I ask a question of a personal nature?

"You may."

"If you suspected that my father was very ill, why did you proceed with the arrangement?"

Mr. Bennet tented his fingers, much as he might have when addressing a client. "I knew him to be an honorable man. He assured me that you were also a man of honor and probity. Lizzy has been out for three years. I believed—and I still believe—that, left to herself, she would never have found a husband to suit her ideas of the ideal mate. She has too much energy, too strong a character to be happy or respectable wed to a man who is not her superior in intellect. Given such a man, she will make a fine wife; bright, eager, and steady in her affections. Your father's illness is sad, but I do not believe it will impact your marriage in any material way. And I can assure you, Mr. Darcy, that if you gain Elizabeth's trust and affection, she will never waver, whatever may occur in the future."

Darcy drew a deep breath. "Thank you, Mr. Bennet, for your frankness. Over the short time I have known Miss Bennet, I have come to the conclusion that I could not have a better companion in life."

Mr. Bennet rose. "I shall see that the announcement is in the *Morning Post* the day after tomorrow. If you have no objection, I shall announce the betrothal to my family before dinner. I trust you are joining us?"

"I will ask Miss Bennet whether she wishes to have our betrothal announced to the family tonight, if you do not mind? And I accept your kind invitation."

"Good man." Mr. Bennet rose. "Wait here, I will send Lizzy to you."

After briefly greeting his family, Mr. Bennet motioned for Elizabeth to join him. "Mr. Darcy is waiting in my study. I think you know the reason."

"Yes, Papa." She smiled a little wistfully. "He really is a good man."

"I agree. Do not be too long."

Having determined not to dress formally for dinner, Mr. Bennet continued upstairs to freshen himself. Better a family atmosphere tonight. Fanny was sure to be upset about the shortness of the engagement period. But he had spent a quarter century dealing with her megrims and nervous attacks, and the grand nature of the match ought to compensate for a loss of triumphant socializing. Lizzy had always been her least favorite child. Marrying her to a man like Fitzwilliam Darcy was enough in the way of success for any woman.

Elizabeth entered the study to find Darcy standing by the window. She left the door ajar and crossed to him as he turned to watch her. "Papa said you wish to speak to me. I imagine it is about the betrothal announcement?"

"Yes. He will have it published day after next. He wishes to announce it to the family tonight. I have no objection, do you?"

Elizabeth gazed past him to the narrow strip of yard between their house and the next. Darcy waited patiently, admiring the way the evening light played over her ebony curls and gleamed on the soft curves of her shoulders and breast. The pang of reluctance she felt had nothing to do with her fiancé and all to do with her mother. Elizabeth knew perfectly well what Mrs. Bennet's reaction to the news would be, as well as her reaction to the shortened time of the courtship.

"I do not object," she said at last, raising her remarkable eyes to his. "I must warn you, however, that my mother's reaction is likely to be…enthusiastic."

Darcy smiled. “I believe I am able to withstand a little enthusiasm.” He took a small box covered in red velvet from his inner coat pocket. “Since we are to acknowledge our betrothal, I have brought this for you.”

Elizabeth bit the corner of her lower lip, a gesture that sent a wave of heat through Darcy. He opened the lid. She caught her breath at sight of the ring it held, a baguette ruby like a single drop of heart’s blood surrounded by small diamonds that glittered in the dusky shadows. Darcy removed the ring, and she let him take her right hand, slipping the ring onto the third finger.

“It becomes you,” he said huskily. “’Who can find a virtuous woman? For her price is far above rubies’.”

Elizabeth looked up at him, her heart thudding in response to what she saw in his face. He bent his head; his lips touched hers, warm and soft. It was a brief kiss, with only a whisper of passion. Elizabeth bowed her head when they parted, resting it on his chest. His heart beat at least as fast as hers.

“We had best go back,” he said gently.

Elizabeth straightened. She felt a tremor different from anything she had ever experienced. This was the final commitment. She was irrevocably bound to Fitzwilliam Darcy; only the vows of matrimony were stronger than this. They returned to the drawing room together, Elizabeth resuming her seat on the sofa. Jane looked at her sister, a sweet smile lifting her lips, but she made no comment. Mrs. Bennet, engaged in retelling some piece of gossip from one of her friends, did not notice either the couple’s entrance or the ring that Elizabeth kept half-hidden in her skirt.

On Mr. Bennet’s return, he moved to stand beside his wife’s chair and addressed his assembled family in a firm voice. “Mrs. Bennet, Mr. Bingley, Jane, Mary, Kitty, Lydia, I have the great pleasure to announce that Elizabeth has consented to become the wife of Mr. Fitzwilliam Darcy.”

Elizabeth was not proven wrong about her mother’s reaction. Mrs. Bennet’s modified shriek was immediately quelled by her husband's hand on her shoulder. Her sisters and Mr. Bingley offered Elizabeth and Darcy their best wishes while Mrs. Bennet dithered in her chair, waving her handkerchief and blessing herself. Her excitement seemed composed of disbelief and delight, each fighting for supremacy.

"Oh, my dearest child, what wonderful news! But is it certain you are to marry Mr. Darcy? Let me see your betrothal ring, Lizzy, oh, my, what a fine ruby, pray take care you do not lose it!"

Elizabeth closed her eyes briefly. Jane gave her sister a sympathetic look. She automatically assumed the role of protector of Elizabeth's feelings by saying, "The setting looks antique. Is the ring a family piece, Mr. Darcy?"

"It was my great-grandmother's. Lady Eleanor left it to my grandfather's wife, and it has been passed down since then."

Elizabeth sat down again. Darcy raised an eyebrow at her, causing mischief to enliven her face. Elizabeth said, "'There is nothing lost, but may be found, if sought.' Except perhaps, virtue, and you have already bespoken me a virtuous woman."

"Only if you are not making a virtue of necessity."

Elizabeth's eyes danced. "First Spencer and now Shakespeare. Am I to live in a wilderness, then?"

"Only Derbyshire," Mr. Bingley put in, and they all laughed.

At dinner Mr. Bennet followed the pattern of placing Darcy at his right, with Elizabeth next to him. Tonight he placed Mr. Bingley to his left and Jane on her husband's left so that the two gentlemen might talk more easily and Elizabeth and Jane could also speak with one another during dinner. Mrs. Bennet contented herself with planning a lavish series of parties, detailing the trousseau and wedding gown to be purchased, and deciding where it would be best for a wedding trip in the spring. Lydia and Kitty attended to her, one with barely concealed boredom and the other even more nervous than usual. Mary sat quietly eating, but Elizabeth thought that she seemed a little sad.

Because Mr. Darcy had frequently dined with the family, Mrs. Bennet had exerted herself even more than usual of late to offer fare she considered suitable to a man of such high social standing. She had not asked his preferences, believing that he must have several French cooks. Now that he was actually engaged to Elizabeth, she felt it incumbent on her to set an even more elaborate table.

"Mr. Darcy," she said deferentially as the turbot with oyster sauce and truffles was served, "pray tell me what you think of this receipt. It is said to be originated by the Prince Regent's favorite chef."

"It is excellent," Darcy replied courteously, tasting the fish.

"Of course," Mrs. Bennet continued, unabated, "I imagine you are quite used to French cooking. You must keep at least one French chef."

"Our cooks are both English," Darcy informed her. "I have no particular preference for French cuisine. There are dishes in both cultures that I appreciate."

Nonplussed, Mrs. Bennet murmured into her turbot, "No French chefs? Imagine!"

Bingley enjoyed his fish as he did almost everything in life, openly and with relish. Darcy found him refreshing after the men of the *ton*. Jane and Elizabeth spoke quietly across the table with the ease of a lifetime's intimacy. Darcy knew that Elizabeth would greatly miss her sister when they went north. Perhaps when the Bingleys visited next spring, he might interest the young man in relocating to the area of Pemberley.

"I am particularly looking forward to the holidays this year," Bingley was saying to Mr. Bennet, "as my brother, Daniel, will be joining us. He should arrive in a few days. You remember him, Elizabeth, do you not? He was at the wedding."

"Oh yes, the serious young man. If there was not a strong family resemblance, I should not have known you were related."

Bingley laughed. "Yes, poor fellow. He graduated Cambridge this year," he explained to Darcy, "and was going on his grand tour this past summer. But with the war on the continent, we persuaded him to wait. My family is from Birmingham, but our mother lives in Scarborough. He is visiting with her."

"Have you only the one brother?" Darcy asked politely. For some reason the name Bingley echoed vaguely in his memory.

"Oh no. I have an elder sister who is married to a Mr. Hurst and a younger sister who wed Sir Aubrey Lanier two Seasons ago."

"They are currently in Italy," Jane said with a glint in her eye directed at Elizabeth that made Darcy think they were more alike than he had thought, "deciding how much of it they can buy. If they can find a chain strong enough, they may just tow the entire country home."

Elizabeth laughed, but Darcy hardly heard her. Memory suddenly supplied an image of a tall young woman with red-blonde hair at a musical evening he had attended the Season before last. She had flirted outrageously with any man near enough to observe her efforts. She was not unattractive, but her choice of colors in her gown and accessories had left Darcy wondering if her eyesight was somehow impaired. Not to mention the collection of feathers nearly overbalancing her turban. Caroline Bingley, someone had told him, nouveau-riche daughter of a tradesman who had parlayed his business into a fortune in investments with the ambition to become a gentleman.

"Daniel wishes to enter the law," Jane added, bringing Darcy out of his remembrances. "He is a most dedicated young man."

"I was quite impressed with his character," Elizabeth said. "He will do well in whatever he attempts."

Darcy felt a pang he hardly recognized at Elizabeth's reaction to the exchange. He chastised himself for it. He had never been a jealous man; such pettiness was beneath him. And this was a man she had met only at her sister's wedding; if she had entertained any interest in him or he in her, surely something would have come of it by now. Besides he was probably no older than she, if that old. Her voice from beside him caught him by surprise.

"You are very thoughtful, Mr. Darcy."

Darcy took a sip of wine and gathered his composure. "I have something to ask of you. If you are free tomorrow morning, I would like you to call on my aunt with me."

"Not the one who dislikes Ben Jonson?" she asked in mock horror.

Darcy's lips turned up at the corners, making him, Elizabeth thought, even more handsome. "No, we will save that aunt for another time. My aunt Lady Madeleine Fitzwilliam, Colonel Fitzwilliam's mother."

"The Countess of Matlock," Elizabeth said softly.

"Yes. She has been very good to Georgiana and me. I want her to meet you before the announcement of our betrothal is published in the papers."

"I will be honored to meet her," Elizabeth said, quelling a moment of anxiety.

"My aunt is very like my cousin Richard rather than her elder son, Viscount Maresford. I have no doubt that she will like you."

Elizabeth said, "I shall probably have to sneak out, however, as I am sure that Mama will want my undivided attention and continual attendance at every modiste and milliner and warehouse in Town from now until the wedding."

"If she disagrees with you," Darcy said, lowering his voice, "tell her that I prefer whatever it is, if that will help."

"So I am to begin blaming you for my choices even before we are married?"

Her father chuckled, and Bingley rolled his eyes. Darcy looked into Elizabeth's eyes. "Whatever pleaseth my lady."

In that moment, something passed between them that altered both irrevocably. It was Mrs. Bennet's voice, a bit loud, that brought the table back solidly to domestic reality.

"So I said to Mrs. Merriweather, you can never be too careful when choosing a goose."

CHAPTER 11
ADJUSTMENTS AND REVELATIONS

Mrs. Annesley watched her charge fidget nervously with the book in her lap, her open face revealing a tension it rarely showed. Georgiana Darcy closed the volume, set it on the table at her elbow, and shook her head. She had come down earlier than usual, and as Darcy had not yet appeared, the two ladies sat in the morning room to await his arrival. Normally the companion would break her fast with the family, but last evening Darcy had asked her to allow him to breakfast with his sister alone. She had already asked for a tray in her room; however, she found herself reluctant to leave Georgiana alone.

"If you do not wish to speak of it, I will not press you, Georgiana, but sometimes our troubles are lessened when we share them. You know I will respect your confidence."

Georgiana nodded. She looked up at her companion, saw compassion and experience in her plain features, and sighed.

"I am worried about my father. Papa was in Town for only a week, but he spent most of the time here at Darcy House. He went out several days to appointments and dined with the Bennets once, and that was all. Usually we go to the theater or opera or a gallery, but this time he seemed so…so tired, so drawn. It frightened me."

Mrs. Annesley rose and came to sit in a chair near Georgiana. She said softly, "You lost your mother when you were quite young, did you not?"

"Yes. I was five when she died. She had not been well since I was born and declined slowly. She was always delicate, Papa says. I hardly remember her."

"It is always very hard for a girl to lose her mother at a young age, especially when she has no sisters. And your brother is quite a bit older than you."

"He is eleven years my senior. We love each other dearly, but he is more like an uncle than a brother. I like my cousin Sofia, but she is older too, and I only see her on occasion. I have always wanted a sister," she finished wistfully. "Now that William is to marry, I hope Miss Bennet is as kind as she seems and we can be real sisters. I could not bear to be shut out of William's life. And if Papa…"

Her voice failed, suddenly filled with tears.

"If I…I lost Papa too, I do not know what I should do!"

Mrs. Annesley took Georgiana's hands in hers and squeezed them lightly. "Do not make assumptions, my dear. It is harvest time; your father may only have been fatigued from the work of getting in the crops and the long journey to London. As for your brother's marriage, I have confidence in his choice. He loves you dearly, I am sure Miss Bennet will love you as well. Have faith in God, and all will be well."

She rose, smiling serenely.

"I believe I hear your brother in the hall. I have some correspondence to attend to, if you will excuse me?"

Georgiana nodded. She rose and preceded her companion from the room as Darcy reached the dining parlor. She wanted to ask William about their father, but fear of his answer turned her cold with terror. She tried to put her fears for her father aside, remembering instead sitting with William in the breakfast parlor the day after his latest dinner with the Bennet family. He looked more at ease than he had been since his return to Town. Not looking at him, Georgiana sipped her tea, aware that he had something he wanted to say and was unsure of how to say it.

"What is your impression of Miss Bennet?" he asked at last.

Georgiana raised her head. "I like her. She is not as dedicated to music as I am, but she appreciates many of the same composers I do. She even told me she reads novels, although not all the time. She seems very kind, and she has a beautiful laugh."

"Yes, she does."

Darcy ate some of his breakfast before putting down his fork to watch his sister closely. "Georgie, I have grown quite attached to Miss Bennet. You know that it is past time I married. Do you think you would like to have Miss Bennet as your sister?"

"Have you asked her to marry you?"

"Yes, last evening. She accepted the formal proposal, but Father had already arranged it with Mr. Bennet."

"So you had no choice." Georgiana fiddled with her napkin.

"I did, but I chose to marry Miss Bennet after spending time in her company. She is a unique lady, very bright, intelligent, witty, and curious. She will make a fine mistress for Pemberley."

Georgiana, who had half-expected the announcement, set her cup down carefully, her eyes on the spotless tablecloth. "Am I to go home with you afterward, William?"

Darcy looked at her intently for a moment. "Of course you are, Georgie. Why would you think otherwise?"

"I know some ladies when they marry do not wish to have younger siblings in the household. My friend Clarissa Lampinton was sent to an aunt when her brother married."

Recognizing his sister's anxiety, Darcy reached out and covered her hand with his. "You will never be sent away, sweetling. I would never allow that, nor would Father. You have no need to worry, Miss Bennet is a caring and generous lady. We will all be a family, I promise."

Georgiana smiled. "Then, yes, brother. I think Miss Bennet will make a very good sister, as she has four sisters already. When is the wedding to be?"

"I do not yet know the exact date, mid-November. I need to return to Pemberley before winter sets in. Miss Bennet understands that and has consented to a shortened engagement period."

Normally Georgiana would be excited for the festivities, shopping for a new gown, meeting the rest of the Bennets, and any family parties she could attend. Instead she continued eating automatically, not looking at her brother.

"Are you unhappy that I am marrying, Georgie?" Darcy asked after several minutes.

Georgiana bit her lip. "No, brother. It is just…it is a great change in our lives."

"It is, but it will be a change for the better. Will you trust me in this?"

"Of course," she answered automatically. "I wish you happy, William."

She wanted desperately to ask him about their father, but the time did not seem right. She felt strangely torn. She wanted to know the truth, yet she did not want to know. Georgiana nibbled a muffin without tasting it. No, she must wait until William's wedding was settled to find a time when he might answer her questions. It would be before they traveled north, she promised herself. Just not now—not now.

Elizabeth had been right about her mother's demands on her time, but the honor of meeting a countess, the aunt of her daughter's betrothed, swayed Mrs. Bennet to release her daughter for the call on Lady Madeleine. If Elizabeth felt any trepidation at this first encounter with the Countess of Matlock, her natural courage in the face of challenge rose to the occasion. Dressed in a calling ensemble of classic rather than current fashion, she accompanied Darcy to Matlock House and was received in the countess's private sitting room.

After the initial introduction and formal curtsey, Elizabeth sat on a sofa beside Darcy, while Lady Madeleine took a chair across from them. The room was not large but exquisitely decorated in shades of lavender, yellow, green, and silver. A large crystal vase held hothouse roses; their scent permeated the air soothing Elizabeth's nerves.

"I am so happy you could come this morning." Lady Madeleine smiled at her guest. "I have been wanting to meet you. My son Richard has spoken warmly of you."

"Thank you, my lady. Colonel Fitzwilliam is a most interesting gentleman. I have found his company very pleasant."

"Yes, Richard can be charming when he is not on duty. I only wish he were able to resign his commission and take up a less dangerous occupation. I hope when Napoleon is defeated, he may do so."

Elizabeth responded naturally, "I asked him if he thinks the invasion of Russia would defeat Napoleon, and he seemed to feel it was quite possible."

For a moment, there was no sound in the room. Elizabeth felt her face flush; she dared not look at Darcy. Then the countess smiled and nodded. "You are indeed a lady of parts, as he said. I had hoped this visit would not be all tea and fashion, and I see I am not to be disappointed. You keep up with the current state of the nation?"

Relieved, Elizabeth responded, "I try to. My father has always encouraged his daughters to read the newspapers and discuss matters of importance. I am afraid I am more inclined to do so than any of my sisters."

"Good. My husband, Lord Matlock, shares matters from the House with me. I, too, was raised to take an active interest in politics and keep abreast of happenings in the country and the world. Your father is a solicitor."

"Yes, my lady. He owns a small estate in Hertfordshire, but his main interest has always been the law."

"A complex study, as much of people as words. If I had been a male I think I should have liked to study the law."

Lady Madeleine rang for tea. When it came and was served, she found Darcy fidgeting, something he did so rarely that she asked him outright, "William, what is it?"

His hesitation intrigued her. After a moment, he said, "I was introduced to Lady Agatha Quintain recently. Richard tells me she is my great-aunt, although she said nothing about it when we met. He also said you may know something of the lady's history."

"Oh, dear." Lady Matlock looked away for a moment. "Yes, a little of it. My mother and Lady Agatha were girlhood friends." She glanced at Elizabeth.

Darcy smiled wryly. "I think Miss Bennet should know what sort of family she is marrying into."

Elizabeth looked uncomfortable for a moment but rallied when Lady Matlock acquiesced and asked, "Do you know anything of your great-grandfather?"

Darcy said slowly, "Only that Father says his father never spoke of my great-grandfather. He assumed they did not get along well."

A small, knowing smile touched Lady Matlock's lips. "From what I have heard, Gerald Darcy did not get on well with anyone except a few men of his own ilk. He was known as a bad man to cross in anything. I fear it was far worse than that for his family.

He was like a throwback to some medieval baron. You know that your grandfather and Lady Agatha were twins?"

"I knew my grandfather had a twin. They were estranged at a young age and never saw one another again."

"That is true. They were estranged when Lady Agatha eloped with Cedric Quintain."

Lady Matlock sat back on the sofa and folded her hands in her lap. She was no longer as reserved as she had been at first, her still-lovely face relaxed.

"It is an old scandal, far too old for most of the *ton* to remember or care about. As my mother told it to me, Lady Agatha came out at seventeen. Her mother wanted a portrait taken, and Cedric Quintain was just beginning to concentrate on that form. He was inexpensive compared to most portraitists, so the commission went to him. During the sittings, the two fell in love. Gerald not only refused to consider Mr. Quintain as a suitor, he went to the studio with a sword, cut the portrait to ribbons, and threatened to do the same to Mr. Quintain if he ever came near Lady Agatha again."

Elizabeth gave a small gasp. Darcy raised a brow. "Other than his profession, were there reasons my great-grandfather disliked Mr. Quintain?"

"He had an uncertain income and might have been a fortune hunter, although that was proved wrong eventually. Mr. Quintain's father was a younger son. He was a printer of art books with a good business but not wealthy. The main objection was that Gerald Darcy had picked out a husband for his daughter, a man of his own generation who had already been widowed twice. Lady Agatha flatly refused to marry him. After the business with Mr. Quintain, he took Lady Agatha back to Pemberley and kept her under lock and key. Mr. Quintain followed. Somehow (no one ever found out how) Lady Agatha arranged to run away and meet Mr. Quintain. She wrote my mother shortly after they reached Scotland. They were married in the church and living with friends of Mr. Quintain."

Lady Matlock sighed.

"Mother lost contact with Lady Agatha after that. There was a scandal, of course, but with only Alexander left, and he the heir, it died quickly."

Darcy nodded. "My great-grandfather died several years after that."

"Yes. He was found by his valet. Apparently he died in his sleep of a heart seizure."

Lady Matlock wondered at the expression of pain that flickered over her nephew's face. It was gone too quickly to be certain, replaced by his usual mask of reserve.

"Thank you, Aunt," was all he said.

To bridge any awkwardness, Lady Matlock said with a smile, "When are you to wed, Darcy?"

He looked at Elizabeth before he answered, "Mid-November. I need to return to Pemberley before winter. Miss Bennet has generously consented to a shortened period of courtship."

"Will you allow me to host a ball in honor of your engagement, Miss Bennet?"

Taken by surprise, Elizabeth said, "I would consider it a great honor, my lady."

"Excellent." Lady Matlock looked at Darcy. "You will certainly agree, William?"

With a wry edge to his voice, he said, "How can I refuse?"

"You cannot. If you will let me know a day when no other festivities are planned, Miss Bennet, I shall begin preparations. Ten days ought to be sufficient, as the Little Season is almost over and I doubt there will be any other large affairs before it ends, especially with the thefts that have occurred."

Darcy looked grave. "I assume Lord Matlock is taking steps to protect the house until the thief is caught?"

"Yes, my dear. Your uncle has hired several ex-military men recommended by Richard to watch the grounds after dark. He will probably add more for the ball. I am sure everything will proceed quite peacefully."

Elizabeth felt a strange chill at the words, the memory of Lady Agatha's comment returning to her mind. *"This is a very clever thief and a ruthless man. He will not be easily apprehended."*

Shortly afterward, they took their leave of her. When they had gone, Lady Matlock sat for some time in silent thought before leaving her sitting room for her household duties. She found it strange that Lady Agatha should enter the Darcy's life once again after so many years of isolation.

Perhaps she is lonely, Lady Matlock thought. *She must be in her seventies at least. Family may mean more to her now than it did in the past.* But somehow she remained unconvinced.

Darcy and Elizabeth spoke of trivialities on the ride back to the Bennet home, as Elizabeth's maid had very properly accompanied them. When they reached the house, Darcy asked if Elizabeth would walk in the small garden with him. Knowing that he wanted privacy, she agreed. The day was pleasant and the garden full of late blooms that sent a quiet perfume through the air. Darcy led her to a shaded bench under a lattice where grape-like clusters of wisteria hung pendant, casting wavering shadows on the flagged walk.

"Do I now know the worst secrets of your family?" Elizabeth teased as Darcy seated himself beside her. She wondered if he was truly disturbed by Lady Matlock's information.

He shrugged. "I expect every family has at least one skeleton in the pantry."

"Still," Elizabeth mused, "it is odd Lady Agatha did not acknowledge the relationship."

"She had no reason to acknowledge the Darcys. She cut her ties to the family a long time ago, it seems with good reason."

"Why? Because of your great-grandfather? I do not expect you have any memories of him?"

"He died two years before my grandfather married. By then his mother's health was failing. She died when my father was four. He has rarely spoken of his father, except to say he was a good man, very quiet and reserved."

"Rather like his grandson."

Elizabeth put her gloved hand in his. He raised it to his lips, pressing a kiss on the back. He said, "I know only one thing about my great-grandfather. Mrs. Reynolds, the Pemberley housekeeper, told me of it once. She came when I was four, but the woman she replaced was there in Gerald Darcy's time. That must be where she learned it."

He stared into the moving shapes on the walk for a moment before continuing, "On the day his father died, my grandfather went to the portrait gallery, took down his father's picture, and burned it."

Elizabeth caught her breath. "Good Heavens!"

"Yes," Darcy said grimly. "It explains a considerable amount, including Lady Agatha's withdrawal from contact with her family, although I am not sure it explains everything."

"What do you mean?" Elizabeth felt his grip on her hand tighten.

"I am not certain. It is only a feeling. Lady Agatha is known for being reclusive, and yet she suddenly appears in society when we are at the point of announcing our betrothal."

Elizabeth said thoughtfully, "She was perfectly amiable when we spoke at the ball. I liked her. She says little, but what she says is to the point."

"Well," Darcy rose and pulled Elizabeth to her feet, "I am probably making much of nothing. We had better go in before Mrs. Bennet sends out a search party."

Elizabeth accompanied him back to the house. But her thoughts went over her conversation with Lady Agatha, to no firm conclusion.

⁂

"I have had another chat with Lydia Bennet," Winter informed Sir Colin as their hackney proceeded along Pall Mall toward White's. "She informs me that Lord and Lady Matlock are holding a ball in honor of Darcy's engagement. She also says that Lord Matlock has the grounds of Matlock House crawling with guards. I have subtracted a dozen or so in deference to her tendency to exaggerate; nonetheless, he will certainly be on alert for any sign of an intruder."

"So you will not attempt the business as before?"

"Not as before, no. But I will still have the prize and ruin the Matlock's party. Remember the irony, Colly—you will pay off Maresford with his own money."

His laugh did nothing to quell the fear rising in his young companion. Sir Colin thought it sounded half-mad. "Why do we not wait for a better chance of success?"

"Because, my timid friend, there will be no better chance. The Little Season is over; no one will hold a large gathering now except the Matlocks. They will be busy worrying about intruders; they will never even think to keep track of guests. That is why, my boy, you are the one who is going to snaffle the sparklers."

Sir Colin stared at Winter in something like horror. "I…I am *what*?"

Winter's genial tone changed instantly to one of open menace. "You are going to steal the jewelry. I cannot be seen at the Matlocks'. Darcy knows me, and so does his damned cousin the colonel. If Maresford sees me, he'll suspect something is up. You are going to go to the ball, and you are going to do the work for a change."

"But if the theft is discovered," Sir Colin was barely able to whisper through a parched throat, "there will be an awful to-do! They will know that no one got in from outside. The magistrate may even have the guests searched! How...how..."

"I will explain everything when we are ready to act. Until then, I prefer to keep my plans to myself."

"But I...I've never done anything l...like that before!"

"There is no time like the present." Winter leaned back, his demeanor now reassuring. "This is the last one. After this, you will be free of debt, and I will be on my way to Scotland. Hopefully we will never see one another again."

Sir Colin devoutly hoped the same thing but kept his counsel. The hackney stopped at White's, and he paid the driver, following Winter inside. Viscount Maresford had left word that Mr. Winter was to be directed to him in the cardroom. When the two men entered, the viscount looked up from his cards, murmured an excuse to the other three whist players at the table and motioned with his head to the corridor outside.

Sir Colin went to find a badly needed drink. Winter moved farther from the doorway so that no one inside could see them. The viscount joined him, a scowl on his face.

"Well?" he demanded shortly.

"You will not have to seek out Miss Darcy. She will be at your residence for the ball celebrating your cousin's engagement next Wednesday week. I expect you will not need any help dealing with her?"

"So long as Darcy is elsewhere, all will go as I want it to."

"Wait until he is dancing with the lovely Miss Bennet and send a footman to summon her to an empty room. Have the footman come back in five minutes so that there will be a witness. That should seal the matter."

"You're a slyboots. I do not think I trust you. You know better than to sell me out to Darcy, do you not?"

Maresford tried to sound menacing, but he only succeeded in sounding like the bully he was. Winter sneered. "I would not sell the Old Roger out to that [he used a very obscene epithet]."

"Well, as I expect you and the devil are old friends, I will not pursue the thought." He turned away. "My congratulations, Winter. When I am successful, I shall find a suitable reward for you."

"Think nothing of it, my lord. I shall find my own reward."

Maresford did not glance after Winter as he departed. It is unlikely he even heard the comment. He was to suffer greatly for his arrogance.

"How was your tea with Miss Bennet?"

Georgiana handed her wrap and bonnet to a footman and turned to her brother, her face glowing in a way that sent a wave of gratitude from that gentleman to Elizabeth.

"It was a lovely tea. She invited my friend Annabelle Nash-Trevane, and all of Miss Bennet's sisters were there, including Mrs. Bingley. She is the most beautiful woman I have ever seen, and so kind." They were walking toward the drawing room, both smiling. "I like her other sisters very much. Miss Mary is quiet but perfectly pleasant, and Miss Catherine and Miss Lydia are quite lively. We talked of books and music and fashions. Oh, it was the best tea I have gone to in ages!"

Darcy loved the enthusiasm in her voice, her face glowing. It came to him that his sister must be lonely, having so few friends and only Sofia in the immediate family. The difference in their ages and activities precluded any intimate relationship between the cousins. Again Darcy wondered at his good fortune in meeting Elizabeth. He took Georgiana's hand as they entered the room and sat with her on a sofa. She noted his more serious demeanor and immediately was all attention.

"Sweetling, it occurs to me that the Bennet family will not meet our relations before the ball, unless we host a dinner for everyone. I think it will eliminate any awkwardness about introductions and make it easier for everyone to enjoy themselves. Do you agree?"

Georgiana's posture grew a little tense. "Shall I have to act as hostess?"

"I would appreciate it if you will. Sofia will be a guest; I can hardly ask her and there really is not anyone else."

In her expressive face, he saw apprehension war with the idea of taking on an adult role. She raised her eyes to his and smiled tentatively. "If you think I can, brother, I shall try."

"Thank you, Georgie. Do not worry about any of the details of the meal. I will consult with Mrs. Adams, as I usually do, and Mr. and Mrs. Burgess know exactly how to proceed. You will only need to decide on flowers and decorations, china, tableware, and a few minor things and to greet our guests with me, as you have done before. If you have any questions, I will be available for you to ask."

"Very well, William. We are only inviting the Bennets and their relatives and our family, are we not?"

"Yes, and that includes Mr. and Mrs. Gardiner."

"Oh," Georgiana sat up a little straighter, "I almost forgot. Mr. Bingley's brother is expected to arrive from Scarborough tomorrow. I shall include him in the invitation."

"Yes, do. It ought to be an interesting evening."

"Another invitation, Mr. Hughes. I am becoming quite the social butterfly."

"Yes, my lady."

Lady Agatha opened the note to find more than the standard invitation. It was personally written by Lady Matlock and expressed her hope that Lady Agatha would be able to attend the ball in honor of her nephew Fitzwilliam Darcy's marriage to Miss Elizabeth Bennet. While the wording was formal, Lady Agatha knew that the countess was sincere or she would not have sent a personal note. With a sigh, Lady Agatha put the invitation aside.

"I suppose I shall have to go, Mr. Hughes. Have you looked into hiring a large coach?"

"Yes, my lady." The butler might almost have resented the implication that he had not done as he was requested. "The Halversen Coachworks hires out coaches; they have a large, well-sprung coach available that I have put on hold until your ladyship decides when it is wanted. I took Thomas with me, and he examined the vehicle. He tells me it is not only roadworthy but capacious and comfortable."

"Excellent, as usual, Mr. Hughes. I shall decide by next week when I wish to travel north. Thank you."

Lady Agatha sat quietly when the butler left her. The situation had advanced from a simple case of righteous anger and revenge to a complex pattern of uncertain emotions, self-discovery, indecision, and wavering purpose. She had never in her life been so torn between past and present. Lady Agatha had always been certain of her feelings about the events in her life. The deep, smoldering rage at the Darcys was as clear as the day that had changed her life forever. She had been given the power to destroy them, not only financially but socially. And yet she hesitated, she wavered, all because of a lovely young woman with the spirit of her own youth and a quiet young man whose respect for women was so very different from any in her experience until she had met her beloved Cedric.

This will not do! I must clear my mind before I take an action I may regret for the remainder of my life. I will go to the ball, and then I shall travel north and find out for myself what sort of man the Master of Pemberley is. Perhaps then I shall know what to do.

The decision was firm, but it brought little relief to her mind. She almost wished that the letter from the parson had never reached her. Almost.

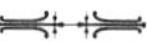

The dinner at Darcy House did indeed provide an interesting evening.

In keeping with the menus at the Bennets, Darcy had indicated to his cook what was required and left the rest to the redoubtable Mrs. Adams. Georgiana was hesitant at first to take on even the simple decisions assigned to her, but as she progressed her confidence rose. Darcy kept a casual eye on her in the event she faltered or became distressed; quite surprisingly, Georgiana proved to have a talent for organization that heartened her brother. By the time she dressed for the dinner, she was glowing with pride.

"You have done a wonderful job, Georgie," Darcy complimented her when they came downstairs to receive their guests. "Everything looks perfect."

"Thank you, William. Once I began, I found that I like overseeing the preparations. I hope our guests will enjoy tonight."

"They are family, Georgie, there is no one to impress. If there were, you may rest assured that you succeeded."

Blushing, Georgiana took her place at Darcy's side as the first carriage drew up to the front of the house. Lord and Lady

Matlock arrived with Sofia and Viscount Maresford. Darcy noted the tension between father and son and suspected that Nicholas had been drinking. Nicholas took Georgiana's hand when she greeted him and kissed it, causing her to pull back slightly and Darcy to meet Nicholas' smirk with a steely glare.

Lady Madeleine kissed Georgiana's cheek and complimented her gown, a nearly sheer white muslin embroidered on bodice and hem with small pink flowers and with a full silk underdress.

"Richard will be delayed," she told Darcy. "General Hartford sent for him this afternoon, and he had not returned by the time we left."

"He's being indispensable," Maresford sneered. "We could not defeat Boney without him."

"He is serving his king and country," Lord Matlock said stiffly. The implication was that the viscount did neither.

Lady Matlock steered her husband and son toward the drawing room in Mr. Burgess' wake. Sofia met Darcy's still cold gaze and mouthed "Later." He inclined his head slightly, and she moved on. Another carriage arrived holding Mr. and Mrs. Bennet and their daughters. Darcy had eyes only for Elizabeth. She wore a deep-green silk gown, and her hair was styled to allow several ebony curls twisted with green ribbon to fall over her shoulder. It was all Darcy could do not to reach out and run them through his fingers.

She, too, complimented Georgiana on her appearance. The younger lady smiled with delight and impulsively took Elizabeth's hands in hers.

"I am so happy to see you. I hope you like the decorations and flowers, I chose them for the time of year and for their simplicity."

"I am sure they are perfect," Elizabeth assured her. She smiled at Darcy and followed her family to the drawing room.

It was another five minutes before the Bingley carriage arrived with Mr. and Mrs. Gardiner and Bingley's brother, Daniel.

Bingley was as ebullient as usual, his open face full of humor. He bowed to Darcy and Georgiana and introduced his brother. That young man seemed to have temporarily lost the power of speech. Recalling himself, Daniel Bingley bowed to Georgiana and murmured a conventional greeting, his gaze never leaving her face. Bingley had to touch his arm to remind him of where he was.

The Gardiners were as natural as always. Darcy welcomed them warmly, and together the last of the dinner guests proceeded to the drawing room where a footman passed a tray of drinks. Maresford had already emptied one glass of brandy and was working on another. Elizabeth sat next to Sofia and Jane on a sofa, with Lady Matlock in a chair across from them. Mrs. Gardiner took another chair next to her. Mrs. Bennet was trying not to stare around the elegantly appointed room from her position on a settee she shared with Lydia and Kitty. Only Mary stood by herself, her eyes on the doorway to the hall. When the rest of the party entered, she turned away, her face showing nothing of the disappointment she felt.

"Have you chosen the material for your wedding dress, Miss Bennet?" Sofia asked.

"Yes, just today. It will be at the modiste's tomorrow." She lowered her voice, "It is a very pale blush-pink silk satin. There is a lace overdress that divides under the bust and falls to the hem. Mama wanted a demitrain and pounds more lace, but Mr. Darcy advised me that if she insisted on anything that I did not want, to tell her he preferred my choice. It worked quite well, although Mama is still unable to reconcile Mr. Darcy's knowledge of fashion even though I reminded her he has a sister."

The ladies laughed, and Elizabeth took a sip of her sherry. She looked up to find Viscount Maresford watching Jane with a hungry avidity that caused her stomach to clench. Her stiffened posture led Lady Matlock to follow her line of sight. Her mouth tightened, she caught her son's eye and shook her head once. With a leer and a half bow, he turned away. Suppressing a sigh, Lady Matlock returned to the conversation, but her mind remained engaged by the tumult in her family.

Nicholas had finally exhausted his father's patience. She had feared for some time that a crisis was inevitable as much as she tried to believe that her elder son would come to his senses before the situation deteriorated to a total rift. Instead he seemed to glory in embarrassing his father with actions designed to undermine Lord Matlock's position in the House. It was unconscionable on Nicholas's part, considering how well his father always treated him and how one day he must take his father's place in governing the country.

"Mother," Sofia's voice brought her back to the present, "are you well?"

'Yes, my dear, quite well. I am sorry, my mind wandered for a moment."

Mrs. Gardiner took up the conversation to give Lady Matlock a moment to recover. She had also seen the viscount's scrutiny of her niece and his mother's reaction. She sensed that he was trying to give offense, barely held in check by his parents' presence, although his reason for doing so was a mystery. She was telling an amusing anecdote about her nine-year-old son when there was a knock at the front door and steps in the hall. Heads turned to the doorway as Colonel Fitzwilliam entered, still in his regimentals. Darcy acknowledged his cousin with a smile; only Mary registered a brief flash of pleasure.

"I see I am not as late as I feared," he said, bowing to the company. "Good evening."

"Advising the War Office on strategy, I assume." Nicholas raised his glass in mock salute.

Richard ignored him. His eyes met Mary's briefly before she modestly dropped her gaze, but what he saw there was enough to bring a smile to his lips. He said quietly as Darcy came up to him, "I see Nicholas is half-foxed already."

"As usual. I had the staff wait dinner a half hour to accommodate your arrival. I know I can count on you when there's a dinner waiting."

"Ah, the price of fame." Richard moved to greet the other guests, took a glass of port from a footman, and moved to stand near Mary. "How are you this evening, Miss Mary?"

"Quite well, thank you, Colonel Fitzwilliam. And you?"

"Better for seeing you and your family." He glanced aside to find Nicholas watching them with his perpetual expression of lordly disdain. Richard turned his back on his brother. "You look very well, tonight. Are you anticipating Miss Bennet's wedding?"

Mary considered seriously for a moment. "Yes. I believe she will be very happy. Mr. Darcy seems devoted to her already."

"And she to him?"

"It is not as easy for a woman, Colonel. We give up any independence we may have when we marry. We trust our lives to our husbands. It can lead to tragedy. In this case, I think Lizzy has found a man she can be happy with."

Richard wanted to ask if Mary had found a man she could be happy with, but it was impossible here, now. He said, "I truly believe she has."

Mr. Burgess announced dinner before Richard had a chance to speak to anyone else. He offered her his arm, and she laid her hand lightly on it. The others were pairing off, Darcy taking in Mrs. Bennet. Nicholas made an attempt to secure Georgiana, but she quickly stepped to Lord Matlock, who smiled paternally down at her and took her in himself. As hostess, she sat at the foot of the dining table. She had placed Lord Matlock on her right and Daniel Bingley on her left with Mrs. Gardiner next to him. As it was a family dinner and not a formal affair, Georgiana had made the seating arrangements to suit the persons attending.

Nicholas was near the far end of the table, where Darcy could monitor his actions. His mother sat on Darcy's right and Mrs. Bennet on his left. Richard sat next to Mary near the middle of the table. As there were more ladies than gentlemen, Georgiana had sat Lydia and Jane next to one another in hopes that Jane's serenity would calm the younger girl's impulsiveness.

With a confidence that belied her inner trembling, Georgiana signaled for the first course to be served. Darcy had complete faith in Mrs. Adams's culinary abilities, and he was not proven wrong. The ragout was excellent; the turbot in lobster sauce and whitefish in Bordeaux were also well received. Only Viscount Maresford moved the food around his plate as if it were hardly fit for human consumption. And he kept demanding that his wine glass be refilled. By the time the meat course with side dishes was brought in, his face had flushed, and his expression had taken on a certain antagonistic edge.

"I see Mrs. Burgess has retained her affection for simple country flowers. And such sweet little flowers on the china. What's the matter, Cousin, afraid some of your guests might break the Wooten?"

Taken by surprise in the middle of a pleasant exchange with Daniel Bingley, Georgiana blushed crimson. She opened her mouth, closed it, and then caught Elizabeth's eye. Elizabeth raised an eyebrow. Georgiana straightened in her chair, turned her face to her cousin, and said firmly, "*I* chose the flowers and china, Cousin Nicholas."

"Oh, charming, dear Georgiana, charming. You grow to be more of a woman every day."

Darcy half rose in his chair, but it was Lord Matlock who spoke with firm authority to his son, "You would do well to remember our discussion, Nicholas."

The viscount sank back in his seat and finished off his wine, motioning for the footman to refill it. Lord Matlock waived the servant away with another hard look at his son. Jane asked Sofia a question about her family's holiday plans, and the dinner returned to some semblance of normalcy. Unconvinced, Richard eyed his brother with a strong suspicion that Nicholas was not finished for the evening.

I will have to keep a closer eye on Nick than usual. He is spoiling for trouble, Richard thought.

Darcy looked down the table to where Elizabeth was talking to Bingley. As if sensing his gaze on her, her eyes met his, and she smiled. He nodded before returning to his guests. She was already influencing Georgiana in the best possible way.

Lady Matlock leaned to Darcy and lowered her voice. "You have chosen very well, William."

At last the dessert course was finished, and Georgiana rose to lead the ladies to the drawing room, while the gentlemen remained for their port and cigars. Nicholas did not sit down again as the women left the room. Instead he made his way to the sideboard, where he filled a glass with brandy and stood drinking, his eyes raking the others with unconcealed contempt. Richard, easily able to read the anger behind Darcy's cold expression, leaned back in his chair and turned his glass of port idly on the tablecloth. He knew the posture aggravated his brother. He wanted the inevitable explosion to occur sooner rather than later so that he might enjoy the remainder of the evening.

Mr. Bennet and Daniel Bingley were talking about the state of the country assizes and needed reforms. Mr. Gardner continued a conversation begun during dinner with Lord Matlock and Mr. Bingley about the difficulty in obtaining good port because of the war on the peninsula. Bingley seemed to be giving only half a mind to the discussion. He kept glancing at his brother with something like impatience.

At last Bingley said, "Forgive me, Daniel, Mr. Bennet, but I want my brother to tell you what he told me last night about two cases he looked into in the north. I think you will find it very interesting."

"Oh yes, let us hear about your cases. Stolen goods, no doubt. Some poor tradesman robbed of his livelihood. Won't be able to rise in the world."

"Nicholas." Lord Matlock's voice was as cold as stone. "Sit down. Close your mouth, and keep it closed."

With a slightly unsteady step, the viscount resumed his chair and his sneer. Bingley looked to Darcy, who said, "Yes, Mr. Bingley, we would be interested in your story."

Daniel Bingley glanced around the table and said, "While I was in Newcastle, there was a case at the assizes of a young man accused of theft and complicity in murder. There had been a series of wealthy homes burgled during various social events. During the last theft, the burglar was interrupted by a maid. He struck her, and she fell against a heavy chest and died of a broken skull. She was only seventeen. An anonymous note to the local magistrate named the young man as the thief, and a few pieces of stolen jewelry were found in his rooms. He came from a prominent local family, had never been in trouble with the law, and claimed that an older man had coerced him into the thefts. The two had been seen together by various people, but as they seemed the best of friends, his story was discounted. Of course the other man was gone, seen riding north presumably to Scotland. He was never traced."

"What happened to the boy?" Mr. Bennet asked.

"Because of his family and the fact that he was not the one who stuck the maid, he was not hanged. He was sentenced to seven years transportation. I suppose in a way that was a harsher sentence than the gallows."

"That is not all," Bingley put in.

"No," Daniel continued. "I was visiting our mother in Scarborough when a friend who had spent part of the previous summer in Bath told me about a very similar case there. A young man of good family, an older man who convinces him to assist in housebreaking during large parties, and then runs out and leaves the young man to pay the price. That time the boy was not so lucky."

Every man in the room except the viscount was leaning forward, intent on the narrative. "Was there a description of the older man?" Darcy asked.

"Tall, well built, brown hair, blue eyes. Attractive to women. In Newcastle he wore a small beard, in bath, a moustache. It might be any one of a hundred men. Oh, except one publican said he wore a distinctive gold ring on the middle finger of his right hand. There was a mark on the maid's temple that looked as if it was made by such a ring. That is the reason the boy was not blamed for her death."

"Was the man named?" Richard asked.

"He was known as Mr. Winter, but it is believed that was not his real name."

Darcy's eyes met Richard's. "He rode, so there is no tracing a post coach," the colonel said. "He could be anywhere in England—but I'll wager he is here in London, up to his old tricks."

"No doubt," Mr. Bennet replied dryly. "The question is, does he have an accomplice and, if so, whom?"

"We know he has a penchant for drawing in young men of good family. If we could discover such a young man with a new friend older than himself, we might be able to find the villain."

"It's all a load of manure." Nicholas banged his empty glass on the table, snapping the stem. "Our burglar climbs in windows, he doesn't mingle with the guests. He would soon be noticed."

"Would he?" Lord Matlock mused. "The athletic thief wants us to think so, but is it true? We know he masqueraded as a footman at the Wendovers' ball for long enough to steal the Kalimar Diamond. Climbing trees in full kit is ridiculous."

"This is all ridiculous!" The viscount rose, facing the table. "This 'gentleman' comes here with a wild story, and you all fall over yourselves to believe him! How d'you know any of its true?"

"Sir," Daniel came to his feet, "are you questioning my word?"

Nicholas spat, "Sit down, little boy, before I teach you how to address your betters!"

The viscount did not see his father rise until an iron grip fastened on his shoulder. Lord Matlock shook him as if he were no more than a disrespectful youth. Nicholas turned on him, only to find a resolve in Lord Matlock's face that partially sobered him.

"You will apologize to Mr. Bingley and to the company for your disgusting behavior. Then you will leave."

Sullenly, Nicholas muttered the apologies. His father walked into the hall with him, stopping where they could not be overheard. "You are a disgrace to your name, your family, and your position. You will go home, Nicholas, and you will stay there. Your mother is involved in the ball she is giving in two days I will not have her distressed now. When that is over I am cutting your allowance by two-thirds, and if anything of this nature happens again I will take even more drastic measures."

He returned to the dining room, leaving his son to find his own way from the house. The men who remained looked disturbed by the scene, some more than others. Daniel Bingley tried to apologize for starting the trouble, but Lord Matlock stopped him.

"Do not trouble yourself, Mr. Bingley. My son is a grown man; he knows how to behave properly. You have been of great assistance in the thefts we have suffered lately. Richard, I think we can begin to scrutinize some of the young men of the *ton*. We may get lucky and find our man before he manages to achieve another theft."

Darcy said, "I think he may attempt something at the ball. He does not seem to be frightened off easily."

Richard agreed. "He does not know that we are aware of the other burglaries. If you loosen security at Matlock House a little, he will believe himself safe enough to attempt another strike."

"I do not like to put my staff in jeopardy," Lord Matlock said, shaking his head, "but the Little Season is coming to a close. If he gets away, he will only start up somewhere else, and there may be another death." He met Richard's eyes. "Very well. We will lay a trap for him. There are no paste copies to substitute, but I can see to it that there is no really valuable jewelry available."

"As the footmen are all your own servants," Mr. Bennet put in, "he cannot playact the role of servant this time. I am sure, my lord, that you are familiar enough with the members of the *ton* to recognize a new face. Let us hope that the Wendover burglary was not the last one he plans."

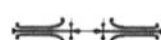

Hunter lay on the narrow bed in his room above a moderately reputable public house, his eyes closed but not asleep. A paper's scattered pages, turned to the society news, rested on the warped flooring. Prominent was a story about the planned engagement ball at Matlock House. He was certain that his quarry had also read of the ball and that he would make an attempt at any valuables left unguarded. Even with extra men watching the house, his arrogance would lead him there like a lodestone to the North Star.

Not for the first time, Hunter considered going to the magistrate and turning the man in to the law. If they knew who they were looking for and where to find him, he was sure to be arrested. Only this was such a clever monster that the law would not find any of the swag on him or in his rooms. He would have disposed of the jewels within a day. Hunter moved restlessly. The only way to make certain Winter was hanged was to catch him with the stolen items on him, and that meant as soon as he left the house.

There was no one Hunter could call on for help. He refused to involve a friend in this business, especially when his prey was known to use violence. The problem was that one man could never watch all the exits from a house. If he stayed in the mews, the front of the house was open. If he stayed in front, the mews was a clear route of escape. Hunter pictured the street in his mind. If he took up a position in the park across from the house and nearly at the end of the block where the drive leading to the mews' entrance met the street, he had a chance of catching his man whichever way he came.

It was not a great plan, he acknowledged, it was the only one available. The ball would not start until after dark; if he gained his position at dusk, no one was likely to see him. There were trees in the park, and he was adept at climbing far more difficult wood. When all the guests had arrived, he would come down from his perch and wait. Hunter silently said a prayer that this time he would succeed. Then perhaps he and Juney could both rest in peace.

⥶

Jane and Elizabeth sat in Elizabeth's room on the afternoon following the dinner at Darcy House. The fire was lit and the room warm in spite of volleys of rain attacking the windows. Because of the storm and Jane's condition the Bingleys' visit had been extended, and it now appeared they were to stay overnight. Charles Bingley and his brother were engaged in a friendly game of billiards, Mr. Bennet was reading over a contract, and Mrs. Bennet was fussing over her inevitable lists of necessities for the wedding. Jane held her knitting in her lap, untouched, her serene face turned to her beloved sister.

Elizabeth smiled. "I shall be forced to attempt to knit some baby clothes myself if that is the extent of your enterprise."

"Oh, I have a number of things at home. Mother Bingley sent us a cradle that she used for all her children. Charles is having it repainted, and I shall purchase a new mattress and bedding. Our aunt Margaret is making a baby quilt and pillow. He will be well provided for."

"He? You are sure it is a boy?"

"I want to be sure. If it is a girl, Charles says he will love her just as well, and I believe him for he is a loving man. I will love her too, but I want to give him a son. Is that not so very conventional of me?"

"Growing up with four sisters will make anyone long for a son!"

Both women laughed, and Jane put her work back into the basket by the padded stool that elevated her feet. She sighed and said, "One of the worst things after the initial sickness is how swollen my feet are. I shall find myself wearing Charles's boots before the baby is born."

"I should think the weight of carrying the baby would be worse. I am sure I will feel like one of those Indian elephants, waddling around the house."

Jane reached for her cup of tea and took a sip. She said without looking directly at her sister, "You are planning on a family, then?"

"Of course. It is my duty to give my husband an heir."

The words sounded automatic rather than a natural response. Jane leaned forward a little in her chair. "Lizzy, are you anxious about...marital relations?"

Elizabeth felt her face warm. Jane was also blushing, but she did not waver. After a moment's awkward silence, Elizabeth said, "Not anxious, exactly. I know enough of husbandry to understand the process, but it must be far different in people."

"Oh yes, far, far different." Jane smiled despite her color. "Lizzy, you can never know how you will feel with your husband until it happens. Charles is wonderful, and I am certain that Mr. Darcy will be as gentle and careful of your feelings. It is the fullest, the most complete expression of love you can experience. If you trust your husband, if you have faith in him, if you love him—I cannot describe the emotions you will feel. Lizzy, do you love Mr. Darcy? I know I have no right to ask, but it is something that will affect every part of your life together."

A gust of wind rattled the panes. The rain increased in volume and then sank back to intermittent surges. Elizabeth hesitated. At last she said in a low voice, "Since we have spent time together, I feel a…a tenderness for him. But how will I know, how can I be certain, what I feel is love and not just admiration or esteem?"

Jane was silent, staring at the fire. She raised her golden head, and her eyes were far away. "If I were to lose Charles, I would survive. But I would not live. Every day, every moment without him, would be unbearable pain. Children help, but it is not the same. It would be as if a part of my body, my mind, my soul were destroyed. I could only wait through the endless years until I joined him. I do not know if you can understand, Lizzy, but that is what our love means to me."

Elizabeth felt her eyes prickle with tears. They sat in mutual stillness for what seemed a long time. Elizabeth felt her sister's words sink into her mind and wondered if she would ever feel that way about Mr. Darcy.

She said at last, "Mr. Darcy is a worthy man, a good man. I am certain of it. He has always treated me with kindness and respect, and he does not attempt to determine how I act or what I think. But a suitor is not a husband. I only wonder if his attitude will continue after we are married."

"Do you have reason to believe him capable of deception?" Jane asked gently.

Elizabeth shook he head. "No, dearest Jane, I think he detests deceit of any kind. I suppose it is just the idea of submitting my life to another's control. I truly hope that one day I may feel about him as you do about Charles."

"I hope you may, too, Lizzy. From what I have seen of him, I believe he will make you a perfect match. There is only one thing: promise me you will not listen to any advice Mama gives you! Nearly everything she told me was wrong. Speak to our aunt Margaret, everything *she* told me was right."

Elizabeth caught her sister's hand, laughing. "I promise, darling. I promise."

CHAPTER 12

LEARNING TO TRUST

As they entered the park, Elizabeth watched Darcy's hands on the reins of the gig. His hands were large, long fingered, and elegant even in gloves. He controlled the bay gelding without seeming effort along the wide driveway of Rotten Row. The gig was painted black, polished until it shone in the thin sunlight, its brass work glittering like gold. The Darcy crest on the side, not large but picked out in gilt, emphasized the importance of the family.

It was the morning of the day before the Matlock ball. Darcy had called at the Bennet home, driving the gig rather than in his usual carriage. At first Mrs. Bennet was reluctant to allow Elizabeth to accompany him alone, but his assurance that they would be in public at all times and that he had matters pertaining to their wedding to discuss with his fiancée convinced her. Now that they had reached Hyde Park without any conversation of note, Elizabeth wondered if his motive was what he stated.

Elizabeth held her shawl around her shoulders. The breeze was cool but not uncomfortable against her face. She said as he pulled the bay to a walk, "Do you find it easier to discuss wedding plans in the open air, Mr. Darcy, rather than in a drawing room?"

A small upward turn of his lips answered her. "I find it easier to discuss certain things without constant observation by well-meaning family members."

"It must be something serious," Elizabeth said, only half jesting.

Darcy did not look at her. "I received a note yesterday from our housekeeper at Pemberley, Mrs. Reynolds. She joined the household when I was four. She is a most trusted and loved woman, almost a member of the family. She wrote that my father has had another episode. It was not severe, and the medicine Sir Ansel gave him helped. But Dr. Morrow, our local physician, confined him to bed for several days."

The wind seemed to have turned suddenly chill. Elizabeth said after several moments, "You wish to advance the wedding?"

"No. That is nearly impossible at this point, and it is only a week away. Under other circumstances we would spend a few days or a week here in Town after we are married; now I must ask you for one more concession. I want to leave for Pemberley the day after the wedding."

All at once his dark eyes held hers. Elizabeth saw pain in their depths, fear; she detected also a flicker of pleading. "I have nothing to hold me here after we marry. I can have everything packed and ready before the ceremony except my wedding gown and a traveling trunk. Mama can send the wedding gown on later."

Darcy drew a shivering breath. He stopped the horse and turned to her.

"You have given up so many elements that most women consider necessary to a courtship and marriage. I did not want to ask you for any more. The circumstances of this entire situation would drive any other woman of my acquaintance to refuse to continue, with considerable justification."

"Have you not noticed, Mr. Darcy, that I am not 'any other woman'?"

"No," he said, his voice dropping to a husky murmur, "you are not. You are my unique and wonderful Elizabeth."

Feeling that another second would have her in his arms in spite of the casual passersby, he slapped the reins on the bay's back and drove on. "I have also noticed that you still do not call me by my given name when we are alone. Will you not do so? I am William to my family."

Shaken, Elizabeth tried to lighten the mood. "If you wish me to, William."

She hardly understood how the sound of his name on her lips affected him. He pulled the horse over to the side, stepped down, and tied the reins to a convenient post. Elizabeth accepted his hand to assist her to the ground. A small copse of trees cresting a low rise stood swaying in the wind. The sound was like voices whispering softly in some unknown language. Darcy led her up the low rise, into the green shadows, sheltering them from view. He loosened the ribbons holding her bonnet, his eyes never leaving her face. Elizabeth felt the bonnet slide down her back as Darcy took her face in his hands and brought his mouth to hers.

With the exception of when he had given her the betrothal ring, Darcy had never touched her in an intimate way. The warmth of his hands on her skin, the engulfing presence of his body, shook her as nothing else had ever done. This kiss was different from the first; that had been a pleasant zephyr, this was a storm. Elizabeth found herself pulled into a vortex of sensation far beyond the melding of their mouths. She clung to him, lost, exhilarated, wanting more of this strange new feeling that woke a need she had never felt before.

Darcy broke the kiss gently at last, breathing hard. He wrapped Elizabeth in his arms, holding her tightly against him. For minutes, they stood that way, her head on his shoulder, his face pressed to her hair, its lavender scent calming him. He wanted to say, *I love you; I adore you, my precious Elizabeth!* But it was too early. Wrapped in the emotions of this first passionate encounter, she might respond with a reply that did not express her true feelings for him. Better to wait until they were both in full command of their senses.

Elizabeth stepped back at last. She kept her head lowered and pulled the ribbons of her bonnet until she could replace it properly. Darcy watched her intently. Was she embarrassed, upset, even angry at his presumption? When Elizabeth looked up at him, he saw that she was shaken, but her smile reassured him.

"I think, William, that we had better return to the gig."

He placed her hand on his arm, and they walked back to the waiting vehicle. Two or three people walking and riding observed them, however the gentleman's stern demeanor and the lady's downcast eyes were the soul of propriety. Darcy handed Elizabeth into the gig, untied the gelding and took his seat beside her. He drove for another quarter mile until there was a convenient place to turn before heading back to the entrance.

When she could trust her voice, Elizabeth gathered her self-confidence to address a matter she had been thinking of for days. The communication from the housekeeper at Pemberley decided her. She would not likely have a better chance to bring up the matter than now.

"William, there is a concession of my own I wish to ask of you."

"If it is in my power, my love, you shall have it."

She drew a breath to continue, "I want you to tell Georgiana about your father's illness before we go to Pemberley. I know it is not my province to make such a request, but I have seen enough of Georgiana to know she is more mature and perceptive than she appears. I believe it would do her a great disservice to allow her to see Mr. Darcy before she is acquainted with the fact that he is gravely ill. She might almost see it as a betrayal."

Darcy was silent. Memory came harsh and bitter to his mind. Even at sixteen, he had not been told how ill his mother was until she was on her deathbed. His father meant to protect him; Darcy's reaction was anger that he had so little time to say good-bye to his beloved mother. He remembered vividly sitting with her in those last hours while she slowly withdrew from life. For months the scene haunted him, while the resentment he felt toward his father faded even more slowly. George Darcy had finally realized the disservice his protective instincts did his son and apologized, but the scars were still there.

Elizabeth sat quietly, waiting for her betrothed's response. He did not appear angry; rather he had withdrawn from her into some place in his mind that was obviously not a pleasant one. As they reached the gate, he drew a deep breath and glanced aside at her.

"You are quite right, Elizabeth. I need to tell Georgiana that father is very ill. She will see the change when we are home, and to tell her then, with no preparation, would not help her to deal with the situation. I will speak with her after the ball tomorrow night."

"Thank you, William, for not rejecting my request out of hand."

"Why should I do so?" He was genuinely surprised. "You are yourself a perceptive woman. I think you are already Georgiana's sister in all but name. She will need your help and support in the months ahead. I still think of her as my little sister, in spite of the fact that she is nearly grown."

"I will do everything I can for her and for you," Elizabeth promised.

They said nothing more until the gig reached the Bennet home.

"This is exactly what you are to do tonight. Listen carefully and do nothing else, do you understand?"

The threat in Winter's voice was implicit. They were in the empty library of the Arthur residence, where it was unlikely they would be disturbed. Sir Colin Arthur nodded, his expression sullen. He would comply because he had no choice and because he knew better than to cross the man he had once thought his friend.

"Go on."

Winter handed him a small leather bag with a drawstring closing. "As soon as supper is announced, while people are sorting themselves out and no one is paying attention, make your way upstairs to the family wing and find Lady Matlock's dressing room. They have the grounds covered with guards, so there will be none in the house to disturb their guests. Find her jewel case; it will probably be in a chest on legs. Break it open and take the most expensive small items—rings, earrings, pendants—nothing bulky. You understand?"

"Yes. How do I break the thing open?"

"There is a large jardinière beside the window at the end of the hall. I will leave a jemmy in it. When you have gotten the goods, put the bag and the jemmy in it. Make sure they are out of sight. You can find some reason to visit the house tomorrow and retrieve the bag. Then rejoin the ball."

"This is the last one?" It was half question, half plea.

"Oh yes, Colly, this is definitely the last one."

Winter laughed. Sir Colin went to the sidebar, poured himself a brandy, and downed it in one gulp. Winter scowled, took the glass forcibly out of his hand, and set it on the tray.

"No more of that until after the job is finished. You can celebrate when you are safely home. We will both celebrate."

Sir Colin shivered. One more time, one more robbery to take him out of debt and Winter out of his life. Only this time he was the one who would carry out the theft. If he was caught…

He desperately wanted another drink, but Winter watched him too carefully. Sir Colin wiped a hand across his mouth and left the library, the leather sack hidden in his inner coat pocket.

Behind him, Winter smirked as he helped himself to a drink. Yes, tonight was the last time in London, for a long while at least. Perhaps he would go to Scotland after all. Money spent there as easily as elsewhere, and English law was nonexistent. Sir Colin was going to find himself up before the beak for much worse than taking a few pretties.

Maybe he can get the sentence reduced to transportation, like that fool in Newcastle. Fools, they're all fools.

He finished his whisky and strolled casually out of the room.

Elizabeth had bathed and now sat at her dressing table in shift and dressing gown while the maid worked on her hair. Never easy to control, the springy curls seemed particularly determined to avoid confinement tonight. She had determined not to take the girl with her to Pemberley. The maid was pleasant and efficient, however Elizabeth doubted her mother would hire another maid for Mary. Once Kitty married, either her and Lydia's maid would accompany her to her new home, or there would be one maid for each young woman. Whichever way it worked out, it was better in her opinion to wait until she reached Pemberley and hire a local woman who was comfortable in the country.

The musing took Elizabeth back to yesterday morning, and prior to that, to her conversation with Jane. Her feelings about Mr. Darcy had changed so completely in the past weeks that she hardly remembered how hurt and resentful she had been at their first meeting. He filled her thoughts as no one else ever had. The memory of his lips on hers and the deep intimacy of his kiss sent a wave of heat through her. At that moment there was a tap on the door, and Jane came in, only to stop at sight of her sister's face in the mirror over the dressing table.

"Lizzy? Are you well?" Jane hurried to Elizabeth's side, concern filling her face. "You look feverish."

"No, no, I am fine, Jane." Elizabeth took several deep breaths. "It is just that I have never gone to a ball held in my honor before."

Not quite believing her, Jane pressed her hand to Elizabeth's forehead. The skin was not hot, and the color was receding from her sister's cheeks. Jane took the brush from the maid and said kindly, "I will do Lizzy's hair, Milly. Why do you not see if Mary requires any assistance?"

Milly curtsied and left the room, and Jane began to arrange her sister's hair. Elizabeth said, "You are the only one who has ever been able to force my hair into compliance. But do you not want to rest before we leave for Matlock House?"

Jane smiled her perfect, serene smile. "I shall do nothing but sit tonight. I cannot dance, so I am confined to the company of other married women who sit and talk instead."

"Lady Agatha Quintain may be there tonight. Lady Madeleine sent her a personal invitation. She is an interesting study, if you care to analyze people. I cannot put her into any context I understand. One moment she is friendly, and the next she will make some satirical comment. I like her—I do not know why."

"Perhaps she reminds you a little of yourself."

Struck by the thought, Elizabeth sat quite still while Jane piled her hair on top of her head and secured it with pins. She began to braid the remainder together, wrapping it around the dark mass of curls then twisting individual ringlets over it and pinning those in place. Last she added a jeweled cap that covered only the front third of the coiffure and teased the small curls around both sides of Elizabeth's face.

"There," Jane stepped back. "You look like a princess. I think Mr. Darcy will approve."

Elizabeth stood up, took both Jane's hands in hers, and kissed her cheek. "Thank you, darling."

Jane sat on the dressing bench while Elizabeth picked up the underdress laid carefully on the bed and slipped it over her head. She turned her back so that her sister could fasten the tiny buttons. The material was a very fine silk usually used for lingerie, but with the overdress of deep-blue velvet covering all but the center of the bodice and the lower front third of the skirt, it was more than respectable by current standards. Jane handed her sapphire earbobs set in silver.

Elizabeth went to find her gloves and slippers, not looking at her sister as she said hesitantly, "Mr. Darcy kissed me, Jane. It was not like the first time, when he gave me the betrothal ring. It was more than just touching my lips with his. Much more."

"He kissed you the way a man kisses his wife. Did you enjoy it?"

"I…I think so. It left me feeling strange, as if there was something more, but I do not know what."

Jane said gently, "That will come after you are married. He loves you, Lizzy. I thought so before, but now I know it. Do you still not feel any real affection for him?"

Elizabeth stood automatically pulling on her gloves, her face showing the uncertainty she felt. "I know there is a bond between us, something that draws us to one another. I know I want to marry him and make him a good wife. I know I want to give him—us—children. I try to think of my life without him, and I cannot. But is that love, Jane? It seems I ought to feel more, what you feel for Charles."

"What I feel for Charles is who I am. We are not the same, Lizzy. You have a stronger, more logical mind. I only know what I feel. You want to know why you feel something. Neither is good or bad. You will have to find your own way, Lizzy. It may mean thinking with your heart and not your head."

Jane rose. Elizabeth came and took her sister's arm as they left the room. They walked down the stairs together and found the rest of the family in the drawing room, except for Lydia, who was, as usual, late. She had only been granted permission to go because the ball was in honor of her sister's forthcoming marriage. She would not be allowed to dance, but as Georgiana Darcy was also to attend, there would be someone for her to talk to. Kitty's fiancé, Mr. Cowper, had made the trip to Town to join them at the ball, leaving Kitty almost giddy with anticipation.

Mr. Bennet was at the point of sending Mrs. Hill to summon his missing child when she appeared, dressed in a white gown of appropriate style but with the bodice lowered considerably further than modesty allowed. Her mother took one look, grasped Lydia's arm, and pulled her out of the room before she was able to say a word. They returned in five minutes, Lydia flushed with anger, wearing a lace fichu that concealed her bosom.

"I take it we are now ready to go," Mr. Bennet said as a coach drew up outside. "That will no doubt be Mr. Darcy."

It was that gentleman. He halted abruptly in the drawing room doorway, his eyes on Elizabeth. She curtsied with a mischievous lift of her eyebrow. Neither spoke, but the heat in his dark eyes mirrored her flush of earlier. Georgiana went immediately to greet Lydia. They left the drawing room together, and Lydia asked her father if Georgiana could ride with them. With Darcy's permission, the party obtained their wraps and separated into the two waiting coaches, Darcy taking Elizabeth, Mary, Jane, Mr. Bingley, and his brother in his larger vehicle. Mr. Bennet transported Mrs. Bennet, a now-enthusiastic Lydia, Kitty, and Georgiana.

"What do you want?" Viscount Maresford snapped as his brother entered the morning room, where he stood with a glass of brandy in hand, his face as surly as his voice.

"Not your company, certainly," Richard replied calmly. "Father wants to know if you are going to stand in the receiving line with the family or remain here soaking yourself in alcohol until you become even more obnoxious than usual."

"He did not say that."

"Only the first part. Personally I think our guests will survive nicely without you."

Nicholas tossed down the rest of his drink and went to refill the glass. "I do not give a fig for our guests. Go stand like a footman and greet the obsequious fools and their ugly wives, overripe daughters, and snot-nosed sons. To hell with all of them."

Richard folded his arms, his face still without emotion. "You have been priming yourself since you came down, Nick. What are you up to now?"

"None of your damned business! Certainly not making eyes at the little sparrow, like I've seen you do lately. Forget her, brother. Darcy may be able to afford to forego a decent dowry in order to bed the delicious Miss Bennet, you cannot. Find yourself a rich widow while there's still a war on to make you look impressive."

Anger flared in Richard's mind, but he was too experienced a soldier and a brother to let Nicholas see it. "You are the one who had better find a rich bride. The way you go through money, once you assume the title the estate will be bankrupt in a year."

"Go back to Father," the viscount's face was reddening with fury, "tell him whatever you like. He has never cared for me, no one but Grandfather ever understood me."

"Grandfather ruined you. He treated you like a princeling and taught you to look down on good people who were not your social equals and to value pleasure and greed above all things. Look at yourself. Thirty-two, a wastrel with no sense of responsibility to your name or the people who depend on the Fitzwilliam family for their livelihood. You are the one who had better marry and get an heir before the liquor drowns you."

"I plan to do just that, brother. A rich, beautiful, compliant wife." He laughed harshly. "Wait only a little longer, and you will see. As for the estate, do not worry about it. Even with the allowance father gives you, you barely have enough to live decently, and when the old man dies, you are on your own."

"I have been on my own for a number of years," Richard replied, only the set of his mouth indicating his rigid self-control. "The prospect does not intimidate me. Father is waiting, Nick. And I am leaving."

Richard stepped into the hall, only to halt in shock. Lord Matlock stood just out of sight of the room, his face pale. He took Richard's arm and walked with him past the ballroom toward the entrance hall, stopping short of the doorway.

"I came to see what was taking so long. I am not in favor of eavesdropping, although it can be instructive. The old man is not dead yet," he added grimly. "We will talk after the ball, Richard. There are going to be changes in this family."

They took their place in the receiving line. Sofia and Lady Matlock both looked at Richard, who shrugged. Sofia rolled her eyes; his mother gave an exasperated sigh. Lord Matlock said nothing. There was no need; his wife knew him so well that she felt his disturbed state of mind. The carriages began to arrive, and for the next half hour they greeted friends and family graciously, with no sign of the conflict raging in their family. The Darcy party arrived soon after Richard returned. Lady Matlock took Elizabeth's hands and smiled warmly.

"My dear, that gown is perfect for you. I am so happy for you and William."

"Thank you, my lady. It is so kind of you to hold this ball for us."

"I should thank you," Sofia put in with a twinkle. "If you had not gotten engaged to my cousin, I should not have had the ball I plagued Mama for."

The line moved on. Darcy saw that Georgiana and Lydia were seated in the ballroom and stood with Elizabeth to receive the congratulations of the guests. He saw no sign of his cousin Nicholas, a fact that bothered him more than it might have. If the viscount had absented himself from the festivities, it would anger his parents while it provided for a peaceful celebration. Nicholas enjoyed causing trouble. Darcy did not want to spoil the evening for Elizabeth dealing with his cousin's outrageous behavior.

Lady Agatha Quintain arrived as the last guests were passing through the line. Lady Matlock greeted her warmly and personally escorted her to a seat in the ballroom. She chose her usual location, near the doors to the garden. Georgiana and Lydia were engaged in conversation, exuberant on Lydia's part, more reserved on Georgiana's. Lady Agatha observed them without seeming to, a talent she had learned early in life. She looked up as Charles Bingley escorted Jane to a chair next to her. He patted her shoulder and departed, concern in his open face.

Jane smiled at Lady Agatha but did not speak. After several minutes, Lady Agatha addressed her in a quiet voice.

"I believe you are Miss Bennet's sister. I am Lady Agatha Quintain."

Jane would have risen to curtsey, but Lady Agatha lifted a hand to stop her. "My dear, at my age and in your condition, curtsies are a useless exercise."

"I am indeed Miss Bennet's sister, Mrs. Charles Bingley."

"And the hovering young man is no doubt Mr. Bingley. Your first?"

"Yes. I would not have come tonight except that the ball is in honor of my dear sister's engagement to Mr. Darcy, and I could not stay away."

Lady Agatha summoned a footman and sent him for a footstool. Jane protested, blushing, but Lady Agatha waived her embarrassment away. "You need to raise your feet, or by evening's end, you will have to be carried to your carriage. One of the few prerogatives of old age is to say and do as one pleases, without regard to anyone else's opinions. A child is a precious gift. You must take all care you can of yourself, for the baby's sake."

Something in her voice arrested Jane's attention. She said with her usual kind interest, "You have children, my lady?"

"No," Lady Agatha replied after a moment when Jane wondered if she was to be reprimanded for her boldness. The single word held a sadness and some darker emotion that Jane could not identify.

"I am sorry," Jane said softly.

The footman brought a padded footstool, and both women watched the milling crowd as the first set formed in silence. Darcy and Elizabeth led the line of dancers. The music was a galliard. With Darcy's tall, elegant figure and Elizabeth's grace and lightness of foot, Lady Agatha was momentarily lost in memory. Conflicting emotions tore at her beneath a calm exterior. They were so young, just beginning life, while she looked ahead to its end. This beautiful woman beside her was to be a mother in a short time; the girls watching the dancers with bright, excited eyes had not even entered Society yet. If she went forward, neither would be likely to do so or to find a husband, have a family of their own. Mr. Cowper had come in time for the first dance and partnered a laughing Kitty. Richard and Mary were two down from Darcy and Elizabeth in the line, his face relaxed, hers quietly happy.

So many lives ruined, so many dreams shattered. Was it worth the price they would pay to avenge an ancient wrong?

Lady Agatha said nothing more as the set proceeded. When it was over, Mr. Bingley brought his wife a glass of punch and stood beside her chair, his whole attention focused on her. His brother had joined Georgiana and Lydia and a young man he vaguely recognized, the four talking with animation. Darcy and Elizabeth came up for a word. Elizabeth continued to where Jane sat, curtseying to Lady Agatha.

"You resemble a princess from a fairy tale, Miss Bennet," she said with a slight smile.

Elizabeth raised an eyebrow. "Not, I hope, the one who sleeps for a hundred years. I recall there was a dragon in that story as well."

"Ah, yes. But you already have your Prince Charming."

Elizabeth laughed, and Jane smiled. The bond between the sisters was obvious to anyone with the perception to see it. Darcy came up and bowed to Lady Agatha.

"Good evening, my lady. It was good of you to attend tonight."

"I find that balls are rather more interesting today than in my youth. I hope our friend the footman does not appear, like the dragon in the fairy tale."

"Lord Matlock has the grounds well covered, and all the servants are on alert for anyone who does not belong to the household." The musicians were tuning their instruments for the next set. Darcy said to Elizabeth, "I must find Sofia. Who is your partner?"

"Colonel Fitzwilliam. Charles, are you dancing this set?"

Bingley watched his wife, who patted his arm. "Go and dance, Charles. I have very good company in Lady Agatha."

Reluctantly Bingley left her and made his way to a young lady he had met previously. She was from a prominent family; unfortunately her less-than-svelte figure left her frequently without a partner. She rose immediately at his approach, and they took their place in the forming line.

A nice young man, Lady Agatha thought. *Anxious for his wife, as he should be, yet still kind to others.*

Out of habit, she watched the room rather than the dancing. The eldest son and heir was not present, a social solecism amounting to insult. It made her uneasy. The instincts of a youth spent in surviving a despotic father gave her the uneasy feeling that some crisis was imminent. A footman brought her a cup of punch sent by Lady Matlock. By the time the set was half-over, Lady Agatha rose.

"I feel the need of a little fresh air." She drew her shawl around her shoulders. "It is too warm for comfort."

Jane nodded. Lady Agatha left unobserved through the doors into the garden. Lanterns were placed throughout the manicured beds and neatly trimmed shrubbery, illuminating paths and statuary. The terrace outside the doors extended down the side of the house, dimly lit by windows at intervals along the way. For a time, she stood without moving and then proceeded slowly toward the rear of the building. She was aware of men watching the house from the farther shadows, Lord Matlock's guards. They hardly entered her perception.

As she neared the end of the terrace where a shallow step offered access to a walkway circling the back of the building, she heard a man's harsh voice and a young woman's frightened response. Lady Agatha hastened to an open door, halting just out of the light that spilled from inside a morning room. What she saw set her mouth in a thin line and clenched her slim hands in her shawl. Just as she had suspected, a crisis was unfolding before her, and she was the only one able to stop it. If she wanted to.

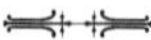

Mary was quietly elated. She had danced the first set with Colonel Fitzwilliam, and at his request reserved the supper set for him. To her surprise, she was enjoying the ball more than any other social event she had ever attended. The colonel spoke well;

he was informed and aware of the world beyond his own social set. He spoke of places Mary had only read about, of Spain and France and Italy, where he had gone on his grand tour before he joined the king's service. Unlike her previous view of military men, he was not fond of war but took it as his duty to fight for his country. His mind was open, and his opinions considered and reasoned.

The colonel was telling her a funny story about a recruit and a bucket of soapy water that almost had her laughing out loud. It was with a jolt that Mary heard her name spoken in a tone of cool reproof. She swung around to find Mr. Cranshaw approaching them. He stopped in front of the pair where they stood at the side of the ballroom, his eyes taking in Richard, in evening dress rather than his regimentals.

"Who are you, sir?" Mr. Cranshaw asked stiffly.

"Colonel Richard Fitzwilliam. Who are you?"

Richard's tone said he was not happy with the younger man's insolent address.

"I am Mr. Cranshaw, a partner in Bennet, Delibes, and Cranshaw. This lady is my fiancée."

Mary gasped. Richard stiffened, and Cranshaw turned a satisfied smirk on Mary. For the first time in her life, she felt a surge of anger at the humiliation that this man imposed on her. She straightened her back and looked Mr. Cranshaw in the eye.

"I have no knowledge, sir, that you have asked me for my hand nor offered for me to my father. You indicated, *some time ago*, that in future you would like to call on me. I have seen you exactly twice in the past four months, and marriage was never discussed. How dare you call me your fiancée?"

"I...I thought you agreed to receive me." Cranshaw sounded more indignant than embarrassed.

"That is not a proposal nor a courtship. And I have changed my mind. Any gentleman who felt respect for a woman would never approach her in public with such an outrageous statement. Goodbye, Mr. Cranshaw."

Mary turned away from him, too upset to notice Richard stepping between her and her now-furious former suitor.

"I think it best if you leave, sir, before you create a scene that attracts the attention of Mr. Bennet."

It was the voice of a senior officer speaking to a new ensign. Cranshaw glanced over his shoulder to where Mr. Bennet was engaged in conversation with Lord Matlock, took notice of several people watching them, and decided that retreat was the better part of valor. He spun on his heel and left the room with what dignity he was able to muster. Richard turned back to Mary, who stood with shoulders slumped.

"I am so sorry," she began; Richard's voice, low and gentle, stopped the words.

"I am not."

She looked up at him. His eyes told her all she needed to know. She laid her hand on his arm and dropped her gaze. The color in her face answered him. Mr. Cranshaw disappeared from her thoughts as if he had never existed.

Darcy found Sofia, and they joined the second set. It was a rather lively reel, which was not as conducive to conversation as some dances. When they reached an interval Sofia said quietly, "I am sorry I was not able to speak with you privately the other night at Darcy House."

"I had forgotten," Darcy admitted with some chagrin. "What was it you wished to tell me, or was it a question?"

She lowered her eyes for a moment before replying in an even softer tone, "Just to watch out for Nick. He has been increasingly troublesome, and Father has given him some sort of ultimatum."

The dance parted them briefly before they again were close enough for private conversation. "What sort?"

"I do not know. He is very agitated about your engagement to Miss Bennet, not about her personally, just the betrothal."

"I know he has wanted my father to allow him to marry Georgie since she turned fifteen. That will never happen. Nicholas thinks that if I die childless, Georgie will inherit Pemberley, thus putting it into his hands."

Sofia bit her lip. "I do not know any particulars; I only know he has been drinking more than usual, and he is in the house tonight, although he refused to attend the ball."

"Thank you, Sofia," Darcy said. "I shall be on my guard."

The supper set was ending when Darcy looked for Georgiana and saw only an empty chair and Lydia Bennet looking uncertain. An inexplicable apprehension gripping him, he took Elizabeth's hand and hurried across the floor.

"What is it, Mr. Darcy?" Elizabeth asked as they neared the seats against the wall.

"Georgiana. I do not see her."

"She has probably gone to the ladies' retiring room." As she said it, she saw Lydia looking around uncertainly. She stood up as her sister halted in front of her.

Elizabeth said, "Where is Georgiana, Lydia?"

"A footman came for her. He said—oh, Mr. Darcy," Lydia suddenly realized Darcy loomed over her, "he said you wanted her in the morning room. But here you are"

Darcy met Elizabeth's frightened gaze, his voice sharp. "Come with me please. She may need you."

He was out of the door before Elizabeth could follow. Knowing if there was the trouble she feared, the fewer people aware of it the better, Elizabeth raised her skirt a little and raced after him. In the morning room Georgiana faced her cousin Nicholas, white faced and trembling. He smirked at her, a half-consumed brandy still in his hand.

"Welcome, little cousin." He waived the glass. "I have been waiting for you. And do not bother to ask where your dear brother is; he will find out about our tryst in due time."

"I will not stay here," Georgiana declared, but her voice wavered.

She made a move toward the door, but Nicholas easily blocked her. Panic clutched her throat. She whirled and put an armchair between them. The viscount laughed, a taunting sound that increased her terror.

"You will not only stay, you will also agree to be my wife, or I will ruin your reputation cousin or no. If it reflects on my family, it means nothing to me. Your dowry and a chance, however slight, at Pemberley are reward enough. Do not worry; once you have given me an heir, you may live your life however you please, as I shall do."

"I will not marry you." In spite of her fear, Georgiana lifted her head. "You are a monster! And you are drunk. No one will believe you."

"They will when they see your condition after I return you to the ballroom. I will announce our betrothal, and you will have no choice but to agree with me or face ruin for yourself and your blasted brother as well as his fiancée."

He started toward her when a voice from behind him froze his advance. "Stop!"

Darcy came into the room and crossed to his sister, speaking quietly. "Has he touched you, Georgie?"

She shook her head. Tears rolled down her cheeks. She turned her head away, not wanting the viscount to witness her distress. Nicholas finished his drink and tossed the glass carelessly on the rug.

"Too late, Darcy. She is already compromised. She has been alone with me for long enough to condemn her in the eyes of the *ton*. Once I spread the story of how she lured me here and promised to marry me, there will be nothing you or your father can do to save her."

"People saw the footman approach her, and Miss Lydia Bennet heard the message. All I have to say is that I came her and then you joined us."

"No, Darcy, it is not as easy as that. A chit like the Bennet girl's word is no good against a viscount's, and yours is not much better,"

"But mine is."

Lady Agatha entered through the door to the terrace, her clear eyes raking the dissolute nobleman. "I was taking a turn in the garden and heard voices. I can repeat the entire nauseating conversation if I have to. You lured this child here for your own disgusting purpose, but you have failed."

"Who are you, you old crow, and what business is it of yours?"

"I am Lady Agatha Quintain, and you remind me of someone I knew a very long time ago."

Nicholas was reviving his confidence. He said with more bravado than was called for, "Who will believe your word against mine?"

"Anyone who knows you or your reputation. I expect my word has far more weight with the *ton* than yours."

Elizabeth had come in quietly and slipped to Georgiana's side. She put an arm around the girl's quivering shoulders and stared in open contempt at Maresford. All at once Georgiana straightened, and her chin lifted.

She said in a strained voice, "I will never marry you, Nicholas Fitzwilliam. I would rather live the rest of my life as a spinster than even look on your face again."

"Elizabeth, Lady Agatha, will you take Georgiana to somewhere she can rest for a while? There is a small parlor between this room and the ballroom, on the right. And thank you, Lady Agatha. I owe you a debt."

With a last withering look at the viscount, Lady Agatha joined Elizabeth and Georgiana and left the two men alone. Maresford did not watch them go. He stared at Darcy with half-closed eyes, disdain written in every line of his stance.

"I can still make enough trouble for both of you to cause talk. How will the delectable Miss Bennet take that?"

Darcy crossed to his cousin in one stride, his body taut, his face full of an icy fury that might have quailed any man less arrogant than his cousin.

"Come near my sister again, speak one word against her, and we will meet at Hampstead at dawn. When I have finished with you, Lord Henry will have to look elsewhere for a whole man to sire the next generation of Fitzwilliams."

Giving Maresford no chance to respond, Darcy suddenly pushed the viscount backward with the full force of his shoulders and arms. Nicholas' feet went out from under him, he slammed into an armchair sending it over sideways. A small table exploded under the combined weight, the Ming dynasty famille rose vase it held shattered. Shards of porcelain, flowers and water cascaded onto the cursing figure of the nobleman. Darcy turned on his heel and left, encountering a footman in the hall.

"See to Viscount Maresford," he said as he passed the man. "He has had an accident."

Darcy found the three women in the parlor he had indicated. Georgiana was no longer crying. She sat on a settee next to Elizabeth, pale and silent. Resentment had modified the shock of the encounter. She had never given her cousin the slightest cause to believe she favored him as a suitor. Why would he offer her such an unforgiveable insult?

Elizabeth looked at Darcy as if expecting to see evidence of a fight. He touched his sister's shoulder lightly so that she looked up at him.

"Are you better, sweetling?"

Georgiana nodded. "Yes, brother. But I want to leave. I cannot stay here any longer."

"You do not have to worry about Nicholas." Darcy's voice made Elizabeth shiver. "He will never approach you again. I have made the consequences of his doing so perfectly clear to him."

For the first time, Lady Agatha spoke, her eyes on Georgiana.. "I am going home myself. These modern balls are too exciting for an old lady. Is there anyone at Darcy House who can look after Miss Darcy until you return?"

"Her companion, Mrs. Annesley. But I think I had better go with my sister."

"No, Mr. Darcy, you had much better stay here with your fiancée. Your precipitate departure will cause a lot of talk and add fuel to any fire that occurs from the recent encounter. If you will have my carriage brought around, with your permission I shall take Miss Darcy home on my way."

Elizabeth rose. "Lady Agatha is right. As the honorees of tonight, if we suddenly leave the ball, it will be fuel for all kinds of gossip and speculation. As little as I relish the idea, we must stay."

Reluctantly Darcy agreed. "Tell Mrs. Annesley as much as you wish to," he told his sister. "You know you can trust her discretion. I will look in on you when I get home."

"I will be fine, brother," Georgiana assured him. "Please tell Lydia that I have taken ill. She was there when the footman came."

"I will speak to her," Elizabeth said. She turned to Lady Agatha, "Thank you for all your help."

"Yes," Darcy added. "We are greatly indebted to you."

He did not see the flicker of uncertainty darkening her gray eyes turn to resolve.

CHAPTER 13
TREACHERY

From the attic boxroom where he had waited out the day, Wickham could not hear the music from the ballroom. Experience told him it was time for supper to be served. He rose, took a modest tot of brandy from a pocket flask, and made his way cautiously to the second floor. He let himself in to an empty guest bedroom and waited with the door cracked open.

This morning had gone perfectly. With delivery men coming and going, one more man with a crate of vegetables on his shoulder was invisible. Once he sent away the mousy scullery maid who showed him to a storeroom, Wickham had put down the crate of vegetables purchased at Covent Garden and stretched his back. He removed the jemmy from amid the cabbages and leeks and left the storeroom for the ubiquitous servants' stairs. There was no one going up and down, as all the staff were engaged in preparing the ballroom and dining room for the evening's festivities. If he did encounter anyone, he thought, hefting the little iron bar, it would be just too bad for them.

As it happened, Wickham made it to the attics without interference. On the second floor, the jardinière sat beside a tall, narrow window at the end of the hall. It was four feet tall, majolica with a painted garden scene. He shoved the jemmy into it, careful not to be seen by anyone in the grounds outside. From there, the path to his hiding place was clear. Wickham made himself comfortable with a meat pie and his flask of brandy. Evening would come soon enough; he was patient when he had to be. He grinned at the dusky shadows all around him. He meant to give Mr. Holier-Than-Thou Darcy a betrothal ball he would never forget.

Now, invisible in his vantage point, Wickham watched for Sir Colin's arrival. He calculated it was five minutes before he heard steps in the hall. Sir Colin moved rapidly to the end of the hallway; there was a rattle of metal on porcelain before his accomplice passed the door again and went into Lady Matlock's dressing room. Wickham checked the hall, found it empty, and slipped to the door of the mistress's bedchamber. Once inside, he made his way to the connecting door by the light of the undraped window. Sounds of someone bumping around in an unfamiliar space almost sent him into the dressing room, but it was too early.

Time crawled past. Wickham heard a harsh ripping of wood and a muffled curse. He opened the door two inches and waited. Sir Colin had lit a candle and knelt beside the wreck of a small cabinet, its door hanging crookedly by one hinge. An open jewel chest sat on the carpet in front of him. He was panting, scooping out jewelry indiscriminately into the leather pouch. Sweat glistened on his upper lip.

Wickham prepared to surprise Sir Colin. The only payout for the baronet's son was to be found unconscious in a ransacked room. Or dead. Wickham did not care which. He saw Sir Colin close the drawstring neck of the bag and stand up, picking up the jemmy. As Wickham's hand grasped the doorknob, the hall door of the dressing room burst in, and a man's voice shouted angrily, "What the bloody hell do you think you're doing?"

The viscount stalked toward the cowering Sir Colin, who stammered incoherently backing away, the sack of jewelry clutched to his chest. Nicholas said in a snarl, "So you're the dirty little thief. Well, you are caught, and the law can deal with you."

He grabbed Sir Colin by his coat front with one hand, tore the bag from his grip with the other, and threw it aside. Terrified, Sir Colin pulled free. He backed into the dressing table, causing the candle to rock dangerously. Nicholas reached to steady it with an oath. At that moment, Wickham entered the room, causing the viscount to round on him, turning his back to Sir Colin.

"Who the blood…Winter!"

"Yes, *my lord*, Winter. You do not recognize me, do you?"

Nicholas scowled. "I thought at first I might know you, but I decided I was mistaken."

"Think back," Wickham purred. From the corner of his eye, he saw Sir Colin pick up the sack of jewelry and retreat a step. "It was a long time ago. One of the rare times you visited your cousin Darcy. You were eleven, and I was six. You took a toy sword from me and broke it. You said I was nothing but a peasant and was not entitled to carry a sword. Do you remember now?"

The viscount's face darkened. "Wickham! Damn you, so this is all your doing."

"It is. You promised me my reward for acting as your spy. It is time I collected it."

Wickham had slowly advanced until he stood face-to-face with the viscount. Before Nicholas could move, Wickham swung his fist with vicious force, catching his old enemy in the side of the head. But Nicholas was not a seventeen-year-old girl or a middle-aged woman. Instinctively he threw his arm up, partially blocking the blow. Instead of taking him on the delicate area of the temple, it grazed his forehead, Wickham's ring opening a shallow cut that sent blood running down the viscount's face.

Nicholas cursed. He grabbed at Wickham, his shadow rising like an infuriated bear on the delicate pattern of the wallpaper. Sir Colin had backed away from the confrontation. Now he snatched up the forgotten jemmy, dancing from foot to foot in an agony of indecision. As Nicholas's hands reached for Wickham's throat, Sir Colin swung the iron bar at the viscount's head.

The jemmy came down on his shoulder, only the end striking him in the back of the head. Sir Nicholas cried out in pain. He folded to his knees with a groan. Sir Colin dropped the weapon, sobbing with fear. Wickham gripped Nicholas's arm and pulled him bodily toward the window.

"Help me!"

Sir Colin stood dumbly shaking his head. Wickham's voice was fiery in the dancing shadows of the candle, a madness of rage burned his mind.

"Help me, or you will be next!"

His paralysis suddenly broken, Sir Colin stumbled forward and took hold of Sir Nicholas' other arm. The viscount tried impotently to struggle. They dragged him to the window, and Wickham unlocked it and threw it open on the night.

"No," Sir Nicholas' voice was a weak moan.

With Sir Colin's help, Wickham boosted the dead weight to the sill. Below a man shouted; there was a stir as other men ran from the darkness toward the house. Laughing, Wickham tipped the viscount's body over the sill, lifted his legs, and pushed. They heard a weak cry, a crash, and shouts of alarm.

"That is my reward, *my lord.*" Wickham turned to his confederate. "Give me the bag. Now!"

He picked up the jemmy from where Sir Colin had dropped it. "Unless you want to join the viscount."

Sir Colin handed him the sack. He stuttered, "W...what sh... shall I do? I've just h...helped you k...k...kill a man!"

"Go downstairs. Wait out of sight. Leave when the others do. I will see you later at Arthur House."

Not caring if the stupid boy followed his instructions or not, Wickham left the dressing room and ran to the end of the hall. He shoved the jemmy into the jardiniere and took the servants' stairs back to the attics. As soon as he had secured the bag of jewelry in an inner pocket, he put the rest of his plan into action. Wickham had chosen this particular attic for a reason. In the far end of the room was a ceiling trapdoor that led to the roof. Installed to give access for any repairs to chimney stacks or roofing, it was concealed at night in thick obscuring shadows.

Without hesitation, Wickham tossed an old rug over the chests he had piled beneath the trapdoor and climbed up, careful not to disturb the dust any more than he could avoid. He unbolted the door, raised it and pulled himself up, kicking the top trunk to the floor before he emerged into the night air. When the door was shut, Wickham lay flattened away from the roof edge, breathing hard. Nicholas had been an unexpected bonus. He would have preferred Darcy but was happy to take what fate offered.

He knew the house would be searched for the killer of the earl's heir. By the time men reached the attic room, even if they noticed the trapdoor, which he doubted, he intended to be out of reach. Crawling across the slates took time. He heard men's voices below, the vaunted guards he had walked right past that morning. How easy it had been! Just as no one looked at servants, no one looked at deliverymen as long as they acted the part.

It took Wickham nearly a quarter hour to reach the front corner of the house. There were no carriage as yet; the guests had not departed. No one wanted to linger with death in the house, they would remain only until their carriages could be called for. That gave him a few minutes to escape. Lying in the leaded gully between joined roofs of separate wings, Wickham carefully peered over the edge. His pulse beat quick time, he felt the elation of success. A man paced by below, looking to right and left. *But never up,* Wickham thought. Searchers rarely looked up.

As soon as the man passed around the far corner of the building, Wickham gauged the distance to the ground. Manicured flower beds curved around the portico. The distance was not as much as from the roof itself but still more than he wanted to drop. Wickham wormed his way to the edge above the portico. He lowered himself carefully and dropped in a crouch, landing with a grunt.

From there, it was a matter of holding on to the decorations around the edge of the portico while he stretched to his full height. With a swift breath, he let go. The moment his feet touched earth, he rolled in the way an itinerant tumbler had once taught him. Flowers flattened under his body; mulched earth clung to his clothing. Wickham did not linger. He stumbled to his feet and ran, clearing the fence palings between Matlock House and the next property in a leap. He kept running until he reached the nearest major street. At that point he slowed to a walk.

He was out. He was free. He had no intention of disposing of tonight's haul; it was too risky. Damn the Dutchman. There were other fences in other places. He already possessed a stash of money large enough to take him anywhere he chose until the hunt was off. Wickham went in search of transportation to his secret bolt-hole. By noon tomorrow he meant to be out of London. He knew exactly where he could hide, and no one would think of it. Especially Darcy.

Perhaps I will pay my godfather a visit on my way. A coming-home gift for Fitzwilliam and his bride.

Chuckling, Wickham hailed a hackney and settled back for the ride.

The first sign of something going very wrong happened as the second course was being cleared. Some sort of commotion in the garden turned heads and hushed conversation. When one of the guards appeared in the doorway of the dining room, visibly shaking and motioned to Lord Matlock, both Sir Henry and Richard rose and joined the man. After a moment of agitated conversation, Richard followed the guard out at a brisk pace, and Lord Matlock faced his guests with a face that mirrored whatever disaster the guard had brought.

"I am sorry to tell you that there has been a serious accident. My eldest son has been badly injured in a fall. I shall have to leave you to attend to him. My apologies."

He followed Richard while talk suddenly rose to a feverish pitch. Lady Matlock sat stunned, her eyes on the empty doorway. She made to rise until years of training and experience as the wife of a political figure kept her in her seat. Darcy, who was sitting at Lady Matlock's right hand, looked down the table and met Elizabeth's shocked gaze. He rose with a murmured word to his aunt.

A commanding presence, Darcy began, "Friends, family, under the circumstances, I believe it is best if we declare this ball at an end. My fiancée and I thank you all for coming and for your good wishes on our betrothal."

He signaled the butler and requested that champagne be served while the guests' carriages were sent for. Elizabeth and Sofia both left their seats and came to stand beside Lady Matlock. Sofia took her mother's hand and held it tightly.

The older woman said to no one in particular, "What could have happened to Nicholas? He has been drinking, I have no doubt, but I have never known him to fall because of it."

Elizabeth looked over the countess's head at Darcy, her expression imploring. "Can you find out the details, Mr. Darcy? I am sure Lady Matlock would feel better for knowing."

"We both would," Sofia added. "Please, William?"

"Very well. I will return as soon as I can."

The night air as he stepped outside struck Darcy's with its sharp chill. Just beyond the small parlor, a group of people huddled around a dark mass on the ground. Lanterns brought from the gardens lit the scene with yellow eyes that cast everything outside their radius into stark shadows, making distorted shapes of the shrubs climb the house's wall. One of the larger bushes was split in half, splayed and twisted. Lord Matlock had gone to wait for the doctor. As Darcy approached, Richard rose from one knee. His face was hard, the face of a warrior.

"He is asking for you. Someone threw him out of a second-floor window. The doctor has been sent for, but he may not last that long."

"Very bad?"

"Talk to him. I will explain afterward."

The men parted as Darcy came up and dropped to one knee beside the viscount. Nicholas's right leg was twisted at an awkward angle, the foot bent outward, and his right arm lay flaccid at his side. There was blood on his face, seeping into the neck of his shirt where his cravat had been removed. His eyes, half-shut, turned slowly to his cousin. Leaning over the broken body, Darcy took his cousin's left hand carefully in his.

"Who did this, Nicholas?"

Nicholas tried to speak, coughed, and groaned in pain. A footman hurried up with a glass of water. Richard knelt on his brother's other side, careful not to touch the damaged limbs. He slid his hand under Nicholas' neck and raised him enough to drip some of the water into his mouth.

He swallowed, looked up at his cousin. "Dar-cy."

Darcy said again, "Do you know who hurt you, Nicholas?"

"Ess…Wic…Wic…am. 'Nother…man…Sir C…c…c…"

His eyes closed, he moaned, and his body went limp. One of the watchers swore shortly. Richard felt for a pulse and raised his eyes to Darcy's.

"He's still alive. Dr. Wyecroft ought to be here any minute; he only lives two streets over."

He stood and said to the nearest footman, "Shelley, find a length of flat board wide enough to accommodate my brother's size. When we move him, he cannot be carried by hand in this condition. Someone get a blanket to put over him."

Darcy stood up, still looking down at his cousin. Neither man saw Elizabeth come up until she handed Richard a throw she had taken from a sofa. With a murmured thanks he covered Nicholas. Darcy put his arm around her; he did not try to send her away. His mind was turning the broken words over, not wanting to believe what they told him. Lord Matlock's arrival with Dr. Wyecroft cleared the area around his patient. Darcy, Elizabeth, and Richard retreated a short way while the surgeon made a brief examination.

"Did you make anything of what Nick said?" the colonel asked.

Darcy closed his eyes briefly. When he met Richard's gaze, his eyes were very dark. "Wickham. And another man, undoubtedly his young protégé. Sir Something, he was unable to speak the name."

"Good God! Wickham? Are you certain?"

"As certain as I can be. Why else would he have asked for me?"

Richard shook his head. "I have heard nothing of him since Uncle George turned him out three years ago. So he has finally gone entirely to the bad."

"He was never far from it. At least we know who we are looking for."

"Who is Mr. Wickham?" Elizabeth asked.

"Someone I grew up with." Darcy glanced at Dr. Wyecroft, still working over his cousin's body. "I will tell you about him later. Now we should go in and see our guests off. I am sure my aunt is not up to it."

"Of course." Elizabeth turned to the house.

Richard said, "I will let you know his condition as soon as I know it. Mother and Sofia will want to be near him."

"I will see to it."

Darcy took Elizabeth's hand and walked with her back to the deserted ballroom. He felt as if it were the set of a play after the actors had gone. The hundreds of candles still burned, empty chairs and settees lined the walls; the decorations declared a celebration, the flowers were bright in their crystal vases. There seemed no place for evil here, and yet it had slithered into the house and struck down the heir almost before their eyes.

Darcy said, "I will see if Lady Matlock's maid has been summoned before I join you."

Elizabeth went back to the dining room to find her family grouped with several other families they knew. Lady Matlock and Sofia were gone. Her father came to her immediately and took her hand.

"What has happened, Lizzy?"

Lowering her voice, she said, "The jewel thieves pushed Nicholas from a second-floor window. He is very badly injured. The surgeon is with him now. I am sure someone sent for a magistrate as well, but I think the family would rather keep the matter quiet for the time being."

"Of course."

"Where are Lady Matlock and Sofia?"

"Lady Sofia took her mother upstairs. As soon as her maid joins her, Lady Sofia will return to tend to her guests. And you, my dear?"

"Mr. Darcy and I will also see the guests off. There is nothing we can do for Nicholas." She noted her mother approaching and said, "I must go now. I will tell you more later."

He nodded, squeezed her hand, took his wife's arm, and guided her back to the group. Elizabeth felt a little dizzy as she went to the entrance hall to stand with Darcy as the various families and single men gathered to depart. The sounds of carriages in the drive outside made a background to expressions of regrets and appreciation. Amid the confusion she noticed a young man whose name she did not remember at the edge of the crowd. He was nearly as white as his cravat, jittering with an obvious case of nerves, something she was more than familiar with although not in men.

She turned to Darcy to ask him if he knew the man, when Sir Colin almost bolted through the door and out into the night. Making a mental note to relate the incident to her fiancé later, she continued to speak quietly to the departing attendees.

Lady Madeleine and Sofia did not return. At some time before the last guest departed, Nicholas was transferred from the garden to a guest bedroom on the first floor. Darcy and Elizabeth were on their way upstairs to find Lady Matlock when there was a knock on the front door. A footman looked to Darcy, who nodded. He opened the heavy panel, and a middle-aged man with a commanding presence entered, followed by two constables holding an obviously furious man in wrist irons between them.

"I am Chief Magistrate Sir James Black," the first man said. "I understand there has been an assault on Nicholas Fitzwilliam. This man was found lurking in the park across the way. I do not know if he is involved, however I intend to find out. If you will direct these constables to somewhere they can hold the prisoner until I am ready to question him, I would be obliged to you."

In the unyielding grip of the two constables, Hunter struggled and shouted, "He'll get away I tell you! Winter, the murdering swine, will get away *again*!"

Mr. Bennet indicated a chair at the table with a nod to Sir James. "Sit down, sir. We need to hear your story before we can proceed. I am a solicitor; I will act as your temporary counsel."

Sir James also took a seat. Reluctantly, the man who had called himself Hunter sat in an abandoned chair at one end of the dining table, Sir James across from him. Mr. Bennet sat next to the young man, while the two constables waited like silent watchdogs at a little distance. Hunter had gained control of his emotions, but the hold was a fragile one.

"My name is Joseph Handley. I was second mate on Bell and Marsden's clipper *China Queen*. When I sailed a bit over a year ago, I left my sister working as a maid in Newcastle. It was a good family, treated her well. She was happy and, I believed, safe."

He wiped a hand over his face, making the handcuffs clank.

"We docked four months ago. There was a message for me at the shipping office that she was killed in a robbery. I went up to Newcastle too late for the trial, but I read about it and the man called Winter." His mouth twisted at the word. "I quit my job, took my pay, and started hunting him. You can ask at Bell and Marsden, they'll tell you that what I say is true."

Mr. Bennet spoke across the table to the chief magistrate. "I can verify the story of the murder and the trial, Sir James. We heard an account from my eldest daughter's brother-in-law several nights ago."

"You know then, sir, that I was at sea and couldn't have taken part in it."

As Handley began his story, Darcy came in and stood silently by the doorway. He thought of Georgiana, his sympathy going out to the young man who spoke through such pain. Mr. Bennet looked up at him; Darcy shook his head. The men at the table turned their attention back to Handley.

"I tracked him north to Scotland and lost him there. I won't go into everything I did, but at last I got on his track again. He's got a woman friend in Matlock, a Mrs. Younge. She runs a brothel where he stays from time to time. I was just too late to catch him there. I found out from one of the women that he was headed for London. I also found out his real name's Wickham, George Wickham. It's taken me over a month to locate him. He's staying with Sir Lionel Arthur's son, Sir Colin. I suspect that's his latest associate."

Darcy stiffened. He reached the table in two strides and spoke to Sir James, "We knew it was Wickham; Sir Nicholas named him as the man who injured him. He tried to give us the name of the other man but could only manage, 'Sir.' After that, he was only able to make sounds. They fit with 'Colin.'"

"Not proof, but significant," Sir James replied. He signaled a constable. "Remove the hand irons."

Handley rubbed his bruised wrists. He said, "I don't know how the snake got in—I've been watching the house all day. He's a clever sod, he must have found a way."

Sir James was silent for a moment. Darcy said suddenly, "We must search the house. The guards would have seen him if he left the premises. He must still be here somewhere."

Handley was on his feet. Anger radiated from his tense posture. He was not an overly tall man, but a hard life at sea was evident in his powerful chest and shoulders.

"If he's here, he has to be found!"

"Constables, come with me." Sir James rose and faced Darcy. "We have not been introduced, but I know your name, Mr. Darcy. We had best gather whatever men are available and go through the house at once."

"My apologies, Sir James." He bowed briefly, "Fitzwilliam Darcy of Pemberley. Lord Matlock and the rest of the family are on the first floor. If you wish to speak to them, I will gather men for the search."

"Thank you, Mr. Darcy." Sir James was already moving toward the inner hallway. He said with a sharp glance at Handley, "You, sir, will follow orders, or I will have you evicted."

Handley muttered consent. Ten minutes later Darcy left a contingent of footmen and grooms in the ballroom and climbed swiftly to the first-floor hall, where Lord and Lady Matlock,

Sofia, Richard, and Elizabeth listened to Dr. Wyecroft. Darcy took Elizabeth's hand and squeezed it gently. She looked up at him, her eyes dark with pain for the family.

Dr. Wyecroft said, "His right femur—thigh bone—is broken. A clean break, but there may also be damage to the hip joint. His knee is dislocated, and his ankle is also broken. That break is more complicated. He is concussed, perhaps badly. The head wound is superficial. I believe he was struck from behind with some object, but his shoulder took most of the blow. The impact must have been relatively light, because it is not broken, only badly bruised. I cannot tell you that he is not in grave condition. He will have to be kept immobile and completely quiet. He is a young man; he may recover. If he does, I doubt he will be able to walk again. I am sorry, but you must be prepared for the worst. I know of a young man studying medicine at St. Bart's, a Mr. Watson. I will send him tomorrow; he will make an excellent assistant in caring for Sir Nicholas."

"Thank you, Doctor." Lord Matlock looked at his wife, who was crying quietly in Sofia's arms. "Do whatever you have to. You will have every facility at your disposal." He tried to smile at Elizabeth, "Thank you, my dear, for your support of my wife and daughter. It is greatly appreciated."

Elizabeth murmured acknowledgment and pressed closer to Darcy. She hesitated before saying softly, "I do not know it is significant, but as Mr. Darcy and I were saying farewell to the guests, a young man I do not know seemed extremely anxious to leave. He nearly bolted for the door. I had seen him earlier talking to my sister Lydia and asked her who he is. His name is Sir Colin Arthur."

Sir James replied grimly, "Significant indeed, Miss Bennet. However, he can wait until we find the main villain."

Darcy said to Richard, "We need to search the house. There is a good chance that Wickham is still hiding somewhere inside."

Sofia reached for Elizabeth's hand, her eyes starred with unshed tears. "Why do you not wait with mother and me? We will use her private sitting room; it is just down the hall."

Murmuring comfort, Sofia took her mother's arm. With a glance at Darcy, Elizabeth took Lady Matlock's other arm, and together they walked with her toward the sitting room. Richard noted Handley and the constables behind Sir James. He had become the senior officer his men knew from the battlefield: grim and solid, without emotion.

Darcy said to his cousin, "I have men below. How do you wish to proceed?"

"As many men as possible to a floor. It is unlikely he is on the ground floor, there has been too much activity for him to go undiscovered. If he is not found elsewhere, we can search there last. This floor should be guarded. If Sir James will lend us his constables? We will split up the rest and search the kitchen and basement and the servants' quarters and attics first. This floor can be searched as well, but with a force of men after all other possibilities are exhausted."

"What if he is armed?" Handley put in.

"It is unlikely," Darcy answered, "or he would have shot Sir Nicholas."

"Very well, Colonel," Sir James approved. "Let us get to it. If he is not found, I will begin to believe he may be a ghost."

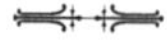

Even after the tragic events that occurred at the Matlocks' that night, it was not until the next morning anyone thought to ask the cook and the kitchen staff if anything unusual had happened on the day of the ball. When Richard questioned Mrs. Bailey, the cook replied that she could not think of anything except a new man had brought in a crate of vegetables. Asked for a description, she tartly replied that he looked like a crate of vegetables, as he had kept it balanced on his shoulder hiding his face and head from view. She had been pushed off her feet with preparations, so the advent of someone she did not remember previously delivering to the house did not make a deep impression. Porters were always changing. She advised Richard to ask the scullery maid, who had shown him where the storerooms were. Mrs. Bailey had been with the Matlocks for fifteen years, knew her worth, and was not intimidated by any of the family except Lady Madeleine.

Frightened half out of her wits to be summoned by the colonel, the scullery maid admitted she had shown the deliveryman where to leave the vegetables, then he had sent her away to her work stating he would find his own way out. Had he left the house? She did not know. No one had told her to stay with him. Could she describe him? Shabby clothes, cap pulled down over his forehead, not as tall as the master, except he might have been because he stooped under his burden. He spoke in a rough voice with a cockney accent. She was sorry she had nothing more helpful to relate. Richard calmed her, sent her back to the kitchen, and quietly cursed the man who had hidden in plain sight.

They knew who they were looking for now, not where to look. When Richard, Darcy, and various others searched the house shortly after the murderous assault, they found an attic boxroom showing signs of recent, brief occupation. It was easy enough to determine how the man had reached the top of the house by way of the servants' stairs. All he was required to do was wait until supper, when everyone was in the dining room making enough noise to mask anything short of an artillery bombardment, go to the second floor, break into the jewelry chest in Lady Matlock's dressing room and take what he wanted. His partner in crime had been apprehended but knew no more than they did.

Well, Richard thought sourly, *Wickham has always been a clever bastard.*

⁂

Lady Agatha Quintain broke her fast the morning after the Matlock ball with a disturbed mind. She had seen Miss Darcy safely home, sending a footman with her to the door. Her admiration for the girl had risen with the ride to Darcy House. Georgiana Darcy neither cried nor bemoaned her experience. She was pale and undoubtedly shaken but in control. Neither lady attempted to make polite conversation. When the carriage stopped, Georgiana thanked Lady Agatha both for her courtesy in seeing her home and for her intervention in the viscount's abortive seduction.

Quite remarkable for a young girl not yet out in Society. She is a Darcy, without a doubt.

Lady Agatha had almost finished her usual morning meal of tea, muffin, and soft-boiled egg when Mr. Hughes brought in the *Morning Post.* "I thought you would want to see this, my lady."

He placed the paper neatly next to her place setting and stood back, waiting in the event his mistress wanted anything else. Lady Agatha, knowing Mr. Hughes only brought the paper at her request, picked up the sheets and turned directly to the society news. Her eyes were caught by a headline in boldface: "Attempted Murder at Engagement Ball." She read rapidly, her expression not changing other than growing more intense. The story was short on facts and long on speculation; the gist was that the scion of a (minor) noble house had been implicated in the robbery and assault on Lord Matlock's heir, Viscount Maresford. A second thief, rumored to be the primary force behind the recent jewel robberies, had escaped capture. The viscount was gravely injured, no specific information was available.

Putting the paper aside, Lady Agatha sat back and contemplated her plans. There was no longer any uncertainty in her mind. She knew what she meant to do. Closing her eyes, she almost felt a feathery touch on her shoulder.

She said to the butler, "I will send a note to my attorney. Have it delivered and wait for a reply. I will be available for the rest of the day or tomorrow morning if he is unable to call until then. Thank you, Mr. Hughes."

"Yes, my lady."

She wrote swiftly and handed the paper to Mr. Hughes, who bowed and carried it out of the room. Lady Agatha returned to her chair. She picked up a book, put aside finding her concentration wandered. The occurrences at the Matlock's ball had fatigued her more than she expected. She felt unusually heavy, as if her body had taken on a physical burden.

I am too old to allow this conflict to continue, she told herself with some vexation. *As soon as I have seen Mr. Witherspoon, I shall take steps to travel north.*

She felt more at ease than she had at any time since the missive from the deceased vicar arrived. Her eyes went to the portrait of her young self, as always seeing not the image but the man who had created it.

Are you pleased with me, my beloved? Although I have tried to view this crisis of conscience as you would have done, I do not know if I will succeed. Be with me, my dearest husband and lover. I need your counsel now more than ever.

That meeting was to happen sooner than Lady Agatha could have expected. Mr. Witherspoon's carriage arrived shortly after Mr. Hughes informed her that the footman had returned and the solicitor was following. Lady Agatha rang for tea. She knew she was an important client, but this was extraordinary service. She had settled back by the time the attorney was announced. He was as unlike the common image of a solicitor as possible—a rotund, rosy-cheeked man who still resembled the amiable schoolboy he had once been. To take him at face value, however, was a grave mistake.

"Mr. Witherspoon, I appreciate the courtesy of your prompt visit."

He bowed to his client and took the indicated seat on a settee, overpowering its delicate upholstery with his presence. "My pleasure, my lady. I am always most happy to attend you at your need."

Mr. Witherspoon of Witherspoon, Woolrich, Hazelmuth, and Gibbs, failed to mention that his calendar had been virtually empty that morning and that time away from the office had a considerable appeal, especially when the client was someone he liked as well as Lady Agatha. They made light conversation until the tea was served and the maid departed. Unlike most of his profession, Mr. Witherspoon was not given to using ten words when two would serve. After sipping his tea and complimenting the blend, he set the cup down and focused his attention on Lady Agatha, noting the tension that had invaded her thin body.

"How may I assist you, my lady?"

She reached for a leather folder on the table at her elbow and handed it to him. "This is in the strictest confidence, Mr. Witherspoon. No word of it is to be spoken to anyone, including your partners. I have confidence in your discretion, but papers will need to be drawn, and clerks are not always so discreet."

"I assume it is of great moment, then? You may rely not only on me but also on my staff. For matters requiring secrecy, any documents will be prepared by a legal assistant whose future career would be destroyed by indiscretion."

She nodded. "Read both documents, please."

Mr. Witherspoon did so, his eyes narrowing. When he was done, he reread them and slowly tidied the edges before returning them to his client. With a deep breath to control his shock, he contemplated Lady Agatha.

"May I know your intentions, my lady?"

Lady Agatha folded her hands on the leather case in her lap. She said firmly, "I want two documents drawn."

She detailed her wishes, sat back, and waited for Mr. Witherspoon's reaction. He was silent for some time, mulling over the implications of what he had learned. At last he said, "You understand that prosecuting such a claim has a large margin of failure? So many years—"

"I understand perfectly. I will not decide which I wish to employ at present. I simply want both options ready. How long will it take?"

"Oh, I can have them ready by week's end. I shall bring them to you myself, if that is acceptable."

"Certainly. I appreciate your assistance, Mr. Witherspoon. It relieves my mind to know matters are in your competent hands."

Lady Agatha rose to walk Mr. Witherspoon out herself. In the foyer, he took a formal leave and left the house, his mind still occupied by the nature of Lady Agatha's revelation. He realized that had he been a man of less ethical inclination, a fortune would have lain at his fingertips. He was not, however. Without fanfare, Mr. Witherspoon considered his client's trust in him a nearly sacred obligation. Shaking his head, he entered his carriage and sent it back to his offices. If the matter ever came to trial, it would be the social explosion of the century.

Lady Agatha stood in the foyer while Mr. Hughes closed the door and returned to her side. Action had always appealed to her above contemplation. She wanted the entire matter settled once and for all. She would see and would act, and all the years of pain and sorrow would be over. Or would they?

Forgetting that she had left her cane in the parlor, she started for the stairs. The staircase was of oak, with a carved handrail and barley-twist balusters. Halfway up the treads, her hand lightly on the smooth wood, a faint gray mist assailed her vision. She swayed, clutching the balustrade. Her legs gave way. She felt pain as her knees collided with the hard surface of the stairs, and the mist darkened to black.

Lady Agatha did not hear Mr. Hughes cry of alarm as he ran to her aid, or feel his support keep her from falling back into the foyer. She was not aware when Marie hurtled down the stairs to her side or when the maid and the butler carried her to her rooms.

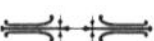

Another breakfast table that morning saw a different reaction to the news of the Matlock robbery and assault. A note was delivered to Lydia, who with a murmured excuse opened it directly. Her reaction was swift and unexpected.

"*No*!" The shriek ran around the table like a small earthquake. "No, no, I do not believe it! I *will* not believe it!"

Voices mingled in astonishment and concern.

"Child, whatever is it?" Mrs. Bennet turned to her favorite daughter, who sat beside her, pale as the paper in her hand.

"Lydie, what has happened?" Kitty, on Lydia's far side, laid a comforting hand on her arm.

Elizabeth, exhausted from the night before and well used to her youngest sister's dramatic inclinations, said quietly, "Tell us what has alarmed you, Lydia, or we cannot help."

It was Mr. Bennet's authoritative tones that calmed the troubled waters. "Lydia, who is the note from? Answer me."

Lydia raised a teary face to her father, her voice so low he was barely able to hear her. "Lettie Gradison. She…she says Mr. W…W…Winter is the robber, and he t…tried to k…kill Lord Maresford. I do not believe it!"

Over his wife's shocked gasp, Mr. Bennet said calmly, "I do not know where Miss Gradison acquired her information, but she is quite correct. Why do you not believe it?"

All at once Lydia realized the error of her outburst, but it was too late to retract the words.

Mrs. Bennet said quite clearly in the hush, "Is that not the man you spoke of so often, my dear?"

Lydia would have bolted, but her father's stern voice held her in her chair. "How do you know this man, Lydia?"

Lydia burst into a torrent of sobs. Beside her, Kitty put an arm around her sister's shoulders, although she was scarcely less pale. Mr. Bennet waited. Elizabeth and Mary watched the participants in this domestic crisis with interest, unalarmed. If anyone, their attitudes seemed to say, could involve herself in such a situation, it was Lydia.

Mr. Bennet rose. "Lydia, I will speak to you in my study. You also, Mrs. Bennet."

Mrs. Bennet stood to follow him, but Lydia remained frozen in place. Kitty took her arm and helped her to her feet. "May I come too, Papa?"

Sensing something unusual in her request, Mr. Bennet nodded. The small party left the room. Lydia had left the note on the table, purposely or accidentally was uncertain. Elizabeth retrieved it, reseated herself, and held it so that both she and Mary could read it. She did not feel the guilt she normally would have in reading someone else's correspondence. In the present situation, any information was vital however gathered.

Lydia,

Say nothing of Mr. Winter. He is proved the housebreaker and last night tried to kill Lord Maresford.

Lettie

Mary shrugged. "Lydia has talked of Mr. Winter for weeks. I believe she met him at the Arthurs' home. He seemed to be her ideal of a gentleman, although that hardly signifies."

"I wonder why 'say nothing'? What could she say so damaging that Miss Gradison must send her a warning at this time in the morning?" Elizabeth folded the note. "I think Papa ought to have this."

Alarm transformed Mary's expression. "Oh, Lizzy, you do not suppose..."

"I suppose nothing, but obviously Lydia knows the man, whose name is actually Wickham, and has had some contact with him. She may have some information to help them find him."

Elizabeth's tap on the door was answered after a moment by her father. She stepped into the study to an atmosphere of tense restraint. Handing her father the note, Elizabeth said, "I thought you might want this."

He nodded. Elizabeth made to depart, but Mr. Bennet stopped her. "Did Mr. Darcy communicate any information to you about this man Wickham?"

"Only that he has a history of dissolute behavior and fraud. He is the son of the Darcys' late steward. They have known one another since childhood."

He nodded. "Thank you, Lizzy."

When the door closed, Mr. Bennet turned back to Lydia. "I want you to tell me everything of your acquaintance with this man."

It was a demand she dared not disobey. Clutching a handkerchief in both hands, Lydia said, "I met him at the Arthurs' home when Lettie and I called on Miss Arthur and her mother. He was so nice! He is a friend of Sir Colin. We...we were in company several times. I did nothing wrong!"

"You were never alone with him? The truth, Lydia."

"No! Never! We walked in the garden, with Sir Colin and Lettie, that is all."

Mrs. Bennet, seeing some unknown disaster hovering on the near horizon, had both hands pressed to her bosom. Her husband folded his hands on the desk, his gaze holding Lydia's.

"Then why does Miss Gradison enjoin you to 'say nothing' about him? I have no doubt that Mr. Gradison will be able to find out from his daughter if you do not tell me."

Lydia began to cry again. "I…I…I told him about the balls, who w…would be there, and about…about the Kalimar Diamond. Lettie told me. It was just talk. He was so interested, and he asked me about jewels, just talking."

She dissolved in further sobs. Her mother moaned, "Oh, Lydia…"

But Mr. Bennet seemed satisfied. "A man like that can deceive even an experienced lady. I doubt he would have any difficulty impressing a child who is susceptible to flattery and attention from a man she believes honorable."

He turned to Kitty, who had kept silent since they entered the study. "You have nothing to add, Kitty?"

Kitty met her sister's eyes. Lydia cried, "You promised!"

All at once Mr. Bennet was completely alert. "Catherine, you will tell me anything relevant that you are aware of."

Slowly Kitty related the scene she had witnessed at the mews gate. She finished by saying to her sister, "You were not to talk to him after that night. Did you?"

Lydia nodded. She was utterly demoralized; for once, all the pretense and self-interest had left her. "Just in the Arthurs' drawing room. Just to say hello."

In the end, Mr. Bennet had the entire story. He was angry, but it was a focused anger. He sat quietly for some minutes while Lydia regained what composure she was able and her mother wiped surreptitiously at her eyes. In the end, he spoke with the authority of the paterfamilias.

"I see that I have been remiss in my duty to you, Lydia. It was shortsighted of me to allow you to leave the seminary before you finished, but since you have seemed to gain nothing of value from the experience, it may not have been a wrong choice. I have trusted your mother to guide your education; however, she has other duties, and you are of an age to exhibit some maturity in your behavior."

Mrs. Bennet looked up at her husband in some surprise. She had expected at least a lecture on her failure with her youngest daughter. Lydia had not moved. She stared into her lap, where the tattered handkerchief lay limp under her hands.

"I do not see," her father continued, "how another school would be of any use. You already are as accomplished as you will ever be in the social graces. What I believe you require is someone with no family connections to see that you are educated in the basic disciplines. I will find a companion for you who will live here and teach you the skills of discrimination, logic, and reason. Your only other choice is to be kept at home until you reach your majority or develop discretion on your own."

His tone told them that he expected that to happen when the elm trees bore apples. To his surprise, Kitty cleared her throat.

"Miss Darcy has a wonderful companion, a Mrs. Annesley. When Elizabeth marries, she will be seeking a new position. If you spoke to Mr. Darcy, I am sure he would facilitate the exchange."

"Thank you, Kitty. I shall do that." He rose. "I am expected at my office. I will be home for dinner, Mrs. Bennet."

The three women sat without speaking until the front door closed behind Mr. Bennet. Two of them were relieved. One was torn between uncertainty and the prestige of having a companion all to herself.

CHAPTER 14
ONE BAD APPLE

"Colin! Good God! What are you doing?"

Sir Lionel Arthur rushed across the library to the table in a bay where his son sat bolt upright, a pistol in a clenched hand wavering next to his temple. The boy raised startled, imploring eyes to his father's white face. Sir Lionel grabbed the pistol and wrenched it from his son's grip. Shaking nearly as badly as Sir Colin, he collapsed into the opposite chair, the pistol falling on the table between them.

It was not yet dawn, that darkest hour of night when the soul wavers between life and eternity. The baronet had wakened with a sense of disaster that sent him downstairs. Some faint sound from the library directed his steps there, only to meet the scene before him.

Sir Colin dropped his head into his hands, sobbing. He was a wreck, clothing disheveled, his hair wildly finger combed, a shadow of beard on his smooth jaw. His father stared at him. Sir Lionel considered his son a bit cocky, even arrogant; to see him like this, utterly devastated and obviously frightened out of his wits, shook the older man to the core.

"What is the matter, Colin? Why would you want to…to do yourself harm?"

Sir Colin slowly raised his ravaged face to his father. "Winter," he gasped.

"Mr. Winter? What has he done?"

The sobs turned suddenly to hysterical laughter. "Killed me!"

Sir Colin gripped the table's edge with both hands. "He has killed me! Oh God, why did you come in? Another minute, and it would all have been over."

"What? What has happened? What has Winter done? I thought he was your friend?"

"So did I."

Sir Colin slumped in his chair, all the emotion of the past few minutes sliding into despair.

"The robberies, the jewels. We did it. He threatened me. I took him to the balls as my guest, and he robbed the houses. Last night he went mad. He threw Viscount Maresford out the window. I was there. I will hang for his death."

The horror of the thought caused Sir Colin to drop his arms on the table and bury his face in them. Stunned, immobile, his father simply stared at the young man as if he had never seen him before, which, in effect, he had not. It seemed to Sir Lionel as some phantasmagorical nightmare. Thoughts like vengeful ghosts hovered around him. The baronet knew without any doubt that his whole family was irrevocably ruined.

His chest tightened until drawing a breath was an effort. Sir Lionel stumbled to the sidebar and poured a glass of brandy, much of which splashed on the silver tray and polished mahogany. The burn of the liquor cleared his head somewhat. Returning to the table, he stood over his son, his voice hoarse.

"What possessed you? Tell me that, Colin. What made a sneak thief of my son?"

Sir Colin mumbled something unintelligible. His father clutched the tumbled hair and jerked his son's head up.

"Answer me!"

Pain and anger twisted the face forced to meet his father's glare. "Money! What else is there? Money, money, money!"

Sir Lionel released his hold. He sank into the opposite chair once more. "I give you a liberal allowance. How can money be the cause?"

"Because I owed gambling debts of nearly two thousand pounds."

Exhausted, Sir Colin sat with his arms hanging loosely. His voice had become apathetic. "Maresford was pressing me. He threatened to go to you. Winter—or whatever his name is—said we could make enough to pay off my debts and have some left-over. Only there was never as much as he promised. I expect he kept the lion's share for himself. When I wanted to quit, he threatened to kill me."

Sir Colin cleared his throat as if it were constricting his words. "Then last night Maresford walked in on me while I was taking the jewelry from Lady Matlock's jewel chest. Winter was hiding in the next room. I did not know he was there. He suddenly appeared and confronted the viscount, some nonsense about when they were children. He tried to knock Maresford out, but only grazed his head. I – I was terrified I'd be discovered. I struck Maresford with the jemmy, hit his head and shoulder. I would have run, but Winter hauled the viscount to the window and threw him out. He took the bag with the jewels and the jemmy and told me to go home. He was supposed to come here later. He never arrived. And now the magistrate will come to arrest me, and..."

Sir Lionel stared at his son in revulsion. He rubbed cold hands over his face as he tried desperately to reason. He felt nauseated.

How in the name of all that was holy had it come to this? His popular, sociable son was a monster. What was he to do? Could he do anything this late in the day? The idea of his son hanging as a thief and murderer was intolerable. It would kill his wife if the disgrace alone did not.

Slowly Sir Lionel rose. He said in a flat voice, "I almost wish I had not interrupted you. It might have been best for all concerned. Since I did, I must find a way to minimize the damage, if I can." When Sir Colin looked up at him with vacant eyes, his father continued heavily, "At last report, Sir Nicholas is alive. Whether he will survive his injuries or not I do not know; it is immaterial."

The baronet went to a desk against one wall and brought back a blotter, paper, pen, and ink. He set them before Sir Colin, who stared at the array as if he had never seen the objects before.

His father said, "I want you to write it down: the gambling debts, Winter approaching you with his infamous proposition, the threats, the robberies, the attack on Maresford, everything. Leave nothing out. I will return in an hour. If anyone calls for you, the servants will be instructed to say that you did not come home last night."

With the first pale dawn light of hope, Sir Colin took up the pen, dipped it in ink and began to write.

Amid all the fittings, teas, visits to friends—chiefly friends of Mrs. Bennet—menus and countless other details of a hastily planned wedding, Elizabeth had not found an opportunity to speak privately with her aunt Gardiner. At last in growing unease, Elizabeth pleaded a headache when her mother went off to look for a special lace to trim the wedding bonnet and instead went by hackney with her maid to visit Gracechurch Street. She was fortunate to find Mrs. Gardiner engaged in playing with her children. At the look in her niece's eyes Mrs. Gardiner turned the game over to their nanny and escorted Elizabeth to the parlor, sitting on the sofa beside her.

"My dear" she turned to face her niece, "what is it? Has something happened?"

Elizabeth took a deep breath and shook her head. "No, Aunt. Mr. Darcy called yesterday to see if I was well after the events at the ball. We are never alone, so conversation remains on a rather stilted level. But he looks at me so…so intensely sometimes, I wonder what he is thinking."

Mrs. Gardiner smiled knowingly; she patted Elizabeth's arm in comfort. "He is thinking of being married to you, my dear, and all that occurs when you two are joined in matrimony."

Elizabeth closed her eyes briefly. "I spoke with Jane not long ago. She could not tell me anything of an intimate nature, of course. She advised me to consult you and ignore anything Mama tells me. I am not certain why, but consulting you has always been good advice."

"I believe I know why." Mrs. Gardiner smiled. "Fanny is a good woman, however she was raised as most women in our society—to think of marital relations as a duty, not always a pleasant one, rather than as they should be. The union of two bodies and two souls, 'Two shall become one,' as scripture describes it. One not only physically, in all aspects of life. That is marriage as it was meant to be and, sadly, not always is."

Elizabeth fixed her gaze on a lovely crystal vase full of late roses. She knew it was gifted by her uncle to his wife, one of many small gestures of affection and gratitude he made often. Seeing her niece's focus, Mrs. Gardiner took her hand and squeezed it lightly.

"Edward and I have a wonderful relationship. I am extremely lucky that he recognizes my abilities as I recognize his, that he encourages me to be myself, to pursue my interests, not just to keep his house and raise his children, although I do that too. We are partners, Lizzy, and that is rare. I believe Mr. Darcy views you in much the same way. I have watched him talk with you, the way that he delights in your quick mind and pungent wit. A man who only wanted a beautiful or wealthy wife would have married long ago. He has been looking for you, Lizzy, and now that you are found he sees what he has wanted made real. He wants you, my dearest, in every way."

For a time, Elizabeth made no reply. At length she sighed and raised her head. "I find that he is also the man I have sought since I entered the marriage market, as it is called. I sense his approbation and respect for me as a person in my own right, not just a reflection of his attitudes and beliefs. My only fear is that the bond of marriage will alter his perceptions. I know there is nothing I can do if it does, if he comes to see me as a possession—a prized possession, but owned nonetheless."

"Do you honestly believe that will happen?"

Elizabeth's breathing was shallow with distress. "I hope not, Aunt. Oh, I hope not! The one thing I could not bear is to be relegated to a state of unimportance except as I provided him physical comfort. To have him reject any intellectual contribution I might make to the marriage or our life together."

"Have you any indication—anything at all, Lizzy—to make you think that Mr. Darcy might do so?"

Elizabeth closed her eyes and held her aunt's hand tightly. After several long moments, she smiled shakily. "No, Aunt. It is just my fear of marriage, I think, of losing who I am. Of all the men I have met, he seems the least likely to impose his ideas of wifely behavior on me."

Mrs. Gardiner watched her niece closely. Elizabeth sat tensely. Her aunt's mind returned to the start of their conversation. She ventured carefully, "Lizzy, are you anxious about the physical side of marriage? Mr. Darcy is an imposing figure of a man, and he is quite obviously completely taken with you."

Elizabeth rose suddenly and paced across the room as if she could not bear to sit still another moment. She stood staring into the fire that burned low in the steel firebox. When she turned, her face was ruddy with more than the heat of the hearth.

"I am not totally naïve, Aunt. I have overheard married ladies talking about...about intimacy with their husbands. It is confusing in a way but not too hard to put the elemental pieces together."

She came back to the sofa and sat down, folding her hands in her lap.

"Men and women are designed to...to fit together. Some ladies do not mind the process, and others quite dislike it. And eventually there are babies, much as with any breeding."

"Well," Mrs. Gardiner said, suppressing a smile, "you have an idea of the basics. It is nothing like breeding animals, of course, except for the mechanics of the process."

Gathering her thoughts she sat back, which caused Elizabeth to relax slightly. Now that the subject was broached and her aunt was neither shocked nor unwilling to share her knowledge, Elizabeth felt less awkward about the information.

"When I was pregnant with Edward Junior, we found a highly recommended midwife, a Mrs. Kellog. She was very experienced, having delivered babies for nearly thirty years. Not long before the birth she was informing me of what to look for when the baby was ready to be born. After she finished, we began to talk a bit about female matters in general. Mrs. Kellog told me things about my body I never knew. I wish we had had the conversation before I wed Edward, it would have made my wedding night jitters far less than they were."

Interested now, Elizabeth turned her gaze on her aunt's dear face. "How is that?"

"She told me that just as all men are not made the same, neither are all women. Brides in our society are generally told that the first time they join with their husbands, there will be pain and bleeding. This is usually true; the amount of either varies from woman to woman. Some experience very little of either, some more, but it is very rare for a woman to be incapacitated by it."

Mrs. Gardiner leaned toward Elizabeth her voice gentle. "It is not a matter of the physical as much as of the emotions. A woman who loves her husband and who is loved by him will find herself immersed in a state so utterly beyond her past experience, so all-engaging, that she may feel nothing beyond the sensations of the moment. Whether she is fully aware of the necessary discomfort or not, it is of short duration and leaves no permanent scars, to either the body or the mind."

Elizabeth sat without responding for a time. At last she said in a low voice, "I do not know if Mr. Darcy is…if he has—"

"Experience? Very probably. He has no reputation for even the kind of behavior deemed normal among his peers, yet he is a virile, healthy young man. Do not let it concern you, Lizzy. It may be better for both of you if he knows what he is about."

Elizabeth blushed profusely. Mrs. Gardiner patted her hand, rose and rang for tea. Dismissing the maid her aunt poured it out herself. Elizabeth accepted a cup gratefully. She was calm now, her naturally buoyant character rising. She was not afraid of the physical aspects of intimacy, as nearly as she was able to anticipate them; it was being kept in ignorance that irked and depressed her. She said as much to her aunt.

"Thank you for your information, my dearest aunt. You have helped me to understand myself better and alleviated my most pressing concerns."

Mrs. Gardiner smiled warmly at one of her favorite nieces. "Go to him joyously, Lizzy. I know he will be all you have wished for in a husband."

Feeling more confident than she had in days, Elizabeth embraced her aunt. If a small, nagging doubt remained, she held it under close guard, deep in her mind.

When Elizabeth arrived home, her mother immediately upbraided her for her absence only three days before her wedding. Rather than remind Mrs. Bennet that she herself had taken on most of the decisions regarding all phases of the ceremony and celebration, Elizabeth chose to apologize and save an afternoon of remonstrations. Responses to wedding invitations were coming in daily, Mrs. Bennet having invited half of London it seemed. Elizabeth picked up the one from Lady Agatha, felt some small object folded inside the heavy paper, and took it into her father's study to open.

Silver gleamed as Elizabeth held the object in her hand. At first she thought it was a brooch, but there was no pin or other way to attach it. Three inches wide and a bit more lengthwise, it represented three stylized lilies, almost a fleur-de-lis, the slender stems twisted into a love knot at the base. The knot was in low relief, standing out half an inch from the rest of the piece. On the reverse, the vertical center had a thin strip of silver that might have been reinforcement, also raised above the surface. She turned to the note for an explanation, only to be further puzzled.

My dear Miss Bennet,

Thank you for the invitation to your wedding. However, I will not be able to attend. There used to be a small French writing desk at Pemberley. It belonged to my mother and was kept in her bedchamber. If it is still in existence, you may find the enclosed of assistance in its use.

Remember always that love is the most powerful force in the universe.
Lady Agatha Quintain

It was surely a strange reply to a wedding invitation, Elizabeth thought, turning the little silver medallion over and over in her fingers. She showed both to Darcy when he called later that afternoon. His long, shapely fingers examined the object carefully before he offered an opinion.

"I know the writing desk she refers to. My mother used it; it was put into storage when she died, as were many of her personal possessions. It is quite beautiful, seventeenth-century French, of rosewood with silver mounts. This plaque probably fits somewhere on the front or top when it is closed. It is indeed an unusual wedding present and a very unusual message."

"When we reach Pemberley, do you think your father would mind if I tried to locate the desk? I would love to return this to its original place."

Darcy shrugged. "I doubt he would object. You can ask him. He may know exactly what happened to it."

Elizabeth let the matter drop and went on to ask the condition of Nicholas.

"I saw Richard this morning." Darcy's face darkened. "Maresford is gravely injured. His right leg is broken close to the hip as well as at the ankle, as you heard. The hip joint was not damaged, and the upper bone did not shatter, which is the only good news, as either might well have involved internal organs. The break to his ankle is worse. Dr. Wyecroft has immobilized the entire leg. He will have to wait to see if any of the blood vessels that service the leg are damaged."

"If they are?"

Darcy's face was stony. "His leg will have to be amputated, if that is even possible."

Elizabeth instinctively took his hand in hers. "I am so sorry, William. I did not like Sir Nicholas, but I would not wish him this terrible happening."

"No more would I," Darcy replied and stroked her hand with his free one.

It was odd that he was able to talk to her so frankly without fear of her reacting to the words with distaste or withdrawal. Richard had come by Darcy House not long after dawn, accepting coffee and one of Mrs. Adam's muffins as he sat in Darcy's dressing room. He was pale, purpose filling his dark-blue eyes. Used to prolonged periods without sleep, Richard had been with the chief magistrate until a few minutes before arriving to appraise Darcy of the latest information about his brother's condition and the hunt for Wickham and his confederate.

"He's gone, of course," Richard had said with a mixture of anger and bitterness. "We went to the Arthur home, only to be told that Sir Colin never returned last night, which I believed no more than I do that he was an innocent drawn in against his will. Sir James ordered his constables to search the house in spite of Sir Lionel's protests, They found nothing except some sign that the library had been used since it was tidied yesterday. Lady Arthur was in hysterics, so Sir James withdrew. He has men watching the house for whatever good that may do. Frankly, I do not expect that Sir Colin will come back. He is either with Wickham or, more likely, secreted away where the law will not find him until his father can assess the situation."

"What about Wickham?" Darcy was in the process of getting dressed, Martin ostensibly oblivious to the conversation between the cousins. "What is being done to find him?"

"Sir James sent an express to the magistrate at Matlock. They will raid Mrs. Younge's establishment, and she will be questioned if he is not found. Frankly I doubt Wickham trusts her any more than he trusts anyone else."

"And Mr. Handley?"

Richard's mouth twisted sardonically. "Gone as well. He has no confidence in the law, or perhaps his quest for his sister's killer is so obsessive that he simply refuses to wait for the law to act."

"Thank you, Martin." Darcy stood before his cousin, perfectly dressed, as Martin bowed and left them. "Are you going north?"

Richard finished the last of the coffee and stood, stretching like a cat. "I have not decided. If Wickham is caught I will ride to Matlock to identify him, unless the chief magistrate has him brought back to London first. Otherwise I prefer to remain with my family until Nick's fate is decided one way or the other. Right now I am going home to get some sleep. If anything changes, I will send word."

"I shall be here after church, until midafternoon, when I intend to call on Elizabeth."

"So it has progressed to 'Elizabeth'?" Richard teased as they left Darcy's chambers and descended the main staircase.

"With the wedding in three days, I felt I ought to become used to calling my future wife by her Christian name. I refuse to follow a custom I find stilted and refer to my wife as Mrs. Darcy."

"Well done," Richard teased. "The one thing a man does not want on his wedding night is formality!"

Georgiana came down from her rooms on that Sunday morning to find her brother waiting for her in the dining room. There was no footman in evidence, a fact that set her senses on alert. Darcy poured her a cup of tea and sat down at the head of the table with his sister next to him. When she had taken a sip and turned her large blue eyes to his face, he drew a steadying breath and began.

"Georgie, I have something I want to share with you. I am sorry I have waited so long. It is because I did not want to hurt you unnecessarily."

The look on her face caused him to hurry on. "It is not about the wedding; it is father. He is…he is very ill, Georgie."

She paled, but her voice was stronger than he would have believed. "I knew there was something wrong when he was here. Oh, William, what is it? Please tell me!"

"He saw Sir Ansel McQuary while he was in Town. I am afraid it is his heart. He has had several episodes of seizures, the last a few days ago. Sir Ansel gave him some medicine to help, but it," Darcy fought to control his voice, "it cannot be cured."

Tears formed in Georgiana's eyes and fell silently down her cheeks. Darcy took out his handkerchief, gently wiped them away, and put the linen square into her hands.

"Does Elizabeth know?" she asked when she could speak.

"Yes. She was the one who encouraged me to tell you before we returned home. We will be leaving the morning after the wedding and should reach Pemberley on Saturday."

Darcy took his sister's hand, so small in his, and held it against his chest. "Father did not tell me when our mother was gravely ill. I was deeply hurt. I felt you would prefer to know the truth rather than have it come to you with no warning."

"She is wise," Georgiana said. "Is there anything we can do?"

"Only remain with him and love him for as much time as God gives us. It may be months or a year, or it may not. And we can pray for him."

Georgiana rose, straightening her shoulders. "Yes, brother, we can. Let us go to church and do so."

CHAPTER 15
MARRIED PAST REDEMPTION

I am to be married within these three days. Married past redemption.

—John Dryden

The morning of her wedding, Elizabeth woke at dawn. She did not rise until she heard her father's door close softly and his quiet footsteps traverse the hall. It took only a moment to leave her bed, slip her feet into house slippers, and put on a robe. His study door was just closing as she reached the bottom of the stairs. Mr. Hill came along from the kitchen with a tray holding a teapot, sugar, cream, and two cups. Elizabeth smiled and tapped on the study door.

"Come." Mr. Bennet looked up from his position in front of the fireplace without surprise as Elizabeth entered behind the butler. "Ah, Lizzy, I thought you might be along this morning."

Mr. Hill placed the tray on a small sidebar. Elizabeth took over at once. "I shall fix my father's tea, Mr. Hill, thank you."

Mr. Hill bowed and retreated, a suspicious moisture in his faded eyes. He had served the Bennet family since Elizabeth was two and Mr. Bennet just beginning to expand his law practice. Miss Jane's marriage was one thing; she still lived close to Town, so they would see her often. But Miss Elizabeth was going to move to Derbyshire, a wild country still and much farther away, Mr. Hill thought, as he closed the door on father and daughter. The family might not see her for years. Shaking his head, he reassumed his professional demeanor and returned to his duties. But a heaviness remained in his heart.

"I see you provided for my presence, Papa."

Elizabeth spooned sugar into her teacup. She added cream to both her cup and his and carried them to the table between the two armchairs before the fire. Her father sat to accept his cup. Elizabeth took the other chair. For a time, they drank in silence, as they had done many mornings in the past. At last Mr. Bennet set his cup aside and turned his dark-blue eyes on his favorite daughter.

"I understand you are to leave for Derbyshire tomorrow morning. Is Mr. Darcy's father worse?"

"He has had another seizure," she said softly. "Apparently it was not severe, although he was bedridden for several days. There is no way to know when another incident may occur. Mr. Darcy needs to be at Pemberley in the event—if he is needed to take over full management."

"Not a particularly auspicious beginning to a marriage." Mr. Bennet reached out and took Elizabeth's hand. "I have thought in the past several weeks that I made a bad mistake tying you to this marriage. A young bride should not spend the beginning of her wedded life in mourning."

"It may not come to that.," Elizabeth met his steady gaze, "or not for some time. If it does," she continued as her chin lifted in a manner he was well familiar with, "I shall deal with it. Mr. Darcy is very close to his father, and there is Georgiana. She has never suffered such a terrible loss. Her mother died when she was five, so this will be very much harder on her than on me."

"And you are determined on your course" He sighed. "You seem to be content with marrying Mr. Darcy. I hope you have come to feel some affection for him. Your path will be a stony one if it is only duty that holds you to him."

Elizabeth said, looking at their linked hands, "Jane asked me if I was in love with him. I was not certain then. She said that if I did not love him, it would affect every part of our lives together." Raising her eyes she smiled, and Mr. Bennet's heart eased. "I am certain now. He is the only man I would ever marry, and I find my love for him growing with each time we are together."

Mr. Bennet leaned and kissed her cheek. "I will miss you so much, my Lizzy. But I know I am entrusting you to a good man."

The quiet suddenly crumbled before the padding feet and strident tones of Mrs. Bennet in the hall outside. "Lizzy! Lizzy Bennet, if you have gone out for a walk, you will be sorry!"

"If I had gone out for a walk," Elizabeth said as she rose, giggling, "I would be unaware of the threat."

Mr. Bennet stood up. He took his daughter in his arms and held her tightly, as he had done when she was a child and came to him for comfort. Releasing her, he stepped to the door and opened it on his wife's vexed countenance.

"All is well, Mrs. Bennet," he said, gesturing to Elizabeth at his shoulder "The lost has been found."

Mrs. Bennet verbally took Elizabeth by the ear and hustled her upstairs. "You need to bathe before the water gets cold and you catch a chill before you can be married!"

"Mama, the ceremony is not until eleven, and the bath cannot be cold as I was only with Papa for a few minutes and Millie had not started drawing it when I went downstairs."

Logic was never popular with Mrs. Bennet, especially when it contradicted her preconceived notions, so she continued in the same tones. "No matter, you must dress and have your hair done, and your hair is never easy to style, and there is the wedding bonnet to think of—oh, I wish Jane were here!"

So do I! Elizabeth thought with asperity. Aloud, she said, "Perhaps they will arrive early." It was more of a prayer than a wish.

The bath was hot, and Elizabeth sank into it gratefully, able to put the events of the day ahead from her mind for a few minutes. When she returned to her room, she found that Millie had brought her a tray with more tea, a scone, and a bowl of berries with clotted cream. Not wanting to hurt the maid's feelings, she drank some tea and ate a few berries, her stomach rebelling at more. Millie seemed pleased as she laid out Elizabeth's undergarments: long chemise, short stays, and stockings. The double dress fell softly on the bed. It did not require a petticoat, as it lay close to the body and provided adequate coverage.

Elizabeth had washed her hair the evening before, so all the maid was required to do was brush it out with a little of the lavender water her mistress used before styling the coiffure. Elizabeth would rather have dispensed with the wedding bonnet, but at her mother's insistence she had had one made of satin a shade darker pink than the wedding gown and trimmed with some of the same lace as the overdress. The hatter had added a double row of seed pearls to the front lace band, making the bonnet more appealing than Elizabeth expected.

Millie put her hair up in a knot of curls on top of her head, with long ringlets hanging down her back. A few small curls framed her face. Elizabeth recognized that the bonnet would fit perfectly over this arrangement and complimented the maid on her ability.

"Thank you, miss," Millie colored, hesitated, and then said, "May I speak frankly, miss?"

"Of course," Elizabeth looked at Millie's image in the dressing table mirror. "Say whatever you wish."

Keeping her eyes lowered, Millie said, "You did not ask me to accompany you to your new home. I just wanted to say that I appreciate you being so thoughtful. I am happy to serve you, but I prefer the city to the country, and if Miss Mary wants me to go with her when she marries, I will. That is all."

Elizabeth smiled warmly at the maid's pink face. "I am happy that you agree with my decision, Millie. Even if Mary does not wed soon, Mama can always use help for Kitty and Lydia."

"Yes, miss."

There was a tap on the door, and at Elizabeth's summons, Mary came in. She wore a gown of gray silk in her usual high-necked, long-sleeved style, but her hair had been arranged in a very becoming coiffure that allowed her to look her age rather than matronly.

She said, "Millie, can you go to Lydia? She needs some assistance with her gown. I will help my sister dress."

Elizabeth rolled her eyes. Lydia always had to be the center of attention. Millie curtsied and left them, from her stiff expression seeming none too happy. Mary turned to her sister, smiling.

"You hair is lovely, Lizzy. Even though we have over an hour until it is time to leave, I fear Mama will be along shortly to oversee everything from your slippers to your earrings."

"I do not doubt it," Elizabeth grimaced. "At least I want to be in my underthings before she arrives."

As Elizabeth put on the long chemise and held her stays for Mary to lace, her sister said softly, "I sent Mr. Cranshaw away at the ball the other night. I was talking with Colonel Fitzwilliam, and he came up and was very rude. He called me his fiancée, as if everything were settled between us, when he has not even asked to court me. I…I grew angry and told him I had changed my mind. I do not want to see him again."

"Good for you," Elizabeth applauded, adjusting the stays for a bit more comfort. She knew that Mary's conscience was bothering her in spite of the provocation. "He has made no effort to secure you in any way. Then to assume you will marry him, no matter what his behavior, is churlish. Did you tell Papa?"

"No." Mary sounded horrified. "I would never want to cause a problem with his work. Papa says he is superb at formulating defenses and may well take silk one day. I have no desire to harm him, I simply have no further interest in accepting his suit."

"Careful, Sister, or you will develop a reputation like mine of rejecting suitors out of hand."

"I do not think so." Mary laid out the wedding gown on the bed, smoothing the silk satin without looking up. "I am not likely to have suitors to reject."

"Not even Colonel Fitzwilliam?" Elizabeth teased and was instantly sorry at Mary's painful blush. She took her sister's hands, speaking softly, "Mary dear, I have noticed the way he looks at you. He is an honorable man, and if he speaks, you would do well to listen."

"I would," Mary said softly, "except that he is committed to this war with Napoleon; until that is over he cannot think of marriage. Even then, he is a second son and unlikely to have sufficient income for a wife and family."

"He is also resourceful and intelligent. And you are not a woman who demands a life of luxury."

"He is also proud," Mary lifted her eyes to Elizabeth's. "I do not believe he could accept a standard of living for his family below what he has now. In any event, he has not spoken, and he may not. I will have to wait and see."

"And hope" Elizabeth hugged her sister.

There was a knock on the door that made both sisters turn to it, Elizabeth fearing that her mother had arrived. She was relieved to find it was Mrs. Hill, with a small package in hand.

"Mr. Bennet took this from the post. He said to give it only to you, Miss Lizzy."

Elizabeth took the parcel with an absent thanks. Obviously Mr. Bennet knew of his wife's propensity to open her daughters' mail and wanted Elizabeth to be the one who received this gift first. She noted that Mrs. Hill still stood in the doorway, a hopeful look on her lined face.

"Come in, Hill. You may as well see what it is."

Elizabeth tore the wrappings from a small leather case. A card lay on top of the box. She recognized Darcy's beautiful copperplate, and read, "Elizabeth, my pearl above price. FD." Slipping the card into the pocket of her dressing gown, she released the catch and raised the lid, her breath stopping in her throat with a soft gasp. Cocooned in blue velvet was a three-inch-wide brooch of platinum with a delicately scalloped edge, each scallop picked out in matching pearls. Inside the ring of pearls were six little rose diamonds, and in the center was a single perfect pearl.

"Oh, Lizzy," Mary breathed, "it is a wedding gift from Mr. Darcy. How lovely."

Mrs. Hill had a hand over her mouth. She backed from the room without either young woman noticing her exit. Elizabeth went to her wedding dress and placed the brooch at the joining of the lace overdress. It matched the ensemble perfectly.

Tears filled her eyes. She did not realize her mother had entered the room until her sharp voice cut through Elizabeth's senses.

"What is the matter? Lizzy, did you receive a letter from Mr. Darcy? Why are you crying? Oh, Lord, do not tell me he has withdrawn from the marriage!"

"No, Mama," Mary put in quickly, "he sent Lizzy a wedding gift. That is all."

"Then why are you crying?" Mrs. Bennet asked suspiciously. She looked at the dress and saw the brooch, her eyes widening. "Merciful Heavens! Is that his gift? Oh, child, what jewels you will have if that is any sample!"

Elizabeth straightened and wiped her eyes with her handkerchief. She was not about to show her mother the note. "It matches perfectly, almost as if he knew what color the gown was to be."

"He could not know," Mrs. Bennet told her confidently. "There is no way for him to find out. It is just coincidence. Now, get dressed child, and be careful you do not wrinkle the fabric or get any stains on it. You must look perfect when Mr. Darcy sees you at the church."

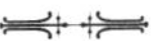

Darcy also woke at dawn on his wedding day. He had spent a restless night, thoughts tumbling through his mind between periods of light sleep that did not register as sleep at all. He had no concerns about the wedding ceremony; all that had been settled with the priest at St. Answyth days ago. The Bennets were hosting the wedding breakfast; his trunks and Georgiana's were packed, awaiting only Elizabeth's luggage to be placed on the servants' coach for the trip to Pemberley. Darcy's genius for organization had taken over, and everything that could be done to facilitate their journey was done.

When Martin came to wake his master, he found Darcy sitting before the fire, wrapped in an old wool robe, his long legs extended to the warmth. Placing a tray holding coffeepot, cup, and accessories on a table, Martin pulled back the drapes to let in the pale morning light.

"Good morning, sir. Did you sleep well?"

Darcy looked up with a wry smile. "Does any man, the night before he marries?"

"I would not know, sir. I have never been married."

Martin prepared Darcy's coffee and handed him the cup, making a mental note to dispose of the robe as soon as his master was out of the house. Generally Mr. Darcy was the soul of sartorial elegance, and Martin had his standards. He began to lay out the clothing he had chosen for the ceremony: a dark-blue coat of superfine, fashionably cut and of perfect fit, a fine cambric shirt, white silk cravat, waistcoat of gray satin with a thin gold stripe, and white trousers. Darcy drank his coffee and paid no attention to his man's activities. Martin was more than capable of putting together an ensemble that would reflect nothing but credit on his master. At the moment Darcy's thoughts were on Pemberley and what he would find when he arrived home with his bride.

Guilt still haunted him for taking Elizabeth into such a situation when they ought to be planning their wedding trip. She had been wonderful in her understanding and empathy for him and Georgiana. He wondered if somewhere beneath it all there was not at least a small sense of resentment, one that might grow rather than fade.

Darcy finished his coffee and set the cup aside. There was nothing he could do about it now. Any chance to release her had gone, they were committed to the marriage. Darcy knew that unless she demanded to be set free, he would never have been capable of letting her go. He wondered if he could have done so even then.

Martin left to draw his bath after inquiring if Darcy wanted another cup of coffee. A shake of the dark head was his only answer. He hoped this marriage worked out well, for all their sakes. Something was very wrong with Master George, all the servants knew it; discussion was guarded and mostly speculation. If the master died, Mr. Darcy would be obliged to take over the management of the estate, as well as observe a year of mourning, all this in addition to coping with a new wife and Miss Georgiana. Shaking his head, Martin retreated to the bathing area and rang for the footmen to begin bringing up hot water.

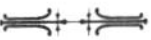

In a small private residence in a less fashionable part of Bloomsbury, Sir Colin waited for the arrival of his father. It was early morning two days after the robbery at Matlock House. He had hardly slept in all that time, starting at any unexpected noise, his eyes wide with fear. The house belonged to Sir Lionel's mistress, a former actress who had requested the residence as part of the bargain for her services. She was a little past her prime, still attractive and of a stolid nature that suited the baronet. He found quite enough drama at home. To Sir Colin's dismay his father had strictly prohibited any liquor, a fact that had the young man even more jittery than his problem with the law alone. In total, between terror of being arrested and withdrawal from alcohol, Sir Colin was a physical and mental wreck.

"Better eat something, ducks." Lettie Cotworthy, stage name Viola Dawn, brought in a tray with a teapot and some toast. Her voice was beautifully modulated, an asset that had furthered her career beyond the bloom of youth. She put the tray on the hassock in front of the chair where Sir Colin sat hunched over, head down, his hands clenched into fists between his knees.

"I don't want it," Sir Colin groaned.

Lettie watched him, her hands on her hips. "Your father'll be here soon. If he has a way for you to leave London, you won't have time to eat, and meals sometimes come few and far between."

The parlor was furnished more sparsely than might have been expected in bright colors with numerous cushions and small knick-knacks. It was a cheerful room, not fashionable but comfortable.

"I don't want anything. I don't think I could keep it down." Sir Colin looked up at her plain face, found sympathy there, and added desperately, "Can't you just let me have one drink? Please, Lettie?"

"Not if I value your father's patronage, and I do. Eat a little, Colin, you'll feel better, I promise."

He shook his head. A key in the front door lock sent him leaping to his feet, his eyes wild with fear. Lettie turned to the miniscule entryway as the door closed, her voice faintly sarcastic. "It's only your da. Nobody else has a key."

As she spoke, Sir Lionel Arthur came into the parlor, his eyes raking his son, who still looked ready to bolt. With a disgusted glare, he nodded to Lettie as he put the key away and spoke to his son.

"I see your condition has not improved, Colin, not that I expected it to."

Ignoring both his father's words and attitude, Sir Colin said tightly, "What have you done to get me out of here?"

Sir Lionel gestured to the chair as he took a seat on the settee facing it. "Sit down. We have not much time, and there are things to discuss."

Lettie discretely withdrew. Not only did she have no interest in the discussion, if the matter ever exploded she did not intend to be hit by any of the debris. Sir Lionel studied his son, sighed, and helped himself to tea. He took a sip while his son sat visibly shaking.

"At seven o'clock tonight, Jonas will knock on the back door three times. He will take you to a ship's boat at a certain dock on the river. I chose Jonas because he is unquestionably loyal. The boat will take you out to the *Fair Winds*, a cargo ship that occasionally takes passengers. I have seen to it that no other passengers are on board for this voyage, so you will have no one else to contend with. I have brought a portmanteau with some clothing and personal items, plain things that will not identify you as a member of the peerage. The bag has a false bottom. Beneath it is five hundred pounds in gold coin. Keep it hidden; you will not need money until you reach your destination, and if any of the crew find out about it, you may never reach it."

"Where am I going?" Sir Colin sounded more frightened than relieved.

"New Orleans, Louisiana. The American president Jefferson recently purchased the entire Louisiana Territory from Napoleon. It is a port city with a good amount of traffic and not yet fully under American control. You speak French well, so you will have no trouble communicating. It is far less likely to have dealings with British law than a northern city. If you are careful, if you act wisely, you may be able to begin a new life there without the threat of death haunting you."

"I—I cannot return home?"

Sir Lionel drew a long breath. "No. Not for the foreseeable future. Maresford is alive but badly injured; he still may die. His family is powerful. They are looking for both you and Winter. Your only safety lies in putting as many miles between yourself and England as possible."

Sir Lionel stood. "I am doing this, Colin, as much for your mother's sake as for yours. We are now the parents of a thief, an assailant, and a fugitive. We have no reputation, your sister's future is ruined, and I will be forced to withdraw from Society and remove to Rathskell for the remainder of my days. Be grateful that I retain enough sense of fatherhood—and guilt—to save you from the noose."

Sir Colin stared at his father, the weight of what he had done suddenly falling on him with an impact he had not felt before. Tears stung his eyes, and he dashed them away. To say he was sorry now was useless, nearly an insult. He only nodded in agreement with the plan, numb with shock at what his future was to be.

Sir Lionel raised his voice enough to reach into the house, "Lettie."

She came promptly, smiling, her voice formal because of Sir Colin. "Yes, Sir Lionel?"

"Have you any hair dye on hand?"

"A little."

"I want you to dye Colin's hair, not obviously, just enough to darken the color a little. He will be leaving tonight."

"Of course." Lettie held out her hand to the young man, adroitly concealing her relief. "Won't hurt a bit."

"Colin." Sir Lionel put out his hand and gripped his son's shoulder. "Take care."

"Yes, sir."

Sir Colin followed Lettie out of the parlor. His father closed his eyes tightly for several seconds, and then he cautiously left the house by the back door.

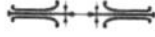

Richard Fitzwilliam arrived at Darcy House in full dress uniform an hour before he and his cousin were due at the church. His face was sober in contrast to his usual jovial visage. Darcy was in his study, sitting at his desk. He was not working, as he had finished all the business waiting the day before. He looked up when his cousin was announced, expectation flickering through his eyes. They shook hands before Richard took one of the chairs before the desk and sat back.

"You look tired," Darcy commented quietly. "Is Nicholas worse?"

"Not specifically. The medical student Wyecroft sent has been a great help. There is nothing that can be done until Nick either improves or…or does not. His ankle is the worst. The broken bone was actually pushing against the skin. Wyecroft could not set the ankle. The usual procedure is to amputate and father was against it. Wyecroft's only other option was to open the ankle like a wound, remove bone chips before they cut the blood vessels or tendons, and reassemble the bones as best he was able."

"Is that done?"

"I have seen similar actions in field hospitals when it was the only alternative to taking the leg, only when the bone was already through the skin. Wyecroft is the best, and he deemed it necessary. Considering Nick's condition, an amputation would almost certainly have killed him."

Darcy said in a low growl, "Wickham has much to answer for."

"He will," Richard vowed. He shook himself. "I apologize for the grisly conversation on your wedding day. I do not particularly like my brother, but he is blood of my blood, and he did not deserve to be thrown thirty feet to the ground by a cur like Wickham."

Darcy shrugged off the apology. "My thoughts have been on Father this morning. I am sorry we were not able to be married at Pemberley. I asked so much of Elizabeth as it is that I could not in good conscience ask her to wed me at Pemberley chapel. Her whole family would have to be transported to Derbyshire, and Mrs. Bingley is obviously unable to travel at all. Also we would have hosted them at Pemberley, and while that is not usually a concern, with father ill I refuse to put him under any additional strain."

"Better here," Richard agreed. "Miss Mary is standing up with her sister?"

"So I understand." Darcy studied his cousin, who avoided his eyes. "Do I detect a scintilla of interest in the modest Miss Mary?"

Richard rose abruptly and paced across the quiet room to the fireplace. He stood unconsciously in the position of parade rest, hands clasped behind his straight back. For years Richard had teased his cousin about his reluctance to marry one of the Society misses paraded for his choice by their ambitious mamas; Darcy realized this was not an occasion for getting even. When he made no further comment, Richard drew a deep breath, his mouth tightening.

"My last conversation with Nick earlier that evening concerned his suggestion that I find myself a rich wife, as he intended to cut me off when he assumed the title. He believed that I have no resources except my army pay and my allowance from father. He is wrong, but I did not enlighten him."

He met Darcy's eyes with the confidence his cousin was used to seeing and said, "That investment you recommended has paid off."

"The improved method of smelting iron?"

Richard nodded. "I had a thousand pounds saved that I invested. It has doubled in a little more than a year."

Darcy grinned as his cousin continued.

"Father overheard Nick's threat. I found him in the hall. I do not know what he intended. He only said there were to be changes in the family. Then Nick was injured. It puts a whole new complexion on the situation."

Darcy rose and went to stand by Richard. He did not offer financial help, as that would not have been taken kindly by his proud cousin. Instead he gripped Richard's shoulder.

"I would like nothing better than to have you as a brother as well as cousin."

"We have been that in all but fact most of our lives." Richard smiled. "She is a fine woman, but I am a soldier. Until this business with Boney is done, I cannot in conscience quit my regiment and my duty. If I survive until then, I will sell my commission and find another, quieter source of employment."

Darcy hesitated. He was not sure Richard would appreciate any advice on the subject of Mary Bennet. However from experience, Darcy knew that asking a woman to wait without any proof of intention to wed was not advisable, however honorable the gentleman.

"Ask her, Richard. Speak to Mr. Bennet, explain your situation. He is a reasonable man, and he loves his daughters. Miss Mary is a constant lady, let her know that you mean to marry her. One man has already lost her by assuming her acquiescence."

Slowly Richard nodded. "My mother has a small silver cross she is keeping for my wife. I will speak to her about giving it to Miss Mary if her father agrees to a future courtship."

"Excellent." Darcy glanced at the mantel clock and turned for the study door. "We had better leave. The last thing I wish to do is be late for my wedding."

A tap on the door that Darcy recognized as Mr. Burgess brought a frown to his face. The butler knew better than to interrupt him this morning of all mornings. He saw Richard stiffen, and Darcy's immediate thought was that Nicholas's condition had changed. He opened the door himself to Mr. Burgess's well-controlled surprise.

"This just came for you, sir."

Mr. Burgess handed Darcy a small package and withdrew. Richard, relieved, cocked an eyebrow. Darcy almost set the parcel aside, until he saw it was from Rundell & Bridge. A sudden certainty made him remove the wrapping to reveal a leather box and a card in Elizabeth's hand. He did not notice Richard discretely step into the hall. Holding the box in one hand, Darcy read the four words on the card: "With all my heart."

Fingers trembling, Darcy opened the little box. The gleam of gold rewarded him; a simple, elegant watch fob lay cushioned in blue velvet. He touched it as if it were the greatest treasure, seeing "EB" and "FD" entwined with the date beneath. When he removed it from its nest and turned it over, his eyes glistened with tears.

"Cousin? Are you ready to become a married man?"

Darcy lifted his head and blinked rapidly,. his voice husky as he joined the Colonel in the entry. "More than I have ever been ready for anything in my life."

⟡

Mrs. Bennet was just scrutinizing Elizabeth from all angles when another tap at the door sent an absent, "Enter," before her daughter could speak. Jane came in, smiling happily at her beloved sister, who promptly left her place in the center of the room and ran to hug the gravid young woman as tightly as possible. Her light-green velvet gown made little attempt to conceal her condition, impossible even if it had, while her classic beauty shone with her joy.

"Oh, Jane, dearest, I am so very happy to see you!" Elizabeth withdrew a little, taking her sister's hands in hers. "I was just wishing that you might arrive early."

"Charles wanted a word with Papa, so we came a little before time to leave for church." She stroked Elizabeth's cheek. "Oh, Lizzy, you look so beautiful. Mr. Darcy will be awestruck."

"I doubt that," Elizabeth demurred. "I think it would take more than a bride to induce such a reaction."

Mrs. Bennet bustled over, kissed Jane's cheek, and with unusual tact, left the room, Mary following her. When they were alone, Jane sat on the dressing bench and looked up at her sister.

"Mary looks wonderful," she said. "It was good of you to ask her to stand up with you, as we determined that I obviously cannot. Not only would it be a strain on my body, I would be embarrassed even though I am married."

Elizabeth smiled. "I have always wanted you to stand with me at my wedding, dearest, but I know your sense of propriety well, having violated it enough times."

"Only mildly," Jane replied. Her eyes took in the brooch now resting between Elizabeth's breasts where the top and skirt of the lace over dress met. "From Mr. Darcy?" It was not really a question.

"Yes, my wedding present. It arrived this morning. I do not know how he managed to match the color of my gown so well, as it has been a closely guarded secret."

She sounded amused. Jane cocked an eyebrow. "Servants talk to one another. Millie knew the color. She has a friend who is an upstairs maid at Darcy House. I expect the color made its way to Mr. Darcy's manservant, if not to Mr. Darcy directly."

Elizabeth laughed. "Poor Mama. She did not know whether to be overwhelmed by the expense of the gift or by the fact that it matched so very well."

Jane smiled. "Mr. Darcy seems a resourceful man. What are you giving him?"

"It is difficult to find a wedding gift for a man who can afford anything he wants. He carries a beautiful old pocket watch. I had a gold fob made with our entwined initials engraved on it and today's date. On the back it says, 'For all eternity.'"

Tears sparkled in Jane's eyes. She rose and again hugged her sister. "Lizzy, I have no doubts at all that you have made the best marriage you could possibly make. I will miss you terribly, but the knowledge that you are marrying a man you love eases my heart."

"You and Charles will visit, perhaps early next year? Promise me!"

"I promise. Now," Jane opened the door as Elizabeth retrieved the wedding bonnet from its box, "we had better go downstairs before Mama marshals the entire household to look for us."

CHAPTER 16

TWO BODIES, ONE SOUL

The Bennets arrived at the little church of St. Answyth a few minutes before the wedding ceremony was to begin. The church itself had begun as the family church of the Earl of Dorsey, built in the late seventeenth century on what was then part of his estate. Over the years it had been renovated and added to, somehow retaining its Gothic character in spite of a square tower, decorated buttresses, carved canopies over the choir stalls, and an Elizabethan altar table. This architectural ecumenism was presided over by the Reverend Mr. Tottingham. He was tall, lanky, and quietly authoritative, and his stiff white hair perpetually looked as if he had just been combing his fingers through it. He had been vicar of St. Answyth for over thirty years and knew all his parishioners well, loved them well, including the occasional lost sheep, and was beloved in his turn.

Darcy and Colonel Fitzwilliam had already taken their positions when Mrs. Bennet led her small triumphal parade to the Bennet pew, consisting of Lydia, Kitty and her fiancé Mr. Cowper, Jane, Charles Bingley, and his brother Daniel. Fully aware that she was the focus of all eyes, Mrs. Bennet took her time being seated. Standing before the altar, the Reverend Mr. Tottingham gave her a tolerant nod from under shaggy white brows, causing her to settle in her seat. Mary waited across from the two gentlemen, calm and serious. She had noted Colonel Fitzwilliam's uniform, and while she would have preferred him to wear civilian clothing, she was not insensible to the figure he cut.

In the other front pew, Lord and Lady Matlock sat with Georgiana and Sofia. Although Dr. Wyecroft had assured them that it was highly unlikely their oldest son's condition would change in the next few days, both showed the nervous strain of sleepless nights and unrelenting pain in lined faces and lavender-shadowed eyes. Although they were not his parishioners, the vicar stepped to their pew and said a few words of comfort before resuming his place.

Mrs. Tottingham sat at the modest organ in the crossing. She was an attractive woman, a little younger than her husband, her glossy brown hair touched with gray. As if at a silent signal, she began to play Clarke's *Prince of Denmark's March.* The doors opened, and Mr. Bennet proceeded down the long aisle with Elizabeth on his arm.

Mr. Bennet had faced the doors as they opened to admit him and Elizabeth, his heart beating like a hard little hammer in his chest. The aisle that he had traversed so many times was suddenly a very long, narrow passageway between pews of smiling, nodding guests. Beside him, her hand on his arm, his Lizzy walked forward with her eyes fixed on the tall man standing before the pastor, her entire being focused in the man she was to marry.

Memories flooded Mr. Bennet's mind. Lizzy wrapped in a blue blanket meant for his heir, her large, dark-blue eyes fixed on his face. Lizzy at six, fifteen feet up in an oak tree, laughing down at him, fearless. Lizzy lit by firelight, intently discussing a book they had both read, focused on her argument. Lizzy dancing, Lizzy flying down the stairs to greet him after a business trip, and Lizzy in her first ball gown. Lizzy's face when he told her she was to marry a man neither of them had ever met. Lizzy that morning, hugging him as she always had for comfort, when it was he who needed comforting.

She has already left me, he thought. *Her place is now with Mr. Darcy, and while that is as it should be, I will miss her more than I realized.*

The wedding bonnet sheltered her face from those in the pews as she passed. It made no difference as everyone had turned at her entrance and observed that her entire focus was on her groom. For his part, Darcy lost any awareness of the congregation beyond a faceless murmur. Elizabeth glided toward him as in one of his dreams, her eyes never leaving his. What he read there left him spellbound. His hand trembled as her father placed her hand in it, and the service began.

"Who giveth this woman to be married to this man?"

Mr. Tottingham's voice reached clearly to every corner of the church. Mr. Bennet responded, "I do."

He squeezed his daughter's hand, placed it in Darcy's, and made his way to his seat. Mrs. Bennet was already sniveling into a lace handkerchief. At the far end of the pew, Daniel Bingley tried not to crane his neck for a glimpse of Georgiana Darcy. Her pale-golden head was hidden behind her uncle and aunt, except for an occasional glimpse. Charles held Jane's hand, both remembering their own wedding. She smiled at him, her eyes starry with tears.

"Lizzy will be happy," she whispered to her husband, "as we are." His response was to lift her hand to his lips.

Kitty surreptitiously held Mr. Cowper's hand, imagining her own wedding day. She was happy for her sister, in no way jealous. Hers was not a covetous nature; Mr. Cowper was her fiancé, they would be married in time. She was satisfied. If she did not have her sister's ability to feel a great passion, she was content with a warm, comfortable affection.

Lydia, on the other hand, kept shifting position in an attempt to find out if anyone was looking at her. She was dressed conservatively in a pale-pink silk gown, her hair pulled back but not put up, and she was proud of the sweep of blonde tresses falling down her back. She wondered how it felt to stand before a church full of people with a handsome man and pledge her life to him. A handsome, wealthy man—perhaps a peer, an earl, or a viscount. Instantly her imagination ran headlong to mansions, carriages, jewels, and dozens of bowing, curtsying servants vying to fulfil her least wish.

Her sister's low hiss waked her as Kitty nudged her sharply. "Lydie, you are grinning like a jack-in-the-box!"

The words brought her back to reality with a jolt. She glanced at her father and saw his stern gaze fixed on her. Without the least remorse, Lydia dropped her eyes and assumed a penitent posture.

"With this ring, I thee wed; with my body, I thee worship; and with all my worldly goods, I thee endow."

Darcy's rich voice spoke the words with reverence as he slipped the wedding ring on Elizabeth's finger. It had been made to match the betrothal ring, a narrow circle of platinum with side diamonds flanking a single ruby. His fingers were warm on hers. Elizabeth raised her eyes to his face, a smile of pure joy infusing her features. His answering smile was promise and covenant.

The Reverend Mr. Tottingham pronounced them man and wife. The blessing was given, and Fitzwilliam Darcy and Elizabeth Bennet were joined in holy matrimony. They walked back down a much shorter aisle together, signed the register, and stepped out into a crisp day with hazy sun spreading a diffused glow over the old gray-stone church. Richard and Mary followed, Mary not looking up at him but feeling the strength of his arm under her hand. She wondered if one day she might walk out of the church again with this man, bound to him for life. It was a sobering thought, yet it made her heart beat faster and color infuse her cheeks. Richard noticed and smiled, the same thought in his mind.

"May I call on you tomorrow, Miss Mary?"

She nodded and then said softly, "Yes, Colonel, you may."

Darcy and Elizabeth stood side by side accepting the good wishes of their guests. Lady Matlock kissed Darcy's cheek and then Elizabeth's, taking the bride's hands in hers.

"You will be very happy, my dear niece. God bless you both."

As Elizabeth thanked her, Lord Matlock shook Darcy's hand. "You know Georgiana is staying with us tonight, along with Mrs. Annesley?"

"It is not necessary, Uncle, with everything else—"

"We are happy to have her. She will lighten the mood, and Mrs. Annesley is a good woman and a pleasure to be around. You need privacy, tonight of all nights."

Darcy colored but did not disagree. They intended to stop for Georgiana tomorrow morning on their way out of London. He said, "Will you be able to attend the wedding breakfast?"

Lord Matlock shook his head. "I am sorry, Madeleine and I wish to return home now. It will probably make no difference, but Nicholas is our son. If anything were to happen..."

Elizabeth said quietly,. "We understand completely. Thank you for coming to our wedding."

Lord Matlock assayed a smile. "Couldn't miss seeing Richard standing at the altar, even if it was not his wedding."

He glanced aside at his younger son, still standing with Mary Bennet. Pain flickered through the earl's eyes. "Perhaps, one day, it will be."

As if sensing his father's attention, Richard said goodbye to Mary and joined his family. He, too, shook Darcy's hand and kissed Elizabeth's fingers with a gallant bow. Georgiana came out of the church, walking with Jane and Charles, her head bent slightly as she listened to whatever Daniel Bingley was saying. For a moment, Darcy frowned; a touch of Elizabeth's hand smoothed his expression. He knew that he was overprotective of his sister.

Now that she had a woman to confide in and seek advice from, he intended to try to be less so.

Mrs. Annesley came up as the Darcy carriage arrived, smiling and wishing them happy. Darcy handed first Elizabeth and then Georgiana in, and then offered his hand to Mrs. Annesley, who thanked him quietly. She sat across from Georgiana, facing her charge and Elizabeth. Darcy took his place beside her. A footman shut the door, and the carriage rattled over the cobblestone street toward the Bennets'.

Elizabeth looked at Darcy under her lashes, wondering that she did not feel essentially different from the woman who had entered the church not an hour ago. Her life had changed forever, yet Darcy was the same man who had called on her, walked with her, taken her to the theater and opera, driven her in Hyde Park, and kissed her in the copse there. At the memory of the kiss, her feelings rose in a spinning haze of color and sensation. She felt Darcy watching her and tried to assume a normal expression. The glow of emotion in her eyes set his pulse racing. It was almost with relief to him when they pulled up in front of the Bennet home, and he stepped out to assist the ladies to the step and the ground.

Mrs. Bennet had a reputation as a skillful hostess. She enhanced the legend with the wedding breakfast, offering a multitude of dishes, English and French, a dozen wines as well as punch and champagne, a table of sweets centered by a lavish cake; fruit, cheeses, and the contents of every hothouse flower merchant she was able to find. She circulated among the guests, laughing, talking at her usual high rate, and enjoying herself immensely. Darcy offered to prepare a plate for Elizabeth, but she declined. She had no desire for food, nor, apparently, did he. She drank a glass of champagne with her husband and otherwise talked to friends and guests who approached to offer good wishes.

Knowing that it might be months before they saw one another again, Jane stayed near her sister throughout the festivities. When Elizabeth went upstairs to change out of her wedding dress, Jane accompanied her, leaning a little on Elizabeth's arm. They entered Elizabeth's room, bare furniture and stripped bed already giving it a look of abandonment. Jane sat in the chair as Millie came in to help her mistress out of her wedding gown.

"It is hard to believe that only this morning everything was as it always has been," Jane said, looking around, "and now there is nothing left of it."

"I packed your traveling trunk, miss—madam—and it's gone to Darcy House." Millie blushed and almost whispered, "Your night things are in it."

She retrieved the ensemble and assisted Elizabeth to change. It consisted of a cream-velvet dress with a plum-velvet spencer trimmed in white soutache. Elizabeth set a small plum-velvet bonnet with a white feather curled around the brim on her dark locks.

"Thank you, Millie." Impulsively Elizabeth hugged the girl. "I will miss you."

"I will miss you too, madam." Millie curtsied and quickly left the sisters, wiping her eyes on the hem of her apron.

Elizabeth took Jane's hand as she stood. "I dearly wish I could be with you when the baby is born."

"So do I." Jane squeezed Elizabeth's hand. "But we will send you an express as soon as it is over. If it is a boy, it will be Charles Thomas, and if a girl, Martha Frances. Martha is Charles's mother's name."

"Both sound perfect."

The two sisters looked at one another, both with tears starting. Their embrace was full of love and farewell. Together they returned downstairs, where Darcy and the remainder of the

Bennets waited. Elizabeth embraced her mother and her sisters, finally turning to her father.

"Goodbye, Papa. I will write often."

"See that you do." He held her tightly for a moment and then stepped back.

Amid the well-wishes of the guests, Elizabeth, Darcy, Georgiana, and Mrs. Annesley left the wedding breakfast for the trip to Matlock House before the newlyweds proceeded on to Darcy House.

Darcy had spoken to Mrs. Annesley the evening before the wedding. Her original plan had been to stay with her sister in Greenwich until she obtained another position. She had sat quietly in Darcy's study and waited for her employer to speak.

He had said, "Mr. Bennet has approached me. He wants to employ a companion for his youngest daughter, Miss Lydia. She requires someone able to instill self-discipline in her and teach her to reason before she acts, as well as any other education she lacks. She is a young woman whose high spirits have never been properly directed, but she is intelligent and not of a poor character. If you are interested in the position, I will make an appointment for you to speak with Mr. Bennet in the next few days. The salary will be commensurate with your present earnings, and the household is a well-run and pleasant one."

Mrs. Annesley had smiled. It was an expression that said she knew exactly what he was not saying and did not resent it. "I shall be happy to speak with Mr. Bennet. How old is Miss Lydia?"

"Fifteen."

"An age when many young women need direction and stability. Thank you, Mr. Darcy, for your kind interest in my welfare."

Darcy had wished her well. He thanked her again for her excellent care of his sister and made her a gift of six months' salary in appreciation.

"If you ever require a reference," Darcy had told the astonished woman, "you have only to write me, and I will provide one."

The speechless companion could only stammer her thanks.

⸻

The major members of the staff of Darcy House were assembled for their arrival and introduced to their new mistress. Elizabeth had already met the Burgesses when she visited with Georgiana and at the dinner party. She met Mrs. Adams, the cook, Darcy's man Martin, and several others. Mrs. Burgess had assigned a maid to assist her that night, with the expectation that Elizabeth would engage a maid on her arrival at Pemberley. It was all done neatly and with minimum fuss, as the household was always run.

Darcy escorted Elizabeth on a tour of the house, as she had only seen the public rooms on the ground floor. He had asked Georgiana to take Elizabeth to view the mistress's chambers on the third floor and note any suggestions or changes she wanted to make. Now he showed her the second floor, wanting with all his being to sweep her into his arms and carry her to his bed. With the iron self-discipline of a lifetime, Darcy reminded himself that, despite the passion he saw in her eyes in the carriage, she was a maiden and he must proceed slowly.

"This is the billiard room." Darcy indicated a door to the left at the second-floor landing. "You private sitting room is here, to the right."

He opened a door to a pleasant room of moderate size. Elizabeth looked around, her eyes taking in the soft colors and pastel shades. "It is as lovely as all the other rooms I have seen." She smiled.

"They are all yours to alter, redecorate, or use as they are, my love."

"In time, perhaps, I shall make some small changes. For the present, they are fine as they are."

The remainder of the wing comprised guest rooms, the breakfast parlor, and a storage closet beyond the billiard room for household items and linens. Elizabeth took it all in, her mind divided between the sights and the man at her side. The warmth of his body seemed to radiate around her; his touch was gentle, yet Elizabeth was aware of the strength inherent in his hands. She was not frightened, she told herself firmly. Still, Darcy's presence nearly touching her was disturbing in a way she had never experienced before.

They did not change for dinner. Mrs. Adams, aware of the lavish wedding breakfast and that neither of her diners was likely to have eaten much of it, prepared a light, nourishing dinner. They sat at one end of the smaller table in the breakfast parlor rather than Elizabeth taking her new position at the foot of the table. Darcy seated her, carefully stroking the soft curls that had escaped her coiffure back from her face. Elizabeth felt a frisson shiver through her. She pressed her cheek against his fingers for a moment, her eyes closed, and then raised her head to find his dark eyes intent and full of desire.

Darcy lifted her hand to his lips, then sat down before the contact evolved into something else. *Not yet,* he told himself. *Give her time, only a little longer.*

Despite Mrs. Adams' best efforts, little of the meal was consumed. Elizabeth drank two glasses of wine, one more than usual. When the meal was finished, they went downstairs to the music room where Elizabeth found several pieces she knew well enough to play without serious concentration. Darcy sat nearby, listening to her easy fingering and clear voice, entranced by the beauty of this woman now his wife. At length Elizabeth finished and rose, meeting Darcy's intense gaze.

"I shall retire now."

He was already on his feet, offering her his arm. Together they climbed the central staircase with its carved oak balustrade and solid handrail. On the third floor, Darcy opened a door carved with a swag of flowers and ribbons. Elizabeth had been in the rooms with Georgiana; tonight for the first time they were her private precinct. A girl named Nell, whom Darcy knew to be one of the upstairs maids, curtsied to both of them.

Darcy said, "I will see you in a little while."

Elizabeth nodded. He left her with the maid, who assisted her to undress and, after she had washed her face and hands, to put on the nightdress packed in her traveling trunk. Nell offered to brush out and plait her hair, but Elizabeth felt that she needed the occupation and dismissed the girl with a smile. She did not put on her robe. It lay neatly folded on the chair by the fireplace in the bedchamber, where little flames snapped and flickered with a rubicund glimmer. The air was not warm nor cool enough to be uncomfortable. The sky had grown heavier all afternoon. Elizabeth wondered if it would snow before morning.

Elizabeth sat at her dressing table to brush out her hair, the brush moving automatically in her hand. She felt detached from the familiar action, her mind hovering between apprehension and anticipation. She had given herself a stern talking-to last night after her mother's fumbling and somewhat contradictory advice of "It is a constant trial every woman faces when she marries. In time you may learn to tolerate your husband's attentions better"; her aunt's kind practicality of "The Lord made procreation a pleasant experience if your husband is kind and you will let it be so"; and Jane's joyful assurance that it was the closest two human beings could come to perfect union. Elizabeth had told herself that she would not behave like a heroine in one of the popular novels, or a silly schoolgirl. She was a grown woman, she had knowledge, she loved Darcy; those were all the elements she required to be a wife. She would go to him joyfully and trust him with her body as she did with her life.

The tap on the connecting door to Darcy's chambers froze her in mid-stroke. Elizabeth rose and laid the brush on the dressing table, and with a single, breathless word, she called her husband to her.

CHAPTER 17
NEW BEGINNINGS

"What in 'ell are you doin' 'ere?"

Mrs. Dorothea Younge, commonly known as Dolly (marital designation questionable), glared at the man in her private parlor, her narrow face contracted in anger, her never-dulcet voice shrill. Dolly's roots in the London slums always emerged when she was angry or upset. At the moment she was both.

George Wickham leaned back in his chair, one arm lying along its gaudy upholstery and the other hand holding a half-empty glass of Holland gin.

"Enjoying your hospitality, my dear."

"No, you ain't! You get your hairy—she inserted a crude description of his male anatomy—outa here, and don't you come back! The magistrate's already been 'ere and threatened to put me in quod for 'elpin you. I want no part o' you, George."

Wickham took a swallow of the liquor, smiled, and threw the remainder in the woman's face. Sputtering and cursing as the raw gin stung her eyes, she groped for something to wipe her face. Wickham handed her his handkerchief. When she was again able to see, he dangled a gold necklace set with tourmaline in front of her blurred vision.

"Sit down, my dear, and listen. If you want this pretty, you will cooperate. It should more than compensate you for any trouble in allowing me a short respite here in your charming premises."

Dolly sat, glowering, torn between greed and fear. Greed, as usual, won. "Why the bloody hell did you have to go after a damned viscount? No maids to hand?"

Wickham scowled. "The maid was an accident, but no matter. In fact, I did not go after Maresford, he generously came to me. Hazards of war."

Dolly was calming. She found another glass and poured a generous tot of the gin, slugging it down in one swallow. "The magistrate searched the place top to bottom. I told 'im I ain't responsible for what a customer does when he ain't here. Somebody musta seen you comin' or goin' and told them."

"Perhaps." Wickham shrugged. "They will not look a second time, and I have no intention of outstaying my welcome. I need a day, perhaps two, and I will be on my way."

"Where to, louse land?" If there was a double meaning to her slur against Scotland, Wickham ignored it.

"Eventually. I have some unfinished business north of here first."

"You ain't on about the Darcys again? What is it with you and them? I thought you was the old man's favorite?"

"So did I."

Something moved behind Wickham's eyes, something cold, inhuman.

"I was the one who sat with him after his sickly goose of a wife died, told him stories, kept him going while his precious son ignored him. When I went off to university, he gave me this ring."

Wickham held out his right hand, where a heavy gold ring shone on the second finger.

"I took it as a promise of future benefits. But when I was sent down for 'immoral behavior,' all he offered me was Kympton parish if I reformed and became a sniveling preacher. When I refused, he threw me out, no doubt at my old companion's urging. I have a score to settle with George Darcy, and I will settle it as soon as I can get to him."

Mrs. Younge shivered inwardly, but her voice was harsh. "Damn your black soul, George. Let it drop, and get out o' the country. You must have enough swag to go anywhere you want to."

The jealousy was apparent in her tone. Had she been a decade younger, she might have convinced this man to take her along. But she was not, and he was dangerous, not only to her personally but also to her business. It had taken her years of working at the same profession to accumulate enough money to buy this small house and fix it up for more affluent patrons. It was a profitable operation, one she had no intention of losing because an old friend wanted a bolt-hole.

"They could be watchin' the place," Dolly told him. "If you're found here, it's the end of me. I'll go to jail for letting you set foot in the door, whether I wanted to or not. That bauble ain't worth it."

Wickham reached out lazily and put the necklace in her hand. "That is worth more than this whole house and every 'lady' in it. Pack up, fence it, and start over somewhere else."

Dolly licked dry lips. She understood that it was not wise to cross this man, and the gold glittered brightly. She licked her lips. His words struck some chord of promise in her stained soul.

"Add a bit to it, and I'll 'elp you. I got a friend who can smuggle you out o' here."

With patent disinterest, Wickham said, "How much more?"

Dolly clenched her hands in her lap. "Fifty pounds gold."

"Twenty."

"Fifty. I'm the one takin' the risk. If you ain't wanted for another murder, you will be!"

"Twenty-five. And your life."

Dolly's face paled under its cosmetic covering, giving her the look of a badly painted doll. After a brief internal struggle, she nodded. "Twenty-five, in gold."

"I never deal in banknotes." Wickham smiled lazily.

"Now" he rose, lifting a small trunk she had not noticed from behind the chair, "take me to the attic room. When you have made the arrangements with your friend, bring me something to eat and a bottle. And—" he suddenly gripped her hand, bending the fingers back until she gasped with pain. "Come yourself. Leave one of the girls in charge tonight. You will be spending it with me. If I have any unwelcome visitors, you, my dear, will be the first casualty."

Wickham released her fingers and pressed his lips to the back of her hand. Shivering, Dolly checked the hallway before preceding him out of her parlor. She would make sure he was gone in less than a day. Dolly knew a peddler who traveled the area virtually unnoticed. He owed her a small debt, enough to take a passenger out of town without asking questions. As long as no one tumbled to Wickham's presence under her roof, she would shortly be considerably richer and quit of the threat of her very unwanted guest.

Darcy woke suddenly, as was his habit, completely aware of his surroundings with one exception. A soft weight pressed against his side, warm and silky curves enwrapped in slumber. A strange mood came over him, tender, protective, sensual. He had slept with a woman before, but this was his wife. *His wife.* Her skin smelled of lavender and faintly of their lovemaking. It was intoxicating; Darcy carefully slipped his arm around her waist, holding her even closer.

Memory flooded his brain. He closed his eyes and let the images of his wedding night cascade through his mind. Elizabeth calling, "Come," at his tap on her door. Elizabeth standing before her dressing table, her beautiful eyes uncertain. This was the moment she would either step into womanhood or retreat from him behind a wall of half-truths he would have to find a way to breach. Not knowing what else to do, Darcy opened his arms.

He felt again the exhilaration as Elizabeth came to meet him, pressing her body against his, her lips opening at his touch. Her light weight in his arms as he carried her to his bed. Elizabeth's wonderful eyes on his, the color of a midnight sky, her delicate hands stroking his face, tangling in his hair as he began to explore her body. She had let him remove her nightdress, the last barrier to trust. He remembered the taste of her, the feel of her, her soft cries and moans, her avid response to his ministrations when his hand parted her legs for the first time. Darcy had worried about the inevitable pain he must cause her, grateful she had only given a little cry nearly lost in more ardent expressions of pleasure.

A euphoria such as Darcy had never felt filled him. They had truly become one flesh. They belonged to one another in a way that nothing would ever change or destroy. Darcy slipped into a doze. Beside him, Elizabeth stirred, mumbled something, and sank deeper into her dreams.

Elizabeth was dreaming of Darcy. The heat of his body infused her flesh, calling up images of her first sight of his naked form. He had lifted her into the center of the vast master's bed, a walnut full tester, it's heavy snuff-colored velvet curtains tied back at the head on the room side. She felt a shiver of nerves pass over her as he untied the sash of his robe and slid it down over his shoulders, laying it on a nearby chair. Elizabeth had prepared herself to show no emotion at this first intimate view of her husband. She had seen statues in museums and private homes, not all discreetly adorned with fig leaves, and she had been around male animals at Longbourn in the summers, so male anatomy was not a total unknown. What momentarily shocked her was her instant fascination with Darcy's body. The statues she had seen were cold, white marble; this was living flesh, defined muscles moving as he turned and came to the bed. He was already in a beginning state of arousal, drawing her eyes for a moment before she raised them to his face, blushing.

Darcy lifted the coverings and lay down beside her. Elizabeth tentatively ran her hand over his chest, the soft scatter of hair across his pectorals under her fingers. He smiled, caught her hand, and kissed the palm softly. That was enough to send a jolt through her belly, both startling and pleasurable.

"Are you well, my dearest love?"

The deep resonance of his murmur raised bumps on her skin. She nodded, not trusting herself to speak. He stroked her hair, running the curling strands through his fingers. With his other hand, he explored her body while his eyes held hers, nearly black with the fire she had seen briefly before when he looked at her. With careful movements, he raised her nightgown to her waist. After only a slight hesitation, Elizabeth pulled the hem up and slithered out of the garment, letting him toss it to the foot of the bed.

Elizabeth slid her arms around his neck. Darcy leaned over her, blocking out the glow of the fire in the hearth. She smelled his cologne as she had before, spice and cedar, mixed with the scent of his skin. It was as intoxicating as wine. Her rational mind slipped into a haze of sensation as Darcy's hand ran gently along the inside of her thigh. His mouth found hers, erasing any reluctance she might have felt. His kisses trailed along her neck from her ear to her shoulder and then to her breasts. Elizabeth heard a soft moan and realized it was her own voice.

Elizabeth lost all sense of time while they touched, kissed, and stroked one another. At length, Darcy's hand on her thighs pressed them slowly apart. Elizabeth knew the time had come for them to join. She tightened her hold on her husband, pressing tender kisses to his shoulder. Desire filled her with a spiraling hunger, irresistible and demanding.

"Love me, William," she gasped. "Show me what to do."

His touch left her blind with passion, stronger than any emotion she had felt in her life. She was caught in a physical storm, William her only reality. There was a moment when his weight bore her down into the yielding bed; she felt a single sharp pain, a momentary burning, and then only the exploding rapture of oneness. Darcy groaned, his body moving rhythmically. Elizabeth wrapped her legs around him as he had told her, drawing him in deeper and deeper, her body instinctively trying to move with his. She slipped into a haze of sensation, will lost, rational thought flown, a being of physical rapture that grew and grew until she cried out and fell away from all conscious thought. Dimly she heard Darcy's shout as he reached fulfillment. For a time there was nothing but a slowly reviving knowledge of where she was and a momentary sense of loss so great tears prickled her eyes.

"My precious wife." His whisper sounded husky in her ear. "My dearest, wonderful Elizabeth. How do you fare, beloved?"

Elizabeth drew what she felt was the first deep breath in hours. She touched his face with wondering fingers. "Oh, my husband—I cannot tell you how wonderful I feel." Her voice caught, she closed her eyes as his breath stirred the hollow of her throat.

"One soul in two bodies," Darcy murmured.

He rolled away from her, leaving Elizabeth suddenly feeling totally bereft. Her soft cry made him pull her into his arms. She nestled against him, no longer lost in the safety of his embrace.

The dreams muted into colors and shapes, and Elizabeth slipped deeper into sleep. Beside her, Darcy pulled her closer, his arm around her waist; cupping a soft breast he let himself drift into sleep as well.

⟡

"Well, Aggie, you seem to have escaped serious injury, thanks to the quick action of Mr. Hughes." Lady Agatha peered up at Dr. MacGregor with an expression compounded of disgust, suppressed pain, and frustration. "How long are you going to keep me in bed, you old quack?"

The doctor smiled. He had known Lady Agatha since the first days of her marriage to Cedric Quintain, he studying medicine at the University of Edinburgh and Quintain just beginning to be noticed as a promising artist. He had had a *tendre* for Agatha then, until he met his future wife. At that point all other women ceased to exist for young Dr. MacGregor.

His pleasant Scottish burr intensified as he gazed with affection at his reluctant patient. "A few days, if I can keep you there that long. Your knees are badly bruised, walking will be painful until they heal a bit. You fainted, Aggie. I've never known you to do that before."

Lady Agatha was about to retort that she had never fainted in her life, but the truth imposed itself. She had indeed fainted. She responded tartly, "I shall stay in bed for a day or two, no more. I am planning a trip to visit a friend."

"Unless your friend lives no more than a day—better yet, half a day-- from London, you will not be making the journey for at least a fortnight. A coach ride, even a short one, could cause you considerable pain and delay the healing process."

Lady Agatha leaned back on the pile of pillows supporting her back. Her eyes narrowed slightly. She said, "What are you not telling me, MacGregor?"

The doctor sighed. He sat in the chair pulled up to the bedside that Marie had occupied until his arrival and took Lady

Agatha's thin hand in his. "Aggie, you seem to be in good health, considering everything—"

"My age, you mean," she interposed tartly.

"Yes, and your general condition, but there is always the possibility that you may have had a very mild apoplexy. Or it may simply have been fatigue. Marie tells me that you have attended two balls in the past week, at both of which incidents occurred that were of an alarming nature. We are neither of us hatchlings, Aggie. A trip to the country, if that is your plan, is a very good idea, but only when you are recovered enough that it will not prove a hazard to your health."

Lady Agatha sighed. She squeezed the doctor's hand and withdrew her own, folding it over the other on the coverlet. "Very well, MacGregor. I will wait. I suppose you intend to leave me a tray full of disgusting medicines to take?"

Dr. MacGregor stood, smiling. "No, Aggie, only a mild sedative powder if you cannot sleep. You need rest now more than anything."

He said goodbye, bowed, and left her, finding Marie in the adjoining dressing room. She studied his face, her own professionally blank, her eyes frightened. The doctor used his most soothing voice. He knew Marie worshipped her mistress; if Lady Agatha was incapacitated or died, the Frenchwoman's life would be shattered.

"She is not badly injured, Marie," he said calmly. "It is only imperative that she rest and sleep for a few days. If she faints again or shows any sign of additional pain, I want you to send for me immediately, day or night. I have left some sleeping cachets on the table. I know you will watch over her well, Marie."

"Yes, sir."

Marie opened the door to the hallway, and Dr. MacGregor left her. She listened to his footsteps recede before closing the door again. She knew her mistress very well; she knew Lady Agatha was unlikely to follow the doctor's orders if they contradicted her own wishes. Sleeping powders; Marie wondered if there was any taste to them. She determined to taste a little of one, and if they could be disguised in tea or some other liquid, Lady Agatha was going to follow the doctor's instructions whether she wanted to or not.

⸻

"Surely, Richard, you must see that in this case, family takes precedence over your commitment to the army."

Richard had known it would be a difficult interview when his father asked him to accompany him to his study after a dinner of which neither man has eaten more than a token. Nicholas was no better, still unconscious most of the time and incoherent during the brief times he was awake. Dr. Wyecroft still held out hope of a recovery, but the likelihood of that diminished day by day.

"No, Father, I do not see that."

Lord Henry made an effort to keep his voice reasonable. His younger son could be every bit as stubborn as his mother, and raising his voice to his wife had never worked in the earl's favor. Father and son occupied Lord Matlock's study, one of his favorite rooms in the house. He had chosen this room instead of the more informal drawing room because it was his sanctum, the place he came to transact parliamentary business, to make vital decisions about the Fitzwilliam estate. It was a masculine room, the walls paneled in walnut, two lined with glass-doored cases holding books and various mementos collected over a lifetime. Firelight caught ruddy gleams in the small panes. Richard knew their contents by heart, but today he was hardly aware of his surroundings.

"We need you, Richard," his father went on relentlessly.

Richard gathered his control, hard won through years of war and command. To meet his father's repressed anger with his own was pointless. Remaining calm was the only way to avoid open conflict.

He said quietly, "My regiment needs me. There has been enough trouble with Northumberland over appointment of senior officers; any more, and I expect Wellington may replace him. Fighting the enemy is difficult enough, without fighting among the commanders."

"He served in the American War," Lord Henry commented. "He has experience, or he would not have been appointed to the post."

"Experience, yes," Richard agreed. "He also has a habit of replacing things that work very well with things that do not. He wants to spend money on a regimental band that could be better spent on equipment or other necessities. Sooner than later there will be a major shakeup, and the Horse Guards will be caught up in the conflict. Wellington has supporters and detractors. Assuming command, however well justified, will cause dissension among the rank and file as well as the officers. I will not abandon my men at such a time."

"And Northumberland believes that his appointment gives him the right to change whatever he likes. Without precedent, I do not doubt he will ultimately fail. What I do not understand is why your military career is more important than keeping the estate running. Surely you understand my position?"

"This has nothing to do with the estate's management."

Richard rose, and his father saw the man his son's men saw in the field, the professional, the commander. Richard Fitzwilliam faced his father across the wide desk in the study, his jaw set and his dark-blue eyes hard.

"I understood your position perfectly, Father. You are concerned for the succession, as you must be. If Nick does not survive or if he is unable to produce an heir, I am the only one who can retain the earldom in the immediate line of succession."

Lord Henry came out from behind his desk. Frustration made it difficult to maintain his composure, but years of parliamentary debates sustained him. He met his son's gaze steadily, and for a moment, they were a mirror image of one another.

"You are perfectly right. If neither you nor Nicholas has a son, our line of the Fitzwilliam family ends. The earldom will pass to your cousin Timothy or his heir. I do not want to see that happen, Richard."

"No more do I. But what you are asking me to do is give up the career I chose nearly a decade ago to become Nick's steward until he either marries and has a son or dies childless."

"And if he does not survive his injuries, you will be my heir. Why can you not see how important it is for you to remain here? Forget Moorlands for the present. I have several other small estates. Resign your commission, and I will deed the best one to you. You can marry then, whatever Nicholas' situation. For God's sake, Richard, listen to me!"

Lord Henry realized how callous he sounded, but he was at his wits' end. As poor an heir as Nicholas had proven to be, he wanted his son to live and recover. But he was a man used to hedging his bets, and he cared for his younger son. To lose both of them was a blow he did not believe he could survive, whatever the outcome of the succession.

"I have listened," Richard said quietly. "Whether or not you believe me, I am also concerned for the succession. You would prefer me to be safe at home, not in peril on a battlefield in Europe. That need conflicts with my sworn duty. And Napoleon is an ever-present threat to England. If he is not defeated, sooner or later, he will mount an invasion. That puts every man, woman, and child on our shores in jeopardy. I am honor bound to protect my country. I could not be the man I am, the man you raised to value honor above all things, if I turned my back on it now."

Lord Henry saw defeat facing him, and made one more effort. "I have noticed that you seem drawn to Mrs. Darcy's younger sister. What of her? If you resigned your commission…"

His son's face told Lord Henry that he had made a mistake. Richard's voice was chill; his words fell like stones between them.

"I have stated my intentions to Miss Bennet and her father. If I survive the war with France, we will marry. With no disrespect to you and Mother, whatever the outcome of Nick's injuries, I never forget that I am a second son. You have been generous in offering help, but whatever life I ultimately live will be achieved through my own efforts. That is the way I want it. Until Bonaparte is defeated, my life is the regiment."

Lord Henry bowed his head briefly. "Very well, Richard. Your mother and I will pray for your safe return. And we shall welcome Miss Bennet into the family."

Feeling old beyond his years, he watched Richard leave the room. One son nearly dead and the other determined to go in harm's way. He sat heavily behind his desk and put his head in his hands. *God go with you, my son, and bring you safely back to us.*

Richard Fitzwilliam walked into the drawing room and stopped at the sidebar. But instead of pouring himself a brandy, he leaned both hands on the solid mahogany and closed his eyes, his head bowed. He did not move until a light touch roused him. His mother stood next to him, her slim hand resting on his arm.

"Did you quarrel with your father, Richard?" she asked gently.

Richard straightened, drew in a deep breath, and placed his hand over hers.

"No, Mother. I had to deny his insistence that I resign my commission and remain at home."

"I see. You do not feel that Nicholas's condition is reason enough for you to leave the army?"

She said it without recrimination, perhaps with a little disappointment. Richard drew a breath as he turned to face her.

"I do not feel that my own interests are more imperative than my sworn word. Bonaparte is a threat to England that must be stopped before we see war on our own shores. I know that one man or one regiment will not accomplish his downfall, but if I were to stay here, whether Nick recovers or not, I would fail myself if not my country."

His mother's still-lovely face was sad. "I could wish you were a little more selfish, Richard, although I know you are not. It is I who am selfish. I do not want to lose both of my sons."

Lady Madeleine turned her head away so that Richard could not see the tears that she refused to shed. "Do what you must, my son. I will always hold you most dear of my children."

She was gone before he found a reply. Slamming his hand into the sidebar so that the glasses on the tray jumped and rattled, Richard damned his brother and the war without the true heat of anger. Like Nicholas, he had made his life, and he must go on with it until its inevitable end. He quit the room, asked for his horse to be brought around, and headed for the Bennet home.

Elizabeth Darcy looked out the window of the Darcy traveling coach at mounds of brown slush pushed into the gutters beside the street. People were hurrying on their individual business, heads bent and shoulders drawn up against the wind that fluttered coat skirts and snatched at hats and bonnets. Next to her, Georgiana engaged her in light conversation that gradually lessened as they left the city. If she missed the familiar company of her companion, it was not evident. This trip was a familiar one to the young woman. She had brought a book to read in the coach, something Elizabeth was never able to do without feeling queasy. Once they settled into the longer stretches of travel, she might also nap.

For propriety's sake, Elizabeth sat across from her husband, whose dark eyes seemed to read her thoughts. She had wakened in the deep hours of the night, the heat of Darcy's naked body pressing her back. With careful motions, Elizabeth had gotten out of the vast bed and looked around for her robe before she remembered that she had left it in her dressing room. There was a bite in the air that told her it had snowed overnight. With gooseflesh prickling her skin, Elizabeth hurried to retrieve it, wrapping herself in the soft woolen fabric before seeking the commode in her bathing area. When necessity and cleanliness had been attended to, she returned to the master's chamber. The fire was nearly out, but Elizabeth did not try to build it up. They had to leave early in the morning; there was no use in a large fire now.

As carefully as she had left the bed, she crawled back under the covers, nestling close to her husband. She felt safe there. William was no longer a figure of intellect, of humor, impeccable, fastidious, an outer image of the inner man. This mass of skin, muscle, bone was the man who had revealed her to herself, who made her whole with his passion that kindled her own. Because of him, Elizabeth thought, she had been given the precious gift of self-knowledge. She was no longer Elizabeth Bennet, she was Elizabeth Darcy; all that went before was only a prelude to this understanding of who she was and who she could be.

Beside her, Darcy stirred, reached for her and pulled her against him, still half-asleep. Elizabeth stroked his hand where it rested on the swell of her hip. His eyes opened, he muttered something, and then abruptly rose on an elbow to stare down into her eyes.

"Are you well, beloved? You are not suffering from…from last night?"

"No, my dearest husband. I am very well."

He sighed with relief. Elizabeth raised a hand to run her fingertips along the stubbled line of his jaw. She moved it slowly downward, along his neck, over his chest, his stomach, finally stroking his wakening arousal. Darcy lowered his head to claim her mouth. The kiss became more intense as Elizabeth continued her ministrations. He groaned suddenly, a sound from deep in his chest. Elizabeth shifted her position to accommodate him. Her arms went around him as he continued to place kisses along her neck, his hands cupping her breasts, pulling him on top of her.

"Love me, William," she had whispered. "Join with me again. I want only to be one with you."

Darcy had obeyed her. At length they had slept the remainder of the night, waking a little after the leaden gray dawn. Now in the comfortable coach, her feet on a heated brick and a thick woolen pelisse wrapped around her as well as a lap robe over her legs, Elizabeth looked across at her husband and saw the corners of his mouth twitch up. Blushing, she returned her gaze to the street scene passing outside, only to hear a low chuckle that made her blush deepen.

Elizabeth cut her eyes at him and tried unsuccessfully to frown in reproof. His face was no longer amused; his eyes held memory and promise. Georgiana, happy to be on her way home, noticed nothing. Mrs. Annesley had removed her possessions to the Bennet residence the day before the wedding to take up her new position. Elizabeth hoped Lydia did not prove too much of a challenge for the companion.

To relieve her feelings, Elizabeth asked, "How long will we be on the road?

"If this snow continues, several days. More if the roads are closed by it. I am hoping that once we leave the area, it will dissipate, as it is still early for snow here."

"At Pemberley, when everything is covered with snow," Georgiana offered, "we hang out wire frames of suet mixed with bits of nuts and other things for those birds that do not migrate. Their tracks in the snow look like pictures I have seen of runes. Some of the small birds nest in the barns, up in the rafters where the barn cats cannot reach them."

Georgiana continued to talk intermittently of Pemberley. The time passed pleasantly, until at length Georgiana fell into a doze. Still feeling the emotional effects of her wedding and the weeks preceding it, Elizabeth longed to sit next to her husband and rest her head on his shoulder while she napped. She had to make do with the padded back of the seat and was finally drawn into sleep.

Elizabeth woke when the coach pulled to a halt at the inn where they were to change horses. Darcy alighted and handed the ladies down, hurrying them into the warm interior. All three proceeded to the ladies' retiring room. When they emerged, the innkeeper's wife showed them to a private parlor, where tea and a tray of scones and small cakes had been set out. Darcy joined them after a quarter of an hour and gratefully accepted a cup of tea. When he was seated next to Elizabeth on a settee, he gathered their attention with a look.

"The innkeeper says that it is snowing north of here, not as heavily as in the immediate vicinity. The weather sages say it will be a long winter—snowfall is already above the normal amount. This storm should lessen before we reach the coaching inn where we will stay the night. Mr. Wilkes is seeing to the horses. When he and the others have had a chance to rest for a bit, we will be on our way."

Elizabeth nodded, relieved. She was glad that they were not to travel much farther in the snow. The roads were in good repair, but even a good road can be treacherous when wet, and even a good driver could have trouble seeing in a heavy fall of snow. After half an hour's rest at the inn, their party returned to the coach. The bricks in their iron boxes were newly heated, warming the air inside the coach enough to take the chill off. Both women wrapped up in their outerwear and covered themselves with heavy lap robes. Snow still fell in a flutter of white flakes that covered the ground. True to the innkeeper's prediction, the storm abated considerably by the time they reached the coaching inn that was their destination. It was a large building of two stories with outbuildings behind the main structure. The innkeeper, Mr. Mitchell, and his wife waited at the door to welcome these important guests. They knew both Darcys from previous journeys. They did not know of his marriage until Mr. Darcy introduced Elizabeth to them in the front hall of the establishment.

"You dear things," Mrs. Mitchell beamed. "We wish you all the happiness in the world."

Her husband echoed her sentiment, leading them closer to the fire in the large stone fireplace that served the entrance foyer where sofas and chairs lined the oak paneled walls. Elizabeth, noting the broad oak planks of the well-used floor, asked the age of the building.

"My grandfather built it in 1728. There was hardly any roads then, and travelers were glad for a place to stay and good food. I'm the third generation to own this inn, and if God is merciful to us our son will be the fourth generation."

"He is in the Royal Navy," Mrs. Mitchell explained, "third officer on a ship of the line. We pray every night for him to come home safe."

"Is he your only child?" Elizabeth asked with instant sympathy.

"No, ma'am," her husband replied. "We have two grown daughters, both married, and three fine grandchildren." He turned to his wife. "Mother, why don't you take the Darcys to their rooms? I'm sure they'd like to freshen up before dinner."

There were only a few other people staying at the inn that night, Mr. Mitchell assured them that the traffic would increase as the holidays approached. When they came down for dinner they were seated in the low-ceilinged dining room at a table with spotless linen and served by Mrs. Mitchell herself. The fare was plain, plentiful and excellently prepared, and the Darcy party enjoyed a wholesome and filling meal. Shortly after they finished dinner, Elizabeth and Georgiana excused themselves to go to their rooms. It was early, however the trip had been fatiguing, and both ladies were glad to make it an early night.

When they had gone, Mr. Mitchell approached Darcy as he sat near the fire, nursing a modest brandy. Darcy indicated the chair next to his. "Sit down, Mr. Mitchell. This is excellent brandy."

"I won't say my son sent it to us from somewhere or other," Mr. Mitchell's eyes crinkled at the corners, "but Mr. Bonaparte may be short a bottle or two."

Darcy grinned. He saw that the innkeeper had some intelligence to impart and waited patiently until Mr. Mitchell cleared his throat.

"I don't suppose it'll be of any concern to you, Mr. Darcy, as well protected as you travel with outriders and all, but we had an incident last Monday se'nnight not far from here."

"What sort of incident?" Darcy leaned forward a little.

"Peddler by the name of Jasper gave a ride to a fella he found walkin' along the road. The man looked a gentleman, said his horse had come up lame, and he was lookin' for someplace to get another mount and go back for his. Jasper knows every farm and village in two counties, so he offered to take the man to a nearby farm where they might lend him a horse. A mile or two up the road, the fella asks Jasper to stop so he can answer a call of nature. Instead he hits Jasper over the head and leaves him alongside the road. Took his cart horse. He found the farm all right," Mr. Mitchell finished, "and stole a horse outa the barn."

"Was the peddler badly injured?" Darcy asked, his attention totally focused on the innkeeper.

"Not bad, shook up and dizzy for a day or two. It wasn't snowing then; if it had been he might have frozen. The constable looked for the fella. They never found him. I reckon he was headed for Matlock or maybe further north."

"Was there a description?"

Mr. Mitchell considered. "Not to say a real accurate one. 'Bout six feet tall, fair hair, blue eyes, dressed well."

"And he wore a distinctive ring on his right hand," Darcy finished.

Mr. Mitchell stared at him. "How in blazes—beggin' your pardon, Mr. Darcy—could you know that? Jasper noticed it especially, said it looked like real gold."

"It is. Where is the constable located?"

"He lives at Highford, six miles east as the crow flies."

Darcy considered. He did not want to divert from their journey, especially if Wickham was on his way to Derbyshire. After a moment's consideration, he said, "Will you get a note to him? The chief magistrate in London and the magistrate in Matlock are looking for this man. He is a very dangerous thief and murderer."

Mr. Mitchell had paled. "I will, sir, as soon as the weather clears. Tomorrow, if it's possible."

Darcy thanked him and went into the parlor to find paper and ink. The peddler had been lucky, or perhaps Wickham simply did not want to draw any more attention to himself than was absolutely necessary. Darcy doubted that the local constable was likely to capture Wickham; he could only put the neighborhood on alert for any other sighting of the fugitive. He had sent an express from London to the Pemberley butler Mr. Niles, apprising him of their departure and warning him to increase the vigilance of Pemberley's defenses against Wickham. But the miscreant knew every foot of Pemberley's grounds as well as the manor house. Vigilance might not be enough. Darcy's only concern now was to reach Pemberley as quickly as possible. God willing, the storm would break and allow them to proceed as planned.

When the note had been left in Mr. Mitchell's competent hands, Darcy went upstairs. They had been given a suite of rooms at the rear of the second floor, two bedrooms with an adjoining dressing room. He knocked softly on the door of Elizabeth's room. Receiving no reply, he opened it only to find the bed turned down, empty. Darcy went through the dressing room where Martin had—with persistent optimism—laid out his nightshirt and robe. Darcy opened the door to his own chamber and found Elizabeth curled in the large bed, already sound asleep. With a smile, Darcy closed the door and allowed Martin, who had just come in, to assist him out of his clothes and into the nightshirt. Darcy had no intention of waking his wife, who was obviously fatigued by the coach trip. Tomorrow they would be in Matlock and by evening at Pemberley. Darcy dismissed his man and joined Elizabeth in bed.

CHAPTER 18

OUT OF THE PAST, INTO THE FUTURE

George Darcy sat before the fireplace in his library, a book resting in his lap, his eyes on the dervish dance of the flames. A small tray with tea and a half-eaten scone sat on the low table to his right. Mr. Niles had discretely laced the tea with a little brandy. George had not had a restful night. William's letter from London said they would be on the road Tuesday morning, expecting to arrive today. George had word that it was snowing south of Matlock. The roads around Pemberley were clear, however, the sky an icy blue.

The Master of Pemberley laid his book aside and leaned his head against the high leather back of his chair, rubbing long fingers over his forehead. The situation with his son occupied his mind more and more as the time for William's arrival with his bride approached. It was reasonable, he thought, to want the Darcy name to continue at Pemberley. It was logical that the only way to accomplish that goal was for his only son to marry and produce a son of his own. But to use his condition as a justification to force William to marry, to actually pick his bride like some Georgian autocrat, was neither.

William sent several short letters during his stay in Town. His admiration for his fiancée was obvious if not overstated. Then the business with Wickham intervened, and his last letter had contained a plea for his father to never be far from assistance in the event George decided to visit Pemberley. He wrote,

> *I know you have no fear of the man, but I beg you, Father, do not allow yourself to be in a position where you are alone with him. He has changed for the worse, committed murder and attempted murder, corrupted young fools to assist him in robbery. He is dangerous and he knows the estate so well that he may easily slip through its defenses. I have written Mr. Niles to apprise him of the possibility of Wickham's presence in the neighborhood. He will have the staff on alert as well.*

As George Darcy closed his eyes, the image of a young, fair-haired boy rose in his mind. George Wickham had always been a charming child, easily making friends, good humored, full of life. George Darcy had thought it well to allow him to be raised with his own son, hoping that the younger boy's easy manners might soften William's reserved and introspective nature. How much of it was a lie from the beginning? Had his namesake always been duplicitous, laughing with them to their faces and at them behind their backs? The elder Mr. Wickham was a sound man, honest, a hard worker, the finest steward Pemberley had known within memory. George Wickham had lost his mother at an early age. Had that changed the boy so drastically, or was it something in his character that only wanted time to emerge, like a hidden disease?

George Darcy knew enough of human nature not to blame himself for the way Wickham had turned out. He had spent considerable time with Wickham, especially after Anne died. The young man had lightened his grief a little, subdued without open sorrow because he was not mourning a family member. But the Master of Pemberley would never have condoned Wickham's licentious behavior. He had given Wickham every opportunity to make a decent, successful life for himself. Instead he threw away every opportunity, wasted himself in dissipation and debauchery, and at last so alienated both father and son that they turned from him, in effect casting him out to make his own way. Apparently that way had been one of crime and dissolution and, finally, murder.

George Darcy pushed aside the weariness that never left him and rose. He hardly stirred from the house these days, dividing his time among the stables, the library, and his study. William would be home very soon with his bride. Did she resent his interference in her life? She was strong willed, much like Anne, without Anne's reticence. If she truly disliked him, she would make it known—and what could he do to change her mind?

A sudden surge of longing for his son's strong, loving presence overwhelmed him. *Oh God*, he prayed. *Let him come home safely. And whatever she feels for me, let them be happy together!*

"Where is Mrs. Younge?"

The woman gave Handley a sour look edged with wariness. "Missus is out for the evenin'. She left me in charge. You want a girl or not?"

Handley considered. He could question this woman or try to talk to the girl he had seen before, who seemed to have no love lost for the proprietress. "Is Belle here?"

"Sure." She put her hand out. It was none too clean, and the nails were broken.

Mrs. Younge's control of the place must be slipping, he thought.

Handley paid her. She turned to a doorway with a heavy red velvet curtain half-open and called sharply, "Belle! Customer!"

After half a minute, the girl Handley remembered appeared in the doorway. When she saw him, her expression lightened, and she came forward readily with a smile a little more natural than professional. She took his arm, and they ascended the stairs to the first floor. Her room was nearly to the end of the hall. It had not changed from his first visit, the wallpaper dull and peeling at the seams, the clotheshorse scarred, bent a bit as if from the weight of carrying years of quickly shed garments. There was a rug of sorts on the floor and a night table beside the iron-framed bed. Belle shut the door and turned to him, her face relaxed. She knew from experience that he would not hurt her.

"I'm glad to see you again," she said.

Handley indicated the bed. "Sit down." When she had done so and looked up at him expectantly, he continued, "The man I asked you about before, Mr. Winter. Have you seen him recently?"

Belle shook her head. She had pretty hair, Handley thought in passing, a soft, light brown, more like a child's than a grown woman's.

"No, not lately. You still lookin' for him?"

"Yes. If you know anything about where he is, Belle, tell me. The magistrates in three cities, including London, are looking for him. He's robbed houses, and he tried to kill a viscount a few nights ago. The man may be dead by now. If you keep back information, you could go to jail. That wouldn't be pleasant for a girl like you."

Belle paled, making Handley ashamed he had frightened her. "Oh Lord, no, I swear I never seen him since he left the last time. He's probably run off somewhere."

"So they think. I don't. He's from Derbyshire. I think he's headed back there. What about Mrs. Younge? The woman downstairs said she's out tonight."

Belle chewed her full lower lip. "That's what we was told. She left Vicky in charge. Never known her to do that before."

"When did she go out?"

"I dunno. I never saw her since dinner. She knows people in town, she must be visitin' somebody."

Handley shook his head. He believed Belle. Mrs. Younge was not about to confide in one of her employees. Still, it was strange. For an abbess to leave her establishment on a working night, especially to leave one of the women in control of things, seemed unlike what he knew of the proprietress.

"Has anyone checked her rooms?"

"Why would they do that?" Belle seemed genuinely puzzled. "She's out."

Handley drew a breath. "Where are her rooms?"

"Downstairs. She has rooms in the back, just past the door to belowstairs. Why…?"

Handley was already at the door. "Just stay here. I've paid for an hour, if I don't come back, you don't have to go down until its up."

Belle nodded. An hour on a working night was a reprieve she was not about to relinquish. She watched Handley leave the room and close the door noiselessly behind him. *Strange man*, she thought, *not like the others.* She wished she had met him before she entered this hell. There might have been a chance for them then.

In the hallway, Handley moved quietly to the stairs. He did not remember them making any noise, still he kept to the inside edge of the treads where they were less likely to make a warning sound under his feet. Fortunately no other visitors were in evidence. He heard voices from the parlor, all women. The velvet curtain masked him as he turned back toward the rear of the building. Handley passed the baize door to the basement kitchen, his hand already in his pocket, closed around the small pistol there. If Mrs. Younge had not actually left the establishment, she was most likely to be in her rooms—if he was lucky, with Wickham.

Handley's heart was racing. He felt a prickling between his shoulder blades, as if someone stood behind him. Chancing a quick glance over his shoulder, he found only the shadowy hall, lit by a lamp in a wall sconce turned low. He drew a deep breath, let it out, pulled the pistol from his pocket, and took hold of the knob on the first door to his right. In a swift gesture, Handley threw the door open and stepped through. The room was dark, empty, silent. Still tense, Handley closed the door and put his back to it. He could make out shapes, a sofa or settee, a sideboard, a chair. As his eyes accustomed to the umbra, he discerned a lamp on a table just to his left. He lit it, and the room took shape around him.

It was a far different environment from Belle's surroundings. The carpet was thick underfoot, the sofa and chair were upholstered in brocaded silk in a bright pattern, the wallpaper looked new with flowers and stripes of yellow, green, and lavender. Mrs. Younge had done well for herself selling flesh. Or perhaps she had another source of income. Handley spared no further consideration on the procuress' finances as he crossed to a second door, pistol in hand. If anyone was in the next room, they had to be aware of his presence by now.

He turned the glass doorknob slowly, flattened his body to the wall beside the opening, and pushed the door in. The inside handle clunked on the wall with a sound that seemed unnaturally loud. For a second or two, Handley stood immobile, muscles constricted, waiting for a shout, a shot, any response. Only a thick silence met him. Carefully he stepped into the doorway. The room was as empty as the parlor, a bedroom of comfortable proportions with a large half-tester bed and a small fireplace. It was as well-furnished as the other room and as uninhabited.

Handley retreated to the hall door, blew out the lamp and cracked the door open. It was still deserted, growing colder as the night progressed. He put the pistol away, eased back down the hall and up the stairs to Belle's room, where he found her dozing on the bed. She opened her eyes when he entered and smiled invitingly.

"You still got half an hour left."

Handley felt suddenly sickened by his surroundings. It was not that he disliked or disdained the woman; he felt sorry for her, but at that moment, all he was able to focus on was the image of his sister's face.

"I appreciate the offer," he said without emphasis, "but I think I'll just rest a bit if you don't mind."

He took the uncertain armchair pushed against a wall and settled as well as he was able on the horsehair stuffing. Belle shrugged. Handley closed his eyes and stretched out his legs. By the time he stirred, Belle had dozed off again. He rose and looked down at her. She looked younger than he had thought, her rouged cheeks bright against her pale skin. Something overcame Handley as he watched her. A darkness inside him that had grown since Juney's death, a disregard for other people, for the law, for what he had long believed were his own principles. He knew without a doubt that it would consume him sooner or later unless he broke free.

"Belle."

She started and sat up sharply before full consciousness returned. Seeing Handley standing at the foot of the bed, she shook off sleep and tried to smile. "You change your mind?"

"How did you come here?"

Belle stared at him. He waited. After a few seconds, she said, "I had nowhere else to go."

"No family, no friends?"

"My mother died when I was little. Eight months ago my father was killed in an accident at the brick factory. The landlord wanted me to give him what Mrs. Younge sells. When I wouldn't, he threw me out."

Her voice was a monotone, but the bitterness in her eyes shook him. She shivered. "I was half-starved when Mrs. Younge found me. She said she had a maid's work at her house if I wanted it. Room and board. I couldn't get here fast enough. Stupid, wasn't I?"

Belle would not look at him. Handley felt as if he were speaking without his own volition, as if a stranger spoke with his voice. "Could you not find other work?"

She hesitated, weighing the question. "He saw to it nobody wanted to hire me, even as a scullery maid." Her voice echoed the despair she felt. "I didn't have money to go anyplace else."

"Would you leave here if you found somebody to give you a decent job?"

"Hire a whore? Nobody's crazy enough to do that."

"If I can, would you leave?"

She shivered. Her eyes darkened. Perhaps she had heard something similar before. "We can't go out unless her watchdog goes with us. She says we owe her for everything. We never have money to pay, so we work it off."

At that moment, although he knew it was not uncommon practice in brothels, Handley thought that Mrs. Younge ought to be hanged alongside of Wickham.

"Yes or no," he demanded, more harshly than he intended.

Belle stood up. "Sure," she said. She took her dressing gown from the footrail of the bed and wrapped it around her. "Why not?"

Belle passed him and opened the door. "I'll be here," she said, and Handley knew she did not believe a word he had said.

She preceded him onto the landing and stepped aside as he continued down the stairs. Maybe, she thought, she should have told him about the room in the attics Dolly kept for visitors she did not want seen by any of the house's inhabitants. As she made her way back to the parlor she rejected the idea. If Mr. Winter was there, they might fight, and who knew how that would end?

⁂

Colonel Richard Fitzwilliam stood at his brother's bedside, gazing down at the slack face. Mr. Watson had discreetly withdrawn to give him privacy. He knew the man in the bed was Nicholas; in spite of that the face almost seemed a stranger's. There were no lines of character, no expression of individuality to distinguish it from a living mask, pale and blank.

"My orders have come through," he told the immobile form. "I'm to rejoin my regiment. I just wanted to say goodbye."

The eyelids flickered. Nicholas made an incoherent sound at the familiar voice and then slipped deeper into unconsciousness. Richard closed his eyes for a moment. It was a useless exercise to stand there talking to a man so near death that he seemed already halfway into another world.

They had never gotten on, he thought. Even in childhood Nick had reminded him more of their aunt Lady Catherine than either of their parents—arrogantly assured, imperious, demanding, always right no matter the facts of a situation. Spoiled and egged on by his grandfather until he believed himself above the rules that applied to lesser men. He was a bully and a braggart, self-obsessed, uncaring for the feelings of those he dealt with, even his own family. He was everything Richard disdained and disliked, everything Richard was not. Blood, they said, was thicker than water; was it thicker than bad character and bad behavior? There had been times in the past when Richard would have been happy to see Nicholas brought down, hard. But not like this. Not by a cowardly act of a cowardly man.

Richard straightened his shoulders. If their positions had been reversed, would he have turned out any better? He reached and took his brother's hand. "Goodbye, Nick. I hope you make it through this. Whether you do or not, I swear to you Wickham will suffer for it."

He turned and left the room, not seeing Mr. Watson reenter from the dressing room, a sadness tinging his professional demeanor. In the hall outside, Lady Matlock waited for her younger son. Try as she might, she was unable to completely hide her distress at his departure. She took his hands in her delicate ones and clasped them tightly.

She looks old, Richard thought with sudden guilt suffusing his mind. *If I do not return, it will be the final blow.* He wondered suddenly if his duty, even his honor, was worth the chance of destroying this strong, brave woman.

"Mother," he began; she squeezed his hands, silencing him.

"Do not, Richard. You are the man you are, you cannot be anyone else. I would not have you anyone else. We will watch over Nicholas. If God grants, he will recover and you will come safely home."

There was nothing he could say. He raised her hands to his lips and kissed them. "Keep well, Mother."

"And you, my son," she whispered.

Richard strode down the hall and descended the stairs swiftly. He had said his goodbyes to his father after breakfast. The earl had maintained a controlled countenance, and the exchange had been brief. As he mounted his horse in the driveway, Richard though of Mary. He had visited her the day before to let her know that he was leaving. She had been stoic until they said their farewells, and then tears had gathered in her eyes.

"I wish I did not have to go." Richard had taken her hands in his, and she had not demurred. "My father wants me to resign my commission and work at our estate. I have refused to abandon my duty to my country and my men.

Mary dropped her gaze to their hands, his large ones covering her smaller fingers. "You must follow your conscience. I want no more than for you to come safely back to me."

Richard's throat constricted. He pressed her hands lightly. "That is all I want as well," he muttered.

Mary withdrew her hands, reached over her head, and drew a narrow silver chain from around her neck, pressing it into his palm. A small silver cross hung from a link in the center.

"This was my grandmother Bennet's. She gave it to me on my sixth birthday. She said that faith would keep me safe. I want you to have it. Wear it or not, just keep it near you. Will you?"

Richard blinked hard several times. He closed his hand around the bright metal, feeling the edges against his palm. He had a sudden mental image of a solemn little girl holding her new treasure, her grandmother's words echoing in her mind.

"I will, Mary," he promised. He slipped the cross and chain into an inner pocket of his uniform tunic. Richard drew her into his arms against all propriety, held her until she gently pulled back.

Mary raised her face to him. "I will pray for you."

Wordless, Richard bent his head and pressed his lips to her forehead. He left the house swiftly, not looking back until he was mounted. Mary stood in the doorway. He raised his hand in salute, trying to keep his face neutral. When he guided the big bay into the driveway, Mary closed the door, leaned her shoulders against it, and let the tears fall unheeded down her cheeks.

At Matlock House Richard put the memory aside, turned his horse out into the street and kicked it into a trot toward the barracks at Windsor. Already the professional soldier took over his mind. Staying alive was a matter of staying focused. And chance. His hand pressed the pocket holding the little silver cross. *And perhaps*, he thought, *of faith.*

"Mr. Darcy?"

George Darcy looked up at Mr. Niles's familiar tap on the door. He had little interest in the ledger before him; Mrs. Reynolds kept the household accounts with exemplary accuracy, requiring only his perfunctory review and approval. Soon, he thought as he called the butler into his study, it would be Mrs. Darcy who kept the accounts. He intended to have William review them at that point. George no longer took an interest in them in any event.

"The gatehouse has signaled, sir. The coach has arrived and is on its way to the house."

George rose and stood a moment more behind his desk. It was time, he told himself, to face what he had created. He followed Mr. Niles into the front hall and saw that the main household servants were assembled, ready to go outside and greet their new mistress. He had not required the more minor servants to attend; he had no wish to overwhelm Elizabeth Darcy with the number of people who would ultimately be under her control.

In the coach, Elizabeth leaned forward to watch out the window for the first sight of Pemberley House. Georgiana was smiling broadly, and William studied her with anticipation mingled with a small reserve of anxiety. How would Elizabeth regard the house, the grounds? He knew she was aware of the size of the estate, but knowing acreage and viewing a home were two very different things.

So far she seemed entranced with the prospect of the woods and lawns. The golden sparkle of the lake in the late sunlight as the carriage slowed for the bridge held her gaze, her lips forming a silent, "Oh." As they left the bridge and the drive turned toward the main structure, Elizabeth looked across at her husband.

"William," she whispered, "I never dreamed anything could be so beautiful."

"I have," he responded, taking her gloved hand and bringing it to his lips. "Do you approve, Mrs. Darcy?"

"How could I not?" Her words might also be taken more than one way.

The coach pulled up in front of the main entrance. Darcy noted the gathered servants, pleased that his father had not assembled the entire interior staff. George Darcy stood at the top of the steps on the semicircular porch, with Mr. Niles to his right and Mrs. Reynolds to his left on the top steps. Below them the servants ranged down the stairs to the drive in two half circles, making a pathway for the arrivals. Darcy assisted Georgiana from the coach and then turned to Elizabeth, taking her hand as she descended.

He felt the pressure on his arm increase as she noted the waiting staff. She straightened and walked sedately at his side, her head up, her smile full of the light he loved. George did not descend to meet them, although he very much wished to. He embraced Georgiana as she joined him, the servants bowing and curtsying to their young mistress. Darcy thought that his father's face seemed strained until George's broad smile as Darcy approached told him that it was a relief for his father to have him at home once more.

Darcy climbed the steps with Elizabeth, the staff executing perfect bows and curtsies as she passed each one. On the porch, Darcy briefly embraced his father. George turned to Elizabeth, uncertain of what her reaction was to be. As he took her hands, she stepped close to him and embraced him in her turn.

"Welcome, Daughter," George said, his voice husky.

"Thank you, Mr. Darcy."

Elizabeth stepped back, and George offered her his arm. Together they entered Pemberley House, Georgiana with Darcy and the others following in order. Inside as a footman and maid took their outerwear, George took his son's arm and spoke too quietly to be overheard.

"When Elizabeth is settled, meet me in the blue suite."

Darcy nodded acquiescence. Mrs. Reynolds had brought forward a maid he recognized as one of the upstairs staff, a pretty girl of twenty-two or -three whose name he recalled was Clara. Elizabeth was smiling at the blushing maid as the housekeeper introduced her. He heard her say that she had assigned Clara to assist Elizabeth for the time being until a proper lady's maid could be hired. Joining his bride, Darcy placed her hand in the crook of his elbow, and together they went upstairs. The third floor held the family rooms. Darcy stopped at a carved and paneled door to the left of the landing. He reached for the glass knob when it was opened by Clara, who had scurried ahead of them by the servants' stairs in order to be at her mistress's command.

Darcy saw that Elizabeth was controlling a laugh with difficulty. He escorted her into the room, spotlessly clean and with new drapes, bed curtains, coverlet, and linen on the full-tester mahogany bed. The green wallpaper, hand blocked with a Georgian wreath pattern in pale yellow, was old but in good repair, as was the green- and gold-striped satin upholstery of the settee and chair. There were several vases of roses and other flowers around the room, gently scenting the air. Elizabeth took it all in, turning slowly until her eyes met Darcy's. She drew a deep, shaky breath, her hand seeking the comfort of his.

"You will be able to change anything you wish," he said. "These were my mother's rooms and have not been renovated for some time."

Elizabeth shook her head. "It is perfectly fine as it is. I shall think about updating it in the future, for now I am content with everything."

Darcy kissed her hand and stepped back. "My father wishes to speak to me. I shall return in half an hour and escort you downstairs for tea."

She nodded. Darcy left her to the maid's ministrations and returned to the first floor where the blue suite was located. George Darcy stood at the window of the small sitting room, staring out over the gardens visible from the room's vantage point. He smiled as his son entered the room at his call, shutting the door behind him.

"You wanted to see me, Father?" Darcy began, before he noticed the desk by the wall with several personal items of his father's on the polished surface. A bookcase held volumes he knew were George Darcy's particular favorites. A miniature of his mother in a silver frame rested on a table next to another vase of glasshouse roses. "What is this?"

"I have moved to the blue suite. You will be occupying the master's chambers. Before you protest, there is a completely practical reason for my decision. Climbing to the third floor is becoming more and more of a burden. I prefer to save my strength for other things. And how can I occupy the master's chambers if Elizabeth is to have her rightful place as the mistress, which she is in everything but name? This suite was designed for a couple, it has more than enough space for my needs. And it is easier for Thalman to reach me when he is required."

Darcy said nothing. He stood with his head bowed, absorbing this new evidence of his father's debility. When their eyes met, his were masked in a way that told George Darcy his son recognized the inevitable.

"Very well, Father. I told Elizabeth that we would have tea shortly. We made the journey in less time than I might have normally taken, and she needs to rest."

"I have ordered tea served in her private sitting room in a quarter hour. I have something for her."

Darcy raised an eyebrow. George grinned in a way that made his son's heart lurch; it was so much the man he knew and loved. "A gift, so soon? She will be overwhelmed."

"I doubt it. I think it would take more than a gift to overwhelm your wife. Come," he strode to the door. "I believe I can make it to the second floor before tea arrives."

With an answering twitch of his lips, Darcy followed his father from the room.

A fortnight after the wedding of Darcy and Elizabeth, Lady Agatha Quintain prepared to travel north. Her health seemed repaired by rest and Marie's constant watchful presence. It was time to go forward with her plans. Sitting once more in her parlor, she rang for Mr. Hughes. When the butler arrived, Lady Agatha handed him a letter composed two weeks ago, held until this moment.

"Send this by express, please, Mr. Hughes, and hire that traveling coach you spoke of. Marie is packing my trunks for a stay in the north. I wish to leave the day after tomorrow. I will leave you the direction of where I will be staying in the event of an emergency."

"Yes, my lady."

As Mr. Hughes withdrew, Lady Agatha saw again the message written in her small, neat hand:

My dear Petti,

We have had some excitement here in Town. Four house robberies during society balls and two assaults, the latest ending with the Earl of Matlock's heir near death. I find the thought of country air most appealing at the moment. Therefore, as you have kindly invited me to visit you several times, I shall accept your invitation.

If it is not inconvenient, I should like to start north Monday next. I shall stop over a day in Matlock and reach you on Thursday afternoon or Friday morning, weather permitting. I look forward to seeing you and any new additions to your collection of "timepieces."
Gratefully, your very old friend,
Aggie

Aristotle Socrates Pettigrew (whose father had an obvious admiration for Greek philosophers), known to his close friends as Petti, awaited the arrival of his guest with anticipation. He had been one of Cedric Quintain's earliest patrons and supporters, the portrait of himself done by the artist hanging in pride of place over the fireplace in the great hall. It depicted him in his scholar's robes, midnight blue with just the *smallest touch* of silver trim. His left hand rested on an impressively thick volume, title not shown, nor could Petti remember what it had been about. His right hand lay protectively on an elaborate automaton. Petti's family fortune had come—as did many in these times—from a fluke.

His grandfather, Samuel Pettigrew, was a clockmaker in Manchester. He was well known, and his clocks valued by the aristocracy and gentry; while he made a good living, it was not a highly lucrative field of endeavor. His son, Lucius, Petti's father, was also a clockmaker, although not as clever as the original. In his twenties, he traveled to France on business and saw a working automaton for the first time.

Automata had been known since at least the ancient Greeks, whom Lucius greatly admired, used chiefly in temples to demonstrate the power of the particular god or goddess. There were examples from later centuries as well, and while Lucius had read of them with interest, this was the first one he had seen in use. It was a relatively simple example of the craft, an elephant in full regalia that walked, turned its head from side to side, raised and lowered its trunk, and made what were assumed to be elephant noises. The fact that its trappings were of rich materials and jeweled added to its appeal. Lucius was captivated and inspired. If the Greeks could do it and the French could do it, a Pettigrew could do it better. He found an automaton he was able to buy and took it home to consult with his father. Samuel Pettigrew agreed with his son in principle, however he had no interest in taking on a new line of work.

Aristotle was possessed of a head for business and a natural charm that made him a perfect salesman. Realizing his son's potential, Lucius sent Aristotle to university. He also had hopes of making lucrative contacts among the upper classes. Without rustling the leaves of the social jungle Aristotle made friends among all ranks of students and faculty, and by furnishing his rooms with several examples of his grandfather's art quietly visible at gatherings held there, he referred orders for clocks from his unwitting customers to his grandfather.

"Oh yes," he would say deprecatingly. "I do not usually speak of it, but my grandfather is quite a superior craftsman. His Royal Highness has several of his clocks at Carleton House."

It was Petti's genius that no one ever accused him of practicing trade. He was simply doing friends a favor. It was his father's genius that he saw an opportunity and grasped it with both hands. While automata were sold as toys to the very wealthy, they took time and delicate effort to construct. This time and the cost made them less profitable than he had hoped. As Lucius Pettigrew experimented with new methods of improving the effects he could produce with his creations, he invented an innovative gearing system.

Mills producing cloth, carpets, and other goods were springing up all over England. Realizing the potential of his new system Lucius patented it and offered it to a local mill owner. From there, it was a matter of time until the Pettigrew system was used throughout the burgeoning industry. The profits had made him a rich man and his son even richer.

Petti's butler, Mr. Turner, knocked on the door of the drawing room to announce that Lady Agatha's coach had pulled up outside. Petti hurried with his bustling walk to the main entry, where Mr. Turner was opening the door to Lady Agatha's footman. Once outside, Petti hurried down the stone steps to greet his guest just as she emerged from a large traveling coach, her maid behind her. She smiled at him with genuine warmth, indicating the wide facade of his home with its two square crenellated towers at the ends.

"Hello, Petti. I had quite forgotten how imposing your castle is."

" 'A poor thing, but mine own.' Welcome, dear Aggie. It has been far too long since we saw one another."

He took her hand, kissed it gallantly, and tucked it through the crook of his arm. "I have several new examples to show you. Do come inside, this weather is growing colder by the day. We shall have more snow by tomorrow."

They mounted the steps to the ten-foot-tall, ironclad double doors. From there, the way was through a small entry, closed by less imposing doors on the far side, which made it a barrier to the cold air from the exterior. As the great hall spread out around them, the butler took Lady Agatha's outerwear and summoned the waiting housekeeper to show her maid to the guest chambers while Petti and Lady Agatha went into the drawing room.

"Was your journey very difficult?" he asked as they were seated before the hearth, where logs hissed and purred amid the ruddy flames.

"Not very. It was not snowing when I left London. We encountered a minor storm by the time we reached Matlock, so it was fortunate that I intended to stay over a day."

Tea was brought in by a maid, a plump country girl in a neat stuff dress and white cap. She arranged the tea tray, poured out, and waited for instructions with a genuine smile on her pink face. Petti dismissed her and turned to his guest. His round-cheeked face, so like a schoolboy's, glowed with anticipation.

"You must tell me all about these robberies." He sipped his tea, leaning forward toward Lady Agatha. "We hardly ever have any crime worse than poaching or petty theft here. And I have seen in the papers that Viscount Maresford was severely injured by the thief."

"Yes." She hesitated, gathering her thoughts. "He was still near death the last I heard of it. The criminal who escaped is a violent, dangerous man. Fortunately, he is probably in Scotland by now."

"I certainly hope so!"

Lady Agatha gave her host a description of the Matlock's ball, leaving out her personal involvement. He listened with interest, without the avidity of the true gossip. When she had finished, he put his cup aside and took her hand.

"I am glad that you left before the crime was discovered," he said. Then, with the freedom of an old friend, he added, "We are both of us getting too old for so much excitement." Petti rose. "Let me show you to your chambers. We keep country hours, and I am sure you would like to rest before dinner. After dinner, I will introduce you to my latest acquisition." His eyes brightened with enthusiasm.

Lady Agatha smiled. "I shall look forward with great anticipation to seeing it."

In her rooms, Marie had everything arranged and ready. After Lady Agatha refreshed herself, Marie assisted her mistress to remove her traveling dress, unlaced the short stays she wore, and helped her into a woolen robe. Lady Agatha lay down on the bed, and Marie spread the coverlet over her. The room had been warmed by a fire in the bedroom hearth. Lady Agatha closed her eyes; she had found of late that she required more rest than previously. Marie knew when to wake her to dress for dinner.

Old age, she thought wryly. But she knew it was more than that. The burden she carried weighed far more heavily on her than her years. She had come here to resolve it. That must be her first and only goal. She slipped into a doze with Cedric's name on her lips.

Dinner was just the two of them, the conversation ranging over several subjects of interest to them both. By the time the dessert course was cleared, Lady Agatha noticed that her friend kept glancing at the windows, where the open drapes were framed against the dusk outside.

"We are losing the light," Lady Agatha remarked. "Perhaps we should look at your new timepiece before it grows dark."

Petti rose as a footman pulled out Lady Agatha's chair. "Yes, let us do that. We can have our coffee afterward."

He escorted her to the central hall, where the butler had already brought his greatcoat, gloves, and hat from a closet in an alcove. Marie came downstairs with Lady Agatha's things and assisted her into them, making sure that she was well protected from the cold. With her gloved hand tucked safely into the crook of his arm, Petti led her down a cross hall to a low, massive door. A footman opened it, and they went out into the chill blue evening, taking a flagged path into a garden set out in the fashion of a Roman villa.

Amid walks lined by shrubs and plants, everywhere one looked were set sundials. Large ones, small ones, some on bases, some on natural elements, such as flat rocks or tree stumps. They were stone, marble, plaster, bronze, decorated with shell, metal, gold, silver, some so simple their age radiated like rays of the sun. A few bore sayings; more had designs etched into their gnomon or dials that were inlaid with semiprecious stones, with mother-of-pearl, with various subtle shades of gold. Petti led Lady Agatha into a side walk, stopping before a low plinth on which rested a sundial so weathered that she wondered if it could possibly be accurate.

"Where on earth did you find this, Petti?"

He was smiling with the pride of ownership, and something more. "It was dug up on the site of an ancient temple on the island of Delos. A man who has found sundials for me in the past contacted me about it. Because of its condition, the owner of the property felt it was not commercially important and had literally thrown it onto a scrap heap. My contact bought it for a small sum, and I bought it from him for a larger one."

"Delos," Lady Agatha murmured thoughtfully. "Is that not where Apollo and Artemis were born in the myth?"

"Indeed. The temple may have been to Artemis, since there is a partial inscription with what appears to be one of her honorifics, Potnia Theron, 'Mistress of Animals,' but it is so weathered and chipped I cannot be certain."

Lady Agatha held her pelisse closer around her body. The wind had a bite of snow in it. Noticing her apparent discomfort, Petti said with concern, "Come, let us go inside. We can tour the garden tomorrow if you like, unless it snows."

She nodded, took his arm, and they proceeded back to the house. Artemis, Roman Diana, the Greek goddess of the hunt, archer, protector of maidens and women in childbirth, the twin of Apollo. She was not a superstitious woman, but Lady Agatha felt a chill in her bones that had nothing to do with the weather.

Did you send me here, Cedric? Or is it only a coincidence, this ancient device for measuring the hours and the days that never come again, dedicated to a huntress who was also a twin?

CHAPTER 19

CHRISTMAS SURPRISES

In a small stand of trees behind Mrs. Younge's, Handley waited with his horse for any sign of Wickham's arrival or departure. Used to long night watches at sea, he was not bothered by the snow-chilled air. He had thrown a blanket he found in the nearby stable over his horse to keep it from stiffening up. His only qualm was that he had missed his quarry. If Wickham had not come to Mrs. Younge's, he might be anywhere, and the trail so long and ruthlessly followed would end, leaving Handley to start over again. He could not allow himself to believe that.

His separation pay was nearly gone. Without a new source of funds, there was no money for bribes, no money to keep up the search. Handley pulled the woolen scarf Juney had knitted him for their last Christmas together higher over his face, tugged his collar tighter around his neck, and carefully walked back and forth in the dense shadows. He could not afford stiffened muscles if he needed to confront his prey.

Shredded clouds drifted across a waning moon low in the sky. It was no more than an hour until the first gray of dawn invaded his hiding place. A bird called fretfully from somewhere nearby. Aware of a rattle of wheels approaching, Handley tensed. He caught his horse's bridle and put his hand over its nose to silence any sound it might make if another horse came near. His body tensed, every sense focused on the noise of the wagon that pulled around the corner from the main street and halted behind the house. The driver clambered down, hitched his cart horse to an iron ring in a post placed for that purpose, and withdrew a large box from the vehicle. Handley watched him carry it to the rear door, pause, and then knock quietly.

Handley knew Wickham's age and general appearance although they had never met face to face. This man was older, smaller, and had a furtive air about him. *Some illegal delivery*, Handley thought. Why else arrive well outside normal daylight hours? Still wary, he waited for the man to return. It was a good fifteen minutes later when the driver shuffled out the door and untied his horse. The animal shied and shook its head, stepping in place. The driver slung a small sack into the wagon, pulled himself up onto the seat, and sat hunched forward. He slapped the reins on the broad rump and drove on in the opposite direction.

The wagon disappeared down another alley. Something nagged at Handley's mind, something not quite right. He knew of Wickham's ability to act out different parts with considerable success. The driver had worn the same coat and hat and walked the same way. Handley's horse shifted its weight, tossing its head against his tightened hold on its bridle. The horse…the horse had not known the man who untied it.

Handley jerked the blanket free, dropped it and swung into the saddle. Cursing silently, he urged his mount forward. Passing the house at a canter, he turned down the same alley as the cart and came out onto the silent main street. Right and left, no sign of the man or the wagon. Handley turned his mount north, desperately scanning the buildings and cross streets. He was almost to the country beyond the inhabited area when he saw it; the wagon stranding alone at the edge of the road, its shafts empty. Horse and driver were gone.

⟡

The letter from Colonel Fitzwilliam reached Pemberley three days after Darcy and Elizabeth arrived. Darcy was in the study, going over wheat production for the past year and proposed future crop rotations, when Mr. Niles brought in the post. His father was transferring much of the estate business to him now that he had married, while Elizabeth was in the process of learning her various housekeeping duties from a very happy Mrs. Reynolds. In Richard's usual manner, the missive was short. After hoping that all was going well with his cousin and Elizabeth, he continued,

> *Sir Lionel Arthur has finally presented the chief magistrate with a letter written by Sir Colin, supposedly left where his father only just found it. It appears to be a suicide note and names Wickham as the instigator of the robberies and the one who attacked Nick, in spite of the fact that the guards saw two men at the window. Sir Lionel insists that he expects his son's body to be dragged from the Thames any day. I am afraid I have to doubt his sincerity.*
>
> *The only useful item in the letter is the name of Wickham's fence, a man known as the Dutchman. His real name is Huygens, a small-time pawnbroker and jeweler. They are looking for him now. He may know where Wickham has gone. I have received my orders and will depart in two days for the Peninsula. Give my best to Elizabeth and Uncle George. As they say in Spain, Vaya con Dios.*

Darcy rubbed long fingers over his eyes. It was so typically Richard, the sunny bonhomie of his nature wintered into the grave discipline of the professional soldier. It had always been so since Richard had taken up his first commission. Duty was more than a word to his cousin; it was a way of life. Every time Richard returned to his regiment he accepted the possibility of death as an elemental part of his commitment to the life he had chosen. Until he finally resigned his commission or died, it would be so.

Darcy put the letter away at a second tap on the door. This time it opened before he could call the visitor in to reveal Elizabeth. Darcy's face lit at sight of her; he rose and came around the desk to take her hands and smile down at her teasing expression.

"I thought you might be ready for some tea," she said.

"That would be most welcome."

Darcy held her eyes, and then he very deliberately leaned to kiss her. It began simply enough; as her arms went around him and his hands stroked her back, the kiss developed rapidly into something much more intimate. Darcy broke the kiss at last, his breath coming rapidly.

"Could we not have the tea somewhere more private? Like our chambers?"

Elizabeth's breathless voice shimmered with laughter. "William! You will scandalize the servants."

"Hardly. I expect that by now most of them know we are married."

She shook her head. "I asked for the tea to be brought here."

Darcy growled, "Oh, hang the tea!" when a knock on the door told them it had arrived.

He quickly returned to his chair behind the desk. It would certainly scandalize the servants should they see him in his present state of anticipation. Elizabeth called the maid to come in when she had seated herself on the settee before the windows. Her face was rosy but sedate. As soon as the maid was dismissed, Darcy joined her. She made his tea as he liked it and poured her own, sitting back.

After sipping her tea, she said, "I wanted to speak to you about Christmas. I have been talking to Georgiana and Mrs. Reynolds, so I understand that the holidays have been celebrated quietly for the past few years. Considering Father Darcy's health, I do not want to initiate any elaborate festivities. I thought a small dinner party for your close friends in the neighborhood might be appropriate. It would give me a chance to meet the people we will be seeing regularly, and for them to meet me. If you and Father Darcy agree, perhaps the week before Christmas?"

Looking into her beloved face, Darcy understood what she did not say. That this might well be the last Christmas all of them were able to celebrate the Season with those neighbors who had been the Darcys' friends for many years. He leaned and kissed her lips lightly.

"Ask him, my love, but I do not think he will disagree. It is the perfect answer to this holiday."

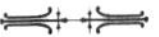

Sir Seymour Rhys-Withers was awakened by his valet at what any civilized human being would consider the ungodly hour of six o'clock in the morning. The valet was apologetic rather than apprehensive. Having been with Sir Seymour for some years he understood that occasionally a magistrate was called out at uncivilized hours, and the tense young man at the door was accompanied by a constable who also requested Sir Seymour's immediate attention. It was, therefore, some ten minutes later that the magistrate entered his study in a dressing gown and house slippers to confront his visitors.

"Well, Rogers," the magistrate spoke directly to his constable, "what is the cause of this rather early visit?"

Rogers stood straighter. "Its that fellow we've been looking for, sir. This man," he indicated his companion, "says he followed the man from Mrs. Younge's to the edge of town in Clark's wagon and lost him."

This rather disjointed statement brought a frown to Sir Seymour's narrow brow. He was a tall, thin man, his brown hair receding around a widow's peak, his thin lips drawn down a little at the corners. He said to the stranger, "Who are you, sir?"

"My name is Handley, Sir Seymour. I've been on Wickham's trail for months, since he murdered my sister in Newcastle. He left London two days ago. I knew of his friendship with Mrs. Younge and went directly there."

"Mrs. Younge?" Sir Seymour rarely allowed himself more than irritation, but the name of the brothel keeper brought out an anger he did not attempt to conceal. "Rogers, I thought you and Gage were watching the house?"

The constable went pale. "We were, sir, me in front and Gage in back." His voice wavered, the words rushing out., "Gage went inside to…to see if there was any sign of anything…"

"To sport with one of the women, you mean. I shall have something to say to Mr. Gage. So, Mr. Handley." He turned to the stranger. "You saw Wickham at Mrs. Younge's?"

"Yes, sir. I also went in and questioned one of the women. No one had seen Wickham—or Winter, as he is known to them—and Mrs. Younge was supposed to be out for the evening. I searched her private rooms; they were empty. I went to the back of the property to wait. Just before dawn a man parked a wagon at the rear of the building. He went in, and about a quarter of an hour later someone wearing the man's hat and coat came out and took the wagon away. I realized too late," he added bitterly, "that the horse had reacted to him as a stranger. By the time I got after him, he'd disappeared."

Sir Seymour digested this intelligence in silence. "Where is Mr. Gage now?"

"Keepin' watch on the house, sir," Rogers admitted reluctantly.

Sir Seymour knew the old saying about the barn door and the horse as well as anyone. He had hoped to be the one to capture the villain and return him to London, thus winning a point over his city compatriots and the gratitude of a prominent local nobleman. Instead, if he did not handle this cock-up carefully, he would look a fool. The magistrate turned to Mr. Handley.

"Colonel Fitzwilliam spoke of you when he was here several days ago, Mr. Handley. I have been asked to offer you any assistance you require, including funds to further your hunt for Wickham. If you will wait for a few minutes until I can dress, I will accompany you back to Mrs. Younge's. Rogers," Sir Seymour's voice altered instantly to something far less cordial, "you will return to Mrs. Younge's and remain on watch with Mr. Gage until I arrive. You will *not* enter the premises. Either of you."

"Yes, sir!"

Rogers decamped as swiftly as if the floor had been on fire under his feet. Sir Seymour called a footman and sent him to rouse another constable. He rang for the butler and ordered coffee brought to the dining room, where he left Mr. Handley to wait impatiently for his return. When the coffee arrived, it was accompanied by fresh scones. Mr. Handley realized suddenly that he had not eaten since a hasty dinner the day before and made good use of the provender until Sir Seymour entered the room.

"If you are ready, Mr. Handley, we will proceed. I intend to arrest Mrs. Younge and her bodyguard for harboring a fugitive."

Mr. Handley said as they left the house, "You know she entices women into her brothel and then keeps them prisoner?"

"I have heard rumors to that effect. Thus far none of the women will testify against her."

"Not with that ex-boxer around she uses to keep them under control. I expect some of them will be willing to speak out against her now."

Sir Seymour nodded. He entered his carriage, which had been brought to the front of the residence. Mr. Handley mounted his horse and followed the magistrate through the waking streets. Lights glowed in a few upper windows where ordinary people were preparing for the day. The law would take care of Mrs. Younge. He had his own priority to follow. As soon as they arrived in the street where the house was located, Mr. Handley tied his horse and followed the magistrate and the two new constables to the door. Rogers and a frightened-looking fellow officer kept to the rear of the group. Sir Seymour nodded, and without warning, the two constables put their shoulders to the front door and sent it crashing into the hall.

The bouncer, who slept in a bed cubby off the hall, came roaring out with a club in one hand, his battered face distorted with fury. As three of the constables subdued him, Mr. Handley slipped past the tangle of arms, legs, and batons and ran up the stairs. He opened Belle's door without bothering to knock to find her pressed against the iron footrail of the bed, her face white and her eyes large and dark with fear. She was dressed in a plain muslin dress with an old shawl over her shoulders. A small satchel sat at her feet.

Handley picked it up, took her arm in the other hand and checked the landing. She made no protest as he led her to the servants' stairs at the rear of the building. In the kitchen a harried-looking woman was preparing dough for the day's baking.

"I don't think you'll be needing that," Handley told her, pausing in the doorway. "Mrs. Younge will be having her meals in the local jail from now on."

When he and Belle stood beside his horse, Handley said, "You believed me when I said I'd be back."

"I wanted to believe you." Belle looked down, not meeting his eyes. "If you had not come back by the time our keeper woke, I was going to leave—or try to."

Handley glanced back at Mrs. Younge's. He set Belle's satchel on the ground, lifted her to sit sideways in the saddle, handed her the bag, and swung up behind her. As the horse moved down the street at a walk, he felt her shiver.

"Is there anyone who runs a boardinghouse where you can stay for a time?"

"There's one woman who'll take me," she replied. "She used to be in the business. You're not staying?"

"I'm heading north after Wickham. I'll have enough money to leave you set for a month or so. After that, if I'm not back, take the post chaise to Lambton, its about two days north of here, and see a man named Fitzwilliam Darcy. His family owns a big estate not far from the town. Tell him I sent you. He knows who I am, he'll see you're taken care of."

Belle said in a flat voice, "You don't want to take me with you."

"I can't. I have to travel fast if I have any chance of catching up Wickham before he makes it into Scotland. I can't let the bastard get away."

Slowly she nodded. "I'll wait here for a month. After that, I'll make my own way."

"As you choose."

Handley felt a moment of sharp regret. Then he took firm hold of his emotions and guided the horse to the boardinghouse at Belle's direction without further comment.

"It is odd that you should be speaking of the Darcys.," Petti leaned back in his chair before the drawing room fireplace.

The small dinner party he had arranged with a few friends and neighbors had gone off well. His cook was superb, his housekeeper made sure everything was up to his impeccable standards, and his staff served à la Russe without in any way disturbing the flow of conversation or dining. Best of all, several of the invitees remembered Lady Agatha from her girlhood in Derbyshire, and others knew of her husband's fame. They treated her with respect and interest. She responded in kind, bringing an added layer to the entire affair.

"How, 'odd'?"

Swathed in a cashmere shawl, the lady sipped her tea and considered him over the rim of the delicate porcelain cup.

"I do not mean it in a derogatory way, my dear Aggie," he assured her. "Just that I very recently had a small business dealing with George Darcy. He asked me to find a special clock for him, a gift for his future daughter-in-law. Or I expect she is his daughter-in-law by now?"

"They were married last Tuesday fortnight," Lady Agatha informed him. A small smile Petti could not quite identify lifted the corners of her mouth. "She will be very appreciative of anything unusual."

"I obtained the clock from a friend of mine." Petti's tone was casual, but pride inflected it nonetheless. "It was made for an Austrian noblewoman. She died before it could be presented, and her husband sold it to my friend. It is quite beautiful, fire-gilt bronze with hand-painted porcelain panels, scenes of a lady in a garden, with side panels of birds and butterflies. There is a golden bird as a handle on the top. He was very pleased with it."

Lady Agatha made no reply for a time, sipping her tea. Lifting her head, she said without looking directly at her host, "How well do you know Mr. Darcy?"

"The son, hardly at all. The father and I have had some business transactions in the past, not recently. He purchased several of my grandfather's clocks for Pemberley at about the time of his marriage to Lady Anne Fitzwilliam. I found a few other items for him over the years until Lady Anne died, and then he withdrew from most social contact. He is hardly seen anymore except among family and close friends."

"There is a rumor in Town that he is ill. He is my nephew, you know."

Lady Agatha put out the words without inflection. Petti studied her face, wondering why the conversation had suddenly centered on a man his guest had probably never met.

"I had not heard of an illness. Of course, he tends to be reclusive, so…" Petti let the sentence fade with a shrug. "Young Darcy is active in managing the estate; he is said to be astute and progressive in his methods of farming. Both men have excellent reputations with their neighbors, tenants, and the local tradesmen."

"No scandals, no whispers?"

She might have been jesting; Petti felt a shade of discomfort color his perception. "No, definitely not," he responded somewhat more firmly than might be expected. "Very moral and upright men. Some of young Darcy's university classmates called him the Monk, because he refused to participate in their revels."

"I made his acquaintance in London recently," Lady Agatha said without emphasis, "as well as that of his fiancée. She is an unusual woman. I do not think she would be easily dominated, so it is as well if he is not the sort to try."

She then let the subject drop and moved on to other casual discourse. Petti relaxed. He wondered if his old friend still harbored ill feelings against the Darcys after so many years. She had suffered from her father's well-known cruelty no doubt, only that had been many years ago. Lady Agatha had escaped him and married happily. With a mental shrug, Petti attended to the conversation. He did not believe her a vengeful person, and what, after all, could she accomplish now?

"I believe," she said finally, "I shall retire. I have not the stamina I once had." She seemed contemplative as Petti walked with her into the main hall. Pausing, Lady Agatha weighed some inner decision before she added, "After the holidays, I believe I shall make a visit to my old haunts. I doubt I shall see Derbyshire again."

"Of course, Aggie. If there is any way I can be of help, please tell me."

As he made the offer, he wondered why she really wished to visit places where her memories could only be painful. Perhaps she wanted to visit her mother's and brother's graves. Petti was an astute businessman, used to reading the subtle shades of meaning beneath words. Some inner voice warned him that, despite her lack of obvious emotion, Lady Agatha's desire to return to her girlhood home was not as innocent as it appeared.

"Thank you, Petti." Her smile was genuine.

As Petti watched her ascend the stairs on the arm of her maid, he wondered for the first time if the reason for her visit Lady Agatha had given was the entire one.

The shop was no more than a narrow oblong between two larger buildings, dark with age and neglect. In the small bay window on the street a few tawdry trinkets tried to assume the look of valuable objects, and failed. The interior resembled a painting that age had blended into a dark chiaroscuro. A long counter ran from front to back along the left side with cabinets lining the wall behind. The only light except the window, which was so dirty it might as well have been opaque, was a lamp sitting on the counter.

The proprietor was scarcely less wrinkled than his ill-fitting suit. Thin, stooped, with a fringe of grayish hair resembling down around his otherwise-bald head, his face was as narrow as his premises and nearly as repulsive. Looks, however, concerned his customer even less than the owner. Wickham kept an eye on the street just visible as motion beyond the smeared glass panes, while the proprietor sorted through the contents of a leather bag, his thin fingers picking over the necklaces, rings, earrings, and bracelets with a jeweler's loupe. When he lifted his head, it was to survey the man before him with calculation. He reached for a flyer lying farther down the counter and slapped it in front of Wickham.

"You might want to read that before you try to flog these to anyone else."

Wickham took up the paper, held it closer to the lamp, and swore. It was his description and a description of the loot he and Colin Arthur had stolen from the Matlocks. There was a reward of five thousand pounds for his capture. Wickham swore again, harshly. He threw the flyer aside and leaned over the counter, his face paling.

"Where did this come from?"

"The local magistrate. I doubt there is a magistrate in any city of size who doesn't have one, and they are being handed out to pawnshops and jewelers. And there are Bow Street investigators looking for you, paid by an earl they say. You are hotter, my friend, than a Guy Fawkes bonfire."

Wickham's face darkened. "I need five hundred pounds."

"And I need to stay out of quod." The older man finished replacing the baubles in the bag, pulled the drawstring tight, and handed it back to Wickham. "Right now I wouldn't give you fifty pounds for the lot. I'd have to hold it for months until the hue and cry died down, and frankly the quality isn't good enough to take the risk."

"What do you mean?"

"They're nice, not top drawer. Settings look fine, the stones are second grade at best. If these are from a nob, he's a cheap bastard."

For a moment, Wickham stood frozen with disbelief. Then he laughed. The sound made the old man shiver. He said quickly,

"We're only about fifty miles here from the border, maybe two or three days changing horses at the coaching inns. Once you're over it, the Scots don't give a damn where the stuff comes from. That's your best chance."

Anger raged in Wickham's mind, a ravening beast with prey in front of him. He had put his hand on the pocket holding his pistol when some scrap of reason stopped him. A shot, especially in close quarters, was very loud, loud enough to bring someone to investigate. He could not afford to be seen and perhaps captured. He picked up the bag and left the shop without another word.

When he was gone, the proprietor pulled out a stained handkerchief and mopped his brow. In spite of the fact the stones were actually quite good, he wanted nothing to do with them or the fugitive. He picked up the flyer, considered going to the magistrate, then rejected the idea. His customers did not tolerate informers. Cold with the realization of how close he had come to death, he looked the way Wickham had gone and then went and locked the front door. He had had enough of business for one day.

On the street, Wickham glanced quickly around at the oblivious passersby before he made his way back to the shabby boardinghouse where he had obtained a room. The owner was a Scotswoman in her forties with a strong dislike of the English aristocracy. Wickham had spun her a tale of losing his Scottish mother who, with her last breath, begged him to return to the border village where she was born. Mrs. Falkirk, he thought with a satisfied smirk, swallowed the story and let him have the room for half price.

The irony amused Wickham. He had taken the Dutchman's advice and had his profits from the robberies converted into diamonds, now sewn very carefully into his hat between the crown and its lining, a small fortune he dared not use until he arrived at some place where English law did not reach. Once in the small, scrupulously clean room, Wickham got out a bottle of cheap brandy and a glass and sat on the bed. The night table served to hold his libation while he thought about what he was to do next.

The need to revenge himself on George Darcy still burned brightly; self-preservation overruled any immediate action against him. Darcy would be at Pemberley by now with his bride; her presence would make both men even more aware of danger. Let them settle in, Wickham thought, grimacing at the burn of the liquor in his throat. He might as well go on to Scotland until their guard relaxed.

Wickham's next move was to shave his small beard and mustache. Before he left the boardinghouse, he meant to use enough tint to color his hair a reddish hue. That and the secondhand clothing he wore was all the disguise available until he crossed the border, where no disguise would be necessary. Wickham finished the glass, rose, and pulled out his satchel. In two days he would be in safe territory, where he did not have to look over his shoulder every minute. Even the Bow Street investigators knew better than to follow him into Scotland. Then, in time, when the hunt died down, Wickham knew he could safely return to Derbyshire and his revenge.

The first impression of Charles Bingley's sleep-drugged mind was a memory: he and his younger sister, Caroline, slipping downstairs on Christmas morning to look at their presents. The sound had the same hushed, furtive rustle. *Nonsense,* his wakening mind retorted. *I am a grown man. I can look at my Christmas presents if I want to. Is it Christmas morning already?*

Somehow that did not seem right, although Bingley was aware that the joyous holiday was close. He raised his head from the bedclothes. With the acute clarity of hearing, sometimes realized when the other senses are dulled, Bingley heard the words, "Do not wake the master." At that moment he found himself out of bed and standing in his nightshirt, shivering with cold, staring in fear at the door to the hallway.

Bingley grabbed up his robe, slid his feet into house slippers and ran to the door. He opened it to find two maids carrying steaming buckets of water toward the room where his beloved wife had been confined to bed for the past fortnight. He caught the arm of the nearest servant, causing her to splash water onto the carpet strip underfoot. She gave a little cry and backed away, her eyes wide.

"Is she…my wife…is she…has she…"

"Please, sir, I have to get the water to Mr. Fortesque. Mrs. Bingley has begun labor."

Bingley stared after her as she scurried down the hall. His lips trembled. He was cold and hot all at once, his stomach clenched, and he thought he might throw up. Jane! His beloved wife, his heart, his soul, was giving birth. Blind and deaf to everything else, he did not hear his man, Lovell, come up until the valet spoke twice.

"Sir, you need to come and dress. There is nothing you can do at present. I am sure Mrs. Bingley is in excellent hands."

Bingley turned stiffly to his manservant. "I need to go to her."

"No, sir, not until you are dressed and presentable. Mr. Fortesque is with her; he is reckoned one of the best accoucheurs in London. I am having your bath drawn. As soon as you are dressed, you can inquire after Mrs. Bingley. Please, sir, before any more of the servants see you."

The last was delivered in something like desperation. Suddenly aware of his condition, Bingley let the valet lead him to his dressing room, where a steaming tub was soon ready. The following half hour passed in a haze of familiar activities. Lovell helped him bathe, shaved him, and assisted him into a comfortable suit, low collar, and house shoes. No use dressing formally when the activity in the birthing room might take hours. By the time the valet finished, Bingley was as irritable as his sunny nature allowed.

"Enough, Lovell!" Bingley turned from his valet's efforts to brush his jacket. "I am going to see my wife, not the Prince Regent!"

He left his dressing room and hurried to the door of the birthing room, fear again possessing him. Jane had been confined to bed by Mr. Fortesque, the accoucheur, for just over two weeks, since false labor pains had left her weakened. The pregnancy had gone well for the most part. Since that incident, Jane had grown visibly wan, her natural calm nature submerged in what Bingley could only believe was a growing debility.

He stopped with his hand gripping the doorknob, all the terror he had not dared acknowledge flooding his mind. *Oh God! What if she is not strong enough;., what if she. . . .* Bingley dared not even think the word. He knocked weakly on the panel, to have it opened by Mr. Fortesque himself. The birthing specialist, a new medical discipline growing ever more popular with the *ton*, opened the door wider and gestured Bingley in.

"Mrs. Bingley is resting. You may spend a few minutes with her." His quiet voice was reassuring. "Be calm. She must not be upset. Once you have seen her, it is best if you do not return until after the event. She must spend all her energy concentrating on bringing forth a healthy child."

"Is she well, though?" Bingley almost whispered the words. "The baby was not due to be born for nearly another week or more."

Mr. Fortesque nodded. "A week is not so very much. And calculations are not always accurate. She is as well as can be expected.

A first confinement is usually the most difficult. Everything to support her will be done—you have my word. I have sent for my assistant, Mrs. Ewell. She is very experienced and a great asset to my practice. Now why do you not see your wife before Mrs. Ewell arrives?"

Bingley moved deeper into the room, past a standing screen that protected the bed from drafts and from anyone opening the door to the hall. Jane lay reclined against pillows, the covers drawn up to her chest. A fire burned with false cheeriness in the hearth, warming towels on a rack before it. A basket of clean rags rested beside it. There was a table covered with a folded sheet and more towels, a large basin ready to bathe the baby, swaddling clothes, and a small blanket. One of the maids waited to run any errands the accoucheur required. It was a scene of organization and control, and it comforted Bingley not at all.

"Jane, my dearest?" Bingley bent over the bed, touching her face gently. "Are you well?"

Jane Bennet Bingley opened cerulean eyes on her husband's face, her mouth lifting in a faint smile. "As I can be, my love. I can only think that it will soon be over."

"Yes." Bingley took one soft hand in both of his, lifting it to his lips. "I am so sorry, my darling," he murmured.

Jane's smile widened a little. "Why? We wanted children, did we not? This is how they come into the world." She raised her hand to his cheek, stroking it softly. "All will be well, Charles. Trust in God, my dearest husband. It will be as He wills."

Bingley bent and kissed his wife's lips without regard to the maid, who found something intriguing in moving the towels around on the stand. Jane's eyes closed. Her body stiffened, and she caught her breath, her hands clenching in the bedclothes. Bingley stood frozen with panic. Mr. Fortesque's hand fell on his shoulder before he could make a sound and guided him away from the bed. Beyond the screen, he faced his employer with grave authority.

"Please go now, Mr. Bingley. I have sent for your brother, he will join you shortly. Your presence here, while it may comfort you, does Mrs. Bingley no material good. She will be afraid of distressing you instead of focusing her mind on her own situation. I will send word as soon as the baby is born."

"If…if…anything…"

Bingley's voice shook so badly he was unable to finish the sentence.

"*When* the baby is born," Mr. Fortesque repeated firmly. He escorted Bingley to the door and closed it firmly behind him. His growing reputation and his professional confidence kept him from informing this wealthy young man with connections to an earl of just how precarious his wife's condition was.

Daniel Bingley waited in the hall. He took his brother's arm and walked with him to the stairs. "How is Mrs. Bingley?"

"In pain. Oh my God, Danny, what am I to do?"

"Wait, Charles. What else can you do? Send word to her family, her mother will want to be here—"

"No." Bingley halted at the bottom of the stairs, shaking his head in definite negation. "Not Mrs. Bennet. If only Elizabeth were here…or Mrs. Gardiner. Yes," he said, heading for his study, "I will send a note to Mrs. Gardiner. And to Mr. Bennet. Thank you, Danny."

His brother remained where he was, watching his older sibling hurry on his errand. With a shake of his head, he entered the breakfast parlor, poured a cup of coffee, put sugar in it, and carried it to the study. Once there, he added a healthy tot of brandy before putting it on the desk where Bingley sat, scribbling. He finished the first note, drank half the coffee gratefully, and took out a second sheet of paper. At that point, he raised his head to stare at his brother.

"Brandy in the coffee?"

"Yes," Daniel replied firmly. "I imagine you will require quite a bit of both before the day is out."

⊰⊱

Snow had fallen all day. Dressing for the dinner party in her rooms, Elizabeth kept glancing out the window. She wondered if some of their guests might not be able to attend due to the storm, even though it had slackened somewhat from the morning. She had felt a little ill when she rose, just a faint queasiness that had departed after a cup of tea and a bath. Now as she stood before the full-length pier glass in her dressing room while Clara fastened the pearl necklace Darcy had gifted her for the one-month anniversary of their marriage, she was again visited by the sensation of impending nausea.

"You look lovely, madam," Clara said, smiling at her in the mirror. "The master won't let you out of his sight."

Elizabeth took firm hold of her feelings and returned the maid's smile. "Thank you, Clara. Do not wait up for me. I do not know how late the party will go."

The maid curtsied and picked up Elizabeth's dressing gown when a tap at the connecting door to Darcy's chambers signaled his presence. Clara hurried to open the door and curtsied as he entered. With a look at the couple, she left the room to occupy herself in the bedchamber. Elizabeth turned to her husband and found his gaze full of admiration. He came, put his arms around her, and kissed her lightly. The gown of blue silk she wore was cut in the current fashion, skimming the body, the décolletage low and the waist high set off by a band of white satin ribbon. Alençon lace trimmed the short sleeves as well as circling the skirt just above the hem. Pearl pins highlighted the arrangement of her dark curls.

"You are the most beautiful woman in the world, Elizabeth."

"You are the greatest flatterer, William, but do not stop on that account."

Grinning, he released her. "The first carriage has passed the gatehouse. We should go down."

Elizabeth took his arm. "I am anxious to meet your friends and neighbors. You will be pleased, I hope, to know that Georgiana has agreed to play for our guests after dinner."

Darcy stopped short in the hallway, staring at his wife. "How in Heaven's name did you accomplish that?"

"I asked her. Just to play Christmas carols. She volunteered to play one other piece, Bach, I believe."

Darcy shook his head, and they continued to the stairs. "I have never been able to get my sister to play for anyone except family and reluctantly at that. For you, my most astonishing love, she will play carols and Bach."

"I left the decision to her," Elizabeth told him as they reached the main hall. "She knows she plays extremely well; she only lacks confidence. These are people she knows, not strangers. If she decides the Bach is a bit too much, the carols will do."

Georgiana followed them downstairs as the first carriage pulled up before the manor house. "Papa is waiting in the drawing room. He will see to our guests until you join him."

Georgiana did not have to elaborate. For a moment, her face was pinched with pain and then smoothed as the footman announced the first arrivals. Darcy wondered briefly if their father's condition had prompted her to agree to play tonight as a gift to him. Darcy had to fight the sadness the thought brought him. Tonight was to be a celebration of life and joy, he was determined that nothing would spoil that.

Elizabeth said to her sister, "That color becomes you very well, Georgie."

Georgiana blushed lightly at the compliment, momentarily distracted as Elizabeth had intended. The gown was indeed flattering, its peach color warming Georgiana's skin and highlighting her pale-blonde hair. The sound of wheels on the front drive focused all of their attention to the present. For the next half hour guests arrived in two and threes. Most seemed pleased to meet the new Mrs. Darcy, and those who were more reserved were the older neighbors who remembered Lady Anne Darcy and could not help wondering how this glowing young woman would measure up to her predecessor as Mistress of Pemberley. Darcy stayed at her side until their last guests came in, a Mr. Wade and his daughter, Susanna Holcomb. She was a pretty young woman of twenty-three, married to the younger son of a local landowner, and a major in the Royal Artillery. They knew Colonel Fitzwilliam, and Elizabeth found herself drawn to the lady's open manner and warm personality.

"Colder than Dante's *Inferno* out there," Mr. Wade pronounced as if the chill seeping in from the front door as it closed behind him was not graphic confirmation enough. "Roads are blocked from south of Lambton to somewhere near Matlock. The post chaise had to turn back, and the regular mail has not been delivered for two days. This is a storm they will talk about for a while, I can tell you."

"What of the Great North Road?" Darcy asked.

He walked with Mr. Wade to the stairs, followed by Elizabeth, Georgiana, and Susanna Holcomb. Mr. Wade shrugged.

"I expect most of it is clear enough for traffic, though I do not think I would want to travel far until the weather lets up."

The remainder of the evening went better than Elizabeth expected. With her open, lively personality and genuine interest in people, she charmed the attendees and began several friendships that would grow and flower over the years ahead, the first and greatest with Susanna Holcomb. After dinner, the guests assembled in the music room, where Georgiana played Bach's *Jesu Joy of Man's Desiring* to enthusiastic applause. She followed with traditional Christmas carols, while most of the listeners sang the well-known lyrics. It was past midnight when the last guest said their goodbyes and left to return to their homes. Darcy had offered overnight accommodations to anyone wishing to avoid traveling the roads at night. As the local roads were still open enough to present minimal danger, and most of their friends lived within a relatively short distance, no one required the hospitality.

Darcy walked upstairs with Elizabeth, entering her bedchamber as the long-case clock in the hall struck one o'clock.

"It was a memorable evening," he said, watching Elizabeth more closely than usual. "I cannot remember a better. Father was more at ease than I have seen him for some time. However, I noticed that you seemed preoccupied several times. Is something amiss?"

When she did not immediately reply, Darcy stopped and turned to her. "Can you not tell me what is troubling you, my dearest wife?"

"It is nothing, William, just my foolishness."

"How, foolish?"

Elizabeth sighed. "All day I have had a feeling that something was…wrong. It is difficult to put into words. An unease, a sense of waiting for some trouble or crisis." She shook her head. "You see why I said nothing."

"Not at all. Is it because of Father, do you think?"

"No," Elizabeth responded slowly. "No, I do not think so."

Hesitantly Darcy asked, "Has it happened before?"

Elizabeth crossed her arms over her chest as if cold. "Only once. I was twelve. I could not settle all day for the feeling of impending trouble. The next day we received word that my grandmother Bennet had died. She contracted pneumonia staying up all night with a favorite mare that was foaling. Papa says I resemble her." She shook herself. "I am not usually so *missish* about things. Come," she said, smiling up at him. "Let us go to bed. I will be fine in the morning."

With some reluctance, Darcy did not press the matter. He knew that premonitions were not always fanciful, and Elizabeth was not a woman to give in to the megrims fashionable with ladies of the *ton*. Darcy helped Elizabeth undress, and they slept well. However, he had cause to remember the conversation vividly the next morning when Mr. Niles tapped on his study door.

"An express for you, sir. And one for Mrs. Darcy." Mr. Niles extended a polished salver.

Darcy accepted the letter with a growing sense of trepidation. "Thank you, Mr. Niles. Mrs. Darcy is in her sitting room with Mrs. Reynolds. A moment, please, before you take the express to her."

Mr. Niles waited patiently for his employer to open and briefly scan the express. Most men of the upper classes read their wives' mail as a matter of course. It was a measure of Mr. Darcy's relationship with Mrs. Darcy that he did not do so.

The express was from Mr. Bennet.

My dear son-in-law,

By now Elizabeth will have received her aunt's letter relating that her sister Jane has given birth to twins, a boy and a girl. Although gentlemen do not usually discuss such matters, I feel you need to know that the labor was long and there were complications that have left my daughter both exhausted and weak. The accoucheur is optimistic of a full recovery, as he needs must be.

At present Jane is in no immediate danger and has constant nursing care. I will inform you directly if there is any change in her condition. My other reason for this letter is to suggest that you discourage Elizabeth from reading any communication from her mother. I am sure Mrs. Bennet will write at any moment with dire

prognostications that will be of no comfort to either Elizabeth or her sister.
With best regards,
Thomas Bennet

Darcy rose and took the second express. "Thank you, Mr. Niles. I will deliver this to Mrs. Darcy."

He found her sitting with Mrs. Reynolds at a small table in her private sitting room, the household ledgers between them. Elizabeth and the housekeeper had developed an immediate rapport with one another. Mrs. Reynolds was gratified to find that the new mistress was well grounded in household management, only the scope of Pemberley's domestic arrangements causing her some trepidation. For her part, Elizabeth appreciated both the housekeeper's experience and her patient willingness to teach her whatever she knew.

Elizabeth looked up with a smile that faded as she saw the two letters Darcy held. She came to her feet, her face pale. "What has happened?"

Mrs. Reynolds had also risen at her employer's entrance. Unlike any other of the servants she did not quit the room. She had known Fitzwilliam Darcy since he was four years old and had been a second mother to Georgiana. She held a unique position in the Darcy household, more friend than servant. Her mentoring was now extended to Elizabeth, whom she had come to consider as a perfect wife for her beloved Master William.

"I have had an express from your father. Your sister Jane gave birth yesterday to twins. She is in a state of exhaustion but in no immediate danger. This," he said, handing her the other express, "is from your aunt Gardiner."

Mrs. Reynolds unobtrusively left the room as Elizabeth sat abruptly at the table, her legs too weak to hold her. Darcy put the express from Mr. Bennet away and stood behind her, his hands on her shoulders in silent support. Elizabeth opened the letter with shaking hands and read,

> *My dearest Lizzy,*
>
> *I am writing on Jane's behalf to inform you that she has delivered twins, a boy and a girl. The birth was over a week before expected; although the girl is quite small, both babies are doing well. Mr. Fortesque, the accoucheur, believes that the calculations may have been incorrect and the birth close to its proper time.*
>
> *As to Jane, she is weak from a prolonged labor and needs rest and care, which Mr. Bingley is providing with a professional nurse and a wet nurse. Mr. Fortesque expects a full recovery in time. I shall stay with her for a few days as well. My sister Bennet offered to move in until Jane improves, however I have discouraged her, as has Mr. Bennet, as such a stay would adversely affect her nerves.*
>
> *I will write to you with any news. Hopefully the next communication you receive will be from Jane herself.*
>
> *With my love,*
> *Aunt Margaret*

He had read the letter over her shoulder. Elizabeth let it fall to the table and bowed her head against his sleeve, trying not to give in to her terror. Birth was always a risk; many women died at the time of their lying-in or shortly after. She knew that Charles would see to his wife's health with every particular care, and yet she wanted—*needed*—to be with her beloved sister. Elizabeth could not bear to think of the worst outcome. Losing Jane was too terrible to contemplate.

"Jane has never been as robust as I." Elizabeth's voice vibrated with pain. She wanted to say, *If only I had stayed behind until the birth, I would be there to comfort and care for her.* She knew, however, that the thought was both unjust and unworthy. Her place was with her husband, and there had been no warning of any problems with the lying-in. She closed her eyes, the warmth of his presence sustaining her.

Darcy's thoughts ran in the same vein. He said after a moment, his voice unsteady, "You sacrificed so much to marry quickly. I would not, for all I possess, have you regret your decision."

Elizabeth heard his anguish. She tightened the grip of her hands on his, and he grasped them as if she were being pulled away from him. "When I chose to marry you, I did so in full knowledge and acceptance that you were to be my family. I love Jane for a lifetime of comfort and companionship, I want desperately to be with her, but you are my life, William. I would not change that if I could."

He lifted her to her feet and pulled her into a fierce embrace, burying his face in her hair.

"If it were possible, I would take you to her. You have heard that the roads are closed or uncertain until the blizzard passes. The express rider only got through because he was able to use country roads and narrow paths that a coach could not negotiate. Your father says much the same as Mrs. Gardiner," he added. "I am sure we will receive any news as quickly as it can be sent."

Elizabeth sighed, almost a sob. "I know Jane is being cared for in the best possible way, and surely twins are more difficult than a single baby. It is just that she has always been there for me, and now that she is in need, I cannot be there for her."

She straightened. Darcy gently wiped the tears from her face with a thumb. Elizabeth assayed a wavering smile. "Does Papa say anything else?"

"You may read the letter if you wish to. He does suggest that I 'discourage' you from reading any correspondence from Mrs. Bennet, although he fails to inform me of a method for doing so."

Elizabeth's smile grew a little more natural. "I am well used to Mama's tendency to see the worst in every situation. As long as Papa and my aunt Gardiner assure us that Jane is in no immediate danger, I shall not take anything Mama writes too seriously."

Darcy felt relief at Elizabeth's words, although he could not be absolutely certain that she knew herself how she might react to her mother's lamentations. He raised his head at the reentrance of Mrs. Reynolds, carrying a tea service. She put the tray down and made Elizabeth a cup of hot, strong tea with extra sugar in it. When Elizabeth was again seated at the table, the housekeeper fixed a cup for Darcy. The homey action did more to calm Elizabeth than any words of comfort.

"Thank you, Mrs. Reynolds," she said with more feeling than a simple act of kindness warranted. "This is exactly what I needed."

CHAPTER 20
PROGRESSIONS

To Nicholas Fitzwilliam's blurred vision, the figure sitting beside his bed took on the appearance of a phantom. His mother rose and bent over him, smoothing the tangled hair from his brow.

"Nicholas? Can you hear me?"

He licked dry lips with a tongue nearly as dry. Lady Madeleine poured water from a carafe into a glass, lifted his head carefully, and trickled the liquid into his mouth.

"Better?"

"M…mother."

"Yes, my dear. Are you in pain?"

"N…n…not much."

He swallowed. His mother gave him more water before she lowered his head carefully to the pillow. She was of two minds as to whether to call Mr. Watson or try to determine her son's condition first. Sitting down again, she took his hand in hers and pressed it gently.

"Do you remember what happened?"

Nicholas's vision was clearing. He stared at the high ceiling with its plaster medallions, grazed with light from barely open drapes. *What had happened? A dark room, a man—no, two men—some sort to fight, and...rushing dark, terror, pain.* "No! Jesus, no, *don't*!"

"Shhh.," Lady Madeleine bent over him once more, her voice soothing, calming. "You are safe, Nicholas. It was all nearly a month ago. Shh, my dear, do not alarm yourself. All is well."

The door to his dressing room opened abruptly to admit the doctor's assistant closely followed by Peters, Nicholas's long-suffering valet. Lady Madeleine looked up with a warning expression as Mr. Watson approached the bed. Nicholas turned his head and stared at the newcomer without recognition.

"Who the devil are you? You look like someone I knew once."

Lady Madeleine almost smiled. "This is Mr. Watson, a senior medical student. Dr. Wyecroft sent him to tend to you while you have been unconscious."

As if to demonstrate his authorization, Mr. Watson took Nicholas's pulse and felt his forehead. He said drily, "You may have known my elder brother. He is Viscount Camberlund now. As a younger son, my father wanted me to join the army; my mother wanted me to become a priest. I took the middle ground and studied medicine. How do you feel?"

"Bloody awful. Sorry, Mother."

She shook her head. For the first time in weeks, her smile was genuine. "Shall I leave, Mr. Watson?"

"If you would, my lady. I will not be long."

When Lady Madeleine closed the door behind her, Mr. Watson examined the fractured limbs. Nicholas groaned once, his jaw clenched to keep from crying out. Peters assisted Mr. Watson as he had since the attack. When the bedclothes were rearranged, Watson straightened up.

"You are healing steadily if rather more slowly than I would like to see. Now that you have regained your senses you will be able to move a bit, which aids in regaining your strength."

Nicholas closed his eyes for a moment and then met the younger man's gaze evenly. "How bad is it? The truth. Peters will tell me anyway."

"The femur—thigh bone—broke cleanly. It was a high break, fortunately not high enough to fracture the pelvis. Your ankle is the worst. The fracture shattered part of the bone. Dr. Wyecroft had to open the leg to try and repair the damage. In fact he could do little. You may walk again but not without assistance. *And pain. But I will not burden you with that now.* If it heals better than expected, you will need a cane at the least. With such a fall," he added, "it is a miracle that you did not break your neck or back. A large shrub softened the impact I am told."

"Mother's forsythia. Well, it was an ugly plant anyway." Nicholas lay back and contemplated the play of light on the walls. "Open the drapes, Peters. I am not dead yet."

"Yes, sir." The valet noted that Sir Nicholas's tone was not as imperative as it should have been.

"They have not caught him, have they?"

"Not yet," Mr. Watson replied. "He is thought to be in Scotland. Lord Matlock has posted a reward of five thousand pounds for his capture."

"Is my brother after the bastard? Richard hates Wickham."

"Colonel Fitzwilliam has rejoined his regiment, sir," Peters responded. "He came to say goodbye to you, but you were not aware of his presence."

"One down for the count and one dancing with death. My father must be in high dudgeon."

"He is coping, sir," Peters said.

"God, yes, he always copes! Damn! I think this is the first time in years I have been completely sober. I do not find it a pleasant experience."

Mr. Watson mixed a powder into a glass of water and lifted Nicholas so that he could drink. "Necessary, I am afraid. Alcohol will only impede your recovery. This will help the pain. Try to rest."

Nicholas made a face as he finished the drink. "Ugh. Like very bad port."

He lay back once more and fell silent. Peters followed Mr. Watson from the room, only to have the medical assistant halt and face him.

"No liquor. None. Dr. Wyecroft has specified that Sir Nicholas is to have only water, tea, or soup to drink. Anything else will harm his progress, as I told him."

"Yes, sir," Peters sounded reluctant. "He will order me to get him a drink, sir."

"Then take the matter to Lord Matlock. He will set things straight."

"Yes, sir."

The medical assistant watched as Peters retreated to the dressing room and whatever duties he found there. Mr. Watson continued downstairs to the library to write a note that would be carried to Dr. Wyecroft, informing him of his patient's condition, as he would undoubtedly want to examine the viscount personally. A period of sobriety might be the best thing that could happen to the viscount, Mr. Watson mused. Sir Nicholas had a long and difficult recovery ahead of him, with no guarantee that he would ever regain his full strength. He needed to concentrate on the battle to come, not dull body and mind with liquor. With his only brother at war in Spain, the viscount might well become not only the heir apparent to the earldom but the only heir.

"Mary, dear, you will not mind waiting at Hatchard's while I look for some lace at the milliner's? I want it to trim Julia's new dress. She is growing so fast. I cannot believe she is nine!"

"No, Aunt, of course not. I shall look for some new music or perhaps a book. Do not hurry on my account."

Mrs. Gardiner left Mary on the doorstep of the bookshop patronized by anyone wanting arguably the newest and best selection of books in London and made her way cautiously across the busy street to the shop. She had temporarily dismissed the carriage, knowing that maneuvering a vehicle through the traffic along Piccadilly took more time than traveling on foot.

Mary welcomed the diversion of accompanying her aunt shopping. She had spent much of the past week with her sister Jane, keeping her company turnabout with Kitty. Their mother visited every day; oddly, her presence seemed to shortly send Jane to sleep. Mrs. Bennet attributed this phenomenon to her motherly presence and took herself off to harry the rest of the household. Now that the danger was over and Jane's health was improving daily, Mary felt that she was able to accept her aunt's invitation without guilt.

Neither woman noticed the two young men lounging at the far corner of the street. Both were well if conservatively dressed; unlike the elder the younger man's clothing was worn with a certain flair, although of lesser quality. They stood rather close together and might have been discussing anything from politics to the latest gossip regarding the Prince Regent and Mrs. Fitzhugh. The only element a keen observer might have noticed was the tense posture of the elder young man.

"Simon." Mr. Cranshaw gripped his companion's arm. "That's her. Mary Bennet, nearly the love of my life. Outside Hatchard's."

The younger man focused his attention on Mary for a moment and shrugged. "She is not particularly pretty, but she has a nice figure." His voice turned sly, "I thought I was the love of your life?"

A middle-aged gentleman who was passing by glanced at them sharply. Cranshaw laughed a little louder than necessary, dropping his hand. "Yes, that is my fiancée. I shall introduce you."

Simon Trent-Davies stiffened, then replied casually, "Yes, I should like to meet her."

The gentleman strode on with the perception that he had misheard the conversation. He had forgotten the young men within six steps.

Cranshaw hissed, "Lower your voice! You'll be no one's love if you get us both hanged."

Mr. Trent-Davies, senior law clerk with Witherspoon, Woolrich, Hazelmuth, and Gibbs drew back, his expression sulky. "I do not know why you care if you see her or not, since she broke off with you."

"I care no more for her than I ever did." Mr. Cranshaw still studied Mary as she entered the bookstore. "She and that jackanapes of a colonel humiliated me in public. I want a bit of my own back."

"Cranny, no." Mindful now of the passersby, Mr. Trent-Davies followed instructions and lowered his voice. "Leave her alone. You'll only get both of us in trouble."

Mr. Cranshaw studied his companion with contempt. "Go back to your office, then. I am not going to attack the woman, only give her a glimpse of what is to come." He turned away. "Wait for me, and we will have luncheon at that little chophouse off Threadneedle Street."

Mr. Trent-Davies watched him walk away with a cold feeling of apprehension. Despite his attachment to his lover, he knew he had no control over Mr. Cranshaw's behavior. Cranny could be willful and was often vindictive. He was dissatisfied with his position despite its advantages and was ambitious for a career in the law courts. It was going, Mr. Trent-Davies feared, to lead him to disaster if he did not control his impulses. Moving a little on, Mr. Trent-Davies stared into the window of a haberdashery and waited for Mr. Cranshaw to return.

Mary Bennet was enjoying her visit to Hatchard's. She had already selected a small volume of poetry by William Wordsworth;

now she perused newly arrived sheet music of Herr von Beethoven, wavering between two pieces she felt she was capable of mastering. *Miss Darcy plays so wonderfully well,* Mary mused. *When I visit Lizzy, perhaps she will be willing to assist me with my fingering.* So absorbed was she that the man's voice behind her nearly caused her to drop the music.

"Mr. Cranshaw." Mary carefully replaced the music sheets. "I did not hear you approach."

"I wanted to surprise you, Miss Bennet. You are Miss Bennet now, of course."

Mary watched Mr. Cranshaw warily, her expression as close to neutral as she could manage. "What do you want, Mr. Cranshaw?"

"Why," he stepped even closer, causing her to stiffen without withdrawing, "to read your future. I am quite the fortune-teller, you know."

"I do not wish to speak to you, Mr. Cranshaw. We have nothing to say to each other."

"Oh, my dear Miss Bennet, you are wrong." Cranshaw made no attempt to hide the sarcasm in his words. "I have a considerable amount to say to you. How is your dashing colonel, by the way? There has been little in the papers regarding the war of late. No new medals to flash at the ladies?"

A totally unfamiliar heat infused Mary's words with anger. "Do not speak of Colonel Fitzwilliam. You are far too familiar, Mr. Cranshaw."

She had begun to feel a little sick. In spite of her apprehension she refused to let her former suitor, if such he had been, discompose her. With as much control as possible, Mary said, "Please leave, or I shall summon the store assistant."

"And what can he do? I am only talking, nothing more. I do not want you to face disaster without some warning, I feel I owe you that much consideration."

Mary's hands had begun to shake. "What do you mean, disaster? There is no disaster, everyone is well."

"Oh, I was not referring to illness—only disgrace. You see, a very well informed source tells me that shortly the widow of a famous artist will take action in the courts against the Darcys. Something about a will, I believe. Perhaps one that was suppressed or 'lost.' I should not be surprised if she ends with a large part of the Darcy fortune, not to mention dragging their respected name through to mud of public censure. And, of course, the Fitzwilliams will be anxious to distance themselves from the affair. You had better hope your soldier marries you before the case becomes public knowledge, or you may find yourself discarded."

He bowed as Mary stared, white faced, at his sneering countenance.

"Good day, *Miss Bennet*."

The volume of poetry fell to the floor from nerveless fingers. Mary did not notice. She swayed against the counter, the room fading and brightening by turns. An assistant who had witnessed the end of the conversation hurried up, unaware of what had passed between the well-dressed young gentleman and Miss Bennet but alarmed by her obvious distress.

"Miss Bennet, please come and sit down in the viewing room. You look quite ill."

Mary tried to clear her vision. The shop assistant's furrowed brow came into focus. She heard the words "sit down" and nodded. He escorted her to the rear of the shop and into a small, comfortable room, where those who wished to examine special orders or books of antiquity or extreme value could do so without other customers interrupting. After seeing her seated in an armchair at the table, he stood back, still alarmed at her apparent condition.

"Is there anyone I can call for you? Would you like a cup of tea?"

Mary raised her head, struggling to take hold of her roiling emotions. She made the effort and steadied her voice.

"My aunt, Mrs. Gardiner, is across the street at the millinery. If someone could ask her to come to me, I would be most appreciative."

By the time she finished the words, her voice had sunk to a near whisper. The attendant said, "Of course, I shall go myself. Please wait here. I will send in some tea."

The attendant left the room. Mary put her head back and tried to gather her thoughts into some coherent form. Why had Mr. Cranshaw done this? Was it all a lie? He must know many people in the law profession and the courts; he might well have information not generally in circulation. What widow? What artist? Why would anyone sue the Darcys? Surely there was no just cause to think such honorable men were involved in anything unlawful or dishonorable.

Her head swam. With the tap on the door a man whom she knew was the manager of the shop entered, followed by another assistant with a tea tray that he sat on the table before her. Mary straightened at once in the chair and tried to smile. The manager dismissed the assistant, poured her a cup of tea himself, added sugar, and put it in her hands. The warmth seeped gratefully into chill flesh. Mary thanked him and drank the tea, feeling somewhat better. The manager did not make conversation. He remained with her until Mrs. Gardiner hurried into the room accompanied by the first assistant, at which point both men tactfully withdrew.

"Mary, my dear, what has happened? You look quite ill."

Mary raised her face to the sympathetic countenance of her aunt as tears began to well in her eyes. "Oh, Aunt, I must see my father at once! Please, take me to his office; he will be there at this hour."

She was on her feet before the words tumbled out. More alarmed than she showed, Mrs. Gardiner took Mary's arm to steady her. "I will take you to your father if you insist. I have sent for the carriage. But why do you not let me see you home, and then we may send for him? I do not think you are in any condition to venture into the City."

Mary hesitated. Mr. Cranshaw might have returned to the office. She did not want to cause a scene at her father's place of business. She nodded. "Yes, that will be best."

Without further questions, Mrs. Gardiner escorted her niece from the room. The manager approached them as they started down the aisle leading to the street door. "Miss Bennet, I believe you had chosen this volume of Mr. Wordsworth's verse. Please accept it as a small compensation for your experience."

"Thank you, sir." Mrs. Gardiner took the book for Mary.

The carriage waited at the curb. A footman assisted them to enter, and the vehicle pulled out into traffic, Mrs. Gardiner sitting next to her shaken niece with an arm around her shoulders while Mary stared blankly out the window, both hands clutching the slender tome.

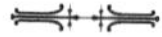

"Mrs. Reynolds, do you know where Mrs. Darcy is?"

Mrs. Reynolds, on her way to her office, stopped when she saw Darcy emerge from the study with a letter in hand.

She smiled. "Yes, sir. She is in the attic storage with Mr. Darcy. I believe they are searching for the writing desk Lady Anne used to use. It is in a room over the ballroom in the old wing of the house."

Darcy nodded his thanks and went upstairs with a faint feeling of trepidation. He did not recognize the handwriting on the envelope; it was not Mr. Bennet's precise copperplate or Mrs. Bennet's sprawling curlicues. It might be from one of her sisters or her aunt, and it might hold good news or bad. Darcy's concern for his wife had remained largely unspoken over the past month. He understood her state of mind all too well. Being so far from her dearly loved sister at a time of crisis wore at her constantly. Every post might bring the dreaded word that Jane Bingley was worse, or dead. Darcy had encouraged Elizabeth's renewed interest in the writing desk when she asked him if he thought his father would object to her using the desk if it could be found, and he had replied she would have to ask his father. At that point any diversion from worry was welcome.

She must have done so, Darcy thought. It surprised him that his father would go with her to locate it. After his wife's death, George Darcy had asked Mrs. Reynolds to pack up her personal items and store them. To the best of Fitzwilliam's knowledge, he had never mentioned them again. It was a concern to his son that seeing them now might trigger an episode with his heart. This was the first time since Darcy had left for London that George had ventured above the first floor. It caused his son a certain amount of foreboding, sending him up the stairs two at a time.

The attics had no windows, which made them ideal for storing furniture. Small fixed vents under the eaves provided what air entered the spaces, little as it was. The storerooms were cleaned once a year. Otherwise, unless items were being stored or removed, they were untouched. Darcy immediately knew which room his mother's things were in from the footman standing by the door. He stepped inside and looked around. Trunks, packing crates, tin boxes, and furniture of all descriptions, shrouded and bare, haunted the gloom. Just enough space was left between the various items and stacks to walk around.

Toward the back, lamplight made a pool of radiance in the semidarkness, where two voices told him his wife and father were sorting through the accumulated remnants of several generations. He reached them just as Elizabeth removed the cover from a small bureau with an inlaid writing desk sitting on it. Her nose was smudged with dust; her eyes were alight in triumph. Darcy wanted to take her in his arms and kiss her until she melted into him before carrying her off to their bedchamber. She was still unaware of him, her entire focus on her search.

"Oh," her voice was awed, "it is lovely. I have never seen such a beautiful desk."

George ran his fingers over the *pietra dura* top, marquetry with semiprecious stone panels in a design of flowers and birds, and silver-gilt mounts. "I had forgotten how exquisite it is. My late wife used it for years. It belonged to my grandmother, Eleanor Darcy, Alexander and Agatha's mother. That is probably how Lady Agatha came by the medallion."

Elizabeth glanced over her shoulder as Darcy approached and stepped back slightly. "Look, William, is it not exquisite? It was kind of Lady Agatha to tell me about it."

Darcy nodded, his gaze on his father. George seemed perfectly calm; he said to Elizabeth, "Do you want the bureau as well?"

"No, thank you, Father Darcy. There is a table in my rooms that will suit quite well."

George said with a glance at his son's face, "I will have Porter carry it down to your room then."

Wondering why he had come, Elizabeth looked at her husband. He answered her unspoken question by handing her a letter.

"This came for you. I thought you would want to read it at once."

A stab of apprehension went through Elizabeth. She took the missive with trembling fingers, her expression immediately transmuted to one of joy.

"It is Jane's handwriting," she said breathlessly. "If she is well enough to write, she must be recovering more quickly than I expected."

She opened the letter and read swiftly,

My dearest sister,

I am feeling much better, as you will know by the fact that Mary did not have to write this for me. She and Kitty and especially Aunt Margaret have been wonderful to me while I recuperate. The babies are doing quite well. We have named them as I told you, Charles Thomas and Martha Frances.

Martha is small, but I expect her to grow swiftly, as she wants sustenance often. Mama gives me constant advice on how to care for them, some of it useful. I wish you could be here to see them, my dearest Lizzy, but I know the weather has been very bad for traveling. When they are older and I am strong again, we will visit with you and Mr. Darcy if you do not travel to London before then. Please give my best to your husband and Mr. Darcy's father.

With all my love,

Jane

Elizabeth's eyes welled with tears. She felt as if a weight had been lifted from her heart. "Oh, William, I am so happy that she is better. I have been so worried. Jane was never as robust as I. Now she sounds quite herself, and the babies are doing very well."

"That is wonderful news," Darcy said, smiling at his wife as George Darcy returned with the footman.

Elizabeth turned to her father-in-law. "I have had a letter from my sister Jane. She and the babies are doing well."

"I am happy to hear it." George smiled at her. If he was thinking of his wife's slow, irreversible decline after Georgiana's birth, there was no evidence of it in face or voice.

Porter lifted the writing desk without effort, waiting for Elizabeth to give him instructions as to where it was to be taken. Instead she stepped past him.

"I will show you where I want it placed," Elizabeth said. Porter obediently followed her to the door. The medallion rested in the pocket of her gown, temporarily forgotten.

Darcy said to his father as they left the attic room, "I am very glad Mrs. Bingley is doing well, as are the twins. It relieves Elizabeth of the anxiety she has felt since she received the express."

"I am happy for them," George said, noting that his son walked closer than was his usual want, alert for any faltering in his father's step. "Now I believe I shall go to my rooms and wash off the dust of years. It was good to see the writing desk again. Your mother loved it, and I believe it will be well used and well-loved again by Elizabeth."

Darcy nodded. He did not speak his thoughts. *It seems a strange object for Lady Agatha to point out to Elizabeth. And strange for her to have the medallion rather than it remaining with the desk. If the stories are true, she never returned to Pemberley after her elopement. Eleanor Darcy must have sent it to her, but why?*

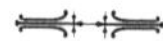

Mrs. Hastings was in the daily process of preparing the elements of dinner. The scullery maid had peeled and cut the vegetables, and they sat in bowls of cold water, awaiting the cooking pot and the baking pan. The meat, a nice roast of mutton, was ready for cooking as well, and the trout from the stream sat in silent splendor covered by truffles and almonds. All the bread was baked; the dessert, apple tart and raspberry trifle, rested on a shelf to await the master's pleasure. Not for the first time, Mrs. Hastings blessed the glass houses for their bounty of ingredients not usually available in winter.

As she stirred the soup pot on the stove, she was disturbed by a step in the hallway leading to the back door. Expecting one of the maids or a footman, she turned her head to find herself facing one of the hunters who were currently acting as guards. He had a young woman with him, her thin face pale with cold, a faded shawl pulled tightly around a muslin dress better suited to summer wear than the frozen world outside.

"Whom have you there, Dean?"

"Don't know, ma'am. She came past the gatehouse, and old Henry stopped her and signaled for somebody to come and bring her up to the house. She claims she wants to speak to Mr. Darcy."

Mrs. Hastings made a decision. Wiping her hands automatically on her apron, she said, "Very well, you can leave her with me. I'll see to her."

Dean, knowing Mrs. Hastings's position in the servants' hierarchy, withdrew. The young woman had not moved. Mrs. Hastings saw the trembling she could not control and pulled out a chair at the big kitchen table.

"Come and sit down. How on earth did you get here?"

The young woman did as she was told, more collapsing than sitting. Mrs. Hastings went to stand facing her. She noted the etching of old pain in the shadowed eyes. This girl, for she was barely more than that, had suffered in her life. The cook went purposefully to a large sideboard and took down a bowl from one shelf. She filled it from the soup pot, retrieved a spoon, and set it before the visitor.

"Get that inside of you. Careful, it's hot. They call it *ragoo de boof*, but I call it plain old beef stew."

It took the young woman only a moment to set to the bowl. When it was nearly empty, Mrs. Hastings put a cup of tea from the kettle always kept on the hob, sat in another chair, and studied the other woman.

"Will you tell me your name?"

She scraped the spoon around the bottom of the bowl, swallowed, and said, "Bel…Isobel. Thank you for the soup, ma'am."

"You're welcome. You don't look like you've had many meals lately. Where are you from?"

Belle hesitated. "Matlock."

"And you came to Lambton to see Mr. Darcy. How did you get from Lambton to Pemberley? It's five miles or more, and in this weather."

"A man gave me a ride. He let me off at the crossroads and told me to walk till I saw a driveway with a gatehouse."

Mrs. Hastings frowned. "He might have brought you that far at least," she sniffed. She rose. "Well, which Mr. Darcy did you come to see? Mr. George or Mr. Fitzwilliam?"

"Mr. Fitzwilliam. If you tell him Mr. Handley sent me, he'll see me."

Belle fervently hoped it was true. She had remained an extra month at the boardinghouse in Matlock waiting for Handley to return. When he did not and men who had known her at Mrs. Younge's began coming around, she took what little money she had saved and caught the post chaise for Lambton.

"Mr. Fitzwilliam has gone out," Mrs. Hastings said, "and Mr. George is—" She did not want to say "resting" or "not seeing anyone right now." At the despair on Belle's face, she quickly added, "Mrs. Darcy is here; you can speak to her if you like."

Belle nodded slowly. She doubted a wife would welcome the intrusion of an unknown woman asking for her son, but she had no other option. "Please, ma'am."

Mrs. Hastings called Mrs. Reynolds. When the housekeeper arrived, she indicated Belle and briefly informed her of the young woman's request. Mrs. Reynolds took in the girl in a glance. *At the end of her tether. Maybe she knows something about Mr. Wickham, she's the kind of young woman he would prey on.*

To Belle, she said, "Come with me."

Belle rose obediently and followed the older woman to a neat parlor that also served as the housekeeper's office. "Wait here. I will be back shortly."

Mrs. Reynolds found Elizabeth in the morning room with Georgiana, discussing the renovation of several guest suites scheduled for the following summer. She looked up at the housekeeper's entrance; something in Mrs. Reynold's expression made her rise to her feet.

"Mrs. Darcy, there is a young woman in my office who came looking for Master William. She says a man named Handley sent her."

It took Elizabeth only a second to recognize the name. "I will come at once."

She excused herself to Georgiana, who watched her leave the room with obvious curiosity. Belle stood up as the two women came into the room. Mrs. Reynolds left them alone and returned to her duties, while Elizabeth indicated the chair Belle had occupied and took another near it.

"Sit down, Miss...?"

"Just Isobel, ma'am."

This was the younger Darcy's wife, she thought, not his mother. She was likely to be thrown out for asking after her husband.

Elizabeth studied the young woman. She said, "You wished to speak to my husband?"

"Y-yes, ma'am. Mr. Handley knows Mr. Darcy. He's been following a man named Winter. We...we met in Matlock a while back. He left me there two months ago to go after the man. He said if he wasn't back in a month to come to Lambton and ask for Mr. Darcy. I waited an extra month," she finished, trying to control the fear she felt. "He never came."

Elizabeth felt an immediate empathy for this young woman. It had taken courage and determination to travel to an unknown town and ask for an unknown man who might simply turn her away.

"I have met Mr. Handley. Do you know where he is?"

"Scotland. That's where he thought the man went."

"The storms have been very bad this winter," Elizabeth said. "He has probably not been able to return. Have you any family or friends here?"

"No one, ma'am. I'm an orphan. My mother's family live somewhere in the south, and my father had no other family."

It was true, and she hesitated, wondering if she ought to admit to where Mr. Handley found her. *That would be the end,* she thought, and she was so weary of losing everything, over and over.

Elizabeth saw the shadow of fear in Belle's eyes and her indecision. She said quietly, "Is there something else?"

Belle dropped her head. A sob escaped her, she knotted her hands together. She raised her head at last braced for the contempt, the disgust, her admission engendered, the looks she had seen on the faces of respectable women who could not cross the street fast enough when Mrs. Younge's women were out.

"Mr. Handley found me at Mrs. Younge's…house. It was a…a…"

"Yes," Elizabeth said, "I know what it must be. How did you come there?"

Startled, Belle could not respond. Mrs. Darcy was watching her with interest but none of the disdain she expected. Briefly she related her story. When she finished, the Mistress of Pemberley felt her chest grow tight. *What if Papa had been a tenant farmer or a factory worker? If he died and the circumstances were the same, would I have fared any better?*

"You were a prisoner, it seems."

"Same as, yes, ma'am."

"Why did you tell me this, Isobel? You did not have to."

"It'd be worse than lying not to tell you." She stood up. "I'll go now. If Mr. Handley comes here, could you please tell him I'll try to stay in Lambton for a while?"

"Please sit down, Isobel."

The woman complied. She had no resistance left. Elizabeth thought for a moment. She might give Isobel some money and make arrangements for her to stay in Lambton for a time until Mr. Handley returned; at the same time she was practical enough to know that it was possible he would not return. Mr. Wickham was vicious. If he found the opportunity to stop the man hunting him permanently, he would certainly take it. And if Handley did return, he almost certainly would contact William. She made a decision and smiled at Belle.

"Would you like to stay here, Isobel? I am sure we could find work for you, until Mr. Handley returns."

"Oh, ma'am," Isobel put a hand over her mouth, tears gathering in her eyes, "that's…that's so good of you. Are you sure?"

"Quite sure. Wait here," Elizabeth said, rising, "while I speak to Mrs. Reynolds. She is in charge of the household staff."

Mrs. Reynolds consulted Mrs. Hastings. The cook was always in need of help, and she welcomed Belle as another kitchen maid.

Belle, too, had learned practicality. She believed that Mr. Handley meant to come back for her. She also knew he hunted a beast capable of murder, a hunt he would not quit short of success or death. And perhaps, with time, Mr. Handley had decided that he did not want to continue a relationship with a woman who had worked in a brothel. Had she thought God would listen to her, she would have prayed for Mr. Handley. As it was, she could only hope and accept the good fortune of a decent job until she knew for certain what the future held.

CHAPTER 21

REVELATIONS

In the drawing room of Mr. Pettigrew's castle, Lady Agatha Quintain sat at a small escritoire with a sheet of paper before her, blank except for the letterhead,. Through the mild distortion of the multipaned windows the ground retained a softening layer of snow. The storms had passed in winds like the howl of distant wolves, blind flurries and piled drifts muting the landscape to a monotone of white. A log fire in the large hearth with its massive stone over mantel kept any chill from the air, but Lady Agatha felt cold in spite of its comfort.

She was committed now. There was no turning back. In spite of her determination her mind was troubled. She had never been a vengeful woman; this anomalous need to revive the past, to in some way assuage old wrongs, was new, and it disturbed the equilibrium of her sensibilities, of her understanding of who she was. In spite of their great loss, she knew that Cedric would not have approved. He would not have wanted her to sink into this pit of old pain from which she could not seem to free herself.

If Elizabeth Darcy was as clever as Lady Agatha believed her to be, sooner or later she was destined to discover the secret of the writing desk. Its contents and her response to them were to determine Lady Agatha's final decision. On consideration, she believed her mother had sent her the medallion so that she might make use of information similar to that in the late Mr. Tweed's missive. How the Darcys would react to it was the only unknown. Or so Lady Agatha believed.

Turning back to the desk, Lady Agatha took up a pen and wrote,

Mr. George Darcy
Pemberley House
Derbyshire

My dear Mr. Darcy,

I will be arriving in Lambton next Wednesday se'nnight. I wish to visit the graves of my mother and brother, who I understand are buried on the grounds of the estate. If you have no objection, I shall call at Pemberley House on the morning of February seventh to learn the exact location of the interments.

Yours,
Lady Agatha Quintain

Lady Agatha rang for the butler and sent the letter to be picked up with the post as soon as a rider was able to get through. At a second summons, her maid came in several minutes later.

"Yes, my lady?"

"We are traveling to Lambton in Derbyshire next Wednesday, assuming there is not another blizzard before then. We will be staying at the Lambton Inn. I will also visit my childhood home, Pemberley House, to call on Mr. Darcy, the present master, and to visit my mother's and brother's graves. I will also be calling on the vicar of Kympton church. You will know what to pack."

"Yes, my lady. How long shall you be staying?"

"I am not sure. Not terribly long, I think. Thank you, Marie."

I will go, Lady Agatha told herself. *I will learn what I need to know, and then I will act.*

Marie returned to her mistress's chambers to inventory the clothing in Lady Agatha's wardrobe to ensure any she packed were in perfect condition. *Lambton,* she mused. She was not sure if Lady Agatha knew, but Marie was more aware of her mistress's past than anyone else except possibly Mr. Hughes. She knew that Lady Agatha was born in the north, that her marriage had estranged her from her family, and that some tragedy haunted her life. This sudden journey when they rarely traveled further than Bath filled her with foreboding. Lady Agatha had been different of late, brooding and distracted. She could do nothing but keep a watch over her lady and try to help her in any way possible, although Marie knew that there was unlikely to be anything of real assistance she could offer.

Marie opened the wardrobe and began selecting garments to be packed. Her hands labored with years of practiced skill as her mind wandered in the past. She had escaped the fire that destroyed the château of her master, along with the bodies of the count and his family, taking the several pieces of jewelry that came to hand in the hope of surviving the Terror. By the time she bribed her way out of the country, she arrived in England with no more than a single gold ring and a few francs.

She had no friends in England, only a spattering of the language, no papers, no idea how she was to live. Men ogled her; one or two made offers she did not need English to understand. Starving, alone, sickening day by day from exposure and fear, she made an attempt to sell the ring at a pawnshop. The owner, seeing her state, decided to take advantage. He offered her a few pounds. When Marie refused, he threatened to call a constable and accuse her of theft.

Marie ran. Clutching the ring in her fist, she hurtled out of the shop and bolted headlong into the street. The following seconds were a blur of dark mass as a horse swerved aside, striking her hard enough to knock the air from her lungs. She fell into the gutter, tried to rise, and then gave up. Nothing seemed to matter at that moment. She was no longer able to fight, nor did she want to. When a footman jumped down from the carriage and came to help her to her feet, Marie only stood swaying, her legs wooden.

That was when a woman's voice said, "Bring her here, Thomas."

Marie was assisted to the carriage. She raised her head to find a striking woman a few years older than herself studying her.

"Are you injured?" the lady asked in English, and when Marie only stared, she repeated it in perfect French.

"No, madame. *Merci.*" Marie started to pull away from the footman when the lady said, "Where do you live?"

"Nowhere," Marie answered in French. "I am an émigré. My master and his family were killed in an uprising of the peasants. I escaped. I have sold what little I brought with me, except this."

She opened her hand to show the gold ring. "It was my mistress's."

"I see." After a moment more of scrutiny, the woman said, "I am Lady Agatha Quintain. What was your position with your master?"

"I was lady's maid to the countess." It seemed a lifetime ago.

Lady Agatha said, "And your name, mademoiselle?"

"Marie Vortier."

Lady Agatha came to a decision. She said to the footman, "Help Marie into the carriage, Thomas."

Marie protested that her clothing was too soiled to sit in such a fine vehicle, but Lady Agatha waived the objection away. "Carriage seats can be cleaned. We will go to my residence, where you can bathe, eat, and rest. Then if you want employment, I have a position as a maid available."

"Madame, you do not know me," Marie said as the carriage jerked into motion.

"My dear," Lady Agatha said, "I know despair all too well."

That had been over thirty years ago. Marie had served Lady Agatha since that day without a single regret, except that she had no way to repay her lady's kindness. Perhaps, she thought as she set her clothing choices aside, that chance would arise now.

⁂

"Well, Bennet, I hope you are not in need of a solicitor."

Mr. Witherspoon, of Witherspoon, Woolrich, Hazelmuth, and Gibbs, knew his fellow attorney moderately well. He was a fresh-faced, jovial man of fifty-five, his thinning hair combed around his face much in the manner of busts of Julius Caesar, except for the laurel wreath. His firm's clientele was composed primarily of the highest levels of society. It was said, not without some justification, that Witherspoon et al. handled more money than the Bank of England. Sitting behind a solid mass of desk, Mr. Witherspoon regarded Mr. Bennet complacently, certain this visit was about some legal matter.

"Can I offer you a brandy or a glass of port?" He indicated a carved sideboard of some antiquity.

"No, I thank you." Mr. Bennet's reserved expression warned his compatriot this meeting might be more serious than he had first expected.

"What can I do for you, then?"

Mr. Bennet saw the change in the other solicitor's manner and approved it. "I have come on a matter of some gravity, if it is proven true. This morning one of my daughters was approached by an attorney known to my family, who informed her that a client of yours, whom I believe to be Lady Agatha Quintain, was contemplating an action at law against a prominent family. He indicated that the matter concerned a suppressed will. I have hopes that it was no more than an unfounded rumor. However, if someone in your office is disseminating private information to outside persons, you will understand the nature of the threat as well as I."

Mr. Witherspoon's face had gone from fresh to bloodless. He rose abruptly, strode to the sidebar, and poured two fingers of brandy into a glass. He drank it in two swallows, set the glass down and turned back, his complexion somewhat restored but his equanimity shattered.

"Can you give me the name of the attorney who approached your daughter?"

Mr. Bennet considered. "My former associate, Mr. Cranshaw." No need to say that Mr. Cranshaw had turned in his resignation only the day before.

Mr. Witherspoon sat down. He steepled his fingers on the leather desktop, cleared his throat, blinked several times, laid his hands flat on the surface, and met Mr. Bennet's steady gaze.

"I handle Lady Agatha's legal affairs personally, have done since well before the death of her late husband. The only other person who has any access to the details of those matters is my senior clerk, Mr. Trent-Davies, who copies out the documents. I find it hard to believe that he would betray the confidence of a client in any way. However, I am ashamed to admit that I have had my doubts about his...ah...*personal life*, if you take my meaning? But one is reluctant to entertain such a shocking suspicion about a young man who has always proven to be very efficient and trustworthy."

Meaning, Mr. Bennet thought, *you know the effect such a revelation would have on your firm's clients.* "I understand completely," Mr. Bennet said aloud. He leaned forward slightly in the chair before the desk, a technique he had used successfully to urge clients' cooperation. "However, the situation obviously cannot be allowed to go on. I do not know the young man. Perhaps you can suggest a solution?"

Faced with a practical challenge, Mr. Witherspoon had regained his composure. "I shall certainly confront him. I will not have any employee here who is not totally loyal to the firm. I may be able to put enough pressure on Mr. Trent-Davies to silence him, as any confidence he breaks will surely come to my ears."

Mr. Bennet rose. He had his doubts that members of the *ton*, that constant vortex of gossip and rumor, were likely to confide to their attorney that they were being blackmailed. He shook Mr. Witherspoon's hand and was on the point of leaving when the solicitor addressed him with some reluctance.

"I can assure you that the only will I have dealt with for Lady Agatha was her own."

Mr. Bennet nodded his thanks and went away. Mr. Witherspoon resumed his seat, thought hard for a quarter hour, and then sent for Mr. Trent-Davies.

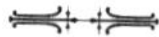

Wickham sat at a roughhewn table in a dusky corner of the small roadhouse some five miles north of Lambton. The shadows suited him; he was indistinct to anyone entering the room from the front or from the passage to the kitchen and cellar in the rear. The roadhouse itself was a place where no one asked your name or your business. He had never used it before, so he was unknown to the proprietor or the other patrons, few at this early evening hour.

He had let his beard grow, trimming it only enough to avoid drawing attention. It had grown out a rusty color; Wickham had judiciously applied henna to his ill-cut hair to match. He wore clothing common to any farmer, hauler, or other workingman, clean enough though obviously well used. While the results would have deceived no one who knew him well, Wickham believed them sufficient to throw off the man following him.

Someone followed. Wickham's instinct combined with discreet questions about a "friend" who might be looking for him had sent him swiftly away from the immediate area of Lambton and Pemberley. In an unconscious gesture, Wickham drummed his fingers on the tabletop, stained by a century of strong drink, scarred with overlapping half moons where metal tankards had pounded on the softer wood. He had no idea who the man was but no doubt as to his purpose. Lord Matlock had put up a reward of five thousand pounds for his capture, enough to tempt many a man to brace him. This one was a tracker. He had come too close at Dolly Younge's, Wickham thought. His escape there left him wary of anyone finding him before he realized his revenge.

That was the crux of it. He discovered in his time at the market town that George Darcy did not leave the grounds of Pemberley House. Fitzwilliam Darcy and his bride were settled in, which would make reaching the older man nearly impossible. With dog patrols of the grounds and no doubt every servant on the place watching out for him, he could think of no way to get through Pemberley's defenses. More importantly, when he had killed his former mentor he needed to be assured of escape. A curse of frustration growled from Wickham's lips. There had to be a way—but what?

Wickham willed himself to think. Since his flight from London, he had not taken the time to do more than plan how to keep ahead of pursuit. He knew the estate intimately. If he gained the inside the house no one would find him if he did not want to be found. Now with the increased vigilance at Pemberley, Wickham was rapidly deciding that it was impossible to reach the house undetected. He still had to find a way to get Darcy away from the house for some little time, leaving George Darcy alone.

It was no longer a question of his going to his prey; he must find a way for the prey to come to him.

He might need help, he thought. There were one or two men in the area with reason to hate the Darcys, and he had enough cash to pay for their services without disclosing his ultimate purpose, if he wanted to trust them. With a five-thousand-pound reward on his head, he was reluctant to chance the purchased loyalty of anyone. Then there was the question of where he should go after the murder. Scotland was safe enough under most circumstances. Since he had little chance of taking down Darcy at the same time as his father, Wickham knew that both Darcy and the bloody colonel would not let a border stop them from hunting him down. He needed a more permanent refuge, the islands or the Americas. In Amsterdam, Wickham knew he could convert all or part of the diamonds into any currency he chose. And ships left the busy port constantly, bound all over the world.

Somewhere at a distance a church bell sounded, ringing vespers. Wickham snarled. To avoid notice, he had to leave the roadhouse before its evening patrons arrived from their work. It would not do for a stranger to be noted and talked about. He started to rise, only to sink back into his chair. That was the answer. Handed to him as if by God Himself.

Seeing that the sour man in the corner looked a bit more cordial, the barmaid approached him, swaying her wide hips. A slatternly blonde of indeterminate age, she called herself the owner's wife. As she leaned forward to speak to him, the neckline of her calico dress scooped so low that she nearly came out of it. Perhaps that was its purpose; her man had no objection to a little extra income if a customer wanted a quick tumble.

"Another, handsome?"

He looked up at her, his mouth automatically lifting in a smooth smile. "Is the church at Kympton still standing?"

She straightened up. "'Twas last time I was by there. You a religious man?"

"Oh, very. At the moment I'm grateful for a revelation." The woman looked at him skeptically, but Wickham laughed softly. "Bring me a bottle of your best brandy."

"You havin' a party?" she asked with what she thought to be a charming innocence. "I love parties."

His face no longer pleasant, Wickham rose. "Just bring it."

When she had stalked off on her errand, he remained on his feet. The Kympton parish should have been his, a nice little flock of sheep to mask other more lucrative activities. It was perfect, Wickham mused, the perfect vengeance. Kympton and George Darcy would die together.

Perhaps someone should have cautioned Mr. Wickham not to blaspheme against something he did not believe in.

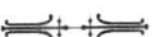

Mary Bennet entered Nicholas Fitzwilliam's sitting room at his invitation. He looked up as the young woman crossed the room to where he sat in a Bath chair[1] a little back from the window. Once he had regained his senses enough to respond to the presence of others, Mary had sat at his bedside in turn with Sofia and Lady Matlock to read to him. Dr. Wyecroft had indicated that some patients recovered more quickly if given such interaction. It seemed to be the case with Nicholas. At first Mary read from the bible then history books and now had progressed to lighter works that he liked to discuss with her.

"Do you read the war news, Miss Bennet?"

1 Bath chair: a chaise with a folding hood that could be opened outdoors, mounted on three or four wheels and pushed or pulled by hand. Named for the spa city of Bath and used by disabled people

A newspaper lay unfolded across the lap robe covering Nicholas's knees. Mary left the door open and took the chair near him with a glance at the *Times.* There was an article about the Marquis of Wellington taking over command of the army in Spain that she had seen earlier in the day at home. It did not specifically mention the Horse Guards, but the indication was that there would be an intensification of the war in Spain.

"I saw it this morning, Sir Nicholas." Mary looked down at the book she held tightly in both hands. "It means more fighting, does it not?"

"Now that Wellington has sorted out Northumberland, he will go after the French with everything he has. Boney lost most of his *grande armée* in Russia over the winter, and now that the Russians are advancing, the German princes are wondering if they can safely change sides."

Mary smiled a little. "I did not know you followed the war so closely, Sir Nicholas."

"Nothing else to do. I can't walk, I can't ride, reading occupies the time. Never did much of that before."

"'Reading maketh a full man; conference a ready man; and writing an exact man.' "

"Sir Frances Bacon. Yes, Miss Bennet, I suffered through university, although my heart was not in it. Richard was quite happy there. He was two years ahead of Darcy and not as dedicated to study, however he did well. Richard has always done well at anything he chose to do."

Mary's gaze turned to the scene beyond the window. Birdsong filled the newly leafed trees. The flutter of wings coming and going from the upper branches drew patterns on a cloudy sky. She missed Richard Fitzwilliam desperately. Not an hour passed that her thoughts were not with him; where was he, was he safe, was there fighting, or was he in camp or on the move? She turned back to Nicholas to find him watching her intently. Blushing lightly, she opened her book; he spoke before she could ask if he wanted her to continue reading to him.

"I think you are a woman who is not easily moved from the path you have chosen."

"I..."

Mary wanted to say she did not understand, only she did. Sir Nicholas's attraction to her had slowly grown as he recovered from his injuries. At first it had been tolerance for her presence as she read to him. The weeks of daily interaction, although completely proper, intensified his appreciation of her quiet, steadfast nature. The thought of her leaving his company grew more painful than the ache in his damaged bones. She was his brother's betrothed in all but name. He knew she was committed to Richard and that to make any open gesture of affection would send her away forever.

"Please, Miss Bennet, read to me if you will?"

Mary nodded. She opened the book, removed the bookmark, and began, grateful for his forbearance. She had come to like Sir Nicholas as a nurse likes a patient, recognizing admirable qualities and accepting those she did not like. He was as he was; she had no desire to change him. God willing, he would one day be her brother; he could never be more.

After half an hour, a maid came from Lady Matlock to request that Mary attend her in her private sitting room. Nicholas picked up the newspaper after she left the room and flung it across the floor.

Richard was always the lucky one, he thought. He closed his eyes, rejecting the idea at once. *No, Richard was the one who followed his duty with honor. He could have had a major's commission, Father would have bought him whatever he chose. He went in as a lieutenant and rose on merit. I have spent my life getting by on my title and my expectation of an earldom. And what has it gained me? This damned broken body and the contempt or the pity of the only people whose opinions mean anything.*

He reached out and picked up the book Mary had left on the table beside her chair. It was Daniel Defoe's *A Tour Thro' the Whole Island of Great Britain,* an amusing and informative volume, suitable for the entertainment of an invalid. Nicholas threw the book after the newspaper.

For several minutes, Nicholas sat without moving, staring blindly at the day outside. Two sparrows were engaged in a battle over a scrap of what appeared to be yarn. Pulling and chirruping, snatching it from one another, hopping and pecking; it would have amused him once. He might even have put a spontaneous bet on which bird would win. Nicholas rang the bell that was never far from his hand. His valet emerged from the dressing room immediately, ready for whatever order his master gave him.

"Pick up the book, will you, Peters? I've dropped it."

Mary found Lady Matlock in her sitting room. Tea was set out on a mahogany tea table. Lady Matlock poured two cups, added cream, and handed one to Mary. She studied the young woman sitting back on the sofa. Not for the first time, she mused that Mary Bennet was hardly the sort of lady she would have thought Richard would marry. Perhaps he was finally ready to leave the army and settle to married life with a calm, steady partner.

"I thought you might want a respite from reading to Nicholas."

Mary colored lightly. "I do not mind reading to Sir Nicholas. He has been very pleasant to me. However, I believe he might now appreciate," she searched for words to convey her reluctance delicately, "reading books that are not suitable for me to read to him."

"Yes." Lady Matlock smiled. "I have no doubt he would. And it will do him good to occupy himself. Mr. Watson and Dr. Wyecroft encouraged him to go outside, but he has not done so. I suppose it is too early in his recuperation to expect it. He does not want the servants to see him in the Bath chair."

Mary nodded. She sipped the tea, a fine bohea, thinking that Sir Nicholas' sense of himself did not allow him to put aside pride for his own benefit. Lady Matlock watched Mary carefully without seeming to do so. She had no doubt that Nicholas was growing too fond of the lady's company and was relieved to see that Mary had no intention of allowing him to encourage the relationship.

"I appreciate your generosity, my dear," she said with a warm smile and then deftly turned the conversation aside to more mundane matters.

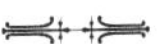

The writing desk sat where Elizabeth had placed it, on a small table in her bedchamber near the windows that looked out over the gardens to the wooded ridge behind the house. In the days since it had been moved to its present location, she had been so occupied with learning her new duties as Mistress of Pemberley that she had not made an attempt to locate the place where the medallion fit. The sessions with Mrs. Reynolds were satisfying. Elizabeth's training at home had been primarily with directing servants and organizing social events and only marginally keeping household accounts. She had taken it upon herself to learn what she could about the latter from her mother. Mrs. Bennet liked to retain control of the funds spent on household items and explained them to her daughters only reluctantly. Not so Mrs. Reynolds. She was more than willing to teach Elizabeth any and all matters concerning Pemberley's domestic finances and more than pleased with her new student.

Her head full of figures and dispositions from their latest meeting, Elizabeth relished the cool solitude of her rooms. She had a letter from Jane, the second still unanswered. The babes were doing well; Martha ate well and was gaining weight, and

Charles Thomas continued to thrive. If her sister could write with two infants to care for, surely she was able to reply. Her eyes fell on the writing desk, and she was captivated again by its beauty; she went to the table, drew up a chair, and laid her hands on the satiny surface.

How many women have sat here as I am sitting, she wondered, *admiring this desk, preparing to write to a friend or relative, accept an invitation, or perhaps pen a note to a lover?* The thought took her to her husband, and she closed her eyes and let Darcy's image fill her mind. *Five months ago I hardly knew his name. I was prepared to marry him with no expectation of happiness, only a hope for an accommodation in the match. Now I understand what Jane meant. I might survive him, but I could never live again without him.*

Her mind went back to that morning as she had dressed for the day. Clara had tisked over her short stays. "I shall have to let out the gussets, madam. They hardly do their job now."

Elizabeth had looked down. Her maid was correct; she was decently covered, by an unusually small margin. She had noticed that her breasts seemed to have increased in size and grown more sensitive. Blushing at the memory of William's attentions the night before, she agreed with Clara. Always with a good appetite, of late she had vacillated between ravenous and peckish. The parsnips in the beef, ale, and parsnip pie at dinner the day before had nearly made her nauseous, and it was usually one of her favorite dishes.

Elizabeth ran her hands lightly over her abdomen. She thought she detected a slight rounding. When she thought back, she had not had her courses for the past two months and was nearly overdue for the third month. Joy filled her, but she determined to wait until she was certain before sharing her news with her husband. If God willed, George Darcy might live to see his first grandchild.

Elizabeth's hands were unconsciously stroking the fine wood of the desk. She opened a small drawer of the table and took out the medallion Lady Agatha had sent her. It gleamed in the clear light of the windows. Aware of the fine workmanship, she turned it in her fingers. With purpose, Elizabeth opened the desk and studied the revealed interior. There were small drawers decorated with painted panels that echoed the outer decorations, a pen tray, glass inkwell with a silver cap, and a drawer for paper. It was not a desk made for work but for personal correspondence.

As she studied it, Elizabeth saw no place where the medallion fit, yet the workmanship was the same as the outer fittings. There had to be a location in the desk for it, she simply had to find it. The center panel held her gaze. It separated the two sides of the desk, four drawers on either side. It was decorated much like the drawers except with a different image, the lily-like design on the medallion. Elizabeth ran her fingers over the surface. She pressed on the love knot at the base of the flowers and felt it give. The panel dropped forward to reveal a secret drawer.

Delighted, Elizabeth examined it carefully. It was large enough to hold a few items of jewelry or other trinkets. Something about it tugged at her mind. It seemed too shallow to occupy the space allowed to it. She pressed the bottom, sides, and back and found a small metal latch hidden behind the back of the drawer. Elizabeth pulled the latch up. The drawer rose an inch. Absorbed, she lifted it out to reveal a lid with a small slot in the center. Elizabeth held her breath. She placed the extension on the medallion's underside into the slot. It fit perfectly. Elizabeth found her hands were shaking as she drew a long, deep breath.

Lady Agatha must have known this secret drawer was here she must have wanted me to find it. Why? What could it hold that she wanted me to have?

She pressed down on the medallion. It gave a small click, and she lifted it up to reveal the second secret drawer. It held a folded piece of parchment, the outer surface as unyellowed as if it had only been placed there yesterday. There was nothing written on the outside. As she lifted it out, Elizabeth felt her hands trembling. If Lady Agatha knew of the missive, it must have been secreted in the desk by either her mother or herself. Slowly, half-afraid of what she would find, Elizabeth opened the letter.

The first lines brought a cry of horror from her lips. She tried to rise and fell back, her knees refusing to hold her. With a dry sob, she continued to read the rest of the message. When she finished, she sat for a long time, dizzy and hollow. At last Elizabeth managed to stand and make her way to the door, still clutching the letter. Her only coherent thought was, *William! I must find William!*

She gripped the knob before her fragmented mind coalesced into a single overmastering revelation. She must not let panic rule her. Elizabeth bowed her head until her cheek pressed the cool, solid wood of the door. When her breathing calmed she opened the door and stepped out into the hallway. Steadying herself on the wall, Elizabeth reached the main staircase. The steps seemed to stretch into infinity. Elizabeth gripped the balustrade tightly to support herself until she reached the first floor.

"Mr. Darcy?"

The footman on duty looked at her strangely. "In his study, madam."

Elizabeth knocked once and went in. Darcy looked up from the papers on his desk and then stood and came to her, taking her arms in his hands to support her. "What is it, Elizabeth? Father?"

"No." She closed her eyes, trying desperately not to let him see how devastated she was.

Darcy led her to the settee before the windows and knelt at her feet. "Tell me, my dearest, what is wrong. Are you ill?"

Elizabeth shook her head. She struggled to calm herself and managed to speak in a strained voice.

"This," she said, raising the letter still clutched in one hand, "I found it in the writing desk, in a hidden drawer. The medallion was a key. You must read it, William."

He rose and sat beside her, taking the old paper from her hand. His eyes scanned the writing; he sucked in his breath sharply and then reached the last paragraph. Elizabeth watched the emotions she had felt flicker over his face; shock, disbelief, fear.

"My God," he whispered. "This will kill Father."

Elizabeth looked up at him. His face had lost all color he stared at the paper as if it were a death warrant. She wanted to scream, to cry out her pain and her fear for him, for all of them, but she was silent. He needed her now as he might never need her again. If he turned from her, however noble his motives, it was the end of any hope for their marriage. Her reason asserted itself. Elizabeth drew a long breath and laid her hand over his where it held the document.

"We do not know if Lady Agatha is aware of this. I do not see how she could be, the letter has been lost for fifty years. And the first part, she cannot know that, no one except ourselves knows. Perhaps she has no interest in Pemberley now. We must speak to her, William. Then we will know how to act."

Darcy laid the paper aside and took his wife in his arms, holding her tightly. For a time they sat that way, silently comforting one another. He said at last, "I was going to tell you later. Lady Agatha sent a note, father received it this morning. She will call tomorrow morning. She wants to visit the graves of her mother and brother at Pemberley chapel churchyard. We will have to speak with her then about—this."

He picked up the letter, refolded it, and rose to put it away in a locked drawer of his desk. Still cold with shock, Elizabeth watched his precise movements. Movement was his way of controlling his emotions; Elizabeth understood from the brittle quality of his movements how very fragile that control was.

She said softly, "If she…if she acts on the information, what will happen?"

Darcy moved to stare out the window. He did not answer for a time before turning haunted eyes on Elizabeth's face.

"I will not allow this to go to the law. We might win in court and still lose everything, not least our good name. This is not a passing scandal. It means disgrace for generations, perhaps forever. It is ruin of everything our family has built for four hundred years. We will not be poor; I have holdings in my own name able to sustain us. The loss of income means nothing compared to the loss of honor. And the loss of everything we love."

He spoke as if the words caused him physical pain. Elizabeth rose; strength flooding through her. "No, William, not everything. Unless I lose you. We swore before God to love and keep one another for better or worse, richer or poorer, in sickness and in health. Those were not empty words, my beloved, I meant them."

"Elizabeth, you must understand—"

"I do understand. You are a good man, the best man I have ever known. Honor has been your life. And there is Father Darcy and Georgiana to think of. I cannot believe that Lady Agatha will destroy our family for a sin committed a lifetime ago; if the worse comes to the worst, we will survive as long as we keep faith with one another. Let us talk to her before we lose hope."

Darcy nodded slowly. "My wonderful Elizabeth. Very well, we will wait and say nothing until we know what to expect. The first part of the letter would have to be revealed; she may not want that, even if the crime was committed as long ago as the sin."

A tap at the door he recognized as Mr. Niles turned Darcy from Elizabeth. The imperturbable butler entered the room. His gaze went from his master to Elizabeth and back, and for perhaps the first time in his career, he hesitated.

"Ah, forgive me, sir, but there is a man waiting to see you. He was sent by Constable Tiggs with a message to be delivered only to you."

Darcy drew a deep breath. There was nothing more to be said at the moment. "Show him in."

Elizabeth touched his hand and felt his strong fingers briefly close around hers. She left the room as Mr. Niles brought a townsman to the study. The man held his hat in both hands and bowed awkwardly to her as she passed and then to Darcy.

As soon as the door closed, he said, "Mr. Tiggs has arrested a man he thinks is the one we all been lookin' for. He'd be most obliged if you could come and take a look and see if it is the fellow."

Darcy found himself on the point of refusing. Mr. Tiggs could have asked any one of a number of merchants and others to identify Wickham. Undoubtedly the constable knew the lure of a five-thousand-pound reward was too much temptation to give anyone else a reason to claim part of it.

"Where was he taken?"

"At the livery. Fellow answers the description pretty well, and he refused to give his name or his business. I'm sorry, Mr. Darcy. I don't know no more."

Darcy thought It unlikely that Mr. Tiggs had arrested Wickham since there had been no fight. He considered in silence for a moment. There was nothing more to be accomplished at Pemberley for the present and a ride to Lambton would provide time to clear his head.

Darcy said, "If you will wait until I have my horse brought around, I will return with you."

"Charles, I am becoming concerned about Lizzy."

Jane Bingley poured tea for her husband, added sugar and cream, and handed him the cup. They were having tea in the small parlor, Jane's favorite room. It was pleasant in the cool afternoon, light coming in through filmy curtains beneath the half-drawn drapes. It was one of the first rooms Jane had redecorated after their marriage. Her tastes were simpler than his sister Caroline's, who had originally done the town house. The colors were now harmonious; shades of pale peach and green, the gaudy Chinese wallpaper changed to a linen texture in cream, the conflicting colors and patterns on cushions and upholstery gone. Bingley studied Jane's face with the attention he always gave his wife, amazed that such a kind, beautiful woman loved him.

My angel, he thought. He sipped his tea and thought before he answered her.

"Have you some reason for alarm, my dear?"

She considered before replying. "Not specifically. She usually writes at least once a week, and I have not heard from her for nearly a fortnight. I know she is absorbed in learning her duties as mistress; that has not prevented her writing at least a note before."

Bingley helped himself to a second tea cake. "Has she mentioned any problems? These are delicious, by the way."

Jane briefly closed her eyes. She adored her husband, but men simply did not comprehend the subtleties of female communication. "Nothing of importance. It is just not her usual behavior. If she was sick, Mr. Darcy would have sent word. I only wonder why she is silent when she has written so regularly until now."

Bingley finished the cake, considered another and rejected the idea. Lately his trousers seemed a bit tighter around the waist than he liked. He held out his cup for a refill before he said, "I suppose you could write her again or send an express. She would surely answer that."

"I am afraid she would think it bad news, and I do not want to alarm her." Jane drank the remainder of her tea, set the cup down and sighed. "I will consider it if I do not hear from her in the next several days. I keep thinking of what Mary heard from

Mr. Cranshaw. Papa thinks it nothing more than pique because Mary cut him."

"Your father is a wise man. If he had any reason to be alarmed, he would surely have gone to Darcy about it, and we would have heard." Bingley put his cup aside and sat back in his chair. "Daniel should be back at any time. I hope his interview with Mr. Bennet went well."

"Papa likes him. And he needs another attorney to handle the work, or so Mama says."

They heard the front door open and a light, quick step in the hall. Daniel Bingley came into the room with the bracing energy of a spring breeze. He grinned at Charles, leaned in to kiss Jane's cheek, and accepted a cup of tea, seating himself on the settee next to his sister by marriage.

"Well," he said, looking from one to the other, "I start Monday at Bennet and Delibes. Not a partner, of course, an attorney on staff, on probation until I prove myself."

"Congratulations, old man." Bingley rose to shake his brother's hand and slap him on the back.

As he reseated himself and Jane added her good wishes, Daniel continued, "The money is generous enough for me to move into rooms. Carrier can do whatever I need. He has been with me since university, and he is a competent man. There is a set on Clarges Street I intend to look at tomorrow."

Daniel selected a biscuit and bit into it. Jane leaned forward a little, her brow furrowed. "You are more than welcome to remain here, Daniel. There is no need for you to move."

"She is right," Bingley added. "You'll want to save money at first, stay here with us."

"Thank you both, but I think I will need the freedom to come and go at all hours without disturbing the household. Its time I was on my own. As for money, Father and you paid my way through university, and I still have my legacy from Father's will.

It was invested in the five percents and was doing well enough. Some months ago a fellow I know in Newcastle put me onto the company that makes Pettigrew Gears. So far I have almost doubled my investment."

"I have heard of the system. I understand they are using it in the manufacture of carpets."

"That and a good many other things. You might look into it."

"I believe I will. As for moving out, think about it at least," Bingley urged.

Daniel took another biscuit and a refill of his tea. "You are a good brother," he said and to Jane, "and a good sister. But it is time I got out on my own. I have hopes that this position will be the beginning of a fine career."

Hopes that one day I can marry as happily as Charles has. That I can give a wife the comforts of a good home, that we can have a family. Even a woman as far above my reach now as Georgiana Darcy. Georgiana Darcy is a lovely dream—only a dream.

"I beg pardon?" Daniel realized suddenly that his brother was speaking to him. Charles repeated patiently, "If you like, I could come with you to look at the rooms."

"Yes, that would be fine, if you have the time."

"Plenty of time right now. We will not be moving back to Netherfield Park until April."

"Are the rooms furnished?" Jane asked.

Daniel recalled the advertisement. "One can get them furnished for an additional amount."

With a practicality that would not have surprised Elizabeth although it made her husband send her a quick glance, Jane said, "There are enough furnishings stored in the attics to fill several flats. Caroline did not care for the traditional pieces. However, there is nothing the matter with them, just a bit old fashioned."

Daniel grinned. He knew his older sister very well. "Thank you again. I accept with gratitude."

The next day was blustery, with a chill wind that made male pedestrians pull their collars up and wind their scarves tightly around their throats, and ladies wrap redingotes or pelisses snugly about them. The rooms were on the second floor of an elderly, well-kept building. As Bingley and Daniel approached a man slammed out of the front door, and with a sharp glance around hurried toward the far end of the block. Daniel laid a hand on his brother's arm to halt him. He followed the departing man with his eyes until he disappeared around the corner.

"Who is that?" Bingley nodded in the departing figure's direction.

"Cranshaw. If he lives here, I will not take the rooms."

"We can easily find out from the landlady." Bingley rang the bell.

After a few minutes a middle-aged woman appeared. She wore an apron, and the smell of cooking followed her. She looked them over with a practiced eye and said, "Yes, gentlemen?"

"I have come about the rooms advertised to let," Daniel told her.

"Yes, sir. If you will follow me, please?"

She bustled away. The entry was plain and clean. They went up sturdy stairs with a central carpet strip to the second landing, where the woman knocked on the door to the right. When there was no immediate response, she knocked again and raised her voice. "Mr. Trent-Davies, are you in?"

The door was opened by a thin young man with a harried look about him. "Yes, Mrs. Hambley?"

"This gentleman," she said, indicating Daniel, "wishes to look at the rooms, if it is not an inconvenience?"

Mr. Trent-Davies stepped back. "No, not at all. Please come in, gentlemen."

Mrs. Hambley moved aside to allow them entrance to the doorway. "If you gentlemen will excuse me, I have to get back to my kitchen. Just knock on the door at the back of the hall if you have any questions."

Mr. Trent-Davies motioned them in with a grimace. "Mrs. Hambley is not rude, gentlemen; she simply knows she can rent these rooms without any effort, so she feels no obligation to enumerate their virtues."

The entry was small, with two spacious rooms and two smaller rooms to the set. A few pieces of furniture had been moved back in one room to make space for a large trunk, already closed. Daniel liked the size of the areas. Windows provided light, everything was well-maintained and convenient. They were returning to the door when he paused and addressed the current occupant.

"As we came in I saw a man leaving who looked vaguely familiar. I think I have seen him in the courts. I was just wondering if he lived in this building?"

Mr. Trent-Davies turned a sudden grimace into a wry expression. "Mr. Cranshaw does not reside here. He used to be a friend of mine, but we have parted ways. If that is all, gentlemen, a hauler is coming for my trunk, and I have a few more items to pack. I am leaving London for a new position in Liverpool."

"Certainly," Bingley answered. "Thank you for your time and your courtesy."

They stopped at the foot of the stairs. Daniel looked around, nodding. "I shall take the rooms. They will do me very well." He added, "Mr. Cranshaw does not seem to have any talent for retaining friends."

"If his performance with Mary is any example," Bingley responded tartly, "I can understand why. Come on, then, let us disturb Mrs. Hambley's culinary preparations. Then we can go home to our own dinner."

With the rooms secured, no time was lost in choosing the pieces needed to furnish them. A carter was hired, and the Bingley footmen moved the furniture into Daniel's new accommodations. His man began to arrange the rooms for his master's convenience while Daniel surveyed the set for any deficiencies to be corrected. That was when he discovered a letter propped on the bedroom fireplace mantel. The name written on it in a clerk's fine hand was "Mr. Cranshaw."

With a sharp breath, Daniel took the missive down. He had no knowledge of Mr. Cranshaw's direction and no desire to contact him. It did not occur to him to burn the letter, only find the least direct way to deliver it.

He replaced it on the mantel as Carrier tapped on the open door of the room and said, "Sir, we will need provisions. Mrs. Bingley has generously sent enough food for tonight and tomorrow. As I shall have other duties to prepare these rooms, I would prefer to stock the pantry ahead of need."

"Certainly." Daniel withdrew his pocketbook and gave his man enough to purchase whatever they might require. "I must report to my new employment. I will return in time for dinner. If you require assistance of any kind, send a note to my brother, and he will send a footman to help."

Carrier seemed to draw himself up. "I shall be quite all right, sir, thank you."

"Carry on, then."

Daniel left the rooms and proceeded to Bennet and Delibes. The afternoon passed swiftly. By the time he took a sedan chair back to Clarges Street, he was feeling confident and a bit pleased with himself. Humming, Daniel approached his new residence. He stopped abruptly on the landing. The door to the set stood slightly ajar, something Carrier would never have allowed. Moving slowly, Daniel pushed the door in. There was no one in sight. Listening intently he heard a faint sound from his bedroom. He briefly debated going for a constable, decided against it, and walked to confront whomever had invaded his privacy.

"Mr. Cranshaw, I believe?"

Mr. Cranshaw's head jerked up from the letter he was reading. Daniel saw his throat move convulsively as he swallowed. He tried to speak, his face pale. No words emerged. Daniel moved into the room to confront him as anger and curiosity struggled for dominance.

"I see you have discovered your correspondence. You have saved me the trouble of forwarding it on to you, breaking the law in the process."

"I…I have a key."

"From Mr. Trent-Davies, not from me. Give it to me."

Mr. Cranshaw handed over the duplicate key with an unsteady hand. "We were friends. I thought he might leave a…a note of goodbye."

"From what he told me," Daniel said as he pocketed the key, "you are no longer friends. You seem to have as little respect for the truth as you do for the parameters of your profession. Were I to do what I ought, I would have you arrested for breaking and entering."

Cranshaw had put the letter away in his inner coat pocket. "I took nothing, except what belongs to me," he said with a growing bravado.

"Gaining entrance with a key you had no right to possess. I will not argue the point with you. I wonder, however, what I might have found had I been unethical enough to read your former friend's letter."

Mr. Cranshaw's reaction amazed Daniel. His knees seemed to give way. He stumbled a step and threw out his hand to grip the mantel for support. His face had turned an ugly gray. He shook his head blindly, staring at Daniel like an apparition.

"No," Daniel said, "I did not. It was unsealed, however as it was not my correspondence I merely replaced it on the mantel." His voice hardened. "Now, take your letter and get out of my rooms. If I ever see you near here again I will give you in charge, and I have the spare key to back up my word."

Mr. Cranshaw blundered past Daniel and fled. Suddenly tired and thoroughly disgusted, Daniel closed the front door and went into the other large room, which was to serve as parlor and dining room. He was quite sure that he knew what the missive held. It explained Mr. Cranshaw's behavior in trying to attach Mary and his spiteful action when she rejected him. It also explained what he knew of the information Mr. Cranshaw had thrown at her and where he had obtained it. Daniel sighed. He did not judge other men's morals unless they harmed the innocent. Mr. Cranshaw was a septic example of manhood, whatever his proclivities.

Daniel heard the front door open and stepped back into the hallway to find Carrier entering the rooms with a shopping basket in imminent danger of exploding. His man closed the door with a shoulder and proceeded to the pantry, giving his master a half bow as he passed. With a smile, Daniel returned to the bedroom and opened a window on the cool spring evening.

CHAPTER 22

DEVICES AND DESTRUCTION

Handley rode slowly along the Lambton high street. He had come from the livery stable where his horse was boarded overnight. The board had cost all but a few coins of his remaining funds. Handley had slept in the hayloft to save what was left. If Wickham ran, he needed the horse to be in good condition even if its rider was not. The stable owner was so impressed with a man who put his mount ahead of himself that he had given Handley breakfast. Most of Handley's remaining money had gone to learn that a man answering Wickham's description had been seen at a roadhouse north of town the day before. The owner denied that any such person had visited his premises. The barmaid took the coins and told Handley that the man had not only been in the place he had also departed with a bottle of French brandy.

"Mean bloke," she added. "And a bit strange, if you ask me. He wanted to know about the church in Kympton."

"Kympton?"

"Aye." The barmaid rested both fists on her ample hips. "Little village 'bout five miles or so west a' here. The Darcys own it, like they own most everything else around here."

Handley halted his mount in the shadow of an ancient oak across from the Lambton Inn. As he waited, his eyes roved over the people passing along the street, intent on their own affairs. Few men were out at that time of day, being already at their work. Most of the shoppers were women. It was too early in the year for the holidaymakers to visit the Peaks or the Lake District. These were locals about simple business, doing errands, buying goods, as they did every day of their lives. Quiet people, God-fearing, upright and honest. The kind of people he had grown up with. Handley was not naïve; he realized that there was always darkness under the calm surface of humanity. That was the minority; this was the majority of country people. Handley felt a kinship with them, something, he mused, he no longer felt with himself.

He had become a man he did not like. Wickham obsessed him. This long hunt for Juney's murderer had slowly drained his ability to judge the importance of any other element in his life. It was as if the man had somehow gotten inside of his mind and pushed out his humanity, his sense of responsibility to others; had turned him into a hunting beast with no purpose except to find his prey and destroy it. And when he accomplished that purpose, what then? Could he ever go back to the ship's officer he had been, to the man who had docked in London that terrible day to find his beloved little sister dead?

Handley mused bitterly that he would have to seek out Mr. Darcy and ask for funds to continue his search for his sister's murderer. The Kympton information should be worth something. The funds he had obtained from the magistrate in Matlock had taken Handley into Scotland. He had barely missed Wickham in Edinburgh. The man tended to hide in larger cities rather than the countryside where any stranger is noticed and remembered. Handley had also ascertained that Wickham was traveling back to the border. The information left Handley in no doubt that Derbyshire was his ultimate destination.

Handley rubbed a hand across his chin. He had not shaved in several days, his clothing was worn and dirty, his hair shaggy without barbering for a month. *The beast is in better shape than I am,* he thought angrily. His decision to seek out Darcy had been reached with desperation; he was still wavering when the clatter of the post coach attracted his attention. It came to a dusty halt in front of the Lambton Inn. The driver got down and went to open the door for his passengers. Handley barely watched him. It was not until his gaze fell on a young woman who had stopped to let the passengers go by that he stiffened so abruptly his horse shook its head in reproof.

Belle looked up as he pulled the horse to a halt and swung down out of the saddle. Her heart began to beat faster as a smile lifted her lips. Handley tied his horse to a stanchion. His eyes took in her dress, plain but of good fabric, her sturdy shoes and warm shawl. Even her bonnet looked new. Belle saw his scrutiny, brief as it was, and pulled back when he offered his arm. She felt cold with shame and a budding anger.

Handley took her elbow and guided her onto the sidewalk, moving back against the building so that they did not block the way. "I asked after you here when I got back," Handley said, "but no one remembered a woman arriving by herself. I decided you were staying on in Matlock."

Not meeting his eyes, Belle gazed into the street. Her voice was as stiff as her posture. "The woman who owns the boarding-house let me work out my board, so I had enough for the room for an extra month. She would have let me stay on and work full-time, but I didn't want to stay in Matlock any more. When you didn't come back, I came here, like you said."

He heard the edge in her words, almost as she had sounded at Mrs. Younge's: bitterness, anger, and despair. It came to him that she thought he had abandoned her. How had she lived since her arrival?

He said, "Its all right, Belle. I'm here now."

Her response startled him in its intensity. "No, Mr. Handley, it's not all right. You didn't even ask me where I've been stayin' or how I've managed. You think I've gone back to what I was."

"No, I..."

He had, he admitted to himself, just for a moment. "I'm sorry, Belle."

"You don't have to be, Mr. Handley. You got me out of that horrible place, only you can't get it out of your head. I told you how I come there. It wasn't my choice, but it happened, and that won't ever go away."

She glanced at a woman who had slowed her pace as she passed them. Handley felt a welling of remorse that threatened to overwhelm him. He had lost Juney, and now he was losing this woman whom, unaware, he had come to love.

"No, Belle, it won't go away. But it doesn't have to be the rest of our lives."

Her eyes met his. Her face was stony with defeat. "No, Mr. Handley, it doesn't—it will. Every time a man looks at me on the street, you'll wonder if is he's one of them. I can't live with that, its like slow poison"

Emotion was beginning to clog her voice. She turned from him and started walking rapidly along the sidewalk. He almost mounted his horse and rode out of town, until the sight of her straight back as she marched away from him sent a pain through his chest that he could not ignore. He caught her up in front of the Lambton Inn and blocked her path. Silent tears glittered on her lashes. Handley closed his eyes for a moment. He wanted desperately to take her in his arms right there on the main street; wisely he knew she would reject him if he did.

"Listen to me, please. I didn't think anything except that you came to find me and I wasn't here." His words sounded desperate in his own ears; he no longer cared. Handley knew he was not going to let this woman walk out of his life if there was any way to prevent it.

Belle hesitated. "You don't owe me anything. I only came because...because...," her voice faltered, dropped to a whisper, "you asked me to."

Something in Handley's mind shifted at the words. He felt dizzy for a moment, as if a burden he had not been aware of was lifted away.

He said, "I asked you to come because I wanted you to. I could have walked away from you in Matlock. I didn't because...you've come to mean more to me than anyone since my family. But if I have faith in you, Belle, you have to have faith in me. If you can't do that, then there's no future for us, and I want that future more than anything I've ever wanted in my life."

Slowly the rigid set of her expression changed, became uncertain. She seemed to be quivering on the edge of a decision that was the rest of their lives. Handley took both of her hands in his and held them lightly. This was her choice only she could make it.

"I want that too."

Handley pressed her hands and released them. It was all he dared in a public place. Belle managed a small smile. It was enough.

"How can I find you?"

Belle said, "I went out to Pemberley like you told me and asked for Mr. Darcy. Mrs. Darcy talked to me. She let me work in the kitchen until you came back. She's a real nice lady. I'll be there if—when—you want me."

A man on horseback passed them, heading along the high street at a fast trot. It was Darcy; Handley knew the upright figure and clean profile. He could not see the man's expression, only a rigid tension in the body. Belle turned to follow his gaze as the horseman moved out of sight.

"That's Mr. Darcy."

Handley released her hands.

"I have to talk to him. I have information about Wickham. I'll do it now if I can catch him up. I'll come out to the house to see you as soon as I can. Will you trust me a little longer, Belle?"

She looked at him, and for the first time, she smiled. "I've trusted you this long. A bit longer won't hurt."

Handley untied his horse and started the way Darcy had gone. By the time he reached the end of the street, Darcy was out of sight. Several passersby were still looking in the direction of the road leading toward Pemberley. Handley kicked his horse into a canter in pursuit. When he reached the open road beyond town, there was no sign of the horseman.

Handley swore; if Darcy had gone across country, it meant a trip to the manor house to find him. Handley urged his horse to a gallop. He came around a wide curve and saw a dust trail in the distance. Encouraged, Handley galloped along the road in pursuit. The dust had settled as he approached. He slowed his horse to a trot and searched for new sign of the rider. As he passed a small grove of trees, Darcy emerged to confront him, a very fine and accurate pistol in hand.

"Handley."

Handley was not sure if his tone was surprise or regret. Without preamble, Handley said, "I saw you leaving town and followed. I have information about Wickham."

Darcy put the pistol away. "I thought you wanted to take him yourself?"

"I do, but I've run out of funds." *Best to be honest with this man.* "I want something for the information."

Darcy nodded. "If Wickham is there, I will see to it that you receive the reward. And I will add a thousand pounds to it."

"I don't want money unless I have to follow Wickham again. There's a woman working at Pemberley. Her name is Belle. If anything happens to me, I want her taken care of."

Darcy studied the man before him. He was a practiced judge of character, and Handley impressed him as a man who put integrity above personal gain. "I have spoken with her. If necessary, I will see that she is cared for."

The man's word was good enough, Handley thought. "I found out yesterday that Wickham is, or will soon be, in a village called Kympton. I didn't go to the constable because he doesn't know me and he certainly does not know what Wickham is capable of."

"I have just had proof of that," Darcy told him with some disgust. "He took in a man who resembled Wickham and refused to identify himself. The constable sent for me to verify if it was Wickham rather than go to a townsman who remembered him from the past."

"Five thousand pounds is a fortune," Handley said neutrally. "It wasn't Wickham, of course. I assume he was behind it."

"That is why I waited out of sight when I realized I was being followed. I thought he meant to either ambush me or make a run at Pemberley in my absence. It is my father he hates. Why, God only knows."

Handley heard a great anger beneath the words. He said after a moment, "We can ride to Kympton. If anyone has seen him, the person will remember. It's as close as I've gotten since Matlock nearly three months ago."

Father is well protected, Darcy thought, *and Elizabeth is with him. If Wickham is in Kympton, I will find him. We have lived in an armed camp long enough.*

To Handley, he said as he turned his horse back to the road, "The turnoff for Kympton is a quarter mile ahead. We can go across country from there. Let us find out if your information is accurate."

Darcy put his horse into a gallop, Handley riding beside him.

Wickham had often said that he acquired more useful information over a card table than at the university he attended, "useful" being a relative term. Shortly before the final debacle in London, he had spent some of his take from the robberies at a gambling hell where he encountered an old acquaintance, one Murray. During the course of the game, Murray had bragged that he knew a way to open any safe, even in a bank. With a little prodding, Murray disclosed that he had figured a way to make a small shell, similar to those fired from field artillery. The device was strong enough to blow the door off a steel safe.

"Why haven't you used it?" Wickham asked.

Murray—collarless, bearded, his shirt stained and rumpled, his hair uncut for weeks—squinted at Wickham, bleary eyed. "Too damn dangerous. Blow your head off if you do one little thing wrong."

"I don't believe you," Wickham taunted.

" 'Struth."

Interested but unwilling to let Murray know it, Wickham ordered another round. When it came, he said thoughtfully, "A shell weighs too much to be carried around in your pocket. And it needs an ignition source."

"Nah this 'un. Jus' a fuse."

Wickham sat back with a short comment on cattle excrement. Murray, suddenly incensed as Wickham wanted, slammed his fist on the table. He proceeded to explain the creation of a small bomb, portable and potentially deadly. His listener was no more certain it would work than before Murray detailed its construction as he filed it away for future reference. Murray was a petty thief and hanger-on, too frightened for his own skin to take a bold step, Wickham thought with contempt, unlike himself.

In the run-down shack hidden in the woods outside Lambton where he currently resided, Wickham spread out his haul from the night before. He had paid a nocturnal call on the local gunsmith, relieving him of several unassociated items: two fuses of the kind used for matchlock guns, a block of sealing wax, two sheets of heavy parchment paper, and a quantity of high-quality black powder. Always deft with his hands, it took Wickham only a few minutes to finish his work.

Satisfied, Wickham donned an old duster that covered his clothing completely, stuffed his makeshift bombs into its capacious inside pockets, put on his hat, and went out to saddle his horse.

Today is the day. I shall have my revenge on George Darcy and his son, and then I will leave England for a good life elsewhere, safe and wealthy.

With a feral grin he turned his mount toward Kympton.

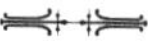

"Lady Agatha, I am most happy to welcome you to Kympton. How can I be of service?"

The vicarage behind the little church was small compared to most such structures, built like the church of wood on a native-stone foundation. Both buildings sat on a low bluff above the river, the town a few hundred yards below. A wood thickly surrounded the area on the north and west, dropping down with the contour of the land to eventually circumvent the village, until it dwindled into farmland. The south was taken up by the churchyard. A gently sloping graveled path led from church to village. Lady Agatha's coach had gained the low grade with ease, depositing her at the vicarage door before pulling into the tree shadows to wait.

Mr. Keene, the vicar, greeted his guest and conducted her into the vicarage. It was smaller than many of its kind, for neither the former vicar nor Mr. Keene was married. Lady Agatha saw an earnest young man, plain of feature, in neat clerical gray. He was not obsequious in his manner, he did not posture. He might have been any well-mannered younger son of a local landowner. Indeed, she mused, he probably was.

"My housekeeper is working with two local ladies, tidying the church for Sunday service. She left tea in my study, if you will accompany me?"

Mr. Keene led Lady Agatha to the first floor, where tea had been set out on a round table near the window. After seating his guest, the vicar poured tea and took a chair, his expression open and interested. Lady Agatha sipped her tea out of politeness and then set the cup aside. She laid her hand on her reticule resting on the table.

"You sent me a document from the former vicar at his instruction."

"Yes, my lady. As I stated in my note, it was found among his papers after his death."

"You have no idea of the contents?"

"No, my lady."

He folded his hands together, an unconscious gesture any person he had ever counseled would recognize as indicating a serious intent.

"I have been thinking back to the time before he became ill, and I can only remember one incident that might have relevance to the document. About ten years prior to his last illness, he was called to a very old lady who was dying. I had just taken the position of curate here, and I was surprised that he did not want me to accompany him.

"Her name was Mrs. Mallory. She had been a local midwife for many years before retiring; indeed she was at least ninety and well-loved in the community. When he returned, Mr. Tweed did not tell me what had transpired. He locked himself in his study for several hours. When he emerged, he looked, quite frankly, as if he had been wrestling with the devil, if you will pardon the description. Nothing was said, and matters returned to normal. The next day we were notified that Mrs. Mallory had passed away in the night."

Lady Agatha considered for a moment. "What do you know of Mr. George Darcy's involvement with this church?"

"Mr. Darcy?" Reverend Keene seemed genuinely puzzled. "Kympton is in his gift, of course; it has been on Darcy land since it was built, over two hundred years ago. Except for generous support he has no direct involvement. I understood from Mr. Tweed that his father, Alexander Darcy, also supported the church with no direct part in its administration."

"And Mr. Gerald Darcy?"

Mr. Keene frowned. "The grandfather. He was before my time, of course. Odd you mention him, now that I think on it. Mrs. Mallory lived out her days on a pension from Mr. Gerald Darcy. Although modest, it was more than sufficient for her needs."

"I have no doubt it was." Lady Agatha sat back, as if some unasked question had been answered.

For a time there was total silence. Lady Agatha started to rise when faintly the sound of a woman screaming came through the window. The words were French, and the voice so familiar Lady Agatha said aloud, "Marie!"

For a second out of time, the air in the room seemed to congeal. Then a blast shook the walls and floor, followed seconds later by another. The window blew out in a shiver of glass. Lady Agatha instinctively gripped the table with both hands to keep from falling. Shock swallowed all other emotions. Mr. Keene grabbed for her arm to steady her, a moment too late. She fell heavily; her reticule slid onto the floor. The tea service followed in a splatter of porcelain shards, liquid spreading over the old planks.

The Kympton vicarage had succumbed to an inferno.

Wickham approached Kympton church from the north, tying his horse in the lower side of the woodland. Except for birdsong and the rustle of activity in the undergrowth, it was silent. He was gratified to see that there appeared to be no one around, until he stepped out of the cover of the trees to find a large coach parked further to the west. The driver dozed in his seat, indicating that the occupant was absent.

If they've gone in to pray, Wickham thought with a lupine smile, *they couldn't have picked a better time.*

He crossed the porch and edged one door open, surveying the interior. Three women were hard at work, cleaning the church, straightening hymnals, dusting the pews, and sweeping around the altar. A bucket of water held what appeared to be several vases. Wickham cursed under his breath. Killing three women in a church would make even Scotland no sanctuary. Wickham backed away and closed the door silently. There was another target he could use.

Walking boldly, as if he had every right to be there, he circled around the vicarage. The back door was unlocked as he had expected. He took one of the devices out of his coat and checked the fuse. He had calculated the time as closely as he could: light the first one, run through the house, light the second one, and disappear into the woods. As soon as word spread, George Darcy would appear.

Wickham took the cheroot out of his mouth and blew on the end until it glowed red. He put it to the fuse and tossed the parchment cylinder against the stairs leading down to the basement where the kitchen and storage were located. He ran down the hall with loping strides without seeing any of the rooms on either side. Coming past the main staircase, he suddenly heard faint voices from the first floor. Wickham checked for a heartbeat, two, and then made for the front door, lighting the second fuse as he paused in the opening. He threw the bomb at the stairs, dived through the doorway, leaped the porch and sprinted for the woods. Behind him, the double concussion tore the silence apart. He did not see the device strike a table and explode, sending a lamp hurtling to break on the carpeted steps. Oil sprayed over the wooden treads and the wall, instantly aflame.

Wickham heard a woman screaming in French as he ran, not losing a stride. *Too late, ma belle,* he thought as he ran. *Too late.*

Mr. Keene helped Lady Agatha back into her chair and then made his way to the door. It was jammed. He gripped the knob and pulled it free, only to see smoke boiling into the hall from both ends in a black wave.

"We cannot get out this way!" The vicar shoved the door shut, wedged it against the jamb as firmly as possible, and ran to the window.

Lady Agatha made a second attempt to stand, only to subside with the room swinging around in her blurred vision. Mr. Keene used a candlestick to break out the remainder of the window glass and leaned out to shout for help. He saw the ladies from the church staring in horror at the vicarage. One of them was holding on to a stranger, a thin woman in the dress of a servant to a wealthy lady, no doubt the Marie Lady Agatha had named. She was still screaming in French, struggling to get free.

"Get help!" he shouted. The low growl of fire invaded his senses—smoke was seeping into the study. The building was on fire, and the women stood frozen. "Go, get help! Tell them to bring a ladder! Hurry!"

One of the women turned on her heel and ran toward the path to the village. The vicar looked down. The ground appeared very far below. He gauged the drop at no more than twenty feet. He might survive a fall from that distance, Lady Agatha would not. Mr. Keene turned back to her. She was conscious; there was a smear of blood on her forehead where she struck the table as she fell. He took out his handkerchief, looked around, and found that the heavy leaded glass water carafe on his desk had not fallen in the shaking. As he wet the linen, he tried to gather his fragmented thoughts.

Something has exploded. There is nothing in or near the vicarage capable of doing so. What must have happened?

Lady Agatha was stirring. He put the handkerchief in her hands, lifting it to her face. The consuming voice of the fire was louder. His throat began to burn from the acrid fumes. Taking Lady Agatha's arm, he guided her to the window and looked out once more. Men were running toward the vicarage from the village, all of them carrying buckets. They would not be in time, he thought.

The sight of two horsemen passing the village men was startling. Mr. Keene recognized the younger Mr. Darcy; his companion was a stranger. Darcy leaped out of the saddle just short of the building. He ran under the window and called up.

"Is there a ladder?"

"In the barn."

Mr. Keene coughed rackingly. The open window drew the smoke in around the door. Lady Agatha handed him his handkerchief, but he pressed it gently on her.

"Help is here," he said. "We…will…be saved shortly."

She tried to nod. Her head pounded, and in spite of the wet cloth her mouth and throat prickled with pain. The air in the room had grown hot. They had a very few minutes before it was engulfed in flames.

Mr. Keene saw Darcy run for the barn, his companion on his heels. The ladder was leaned against the hayloft. Darcy pulled it free, took up one end as Handley lifted the other, and carried it to the vicarage. As soon as it thudded against the building, he tossed his hat aside and began climbing. The ladder was several feet short of the window, but Darcy's height gave him an advantage. He reached up as the vicar lifted Lady Agatha to the windowsill, gripping her waist with both hands.

"Hold on to me," Darcy said.

She tried to nod. Her arms went around his neck, and her head drooped against his shoulder. She murmured, "Alex," and fainted.

Handley held the ladder steady while Mr. Keene found a foothold and descended. A great blast of searing heat followed him as the door to the hall gave way. The flames had invaded the ground floor rooms as well, and the temperature radiating from the outer wall was nearly unbearable. Handley caught the vicar's arm and pulled him away from the wall, throwing the ladder out of harm's way.

They retreated toward the church, Mr. Keene glad of the stranger's supporting arm. His face was flushed from the temperature in the room, his hair singed where the last banner of fire had brushed him. Men were throwing water on the vicarage, to little avail. The old wooden structure was well and truly destroyed.

"I…I cannot think what caused it," the vicar muttered. "There were two explosions, and then the fire seemed to come from everywhere."

"Explosions?" Handley stopped short. "What kind of explosions?"

"Loud ones," Mr. Keene replied with some bitterness. "I am not familiar with munitions. I should say rather like some sort of gun."

Handley looked around. Darcy had already carried the unconscious woman into the church. "Do you know if anyone saw anything?"

The vicar closed his eyes briefly. "There was a woman, I believe Lady Agatha's maid, who kept screaming in French. She was terrified for her mistress. Let me try to remember."

Mr. Keene swayed a little on his feet, Handley keeping a firm grip on his arm. After a moment, he said, "My French is not the best. But I heard 'fire' and 'madam' repeated, and I believe she said, 'l'homme,' several times and then, 'Il a couru dans les bois.'[2] It does not make much sense, I am afraid."

"It makes sense to me." Handley saw one of the women emerge from the church and beckoned her to them. "Can you take the padre inside, ma'am? There's something I have to do."

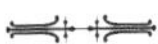

Mr. Niles tapped on the door of the library and waited to be called in. He felt a certain reservation about his next action, although he knew very well that Mr. Darcy would not be happy with him if he kept silent. Mr. Niles entered to find his master sitting in a comfortable chair in a window bay with Mrs. Darcy across from him, both reading peacefully.

George Darcy looked up, unalarmed. "Yes, Mr. Niles?"

Drawing a breath, Mr. Niles said as neutrally as possible. "Excuse me, sir, there seems to be a fire in the direction of Kympton."

George stood up and turned to the door. Behind him, Elizabeth put her book aside and also rose.

"How big?" George asked.

"I should say, sir, at least one structure."

"Very well. Have the gig brought around and get every man who can be spared into a wagon with all the buckets available. They will need all the help they can get. If its in the village, the whole place is in danger."

2 "The man, he ran into the wood."

"Father Darcy." Elizabeth moved to block his way as Mr. Niles departed. "You cannot go. You promised William you would stay at Pemberley."

"William is not here," George told her, not unkindly. "Kympton is on Darcy land, it is our responsibility to assist them. I will not send my men into danger and stay here."

At that moment Elizabeth clearly saw her husband in his father. Her chin rose. "Very well. Then I am going with you. My help will be needed as well."

At that moment George Darcy clearly saw Lady Anne in his daughter-in-law. He smiled. "Get your things."

In the entrance, Georgiana caught her father's arm, alarm clearly printed on her delicate face. "Papa, you cannot leave! Let our men go., they are trained, they will do everything necessary. Please, Papa!"

George touched her cheek gently. "You know I must go with the men, Georgie. We have a duty to our dependents. I cannot set that aside because there is some risk involved."

She hung her head. "I know. I am just frightened."

"I will look after him," Elizabeth promised as George continued on to his rooms. "When William returns, tell him where we have gone, although if he sees the smoke he may go to Kympton first."

Georgiana hugged Elizabeth swiftly. "Be careful, Lizzy. I could not stand it if you both did not come home safely."

A quarter hour later, they were on their way. The road to Kympton was in good repair, like all roads on Pemberley, and the gig made good time. A quarter hour saw them pulling up the slope from the village. Elizabeth caught her breath at sight of the burning vicarage, already nearly gutted. She saw Darcy's horse a moment later. A boy was standing near the big stallion, talking to it quietly. In both hands, he held a top hat that Elizabeth instantly recognized.

"That's Erebus," she pointed out. "And the boy has William's hat. William is here."

George called to the boy, who ran over and stopped beside the gig. "That is my son's horse. Where is he?"

"In the church, Mr. Darcy. A lady was hurt, and he took her inside. Vicar's there too."

"No one died in the fire?"

"No, sir."

"What happened?"

"Don't know, Mr. Darcy. There was two turrible loud explosions and then the fire. Vicar and the lady was on the first floor. Mr. Darcy got 'em out, down a ladder."

"All right, thank you, son."

Elizabeth prepared to climb down, speaking over her shoulder. "I am going to find William. Please come with me?"

"As soon as I tie the horses. I do not like Erebus standing alone, although our small friend seems to have kept watch over him."

George came around the gig and handed Elizabeth down. She extended her hand to the boy, smiling. "May I have my husband's hat? I am sure he will be pleased to have it returned to him in such good condition."

"Yes, ma'am." Blushing lightly, he handed her the hat.

Elizabeth held it tightly in both hands as she walked the short distance to the church. Behind her, George strode to where Erebus waited with restless patience. He snorted at the familiar smell of the man and tossed his long mane. George stroked the sleek black nose before he took up the reins. The boy had accompanied him. His eyes devoured the stallion, admiring and wistful.

George said, "You did not see what actually happened in the vicarage, then?"

"No, sir." A tentative hand went out to stroke the black satin shoulder. "My ma was cleanin' the church, she does every week, and she set me to pull weeds in the churchyard. I come runnin' when it happened. A woman was screamin' in some foreign language, and the vicar was shoutin' for help. Then Mr. Darcy and another man rode in and got a ladder and saved the lady and the vicar."

George frowned. "Another man? No one you know?"

"No, sir. Looked rough, but they come together. After Mr. Darcy took the lady into the church, the man got on his horse and rode into the woods farther down."

"Toward the village?"

"Yes, sir."

As if he meant to circle that part of the grove without being seen. George dug in his waistcoat pocket and produced several coins. "Thank you, son. You had better go and find your mother, she may be worried about you."

The boy's eyes widened. "Thank you, Mr. Darcy."

He clutched the coins and ran to the church. George led Erebus to the gig, tied him to the rear, and led the carriage horse to a large oak out of the way of the men still pouring water on the ruins. The wagon from Pemberley drove up, and his men jumped out, running to the bucket line to relieve the men there. He did not need to direct them, they were well trained in fighting fires. The safety of the manor house depended on them.

Wickham. George's face set in grim lines. *This is his kind of deviltry. And his only purpose in firing the vicarage was to bring me out of Pemberley. I have no doubt he decoyed William away for the same reason. He has never been as clever as he believes himself to be. If he is here in the grove, I will not allow William to spring his trap in my stead.*

George bent and ran his hand down the hind leg of the horse, using the movement to check the small pistol he had taken to carrying in a waistcoat pocket. If Wickham was watching from the trees, he would see nothing amiss. The pistol was of the Queen Anne type, with a screw plug in the barrel for loading, accessed by revolving the trigger guard. He had sent to Manton for the pistol on a special order when an attack by Wickham became probable. The frame was skeletal, so there was nothing to reveal its presence. George had said nothing to William or Elizabeth, preferring to let them think that he relied on the security of Pemberley's staff. He did; he also knew George Wickham well. There was always the chance of a confrontation, as now.

George tied the horse and walked slowly into the trees. He counted on Wickham wanting to confront him rather than shoot from ambush. The sharp, clean smell of pine surrounded him, his boots stirring dead needles, twigs, and the garnered leaves of the winter storms. Here and there in the stippled light, a small white flower nodded shyly. Every sense was preternaturally attuned to his surroundings. Wickham would not have retreated far.

George had gone some fifty feet into the woods when he smelled the smoke from the small cheroots Wickham affected.

"Come out, George." The Master of Pemberley stopped and turned slowly. "Unless you would prefer to shoot me in the back."

Wickham stepped into the open, a pistol in his hand aimed at George Darcy's heart.

"No, Godfather. I want to see your face when you die."

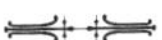

Elizabeth entered the church to find her husband in the family pew in his shirtsleeves, speaking quietly in French to a thin woman who stood over Lady Agatha Quintain. Marie's face was streaked with tears as she gazed at her mistress. Lady Agatha lay very still. Elizabeth could see her chest rise a little with each breath. There was blood on her forehead; William's coat was rolled as a pillow under her head.

"The doctor will be here shortly," he told Marie in French. "He is a very competent doctor. I am sure she will be well."

Two village women were attending to a man in what had been a neat gray suit but now showed the ravages of the smoke and flames of the fire. He stood when he saw Elizabeth and reassured the women he was not in pain while one of them bandaged a long cut on his hand.

Elizabeth said, "Is there anything I can do, Mr.…"

"Keene, David Keene. I am the vicar of Kympton church. Mrs. Darcy?"

"Yes."

"I am not in need at present, thanks to these ladies. I wish I could say the same for Lady Agatha. When the explosions shook the vicarage, she was just standing. She was thrown to the floor, and I believe she struck her head on the table."

"Dr. Morrow will be here anytime, Mrs. Darcy," the woman bandaging the vicar's hand said, straightening up. "The lady's poorly, I'm afraid."

Elizabeth nodded. "I am so sorry for the loss of the vicarage, however structures can be rebuilt. It is a miracle that you and Lady Agatha escaped. You said 'explosions'?"

"Two." Mr. Keene wavered between outrage and disbelief. "I have no idea what caused them. Apparently there was a man involved, Lady Agatha's maid saw him run into the woods."

Elizabeth felt cold creep into her chest at the words. She turned toward her husband, who had exited the pew, leaving Marie to tend her mistress. He saw her, and his eyes widened.

"Elizabeth? What are you doing here?"

"I came with your father. When he saw the smoke, I could not keep him at Pemberley. He brought out men to fight the fire. He should be here at any moment, he said he would join me as soon as he tied the horses."

She looked toward the side door, but the figure who came briskly in was not George Darcy. He was a big man, his thick brown hair salted with gray. Eyes of a strange gray green surveyed the room in a glance. The man dismissed the vicar as not in need of immediate care and strode to the Darcy pew, his medical bag in hand.

"Darcy," he greeted Fitzwilliam. "What happened?"

"Some sort of explosions," Darcy replied grimly. "This is Lady Agatha Quintain. She was hurt when the vicarage burned."

"So I see. And you, miss?"

Marie looked up. She felt immediate confidence in the large man. Her English had abandoned her, she said in French, "I am madam's maid. Please help her, *m'sieur le docteur.*"

"I will do what I can," Dr. Morrow promised in the same language as he set his bag down.

Darcy had gone to Elizabeth, his eyes on the side door. "How long ago did you leave Father?"

"I do not know. A few minutes." She held tightly to his arm. "You do not think he might have…?"

Darcy said, "Stay here. That is just what I think."

He was halfway to the door when they heard the shot.

CHAPTER 23
RETRIBUTION

Handley found Wickham's horse tied just inside the tree line on the far side of a tongue of wooded area above the village. He took it with him into a thicker growth, tied it to his own horse, and continued on foot back toward the church. Wickham was in here somewhere, to what purpose he was not certain. That the man had a purpose he had no doubt, and one of evil intent. Arson was a hanging offense, although Wickham probably felt no compunction on that account, having a noose waiting for him already.

Silently Handley cursed the mat of vegetation underfoot. He found it almost impossible to move without making some noise. Slowing his pace gave Wickham time to accomplish his intent and perhaps run before Handley found him. Or to set up an ambush. He wondered if Darcy knew he was gone. Maybe he should have said something. Everything had faded except the fire burning in his mind to catch Juney's killer, raging hotter than the one at the vicarage. There was no time to gather men and beat Wickham out of the woods like a wild beast. He had escaped too many times before; Handly swore that his prey was not going to escape again.

It seemed an hour passed before he heard a mutter of voices ahead. Handley halted and brought his pistol up. Was there a confederate? Was that why Wickham was hiding here? Handley crept forward, intent on every step. A breeze from the river rattled the pine branches and sent stippled light fluttering like birds. He came to the trunk of a venerable oak and eased around it enough to see that a small glade lay ahead. Two men faced one another in the center. For a second Handley thought one was Darcy until he realized this man was older and looked ill.

The father, he thought, *the man Wickham wants to kill.* And with Wickham's gun aimed point-blank at his chest.

"Keep your hands away from your coat," Wickham snapped.

George Darcy slowly pulled the fabric open, showing the inner lining. "What are you afraid of, George? I do not carry explosive charges."

Wickham's eyes narrowed. "Clever little devices. I learned how to make them from an old friend. I'm afraid I blew up an old woman with them, not that I intended to."

"A noblewoman," George said, "and my aunt. What you intended was to get me here, away from Pemberley. What happened to you, George? I do not understand."

"You happened." Wickham's voice vibrated with hate. "You brought me up to live the life of a gentleman and gave me no way to do it. I should have had a share of Pemberley or at least an income from it. I earned it, truckling to you and your son for years, until I found out that I was no more to you than any other servant."

George said slowly, "You were much more. You were my godson. I wanted you to have a good life, and I gave you the means to do so. You had the opportunity of an excellent education, had you made use of it. I hoped you would have an inclination to the priesthood. I would have seen to it that you had Kympton when it became available. If that was not to your liking, you could have studied law or taken a commission in the army, or joined the Royal Navy. You could have lived as well as any younger son. But only blood inherits property."

"Priest, lawyer, army—wasting my life for nothing. I was entitled to more than that. I was raised like a son; I deserved to live like one. My father never wanted me to be what he was, just another piece of Darcy property! He encouraged me to take all you gave me and use your influence so that I never had to work like he did. 'A good life'," he mimicked. "Well, I've found the good life for myself. I have enough money to leave England and enjoy myself somewhere the law can't follow. And when that's spent I can get more, without bowing and scraping."

Wickham's cheroot had gone out. He threw it down and raised the pistol. "Time to go, *Godfather*."

"It would have happened soon enough in any case, George. I am dying."

The words took Wickham completely by surprise. For two seconds, three, he stared at the man he had determined to kill, before the truth struck him. In that time of distraction, Handley stepped out of the shadows and spoke in a voice that snapped his prey's head toward him.

"Let the gun fall, Wickham, or I will put a bullet through your rotten brain."

George Darcy was not startled by the stranger. A countryman, he had caught the movement from the corner of his eye as Handley slipped into position. Darcy's hand fell to his waistcoat pocket and gripped the little gun. With an animal cry of rage, Wickham swung toward the new threat. George Darcy pulled the miniature gun out and fired, the sound no louder than a handclap. Wickham's right arm fell useless to his side, blood running from under his coat sleeve as the pistol fell. It hit the earth and discharged harmlessly.

Handley reached him in a stride. Wickham struck at him with his left fist, the blow glancing without effect from Handley's shoulder. Handley hit him with the barrel of his own pistol, under his hat brim. It was not a hard enough impact to kill or severely injure. It sent Wickham to the ground, his hat falling aside. Handley put the pistol back in his waistband and then rolled his quarry onto his back, tying the man's hands with Wickham's own cravat. He checked Wickham's duster and coat and pulled a knife from one boot. As the prisoner began to groan, Handley bent over and picked up the hat, then gave it a hard shake. His fingers explored the inside and found the packet sewn into the crown.

Someone was running. Darcy's deep voice rang through the quiet, "Father! Where are you?"

"Here, Son," George called in a tired voice. He put the small pistol away and walked to meet Fitzwilliam, who rushed into the glade with his own pistol drawn.

His son gripped George Darcy's arm and scanned his face. "Are you hurt? There was a shot."

"A misfire by Wickham's gun. There were two shots." His father showed Darcy the skeleton gun. "When dealing with Wickham, it is always wise to provide for contingencies."

As Darcy grinned, his father turned to the other man. "Mr. Handley, as I presume you are, do you need assistance?"

"No, thank you, sir." He handed George Darcy the hat. "There's a pocket sewn into the top. I think it has whatever's left of his loot in it."

George smiled as he took it. "I will see that it is restored."

Several men from the Pemberley contingent arrived from the fire line. Darcy motioned to Wickham who was sitting up and moaning.

"Get him into the wagon, Dr. Morrow can see to him there. When the doctor is finished take him to the constable in Lambton and tell Mr. Tiggs the reward has already been claimed. Do not let Wickham out of your sight. I am going for the magistrate."

The men jerked the prisoner roughly to his feet. Darcy stepped in front of Wickham, and the two men who had grown up together faced one another for the last time. He lifted Wickham's right hand, ignoring his grimace of pain, and pulled the gold ring off his finger.

"My father gave you this as a token of his belief in you. I will not see it on your hand when you stand on the gallows."

"I'm going with them," Handley told Darcy as the men led a cursing prisoner away. "As much as I want to see him hang, I'll shoot him if that's the alternative."

Darcy turned to his father. "Come back with me. Elizabeth is waiting."

"I have to differ with you, Son." He nodded at his daughter-in-law, who was just making her way through the near trees. "I doubt you will ever be able to enforce the 'obey' part of the wedding service."

"I will settle for 'love' and 'honor.'" Darcy extended his hand to his wife, who ran to grasp it. "I would not have her any other way,"

When the party entered the church, Dr. Morrow was rebandaging Mr. Keene's hand. The minister was still pale; however, he had regained much of his composure. The wife of his sexton had extended the hospitality of their spare room until other arrangements were made, and the vicar was preparing to accompany her there. Marie sat in the Darcy pew with her mistress. Her face was very still while her lips moved with the words of her prayers.

"She's in a bad way," Dr. Morrow confided to the Darcys out of Marie's hearing. "At her age even a minor fall can be devastating, and if I understand her maid, she had a fall down some stairs at her home not too long ago. They are staying at the Lambton Inn. That will not be suitable for her now. The woman in Lambton who takes my nursing patients already has a case that will go on for another several weeks. Dammit, I wish we had a hospital near here. The closest is Derby, and she would never survive the trip."

"Her coach is outside," Elizabeth said. There was purpose in her face that Darcy instantly recognized. "It is only about four miles to Pemberley. We will take her there. It was once her home, it is only fitting that she return in her need." She went to one of the women who still waited with the minister and said, "I am Mrs. Darcy. I do not know your name."

"Mrs. Williams, ma'am."

"I need several quilts or other bedding. We are going to take Lady Agatha Quintain to Pemberley, and I will need something to pad the coach seat."

Mrs. Williams turned to the boy, who came immediately at her call. "Tad, run home and have Dorry bring two quilts and a blanket. You can help her."

He was gone on the words, and Mrs. Williams turned to Elizabeth. "It won't take Tad ten minutes, ma'am. He's real fast on his feet."

Elizabeth smiled at her. "Thank you. I am afraid this has been a very poor way to meet."

"Yes, ma'am, but things will get better. We'll build a new vicarage, its been done before."

"You will have all the help you require." Darcy came up to them. "I will speak to the vicar when he is recovered, and Pemberley will provide whatever is necessary."

He said to Elizabeth as he led her a little way away, "I have to get the magistrate and have Wickham transported to Derby as soon as possible. I do not trust him to the local jail or the local constable. Can you convince Father to go home?"

She smiled. "I will take him home. Do what you must do."

He lifted her hand to his lips. Elizabeth spoke briefly to Marie, retrieved Darcy's coat, which Marie had removed in favor of holding her mistress's head in her lap, and lifted his hat from the finial of the pew where she had hung it. Dr. Morrow had gone out to see to the prisoner. A brief examination told him that the bullet would need to be removed in his surgery. Handley took Darcy aside when he emerged from the church. His face set in grim lines, he said, "The doctor wants to take Wickham to his surgery. I'd like a couple more men to watch him. He's deadly as a wounded snake—no telling what he might try."

Darcy called one of the men he had assigned as guard and spoke to him briefly. The man hurried off to the fire line.

"Gage will find two of our gamesmen to go with you. I cannot arm them at present. When my father returns to Pemberley he can send pistols for them. They are deadly shots, and Wickham's attempt on my father has left them ready to keep him in custody in any way necessary."

Elizabeth walked to the coach still parked out of the way. The coachman had joined the bucket line, but his age and condition released him as soon as the major fire was under control. She explained briefly what was planned, to his ready agreement. Dr. Morrow intercepted Elizabeth on her way back to the church. Darcy rode past them on Erebus, kicking the stallion into a canter. She smiled unconsciously at the image he made, the tall man on the tall horse, one perfect unit.

"Mrs. Darcy," Dr. Morrow addressed her with some gravity, "I appreciate your wish to help Lady Agatha. I do not remember her, of course, but her story is fairly common knowledge among the older citizens. However, you have someone of great importance to care for. Do not over expend your energies."

"I assure you, Doctor, my father-in-law is well looked after."

"I was not referring to Mr. Darcy."

Elizabeth frowned and then colored as his meaning became clear. "How—why do you think…"

"I have delivered a good many babies in my time. I do not need to be told when I will eventually be called on to deliver another. How far along are you?"

"A little less than three months."

"Then you have nearly passed the first challenge. The first three months are the most hazardous for the baby. Any sickness?"

"At first there was nausea when I woke in the morning, now only with certain foods. And I tire more easily than usual."

"That is to be expected. Consult Mrs. Reynolds when you are ready, she knows more than most midwives. If you need anything, please call on me." He tipped his hat, "Take care of yourself, Mrs. Darcy, for all your sakes."

Elizabeth looked down. "I will, Doctor."

In the end, Elizabeth drove the gig back to Pemberley at a walk, the coach following with Lady Agatha swathed in blanket and quilts. Two footmen carried her to a suite on the first floor, across the hall from George Darcy's rooms. After Georgiana's concerns were calmed, George was turned over to his valet, who ushered him away to wash and rest. Georgiana waited while Elizabeth explained the situation to Mrs. Reynolds. The housekeeper took charge at that point, sending a maid to assist Marie and making arrangements with Mr. Niles to have Lady Agatha's luggage retrieved from the Lambton Inn.

When they were alone, Georgiana burst out, "Papa could have been killed by *that man*. Why, Lizzy? I do not understand. I remember Mr. Wickham as a pleasant young man, always laughing and jesting. He has done such terrible things! Father was so kind to him. Why would he do this?"

Elizabeth took the girl's hand and spoke slowly. "Some people have a hidden fault in them, like canker in a tree. When the tree is young it cannot be seen; when the tree grows so does the canker, until it destroys the tree. Your father did nothing to justify

Mr. Wickham's enmity or to cause his actions. It was a flaw in the man himself that destroyed him."

She smiled sadly.

"Why do you not see if Father Darcy would like you to read to him? He may need some company after today."

Georgiana went to her father. Elizabeth suddenly found herself with nothing to do except wait for William's return. She went to her own rooms to find Clara drawing a hot bath and was grateful to have someone take care of her. In the bath, Elizabeth's thoughts drifted.

Lady Agatha has returned to Pemberley. If she lives, we will have to give her the letter and abide by her decision. Her father must have been a monster. I am so fortunate to have Papa's love and understanding. She is old. Was she injured so badly that she will want to take Pemberley from us now? We could not have planned what happened, but William saved her life. Surely that will mean something. And the baby, our baby, the creation of our love, will William want him, or her, if we are dispossessed and shamed by the past?

Clara found her dozing in the cooling water. Roused, Elizabeth dried herself and put on a dressing gown before lying down to rest until time to dress for dinner. She came downstairs two hours later to find Georgiana waiting and William still absent. A vague unease possessed her, however Elizabeth set it aside and sat with her new sister in the drawing room. She took up her needlework, put it down and leaned back in her chair, more weary than she might have expected.

"Papa is sleeping," Georgiana told her. "Thalman will see that he eats later. I have never seen him so sad since Mama died, and I was quite young then. I...I hope this does not affect his condition."

Her voice dropped on the last word. Elizabeth considered her words before she answered, "Father Darcy is aware of what I told you earlier. To be betrayed by someone you have trusted and felt affection for is a bitter thing. I think the first shock of it will pass, and he will recover with no lasting harm. Your mother's death was different. To lose a dearly beloved person is something you never truly get over." *Like Jane and Charles, like myself and William.*

They heard steps in the hallway, and Darcy came into the room, his face pale. He had come directly from the stables, the dust of his ride on his clothing, a smell of horse and leather around him. Elizabeth hurried to him, to be met with a rueful smile.

"I apologize, my dearest, for appearing in this condition. I could not wait to see you." He pressed his lips to her forehead in spite of Georgiana's presence, not seeing her sly smile as she rose.

"Are you well, William?" Elizabeth's concern darkened her lovely eyes.

"Yes, as well as can be expected. The magistrate was engaged when I arrived so I had to wait. He accompanied me to Lambton, to Dr. Morrow's. There was a slight altercation when the doctor had the prisoner untied so that he could remove the bullet."

Darcy glanced at his sister, who was listening.

"If you will excuse me," Georgiana said in her most adult tones, "I will inform cook that dinner should be delayed for half an hour."

Elizabeth could not suppress a smile. Georgiana left them, closing the door behind her. It had not touched the jamb before Darcy was kissing his wife hungrily. He released her and stood back, grinning.

"My apologies once more. I hope you will not have to change again."

"A little country air is always welcome," Elizabeth teased. She sobered. "Is all well, William?"

"Yes, now. Wickham tried to get hold of Dr. Morrow's scalpel. Our men and Handley subdued him, and he was forced to take a dose of laudanum. The wound is not serious. He is being kept at the surgery, in shackles and under guard, until he can be transported to Derby where there is a proper jail. Whether he will be tried there or in London, I do not know. It is over, Elizabeth. Father is no longer in danger from him, nor is anyone else."

"It has affected him deeply, William."

"So it would. He is a rational man he will come to terms with it in time. Now, I am going upstairs to remove the evidence of most of a day spent in the saddle. And then I will eat, and sleep until at least noon tomorrow."

Elizabeth walked him to the door. "Eat," she said. "Sleep may be delayed for a short time."

H husband grinned. "I am more than willing to make the sacrifice."

CHAPTER 24

COMMUNICATIONS

Elizabeth sat in the morning room, reading a letter from her sister Kitty. William was riding the property with Mr. Standish, assessing the progress of the crops and talking with the tenants. The room was bright with sunlight from undraped windows open to the breeze that smelled of green growing things. George Darcy had gone out into the gardens to visit his favorite area, the rose garden that had been Lady Anne's special domain. In the fortnight since the burning of Kympton vicarage, William and his father had organized its rebuilding with the assistance of the village elders. With numerous volunteers to do the labor, the new residence was to be finished by fall.

Elizabeth's hand unconsciously rested on her abdomen. She had to tell William soon, she thought uneasily. Clara had let out two of her looser gowns so that nothing showed. However, Elizabeth knew that before long she was going to need more than adjustments to her wardrobe. Smiling, she returned to her letter.

I am so excited for my wedding, dear Lizzy. Of course we will live at Danekirk, Mr. Cowper's estate in Kent. Mr. Cowper has put a number of acres into hops, which grow very well in our part of the county, and expects a healthy cash crop. The manor house needs repairs to the roof, but it is entirely suitable for the time being. We will be so happy, Lizzy!

Mama says there is hardly enough time to arrange everything; you know what she is like, and I say everything will be fine so long as Mr. Cowper, I, and the minister are at the church. Lydia is doing better with Mrs. Annesley than I expected. Her French has improved greatly. She practices the pianoforte an hour a day, and Mrs. Annesley is instructing her in logic. I daresay if anyone is up to the task of teaching Lydie to think clearly, it is her companion.

Elizabeth laughed softly. Kitty's ebullience lifted her spirits. If scandal came, perhaps it would not touch her family too heavily. Lady Agatha was improving, although she still slept most of the time. Elizabeth began to suspect that her maid had something to do with her continued somnolence. The woman was so obviously devoted to her mistress that there was no question of Marie harming her; perhaps it was only Lady Agatha's age and the severity of her injury. As Elizabeth continued to read, the next part of Kitty's letter sobered her mood.

Mary does not speak of it, but she is growing more concerned for Colonel Fitzwilliam. His family has heard nothing from him since his departure, and while there have been no major battles of late, there are always small engagements. Papa tries to reassure her, to little avail. She is with Lady Matlock much of the time. They have grown quite close. We all hope there is nothing to his silence except the difficulty of sending mail home during a war.

Elizabeth closed her eyes in a brief prayer. The loss of Colonel Fitzwilliam would be a terrible blow to William. He and his cousin were as close as brothers; to deprive William of the one man he trusted and loved above all others was unthinkable. She knew as well that if he should die, Mary would live out her life as a spinster. Her sister was not one to give her heart twice.

> *Lord Maresford continues to improve. Mary says he seems to have a new purpose to his life. He still cannot walk, he gets around in a Bath chair pushed by his man. His right leg was badly damaged in the fall. The doctor has told his family that he will never be able to walk without a crutch. Otherwise they have been assured he will fully recover.*

Elizabeth thought that Nicholas was one more man to find salvation in disaster. Again the question came to her, how badly would a scandal in the Darcy family affect the Fitzwilliams? For a moment her mind raged against the idea. *It was so long ago!* The remainder of the letter consisted of well-wishes for her and William. Elizabeth put the missive away and tried to think clearly. She must talk to William. They had to decide whether to tell Father Darcy about the situation before Lady Agatha fully regained her senses and the decision was taken out of their hands. Elizabeth was certain that he would not thank them for keeping such a secret from him. Any more, she told herself with some trepidation, than William would thank her for keeping the secret of her condition from him.

In the rose garden, surrounded by the heady fragrance of early blooms, George Darcy sat on an oak bench where he and Lady Anne had often sat of a spring evening. The bench was cut from the trunk of an ancestral oak that had fallen in a storm when George was a boy. A local carpenter had formed it, and his father had carved the back himself, shapes reminiscent of rose petals and leaves. Alexander had always been creative. George's grandmother Eleanor kept a beautiful watercolor in her private sitting room, a view of Pemberley from the lakeshore. Although It was not signed and Alexander never mentioned it, George knew instinctively that it was his father's.

He closed his eyes and let the peace of the garden take over his mind. Bees bustled from plant to plant; birds trilled sharply in the Spanish chestnuts beyond the old stone wall. When he was troubled, George came here to commune with the memory of his wife. It was his greatest hope and comfort that when his time came they would be reunited.

Something is troubling William, Anne. You always had an instinct for people, especially our son. I do not believe it has to do with Elizabeth, they are so obviously in love, as we were. Perhaps it is only my illness that wears on him. He is all I could have wanted in a son he makes me proud every time I look at him. And Elizabeth has become like my own daughter. I suppose I ought to talk to him, but I would rather he come to me if it is anything of importance. Perhaps he will; he has become more open since his marriage. How I wish you were here with me! There is not a day, not an hour, I do not think of you and miss you with all my being.

He must have dozed. George felt the warm, slim weight of his wife's body against his side. Her sweet voice murmured, *"Our children are strong, my love. Whatever adversity comes, they will survive and grow stronger."*

The serene confidence of her words filled him. He tried to draw her nearer when an alien voice intruded.

"Sir? Are you well? It is growing dark. Do you wish to come in now?"

George raised his head. His valet stood beside the bench, proper as always. The sun was declining behind the manor house., purple shadows painted silhouettes of flowers and leaves on the stone wall.

"Yes." George stood. "I will go in now. Thank you, Thalman."

The man gave a silent sigh of relief and followed his master back to the house.

⸻

Darcy also had a letter, from his uncle Lord Matlock, of less pleasant content than Elizabeth's correspondence. He read it in his study, and when he was done Darcy sat for some time, staring into a silence of memories and conflicting emotions.

Wickham was hanged at Newgate at dawn yesterday. I would not have had you there, for I know, in spite of everything, you grew up with the scoundrel and his end was no more honorable than his life. I was told he spent the night before his execution raving and screaming curses against the Darcys, the Fitzwilliams, and the courts. When they brought him to the gallows he had to be dragged up the steps by two turnkeys. I will not go into further description. He is dead; that is the end of it.

Mr. Handley was there as well. I have seen to it that he has the reward. He is staying on in London, having newly married a young woman named Isobel. I believe he intends to become a Bow Street investigator. He seems to have a talent for finding miscreants. I wish I had better news of Richard he has not sent any word since leaving us in November. Madeleine says nothing, but I see the worry in her eyes. Perhaps we shall hear something soon. Miss Bennet is with her almost daily, and a great comfort. We are all very fond of her. My other son is progressing, physically and, I am happy to say, mentally. Wyecroft has done all he can, and Nicholas is making every effort to recover as much of his physical abilities as it is possible for him to do. He has even evinced an interest in politics. Perhaps his misfortune will have some positive effect after all.

Darcy refolded the letter and laid it aside. He would ask Elizabeth if she wanted to read it later. Wickham had gone completely to the bad, but Darcy knew he would not have wanted to witness the man's death. Whatever his crimes and sins they had been friends once, and he could not divorce himself completely from those memories. Slowly Darcy opened the locked drawer of the desk and withdrew the ring he had taken from Wickham. He stared at it for several minutes, some dark emotion stirring in his eyes, After the trial, where it had been used in evidence, the court had returned it to him. It looked no different than the day Wickham had left for university, when George Darcy gifted it to his godson.

Abruptly Darcy rose and quit the study, walking swiftly over the lawns to the lake. He stopped at the end of the stone pier extending twenty feet into the water. Ripples moved against it, the soft sound of their endless passage soothing his turmoil. He reached into his waistcoat pocket and took out the ring Wickham had worn. Darcy turned it in his fingers, staring unseeingly at the lapping water. Then with a sudden violent movement, he threw the ring far out into the lake, turned on his heel, and returned to the manor house.

Elizabeth was unusually quiet during the evening. When Darcy rose to retire early, she followed. They climbed the stairs together, still in silence. At the door to her rooms, Elizabeth drew him inside and closed the solid panel. She looked up at her husband's face, so well known and loved, and touched his cheek with gentle fingers.

"William, there is something I must tell you and another matter we must discuss very soon. I would not trouble you with them tonight, except Mrs. Reynolds tells me Lady Agatha is improving rapidly and will soon be sitting up."

"You want to tell Father about the letter."

"We must. We cannot keep such a secret from him only to have him find out in the most shocking way."

Darcy turned aside but he did not leave her, although she knew his impulse at such times was to isolate himself.

He said, "When I received her note, I hoped we might speak with Lady Agatha privately during her visit. If she was intent upon proceeding, we could then tell Father and make whatever arrangements were necessary. With the fire and her current residence here, that option is no longer open to us." Darcy met her eyes, those eyes a man might drown in. "Yes, beloved, we have to tell Father everything."

Elizabeth felt the pain behind his calm words. He knew the risk to his father's health in spite of George Darcy's strength of character. His son's love fought against the necessity of disclosure, even as he accepted it. He put his arms around Elizabeth and held her to him, his face resting in her hair.

"What did you want to tell me?"

Elizabeth wished fervently that she had not mentioned it. He was not to be put off now. She swallowed against a throat tightened by apprehension and leaned back a little in his arms.

"Have you noticed that my breasts are increased of late and more sensitive?"

"Have I hurt you? I know I am sometimes a…bit…enthusiastic."

Elizabeth almost smiled. "No, my love, you have not hurt me." She freed one of his hands and pressed it to her abdomen. "You will feel nothing yet, but soon I shall no longer be able to hide my condition in let-out gowns. William, you are to be a father."

Darcy stood, stunned. Thoughts cascaded through his mind, he felt his hand on her stomach tremble. A child, a miracle of their making. Now when the world he had always known, always taken as his heritage, rested on the brink of dissolution. Elizabeth's voice jolted him back to her presence; it quivered on the verge of desperation.

"William, please tell me you want our child."

"Want—oh, my soul's heart, why would I not want our child?" Darcy folded her in his arms, holding her fiercely.

Elizabeth clung to him, her voice a whisper. "I was afraid, with everything as it is, you would not want our child raised in the shadow of scandal. I was terrified you might try to send me away."

He eased his embrace so that he could see her face. "Could I have sent you away?"

"Never! I swore before God to be your wife until death parted us. I will never leave you so long as I live."

"And I will never let you go, my Elizabeth." Darcy looked into her lovely face, impassioned with purpose, and felt tears prickle his eyes. "I believe something sent us to one another after all our searching when the time was right for both of us. We are one, we shall always be one. If our son, or daughter, grows up the master of ten thousand acres or ten we will love him, or her, no less."

Darcy kissed her tenderly and felt her body relax against him. A tap at the door parted them, although their hands were still joined.

"That will be Clara," Elizabeth said. "I will come to you shortly."

Darcy left her and returned to his chambers through the connecting door. *A child! Now more than ever, this business with Lady Agatha must be settled.* Fear had entered into the equation as well. Childbearing was dangerous; Elizabeth must have the best care. There was much to plan for. But tonight they would comfort one another, renewing their vows in a different way.

The Fitzwilliam ladies were having tea on the terrace of their Mayfair home, enjoying the spring day. Mary Bennet sat quietly while Sofia related the latest foibles of one of her friends. Lady Matlock held a piece of needlework in her lap. She had not put in a stitch since they had come out, and Mary doubted she even remembered it was there. Her own thoughts were on Richard, as no doubt were his mother's. They still had no word from him, raising their anxiety daily. Mary's hand rose to her throat, where the little silver cross had rested for so many years. She said a silent prayer that it would keep him safe.

Sofia broke off in midsentence, her eyes going to her father who had just come out of the French-style window onto the shaded flags. His face was gray in spite of his attempt to keep countenance. Lady Matlock drew in her breath so sharply that it was almost a cry.

"I have heard from a friend at the War Office. Richard has… has been missing from his regiment for nearly a week. He was on a special mission to contact some Spanish partisans. A search party found evidence of a fight, possibly a French ambush. There were no casualties found. They believe the partisans have taken him with them into the mountains."

"But if he were able," Lady Matlock's hands clenched in her lap, crumpling the piece of fine linen she had been embroidering, "surely he would send word to his commander."

"Unless the partisans are on the move. We can only wait until something factual is known."

"Wait!" Lady Matlock stood, her needlework falling unnoticed to the flagstones. Her voice rose, shaking. "How many times must we wait for official notice before our worst fears are confirmed? What if he was wounded and the French captured him?"

"The local partisans detest the French. They would never leave a wounded man to be captured."

He did not add that if it seemed inevitable, they would likely kill the man first. His wife was growing as near hysterical as he had ever seen her.

"I could have pressured him to stay. He might have listened to me…!"

"Maddie.," Lord Matlock took her hands in his, "he would not have listened to anyone. Duty has been his life since university. Even with Nicholas so badly injured, he had to go. If God wills, he will come home alive and well. We can do no more than pray and hope."

His wife bowed her head in acceptance. Sofia went to her mother and then extended her hand to Mary, who grasped it with cold fingers. Her body felt stiff, as if she were half-frozen. *Richard!* she thought numbly. *Please, God, not Richard!* He had not stayed for his family. Would he have stayed if she asked it of him? And if he had, would he have been the man she loved?

Sofia put an arm around her mother. Mary took Lady Matlock's other arm, and together they led her, unresisting, into the house. As she passed, Mary touched Lord Matlock's arm. He patted her shoulder but did not follow. His two daughters, as he thought of them, would see to his wife. There were things he had not told the women. True, there were no bodies; however, a significant blood trail led away from the site of the conflict. A man that badly wounded, without professional help, was unlikely to survive. Until the facts were certain, he would wait and watch alone.

George Darcy looked from his son to his second daughter expectantly. "Have you finally decided to tell me what has been troubling you, William?"

A breeze blew in through the open windows of the sitting room in George's chambers, bringing a scent of flowers to mingle with the roses in a crystal vase Elizabeth had placed on the table earlier. They were pale blush blooms, cream with light red centers that would fade as they opened to a lovely pale pink.

George wondered in passing if Elizabeth knew they had been Lady Anne's favorite.

Darcy gathered himself. Controlling his voice with the self-discipline of a lifetime, he said, "Father, you remember the writing desk you helped Elizabeth find?"

"My grandmother's desk, of course."

"The morning of the Kympton fire, she found a secret drawer, opened by the medallion Lady Agatha sent her in London. There was…" his words faltered for a second before Darcy forced himself to continue, "a letter in it. It was not addressed to anyone. Elizabeth read it; it was for Lady Agatha from her mother. I have also read it. It contains information that…that could change all our lives forever. I have hesitated to tell you, but when Lady Agatha regains enough strength, the situation will have to be faced."

Quietly George said, "Let me have the letter."

Elizabeth handed him the folded parchment she had been holding. George opened it and began to read. His expression grew steadily more withdrawn until he refolded the missive and laid it on the table next to him. Darcy and Elizabeth watched him with ill-controlled anxiety. At last he rubbed a hand across his eyes, meeting theirs one after another.

"I always knew my grandfather was an aberration in the line, a very bad man. I never suspected he was a cheat, a liar, and a blackmailer, for that is what it amounts to."

His determined gaze held his son's. "William, we must make this right. I do not know what Lady Agatha will say or what she may do. I only know we cannot live with this stain on our name."

"No, Father," Darcy agreed quietly, "we cannot. As soon as she is able, we can give Lady Agatha the letter. When she has read it, we will meet with her."

George said slowly, "It is hard to know how badly she was hurt, growing up in such a household. She cut all ties with the family, even her twin brother. I sent her word when my father died, she did not respond. The fact that she wanted to visit the graves of her mother and brother speaks of some sense of reconciliation. Whatever her decision, we will abide by."

They agreed silently, having expected nothing less. Elizabeth leaned and kissed her father-in-law's cheek before they left him.

Alone, George sat without moving, his eyes closed. He knew William had already begun to plan ahead if the worst should happen. There was the Staffordshire estate and the one in Scotland, both now safely in his son's name. The blow to William's pride if it should all come out disturbed him more than any reduction in their circumstances. And Georgiana had not entered society yet, perhaps for the better. Even Elizabeth's family and the Fitzwilliams could not escape some calumny.

I hope you are right, my darling Anne, and this disgrace from the past only makes our children, and their children, stronger. I wanted to die at Pemberley and lay my bones in her earth next to you, my dearest wife. Now it is no longer my life that matters—it is the lives to come.

George sent for Mrs. Reynolds and gave her brief instructions.

CHAPTER 25
REDEMPTION

Marie answered the tap at the door, expecting to see the other maid. Instead she found Georgiana Darcy standing in the hallway, a book in her hands.

"May I see Lady Agatha?"

Marie glanced over her shoulder to the bed, where her mistress lay propped on pillows. Lady Agatha called, "Who is it, Marie?"

"Miss Darcy, my lady."

Lady Agatha's brows rose. She nodded, and Marie stepped back with a curtsey. Georgiana approached the bed with some trepidation. She had only met the elderly lady once, under circumstances that could accurately be called unusual. She was unsure of her reception, in spite of the fact that Lady Agatha was a guest. The woman had impressed her as someone who made her own rules.

Gray eyes of intense clarity surveyed her. Lady Agatha said, "Sit down, child," with a gesture to Marie, who moved a chair to the bedside. She properly withdrew, and Lady Agatha continued to watch her visitor with interest. "I take it you have suffered no lasting ill effects from our last meeting. It was the gentleman who was so desirous of your hand who was badly injured, was it not?"

"My cousin Lord Maresford." Georgiana seated herself, the book in her lap. "He nearly died. My brother told me he will never walk again without a crutch."

Lady Agatha was silent for a moment. "I am afraid that sometimes when the chickens come home to roost, as they say, they are not chickens but dragons. The man who attacked him was never caught?"

Georgiana shivered. "I am not supposed to know, but one hears things."

"Especially if one listens in the right places."

Georgiana blushed. She continued in a restrained voice, "It was the robber, the one who attacked Lady Wendover. His name was Wickham. He killed a young housemaid in Newcastle some time ago. He is the one who burned the vicarage at Kympton and tried to kill my father. He used to live here, his father was our steward when I was a child. Oh, it is a terrible story!"

"Then perhaps you should tell it to me instead of whatever it is you brought to read. Did he escape?"

Georgiana lowered her eyes. She shook her bright head. "No. He was captured and sent to London. He…he is dead."

Lady Agatha nodded slowly. "Well, the book may be a better choice after all. I have known very bad men in the past, none of them murderers so far as I know. It is not a fit subject for a young girl."

"Elizabeth—Mrs. Darcy—says that some people have a kind of canker in them, like a tree, that cannot be seen when they are young but grows as they do until it destroys them."

"I have met your sister-in-law. She is an exceptional woman." Lady Agatha folded her hands on the coverlet. "What did you bring to read?"

"Mr. Wordsworth's poetry. Elizabeth likes it particularly."

"Then," Lady Agatha said, smiling, "we must have some of it. I am not fond of the daffodil one, although they are showy flowers. My maid tells me the gardens here are spectacular. I am glad they have been kept up. My mother loved them, they were her greatest pleasure."

"My mother also loved the gardens. My grandmother Darcy expanded the rose garden, and my mother added some rare varieties to balance the old roses. I remember sitting there with her. She would tell me about the flowers, where they came from and what they were called. It is one of the few things I do remember of her."

"She died when you were young?"

"I was five. There is a portrait of her in the gallery, if you wish to see it."

"Perhaps I shall." Lady Agatha lay back on her cushion of pillows. "What of Mrs. Darcy, as you so properly call her? She has been at Pemberley for several months. Is she happy here?"

"Oh yes. She and my brother are very happy. I hope someday to find a man I can feel such affection for. They talk about everything together. He has never been so happy. If it were not for Father—"

Georgiana stopped abruptly, her fair face coloring. She did not understand why it was so easy to talk to this elderly lady, not realizing that Lady Agatha had learned the art of listening.

"He is not well, yes, I know. But I am sure he is well cared for here. Were your mother and father well suited as they say?"

The girl nodded. "He still mourns her. Sometimes he sits in the rose garden for hours. He says he feels close to her there." Tears gathered in her eyes, and she dabbed them with her handkerchief.

"When you marry, child," Lady Agatha went on quietly, "find a man who will confide in you. That is the secret of a good marriage. There will always be conflicts and disagreements—that is human nature. It does not signify. If you cannot trust one another with your deepest thoughts and feelings, you can never be more than strangers." She motioned to the book Georgiana still held. "Let me hear some Wordsworth, then. I will tell you when I tire and need to rest. The old take more healing than the young." *Sometimes a great deal more.*

Mrs. Reynolds did not return to George Darcy's rooms until late that evening. The house was quiet, everyone except a few servants in bed. Thalman dozed in George's dressing room, waiting until his master should decide to go to bed, in spite of the fact that George had dismissed him an hour before.

Mrs. Reynolds's soft tap at the door roused George from a light doze. She entered at his summons and stopped near the door. "Marie has gone downstairs for something to eat. I can keep her for a few minutes if you wish me to?"

"Only if she starts to return in the next quarter hour. Thank you, Mrs. Reynolds."

She dropped a small curtsey and left him. George rose, took up the letter that still lay on the table by the roses, and crossed the hall. Lady Agatha's room was dark except for one candle lamp burning on a night table. He stood at the bedside and looking down at her, remembering his father. A good man, a fair man, quiet, soft spoken, of unbending propriety and unquestioned honor. She looked so frail, small and delicate, her hair hardly less white than the snowy linen of the pillowcases. She had suffered much in her lifetime and survived. George could not help admiring her.

He leaned over and slipped the letter under her hand where it lay on the coverlet. Her maid would never think to read it. In the morning Lady Agatha would know the truth. She would have time to consider her feelings before they met. At that time William would take charge and make whatever decisions were necessary.

George left the chamber as quietly as he had come. In her still, cool room, Lady Agatha smiled softly.

Lord Matlock struggled with the question of whether or not to send William notice of Richard's disappearance. Whatever illness George Darcy suffered, it troubled his son greatly, and to be newly married as well, however felicitous the match, must cause some additional strain. Wickham's death had ended one source of anxiety, he hesitated to introduce another. However, Lord Matlock knew how close the cousins were. If it came about that his son was dead, it was unfair to notify William without warning.

It is the waiting that is so terrible. Maddie is growing thinner day by day, she has none of her usual quiet contentment. Sofia and Mary do what they can, but only definite news will bring her any kind of peace.

He took up his pen and wrote briefly, emphasizing that they knew nothing definite. When the letter was dispatched, he sat at his desk for a time, thinking about both of his sons. How strange life was. From a boy, Nicholas had always been absorbed by his status; the knowledge that he would one day inherit the earldom dominating his actions and his relations with other people, including his younger brother. Richard, who might well have shown the jealousy of many second sons, had reached out to others. He had chosen a difficult career, refused to allow his father to buy him a major's commission in favor of beginning as a lieutenant, and made his own way up the ranks on merit.

Lord Matlock knew another factor in his son's military success, one he was sworn not to share with anyone under penalty of prosecution for treason. Richard's excellent command of French and Spanish made him invaluable as an agent behind enemy lines. It was a dangerous occupation, especially if he was taken prisoner. He might well be tortured for information and shot or hanged without any chance of being traded back to the army in a prisoner exchange. Lord Matlock shoved the idea roughly aside and rose. He had a meeting at the House of Lords in an hour on the question of abolishing slavery in the islands. It did no good to worry about his son when there was no chance of influencing the outcome.

He started to rise when a tap on the door admitted his butler. The man's face was paler than usual, and his manner almost tentative. Lord Matlock raised an eyebrow.

"Yes, Hartman, what is it?"

"This, my lord." The butler extended a note on a salver. It was on heavy, official-looking paper. "It was just delivered by messenger, sir, from the War Office."

Lord Matlock felt the blood leave his face. He took the missive, his hand trembling. "Thank you, Hartman."

The man bowed and left him, closing the door. Lord Matlock recognized his friend's writing. He broke the seal and opened the note, his throat too dry to swallow.

The lost are found. Badly wounded, with the partisans until they could get him back to an English regiment. Will be invalided home as soon as fit to travel.

Richard's father bowed his head in his hands, said a fervent prayer of thanks, and went out into the hall. Hartman waited a little distance away, ready for whatever capacity he might be needed to fulfill.

"Colonel Fitzwilliam has been returned to an English regiment. He is wounded but alive. You may convey the news to the other servants. I know they have been concerned for his safety."

"Yes, sir. Thank you, my lord."

Against all protocol and training, Hartman was smiling as he made his way to the baize door that led belowstairs. Lord Matlock retrieved his letter to Darcy and went to find his wife and daughters. They were in the drawing room. Nicholas had joined them and was listening quietly while Sofia read from a volume of Shakespeare. He had lost weight during his long recovery. Oddly enough, the difference made his resemblance to his brother more pronounced.

Lady Matlock looked up from her needlework, saw the missive in her husband's hand, and stiffened, fear darting through her eyes. Lord Matlock smiled, and she shuddered.

"Richard is alive. He was wounded with the partisans., They took him to another English unit. He will be sent home when he can travel."

Nicholas closed his eyes briefly. Sofia began to cry quietly, reaching out to grasp her mother's hand.

"How badly wounded?" Lady Matlock asked when she could control her voice.

"My friend does not say. We will probably receive official word within a day."

Nicholas looked at his father with a wry smile. "So my little brother will come home to vex me again. Well, life would be boring without him."

Sofia, drying her tears, slapped his arm in mock reproof. She said, "I must send word to Mary at once. She has been terribly worried."

She left them, while Lord Matlock remained by his wife's side. "Whatever has happened, they expect him to recover. We will deal with the outcome as we have to."

Lady Matlock nodded. She squeezed her husband's hand, her face still strained. He brought her hand to his lips and kissed the pale knuckles.

"I think," she said, "I shall go to church and thank God for sending our son back to us."

Mary Bennet was also sitting with her family when the note from Sofia arrived with a footman. For once, seeing the fear in her daughter's face, Mrs. Bennet did not immediately demand to know the contents. Mary opened the note and read swiftly; her sobbing response was answer enough.

"Oh, thank God, thank God! He's alive!"

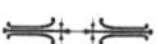

Lady Agatha sat in a chair by the window in her bedroom, her feet raised on a small hassock, a lap rug covering her legs. Chairs had been arranged at a comfortable distance in front of her position. She was dressed in a silk robe, pale blue trimmed with pointe d'Angleterre lace, her silver hair put up in a simple knot and braids. She looked every bit the matriarch. The letter lay in her lap, one thin hand resting on the aged velum. She did not need to read it again—she could almost recite the contents verbatim. She closed her eyes and saw her mother's fine, delicate hand as she had sat at the writing desk putting down in ink words that condemned both her and her husband.

My dearest Aggie,

The monster is dead. I have killed him. Since he can no longer reach you, he has tortured Alex. Yesterday he invaded Alex's rooms and found his paintings. He burned all except one I managed to save, while Alex watched. It was as if a piece of your brother's soul were being torn from his body. Gerald called him terrible names, but Alex was silent. When it was done, Alex went into the house. I found him in the gun room loading a pair of dueling pistols. I convinced him to go to a friend's home for the night and wait until today to confront his father. I realized at that moment I must either lose my son or commit the ultimate sin.

Gerald blamed me for everything, of course. When he left me last night, he was nearly too drunk to walk. I knew he would fall into bed in a stupor from which little might wake him. I waited until well past midnight before taking a pillow from my bed and going to his chambers. I knelt on his chest and pressed the pillow over his face. He hardly struggled. I waited until I was certain and then returned to my rooms. The doctor, who knows well Gerald's penchant for drink, said it was a heart seizure. I will have him buried in Lambton churchyard. I will not share even so little of Pemberley soil with him.

His crimes against Alex were great, but his crime against you was greater. My dearest daughter, you were not second born, you were first. Alex came a quarter hour after your birth. Gerald was mad with fury. Because of the entail, you were entitled to inherit Pemberley. My only way to save your life was to agree to the lie. Gerald terrorized the midwife into agreement, and he eventually paid her for her silence. But you are the rightful heir.

I shall leave this letter in the secret drawer of the writing desk. I will send you the key with a note to ask Alex for the desk. He will give it to you and then you two can make whatever accommodation is possible. Your brother is a good man; he will not deny you. God bless you, my daughter.
Mother

Darcy and Elizabeth found George Darcy in his sitting room, standing at the window overlooking the gardens. He called them in without moving, as straight as ever but without his usual effort to appear untouched by his condition.

He looks so old and tired, Elizabeth thought. She watched her husband's face, the play of emotions in his eyes quickly hidden.

George turned to face them. He said, "The letter is not here. I left it with Lady Agatha last night while she was asleep. I am sure by now she has read it. I wanted to give her time to think before we met with her."

Darcy's shoulders stiffened. He said nothing for a moment and then shrugged. "It makes no difference. If we had taken it to her now, she might have delayed the meeting. I would rather have it over with."

He looked down at Elizabeth. She slipped her hand into his and felt strong fingers tighten on hers. They crossed the hallway, George following them. Darcy knocked lightly on the door. It opened so quickly that he knew the maid must have been waiting for them Marie stepped back and curtsied as they entered, and then closed the door and went into the adjoining dressing room, closing that door as well. They sat in the chairs, Elizabeth in the middle. For a dozen heartbeats nothing was said until Lady Agatha spoke, without inflection.

"You found this in the writing desk?" she said to Elizabeth, hardly a question.

"Yes. As you must know, the medallion is a key. No one would put a decoration under a secret drawer unless there was another compartment. There was no name on the outside, and when my eyes fell on the first sentence, I kept reading. Did you know it was there?"

"No. I knew my mother had left some communication she considered important hidden there; she sent a note telling me so in veiled terms, along with the medallion. At the time I thought it was a plea to reconcile with Alexander, perhaps to request compensation from the estate. I did not receive it until after her death, and then it did not seem important. Apparently I could not have been more wrong."

"You have read the letter," Darcy said, his face its old reserved mask. "You know our question. What are your intentions for Pemberley?"

Lady Agatha considered him, her expression as masked as his. "You remind me of my brother. You favor him, as does your father, although you have not the same temperament. Alex was an artist, or would have been had he been allowed to follow his own wishes. That is how I met Cedric, he and Alex were friends."

She drew a breath that seemed to shake a little. "If you will allow me, I will tell you the story, as briefly as I can, of how Gerald Darcy destroyed his family. It is relevant to the crux of our current situation."

"We will listen to whatever you have to say," George assured her. He looked at his son and daughter. "And we will abide by your decision."

For the first time, Lady Agatha face showed emotion. It might have been surprise or satisfaction, it was impossible to read in the seconds it lasted.

"Very well. You probably know that my father was a tyrant, a cruel, selfish man obsessed with power who cared for no one; not his wife, not his children, only himself. He abused my mother all their married life, he bullied and browbeat Alex. I was the only one he did not try to dominate. I never knew why until now. It was fear, fear that somehow I would discover what he had done and call him to account for it."

She paused. Elizabeth rose, poured a glass of water from the carafe on the night table and brought it to her. Lady Agatha murmured thanks before drinking a little.

"When I was seventeen, Alex introduced me to Cedric Quintain. My mother wanted my portrait taken, and Cedric was just acquiring a reputation as a portraitist. It would have been an important commission, leading to others, for the Darcy name had power then as now. During the sittings in London we fell in love. When he asked Gerald—I can never think of him as my father—for my hand, Gerald nearly went berserk. He destroyed the painting and threatened Cedric's life.

"Cedric had to leave, but we were determined to be together. I could not trust my maid, or my mother's maid, to carry a message to him. Gerald had all the servants terrified of him. So my mother took a note on her next trip to church and gave it to Cedric. She also gave me what little money she had managed to hold back from her pin money without Gerald's knowledge and a few pieces of jewelry inherited from her mother. I ran away with that and the clothes on my back, and we went to Scotland. We were married there, in the church. We lived in Scotland until I reached my majority. Cedric sold landscape paintings and some portraits, and we got by. Then we returned to England."

Lady Agatha drank another sip of water. The narrative brought back memories she had kept at bay for over sixty years. They wore on her more than she might have imagined.

After a short pause, she continued, "For the next year, Gerald did everything in his power to destroy us. Commissions promised were withdrawn, supplies were no longer available, friends turned from us. I do not know how many times we moved. We would no sooner find accommodations than the landlord would evict us, with no reason given. When we finally reached the end of our resources, we took ship for Italy where Cedric had a friend who would assist us."

Her keen eyes found Elizabeth's. "I was six month gone with child."

William instinctively caught his wife's hand. George shook his head, the memory of his dear wife's near death at the birth of Georgiana and her lingering ill health fresh in his mind. Lady Agatha went on in a soft voice, without hesitation.

"I did not have an easy time. Normally I would never have attempted a sea voyage, and at first it was not too bad. As we left the

Bay of Biscay, a large storm blew up suddenly out of the Atlantic. I was on my way to our cabin when a huge wave struck the ship so violently that I was thrown down the companionway. The ship's doctor did what he could, but it was too late. I lost our child. A little girl."

She held off any expressions of sympathy with a sharp gesture of her hand.

"Although the ship was badly damaged, the captain somehow made port. I was sent to a maternity home until I recovered enough to continue. We had to leave her there, buried in a foreign land. We continued to Venice and then to Rome. We lived there for eight years while Cedric built a reputation. By the time we returned to England, Gerald was dead, my mother was dead, and Alex had married. Despite my mother's note and the medallion, I had no desire for any communication with my brother, since I was not certain how like or unlike Gerald he had become. Cedric and I were happy. I needed no one else."

Lady Agatha leaned back in her chair. The story had tired her, and Elizabeth wondered if they should leave her alone for a time. As if reading his wife's mind, Darcy said, "If you wish to continue this meeting later, we can leave you to rest."

Her lips lifted in a half smile. "I am sure you would prefer to have this matter settled expeditiously. You see, I knew about the substitution of birth times before I came north. The midwife made a deathbed statement to the former vicar of Kympton. He suppressed it out of respect for my brother and the Darcy family, but his conscience made him leave it sealed, with a note that it was to be forwarded to me after his death. The current vicar followed his instructions."

"So you knew when we met in London?" Darcy's deep voice sounded strained.

"Yes. I wanted to see what sort of man you were. I knew your father was ill; I was interested to find out if you were anticipating your inheritance or sincerely concerned for him. And I wanted to know what sort of woman you were to marry and how you treated her. I was not about to turn Pemberley over to another Gerald Darcy."

"So you came here to consult the vicar and undoubtedly others about the current family?" George spoke for the first time. "And you already have proof of the deception."

"I did. And as I stated, to visit the graves of my mother and brother. As for proof, I had the statement in my reticule. It burned in the fire at the vicarage. This," she said, touching the letter, "is all the proof that now exists. Why did you not destroy it?"

All three of her listeners looked at her with varying degrees of affront. Lady Agatha laughed lightly.

"Very well, I withdraw the question. For the same reason, you do not remind me that you saved my life, or tell me if I make this letter public, my mother's name will be disgraced along with the Darcys, although that fact in itself does not concern me. She has been dead for many years, any judgment of her actions is long past."

Lady Agatha said to Darcy, "Will you bring me the portfolio in the second drawer of the armoire, please?"

He rose to retrieve it and handed the slim leather case to her. She held it with the letter, gathering her strength. Her sensitive hands were steady when she opened it and withdrew two documents.

"Before I left London, I had my solicitor prepare two legal documents. This," Lady Agatha said and held up the first, "would begin proceedings in law to regain possession of Pemberley. This," she held up the second legal paper, "is a statement to be signed by both of you," she indicated George and Fitzwilliam, "transferring ownership of the estate to me. I will then be able to dispose of it however I choose."

Lady Agatha turned to George. "They were created in a spirit of long-held anger and bitterness that ought to have been put to rest when I realized your son," she spoke to George, "was a man of honor." She handed both documents to Darcy. "Destroy them. I want nothing from you. I have realized that I no longer desire to nurture such bitterness of spirit. My dear Cedric would not be proud of me."

Darcy took the papers. He did not thank her; it would have been insulting to do so. Instead he said, "What are your plans now, Lady Agatha?"

"I have been staying with a friend who lives near the border with Nottinghamshire, Mr. Pettigrew. I should send him a note before he comes looking for me. When I am well enough, I will return there and eventually to London. This is not and will never again be my home."

George Darcy rose. "We will leave you before you tire. You are welcome here for as long as you wish, whenever you wish."

She bowed her head briefly in acknowledgment. As Darcy and Elizabeth stood, Lady Agatha said, "Mrs. Darcy, may I speak to you alone?"

Elizabeth waited while her husband and father-in-law departed. "Yes, my lady?"

"You are with child."

"Yes, my lady."

"Your husband knows. He is most solicitous of you."

Elizabeth colored. "He is the only one I have told."

"You are happy, I can see that. You have chosen well, he is a good man. He will be a good father."

"Yes," Elizabeth agreed, "he will."

"This is a time of joy. Share it with those you love." Lady Agatha extended her mother's letter to Elizabeth. "This is my last link to the past. I am done with evil memories. Burn it."

Slowly Elizabeth took the old paper. Lady Agatha smiled up at her, her expression serene. Her throat tight, Elizabeth said, "I will."

Alone, Lady Agatha called for Marie. The maid came quickly, concerned for whatever had passed between her mistress and the others. Lady Agatha regarded her maid sternly.

"I am going to nap for a while, Marie. You need not slip any more of the doctor's sleeping draught into my tea. I am quite past needing it."

Unintimidated, Marie replied, "Yes, my lady."

CHAPTER 26

JOURNEY'S END

One week later Lady Agatha made the trip to Pemberley Chapel churchyard in an open barouche with Darcy and Elizabeth. The spring sunshine was warm, and the air smelled of new growth. Elizabeth had made a visit to Lambton and was wearing one of the new gowns she had ordered, slightly less fitted, with an expanded bodice. Her straw bonnet patterned her face with latticed light. Looking at her, Darcy thought that she was the essence of life and joy.

"Your sister was with child when we met in London," Lady Agatha said, watching her. "I trust the birth went well?"

"She had twins, a boy and a girl. The girl was small, however both are now doing well."

"I am glad for her. She seemed a very gentle woman, she will make a fine mother." Lady Agatha gazed at the passing grounds. A hawk soared suddenly above the trees, turning with deadly grace before it plunged down on whatever prey it hunted. *Life, and death, and the future. She is hunting for her chicks, a new generation that will, in turn, hunt to feed their own offspring.*

When they stopped, Darcy handed her down and then Elizabeth. He led the way to where Eleanor Darcy and her son were laid to rest, along with Alexander's wife Millicent. Elizabeth had brought a bouquet from the cutting garden that she handed to Lady Agatha to lay on the graves. They stood in silence for a time. At last Lady Agatha turned away. She felt no sadness, only a sense of gratitude and the peace of the old who know they will shortly join their loved ones in eternity.

"I shall be buried in London with Cedric," she said. "I am pleased to know that my family is well cared for in death. Thank you."

Darcy bowed and offered her his arm. They returned to Pemberley. Three days later Lady Agatha set out for Mr. Pettigrew's estate. She had sent a note of explanation to Petti, who had immediately extended his hospitality. George Darcy watched the coach depart, standing on the porch beside Darcy and Elizabeth, with a small sense of regret. When the big vehicle was out of sight, they turned to go in. Elizabeth took her father-in-law's hand and looked up at him.

"Father Darcy, I am with child."

George looked from her to his son and pulled her into a strong embrace. When he released a somewhat breathless Elizabeth, he reached out and slapped his grinning son's shoulder. "I could not be happier. When will you tell Georgiana?"

"Now is as good a time as any," Elizabeth answered. "I am sure Mrs. Reynolds suspects, and she can make it official with the servants. Pemberley will have another heir by late summer."

"The one it has now," George said, "is the best it will ever have. Nor could it have a finer mistress."

Mary Bennet waited with Lady Matlock and Sofia for the arrival of Lord Matlock and Colonel Fitzwilliam. Richard had refused to allow any of the ladies to meet him at the ship bringing him home from the continent. Lord Matlock had taken his younger son to Dr. Wyecroft immediately from the docks. It was now late afternoon, and all three women showed the nervous strain of the prolonged wait.

When the carriage pulled into the driveway, they were all on their feet. Lord Matlock's voice sounded in the entry hall, but not his son's. Mary felt the cold waste in her chest tighten. She knew only that his left hand and arm were damaged, not how badly. He was such a proud man. Did he still want her as his wife if he was not able to provide for her, if he was not whole?

The two men appeared in the doorway. Richard was thin and worn, his left arm in a sling, the wrist and hand heavily bandaged. Tears streaking her face, Lady Madeleine hurried to embrace her son as her husband stepped aside.

She touched his cheek gently. "Richard, I am so very happy to have you home."

Uttering cries of welcome, Sofia followed her mother. Richard smiled at them, laid a hand on his mother's shoulder, and spoke quietly to his sister. His gaze rose to Mary's face. They spoke silently for endless seconds, and then he extended his right hand, and Mary ran to him, caught against his side as he murmured into her hair, "My dearest one."

None of them saw Nicholas enter the room, leaning on a crutch. When Richard released Mary, he said, "Well, little brother, we seem to have three good arms and two good legs between us. That should put the odds a bit in your favor, for once."

Richard turned to his brother. Nicholas held out his hand, and Richard took it, careful not to compromise Nicholas's balance. "It's good to see you too, Nick."

Lady Matlock had ordered a special tea, and they sat in the drawing room while Richard told them a modified version of his injury. "Somehow the French learned of my rendezvous with the partisans and set up an ambush. They were not as close as they thought, and their muskets are wildly inaccurate over one hundred yards. They lost several men, the partisans lost one, and I was wounded when a bullet struck my musket. They took me to an old woman in one of the villages who poured the local brew over my hand. When I was able to see again, she had wrapped it with a bunch of herbs and some sticks to keep my wrist straight. It was several days before the partisans got me to a mixed English and Spanish regiment. The surgeon did what he could, set my wrist, and wrapped everything up. I am seeing Dr. Wyecroft again in the morning. He will do what has to be done."

"Your hand?" his mother asked. She tried to keep the fear from her voice, but Richard heard it.

"I dislike going into detail with ladies. I will say that part of my left hand was shattered. I lost the last two fingers and part of the palm. Wyecroft will make sure what remains is as able to be used as possible. The wrist was also broken."

"Wyecroft is the best," Nicholas offered. "He did damn well by me."

Sofia leaned a little forward in her chair. "Surely you cannot go back, Richard."

Richard looked down before he responded. "No, I cannot go back. I will be able to ride but not handle a horse and sword at the same time with any degree of control. And I do not think I would care to spend my days at a desk inside the War Office, or any other government enclave."

"We can discuss this later," Lord Matlock said. "For now, you need to rest and heal."

"We will find something for you, little brother," Nicholas said. "We can always use another groom."

Richard threw his napkin at his brother. For the first time in what seemed an eternity, Mary smiled with genuine humor. She took her leave shortly afterward. Richard rose and walked out with her. As they waited for the carriage to be brought around in the discretely empty entry, he pulled her to him and lowered his face to hers, kissing her as he had long wished to do.

"I still have your cross," he said when he released her. "It kept me from giving up hope when I thought I would lose my hand. I do not know when we may marry, but if you will wait a little longer, I can think of nothing in the world I want more than to make you my wife."

Mary's answer was to pull his head down and return his kiss with a passion she had never suspected she possessed.

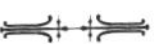

The wedding of Catherine Bennet to Robert Cowper was a joyous affair. Lydia stood up with her sister, and a cousin acted as Mr. Cowper's best man. Elizabeth and Darcy made the trip from Derbyshire to London with Dr. Morrow's assurance that it would do their child no harm so long as Elizabeth was careful not to exhaust herself; with Darcy at her side, that was assured. Georgiana came with them. George Darcy was invited; reasonably, he elected to remain at Pemberley rather than face the long journey to and from the city. The Darcys' collective gift was a month's use of their cottage at the lakes, complete with staff and every amenity. The newlyweds had to do no more than travel there and enjoy their wedding trip. Elizabeth also gave her sister a diaphanous silk nightgown and matching peignoir, causing Kitty to blush profusely when she opened the gift.

At the lavish wedding breakfast, Daniel Bingley found a chance to talk with Georgiana. He was now a junior partner in Bennet, Delibes, and Bingley and showing more promise of an outstanding career than Mr. Cranshaw had ever done.

"You are coming out this year?" Daniel asked as they stood on the terrace of the Bennet home, trying to sound casual and not entirely succeeding.

Georgiana shook her golden head. "No, I have decided to wait at least a year. You must know my father is ill, and with Elizabeth...she will need my help, and I so look forward to being an aunt. I may not come out until I reach my majority."

A brief look of relief crossed Mr. Bingley's face. "I am happ... that is, I think it a wise decision on your part, considering everything. If you are not particularly attached to anyone or, I mean, if you do not wish to marry soon, that is..."

Georgiana took pity on the customarily articulate solicitor and smiled kindly at his confusion. "There is no one—in particular. When I marry, I want to find a man as good as my brother, and that is not easy. Although I am certain he is out there, somewhere, perhaps nearer than I might expect."

Daniel's day brightened considerably. "I hope he is. Given a little time, he will find you."

Richard and Mary sat together at one of the small tables Mrs. Bennet had situated around the dining room and sitting room, now united by opened double doors, for the use of anyone who did not wish to eat standing. Elizabeth and Jane occupied another of the tables at a little distance, their heads together as in the past, their laughter falling softly on the general noise of the celebration. Richard's hand was healing; the maiming was not as radical as Mary had feared. His wrist would be stiff, and he had lost some function in his remaining fingers. He had a glove made with the two missing fingers and palm packed tightly with lamb's wool and sealed into the leather. He was not able to wear it for long at present, and Mary believed he would eventually abandon it when he grew more used to living with his injury.

"Father wants to give me one of his small estates, the one in Dorset, but I am inclined to refuse. I do not want to take any of Nicholas's inheritance, especially since he has shown so much change in his behavior. I realized a decent sum from the sale of my commission, and I have some savings. I also invested in a company Mr. Bingley recommended. It has brought in more profit than I expected. I am far from wealthy, my love, but I can afford a wife and family in a modest way."

"Elizabeth says that now she is expecting a child, William wants to divest some of the property in his name, especially an estate in Staffordshire. I am sure he would sell it to you for a reasonable sum. It is more business than farm because of clay deposits, although there are cattle and horses. I think you would like to breed horses, would you not, Richard?"

Richard looked at her with a kind of wonder in his eyes. "Breed horses! Darcy promised me the first male foal of the stallion I found for him in Spain. With the right mares, what a line he would produce! It needs time to build a herd and a reputation, and that is something I have now. By Heaven, it is the answer!"

He lifted her hand to his lips. Mary beamed. "They are staying until next week, if you want to talk to him about it. And I think this fall would be a lovely time for a wedding."

On August 16, 1813, Elizabeth Darcy was delivered of a son, George William Darcy, after a long but not dangerous labor. The Bingleys had arrived a week previously for Jane to help her sister through the lying-in. Bingley was there to help Darcy through the ordeal of a man with a beloved wife bringing forth his child in suffering he was unable to share. Both Darcys survived, and their son was well formed and healthy. He had his father's coloring and his mother's eyes, and he was the pride of every soul at Pemberley, especially his grandfather.

George Darcy not only lived to see the birth of his grandson he also survived until the birth of his granddaughter, Agatha Jane Darcy, a little over two years later. He passed quietly in his sleep three months afterward, a faint smile on his lips, as at the appearance of someone deeply loved.

FINIS

Made in the USA
Middletown, DE
19 July 2020

13189797R00256